I0822392

ARCING THE FLATLINE

MICHAEL WOODRUFF

ARCING THE FLATLINE

Arcing The Flatline - A Human Potential Fable

First Printing, 2024

ISBN 979-8-9918497-1-5

For Millie...
...my champion of change

To that obtrusive companion within you,
the playful presence pleading for 'more' when you think you have 'less' to give...
...persuading you to venture out a little further.

Contents

PART ONE:

THE LIFE OF BUSINESS

ONE YEAR AGO...

1

Tickers

He wasn't dead yet.

With the opening bell on his mind, uncertainty from a mass-selloff in the overnight foreign exchanges in his head, and thoughts of the consequences from another volatile down day, Jacob Paisley had a little space remaining in his intellect to process more. But he found a way. It was what he did. The leather soles from his nine-hundred-dollar shoes yielded a trajectory of confidence as he crossed the intersection at Pearl and Broad.

He slipped on a silver pair of earbuds, reached within his pocket for the phone and tapped the music icon on the glass screen. *Madness*, from the rock group *Muse* beat deeply into his ears and his steps aligned to the music's cadence.

The New York Stock Exchange was three blocks away. His driver always dropped him off and picked him up, as instructed, at Fraunces Tavern. The next crosswalk on this purposeful early Monday morning walk was at Stone Street. Then Marketfield, then Beaver and finally: Wall. His offices faced west and overlooked the 4–story American flag covering the alabaster columns of the New York Stock Exchange.

Sunlight was limited down here, with gray buildings limiting direct rays and capitalism's demands filtering much of what found its way to the street. The climate was more of a heavy dampness than anything else. At the same time there was a dry sense of mysterious opportunity, and much about making money by any means possible. Do it, or else. Drive for the dollars. For a historical sense, this location still represented the capital of capital. Although the digits technically exchanged in their buys and sells at data centers in nearby New Jersey. Trillions of dollars exchanged hands each day. All actions taken with any form of progress, direct or indirect, were chronically logged with voyeur-like detail. As far as U.S. capital generation, what happened in the Wall Street of the west, Silicon Valley, was a different story altogether.

December weather meant that nearly everyone outside in the elements, moving with or against their purposes, were dressed in stylish dark overcoats. The pops of color were sparse. It could be mild in the early morning when the investment community came to work, and frigid late in the evening when everyone headed for home, or lately, to the bar to drink the pain of a day away. Rain or snow flurries or sunshine. This particular morning was mild with a slight breeze.

Random thoughts of investment opportunities launched, dashed and darted as he sensed the sea of money all about him. Some ideas landing for a short period of calculation, most moving on. Nearly everything that he did was met with what financial trade or investment could be gained as a result. He found the ticker in all things that he saw, heard, smelled, felt. From the sky to the subway – all things he sensed were related to a public or private equity trade. All things were relative to what could be gained by manipulating trading symbols. At any moment, a dozen tickers of stocks or options, mutual funds or ETFs were in play.

It was what he did best. He took it all in, made sense of it, developed a strategy, and produced results. Observing the aging yellow taxis dashing up and down the pre-dawn New York City streets, he considered a trade stemming from the Governor's recently revised regulation to refit all public transportation fleets to more efficient green-energy hybrids. Decarbonization was not a new concept. Thirty years ago it was simply called pollution. There was a need to confuse it's meaning: commoditize it; regulate it; legislate it. Ticker symbols were streaming through his thoughts: TSLA as in Tesla; NIO as in Nio; RIVN as in Rivian and the wannabes, struggling to catch up in hype, but producing units: TM as in Toyota; GM as in General Motors. He quickly determined that this was a hand outplayed and switched gears. A new line of tickers, lithium battery producers invaded his thoughts: LTHM as in Livent; LAC for Lithium Americas; and ALB representing Albemarle danced across his thoughts. Fuel cell companies in the alternative energy sector. Small market caps that he could easily leverage into herd plays. It had slight potential if he could sway institutional investors to follow what the insider's whispers were saying. This was a trend. This was where a massive influx of idle cash could flow. Maybe. Perhaps a play on the upcoming NYC Clean Energy municipal bond instead. It was a better strategy for the tax triangle. This bond would fit into the GreenWorld mutual fund his firm was launching. Better? *Far too many competitors are already at this table*, he thought. *It's a pass.*

He saw few other market professionals on this 5:30am stroll up Broad to Wall. He was almost always the first to arrive at the offices of Paisley & Pierce Capital Management. Recognizing some of the other early-morning money managers, traders, analysts, members of the media, and a contingent of financial admins on their commute to work. Gesturing little more than "Good mornings" and frosty glances, they all made their way to their way of life. Conversation could always lead itself to opportunity. Not knowing someone within this well-known circle of power, not being placed in a position of small-talk was – well, it was charming and welcomed as it featured rare moments of the perpetual daytime grind.

With a crisp Wall Street Journal tucked under his arm, and a tight grip on his attaché Jacob crossed Stone. A shiny black limo slowed to a stop. Looking down at the tires of the vehicle he thought of Goodyear Tire (GT). *GT's cash flow is shit – has been - they're going to need to take the deal. Bring that degradation of margin to a crawl, opposed to the freefall it's in. That industry needs massive consolidation, less competition*, he assessed, and wondered how he might help broker the deal. He had a soft spot in his heart for the blue collar Midwest companies and anything from Ohio.

He smelled coffee and pastries from an early morning street vendor, and remembered the scorching he took on SBUX: Starbucks in Q2 of 2006. As soon as his firm placed a "buy" rating on the Seattle-based coffee company, the up-trending $40 stock price fell to $30. *Had to fire that chartologist*, Jacob thought. *He gave me no choice.*

A tangelo rolled around within his briefcase. Eating one healthy thing while at work each day was a recent insistence from Adele, his loyal and longtime administrative assistant. He thought about her for a second, and shrugged. *She cares about me.* Feeling it bump and roll he thought of the IPO he generated in a deal with Tropicana and Sunkist. The ticker FRUT was his idea, generated over cocktails with a couple commodity traders at Bobby Vans, his favored Wall Street steakhouse and drinking hole.

A simple pleasure – zipper skin Minneolas were in season and shipping in from Australia. Paisley thought of the deep ocean container haulers required to ship bulk commodities, such as DryShips Inc. (DRY), debt-restructured Eagle Bulk Shipping Inc. (EGLE), and his new champion: Genco Shipping (GNK). They were great global plays with returning and handsome dividends, yet risky business models. Like floating real estate investment trusts, the shipper contracts and profit were determined primarily by the quantity of vessels available to negotiate transportation fee deals. From Florida oranges to Brazilian wheat to Australian iron ore, bulk shipping was a delicious mix of risk for Jacob.

His phone buzzed in his jacket pocket. He reached for it, and the name on the phone's face put a smile on his own. The loud cadence beat of the music went silent as the call came in, "Tommy B, talk to me." He was referring to an Indian trader name Vivek Banghama. His nickname was Tommy. Few traders had the Midas-touch at this time. Tommy was rolling.

"Looking for a double-triple from you Tommy", Jacob paused to listen for a minute and then added, "Let's put it in the incubator. Let it hatch. Good idea. You're thinking differently. You're thinking like Sammy used to." He listened, then spoke again, "Sammy is...Sammy was one of our GOATs. That's why your clients love you right now. You are killing the benchmarks." After more listening while Jacob walked toward Marketfield Street, he added, "Let's discuss that further tomorrow. You'll have to walk me through the drivers and put some color on it. Let's safeguard to be part of the quantitative trading, not against it."

With a few seconds of listening while glancing at the surroundings, Jacob interrupted his caller with, "Exactly. That's how we make money. People love you Tommy. The fuel of our success is your portfolio's growth. Let's talk later." Jacob ended the call with reassurance, but sighed deeply while slipping the slim platinum phone into his trousers. The loud beating music resumed. His stride was in tandem with the beat.

He squinted, thinking of the opportunity. In this early morning void of daylight, his eyes were more green than blue. They changed slightly with different surroundings. At this moment, the flecks of green resembled the bluff color of cash.

Jacob Paisley's money never slept. It was always transitioning from one creative instrument of wealth to another. His stock-picking prowess was not just textbook, not just the thesis for seasoned traders to follow, not just the influence upon billions of mutual fund dollars, not just hedgie methodology, it was the power of the example. What to do and how to do it. Jacob Paisley was the market mover that many investors, from institutional to individual, aspired to become. His respect garnered calls from sovereign wealth funds, oil-producing country foreign investors, and many private equity firms. A steady flow of criticism and sarcasm followed the fame and fortune. *Pressure comes to those that deserve it*, he'd say.

"What's Jacob Paisley Thinking NOW?" was a random segment in Smart Money. Random because Paisley didn't want a journalistic deadline. CNBC featured Paisley in short segments titled, "Paisley's Pulse". Fortune and Forbes recently did bios on Jacob. He was a regular of interest in Trader Monthly and other trade pubs.

It seemed, at times, that there was a little Paisley in all financial decisions made, and a lot of Paisley in many. He provided a provocative message and extraordinary insight in representing PPCM, short for Paisley & Pierce Capital Management. There was even one well-known competitive financial advisor that made a comment about Jacob Paisley that others recited: *It appears that you're constantly in a privileged state, knowing something just before someone else, acting upon that knowledge with a speed and accuracy second-to-none... We hate you for that!* It was in good fun, and a compliment that added to the awareness of one of Wall Street's brightest stars: Jacob Paisley.

Noah Pierce, his former partner, had cashed out. Now, it was Paisley and his team to market-master the results. Or to try to.

The fame-junkie's cell phone buzzed in his pocket again. He checked the screen, determining who was calling early, and pushed the energy sector analyst's call to voice mail.

He made a call of his own, and due to the time of day, it went to voicemail. "Ripley – Jacob here. I've just heard from Tommy. He's going forward with the ME trade we spoke of yesterday, he just – doesn't – know – it – yet. We'll firm up the detail today and buy shares off the run, and place the shorts off the grid. I'm going to ask you to monitor any erroneous feeds and give me a heads up early with this one. Send me a text to confirm. Thanks. Oh – sorry about the Giants loss. Hope you're still wearing shorts when I see you next. There's always next year. Out."

He ignored the advertising that dressed the windows of nearby office buildings. It was common knowledge that Gannet (GRN), Omnicom Group (OMC) and Interpublic (IPG) were near-term targets for an unsatisfied acquisition appetite from Alphabet, also known as Google, ticker: GOOG and GOOGL. But those mavericks at the Mountain View, California tech company were far too crafty to pick them up at their current price. "Let the current economy bring M&A deals to Alphabet", one tech sector analyst recently reported. Jacob decided they'd be interested at another 25% discount below their current valuations. A PE ratio of sub-5 for a marketing monster was a potential play for the next calendar quarter.

Daniel Fianacca, one of the junior traders with the firm approached Jacob. "Hey Mr. P – how was the weekend?" They were each dressed in black overcoats, navy Ralph Lauren suits, crisp white dress shirts, and were wearing similar silk ties that had rich red designs. They donned an affluent fat cat look, providing an appearance of having just crawled out of a Gentlemen's Quarterly advertisement.

Not answering his question because neither of them really cared for weekends, there was less money to make than on a weekday. Jacob had more pressing curiosity to settle, "Danny-boy. How'd you make out on the Seamaster?"

They both stopped walking. "I got it. I talked your connection down a little, to $3,900. Hope that's alright. He seemed like a reason able-enough guy. So, like you always say, I had to take advantage of his soft side. Thanks again for the suggestion." Daniel was excited, referring to an Omega yacht watch that he purchased over the weekend as a birthday gift for his father.

Jacob and Daniel stood the same height, an inch or two above six feet. Daniel avoided looking directly into Jacob's penetrating blue eyes as they were too intense and were continuously seeking a deeper meaning to things.

"Last year you bought him a yacht – a Beneteau. This year you bought him a timepiece. Hope he's not disappointed. Is that the definition of a down market, or not delivering your call?" Jacob deliberately cocked his head to one side and gave Daniel a crooked and teasing smirk. He was referring to Daniel's most recent quarterly bonus but wasn't pressuring him with much of a degree of seriousness. Times were very tough in the world of highly mobilized capital. Nothing stayed the same or was taken for granted.

"It's a beautiful timepiece, Jacob. Pop's gonna' love it."

Jacob offered an idea for one of his favored traders, "Danny, you ought to get him a film solar charger." They shared an admiration for gadgets to adorn the company's Oceanis which was docked in Boca Raton.

"Yeah, that's a good idea. I'll look into it."

"Just ask Adele to send him the same one we ordered for Trade One," This was the name of the company's yacht. Each quarter several of the most successful traders from PPCM would invite a select group of their new clients to fly to Florida on the company's private jet and take them out for a fishing boondoggle day trip into gentle waters on the 55' luxury sea craft. Premium champagnes, heavy hors d'oeuvres, and cigars. Danny was a regular in attending the weekend excursions on Trade One.

"I'll do that, Mr. Paisley. Thanks. I know he'll appreciate that. He likes toys."

"Instead of Adele, get with," he paused searching for the name, "...what's her name...the new one..."

"Shelby?"

"Yes, thank you. Get with Shelby. She ordered it and will know which one. Have her take it out of my petty cash account."

"You sure?"

"Sure."

The young trader's face lit up. "She's..."

Paisley looked away toward the office lights within the buildings above. It was never really night in Manhattan. "She's what?"

"She is," he paused, "...mighty fine, if you know what I mean. Good hire."

Jacob looked back at Danny nodding slightly. "Yeah. I guess."

The young trader went on, "I mean, she's – well, quite exceptional..." Daniel was attracted to an oncoming automobile driving well below the speed limit. "And - speaking of beautiful, *hello gorgeous.*" A glossy Nevada-silver Maybach 57S slowly crept by them both. "You know it takes five months to put one of those workhorses together?"

"Keep dreaming big, Danny. As they say, never lose faith in your future. Seed it into your consciousness. Or better yet Daniel, just go get yourself one. You'll figure something out." Jacob retreated to a well-traveled theme of getting his favorite traders deeper into debt so that they felt an obligation to hyper produce more gross profit.

" Mr. Paisley, what was it like when you bought your first Ferrari?"

Jacob looked down at the asphalt and smiled. He took a moment to remember the moment before he replied. "For me, it was the day I entered the Cool Car Club. I remember looking at the salesman after I ground him down to basis points on the deal, stating, 'I'll take it.' Those words became empowering. But, never felt as good as saying it the first time." He looked back up to the young trader.

"I'll take it." Danny recited the words, picturing himself at some point saying something similar. "That fits."

The phone buzzed in Jacob's pocket again. He checked the screen. An international number blinked on the screen. He ignored it.

Daniel knew this drill well and looked for an exit. He had no intentions in accumulating debt toward a $425,000 car anytime soon, and he especially didn't wish to spar in this sort of verbal volleyball with the boss. Reciting some of Jacob's material, he watched the car roll away and finally replied, "Well, there's nothing wrong with calculated inaction. Caution is sometimes king. You gotta' use stealth in building wealth. Right Mr. P?"

Jacob replied, "How can you begin to finish what you haven't started?"

"Listen, I got to catch up with someone. I'll see you in there." Before he departed, he stalled, and added "Trader danger..."

A competitive trader approached Danny and delivered an insult, "I wouldn't want to work for a company with pee-pee in its name." The trader looked like the pair in that he was nicely dressed, well groomed, but differed in that he had light blond hair with too much product.

"Oh yeah?" Danny replied while raising his voice just short of an angry scream, with spit flying from his lips, "Well you're working for a number two – and you know what that is? It's shit. Get the fuck outta' here ya mongrel. You're JV. Not varsity, not collegiate, not professional. JV. You're bush league..."

In a calm voice with a smirk, his competitor spoke intentionally and slowly so that Daniel would hear him, "When you want to come to work at a real trading house, call me - so that I can ignore your call." The trader muttered something else undetectable under his breath, leaving nearly as soon as he arrived.

"I don't work with amateurs." Danny looked in the direction of the parting competitor. There was a story behind the exchange Jacob didn't need to know of but made the assumption it was competitive banter between like-minded arbitrageurs. Perhaps it was bar room banter, a girl, frat bravado. Danny double-patted Jacob on the arm and dashed off.

Jacob felt a smile fade from his face, as he watched the second-hardest-working trader of PPCM depart. He also felt a tingle in his left pinky. *Odd*, he thought. It crept up his arm, stopping at his elbow, and then became a piercing pain on the top of his left shoulder. Jacob took a deep breath and it diminished. His thoughts were suddenly on healthcare companies such as Johnson & Johnson (JNJ), Novartis (NVS) and Merck (MRK). The dividend on Merck had reached an irresistible level of 6.2%. With a market cap of three hundred seventy five billion, he was advising all twenty two of his traders to get their clients on board. He took another deep breath. *What the hell was that?* Better. He kept walking.

Jacob remembered the bull run in pharmaceuticals and biotech stocks – it was a long time ago, and a significant piece of his pinnacle.

Longing for a good thought he continued thinking of his storyline: the transition to day-trading during the dot.com bubble, where he was as the World Trade Center's came crashing down on September 11th. He paused in thought. He then remembered the next splurge in trading, the demographic explosion in the emerging markets, commodities swelling, housing, real estate, CDOs, and the short selling spree as it all came down. Sitting in a bath tub of hundred dollar bills with a stripper while watching Ben Bernanke, the Former Chair of the Federal Reserve, discuss quantitative easing, the transition in to shadow banking, and clandestine batching – and the unique categories of ETF pops which Jacob developed and leveraged. Then, there was the high-frequency trading debacle and the dark pool investigations. So, many regulatory issues that they had acted upon that in the end led, yet billions of dollars in profits later, led to disappointments.

Daniel was no longer in sight. He knew that many of the junior traders had the same opportunities to make their millions. But, things sure felt different all of a sudden. With scrutiny and what was suddenly described as uber-regulation, it wasn't apparent that they'd be able to clean house with a reckless agendas they had over the past two decades. In his heyday, Jacob was honored by premiering in the Trader Monthly Top 100 in eight of ten years before dedicating himself to the commercial development of the firm as the CEO. *Is this a great country, or what?*

The phone buzzed in his pocket again. For just a split second he thought Apple (AAPL) *pure and longstanding genius.* He pulled it out of the pocket, touched the illuminated apple icon and sternly told the caller he'd provide guidance after Boeing (BA) announced to the general public at 9am. If it was a client of the firm, the call would have gone differently.

Thinking about the Monday morning huddle message with the traders in the firm, he didn't know what more he could do to persuade and encourage. He often thought that his material, original and borrowed, was nearly exhausted. But, he was also sure that something would come to him. *Team, history equips us with levers to operate and manage forward, this moment and the next. We cannot allow doubt to squelch what we should support, our clients... What we need to believe in is the value of the service that we provide toward those that choose to employ us. And by the way, oh yes, they have many choices. More avenues to turn than ever. The clients of PPCM...* That was the way it would go. The sales huddle would circle back to a familiar topic of late – the numerous investment firm choices that were available. The sanctity of service differentiation didn't age. Then, he'd drop a few of his favorite tickers on the small crowd. They'd applaud with fervor, and retreat to their phones minutes with a sense of purpose and bravado before the official opening bell.

He checked his watch, a gift from his favorite congresswoman, for a tip. The black-faced white gold Atlas chronograph punched out at $19,000. Tiffany: once the ticker TIF before the acquisition by Louis Vuitton. *What a riddled brand*, Jacob thought. The beautiful timepiece glistening in the streetlights. 5:35am. Jacob's admin, Adele, should be rolling in around 7am.

A text message chimed in his pocket. It was a unique low tone of a bell. He checked the screen: from Victoria: *see you tonight Santa baby...naughty or nice?*

Oh my - how she's relentless, he thought. A slight smile formed and, as quickly as it came, slid away. His contemplations transitioned to the Monday morning battleground that called for a different form of pleasure and a different pursuit of happiness. Slipping the flat silver open-faced phone into his trousers his mind met thoughts of determination: *Battle. Focus. Nothing else. Naughty. Yes, please - naughty.*

Nearly four hours before the markets opened. Thousands of options orders to place, dozens of calls to make, puts and calls to leverage, plenty of justification to seek from last week's losses, and several creative plays to concoct. *This week can be better. Has to. Much.*

The phone buzzed again. His tone was terse and abrupt with the caller because the subject was repetitive and unnecessary: "Again? Really?" Jacob listened briefly, then came off the ropes, fists drawn, swinging: "Rick, what cures a suppression of confidence? A million-dollar performance bonus for the quarter. Losers have a passion for finding scapegoats. Rick, don't be that guy." His displeasure was not that this was a third call addressing the same topic. Dissatisfaction was in the emotion that surrounded a linear decision that they had agreed upon together just fifteen minutes ago. He sarcastically asked if Rick, the trader with a confidence problem, needed another call of reassurance. "So we agree you've got it this time? That's right, flush it out. Model it if you can. The more you sweat in practice, the less you bleed in battle. You've got the aptitude for this..." He listened to the interruption, but clearly didn't care for verbal volley with the caller and continued, "You cannot solve your problem until you quantify it. It's why we picked you. Let's make some money." He listened to the caller for a few seconds, and closed with, "Something from nothing. That never gets old." He touched the glass surface of the phone ending the call.

Jacob had recently been giving much consideration to the bullishness of his trading style throughout the twenty-five years he had been in the financial district. And the contrarian and cautious actions that his former partner and mentor, Noah Pierce had countered with. Paisley & Pierce. They were a good fit. *And now? Am I second-guessing myself or shoring up the way forward?* He quickly deduced that he was firming up his instinctual style of trading. Getting it right, making a lot of high-net-worth investors' truckloads of money. He had done very well for himself along the way.

Jacob again contemplated his edgy trading style, pairing it against this current day rough market. *No Noah Pierce to talk me off of the edge anymore. Miss you, pal.* He remembered once telling Noah: "*We're constrained by the potential recessionary impact of our own actions. Each trader and each client does better when all traders do better. And to do better, to build a better firm, we have got to act upon sensible trends that have demographics, legislation and any other economic factor backing to support our leadership in this marketspace. But data isn't always the DNA that we can rely upon. We must think for ourselves. Act upon a measurable degree of risk. We've had a responsibility to deliver that difference".* Delivering The Difference. Their tagline was born.

Those days were gone. *It's got to turn. Really needs to turn. No cutting and running. Out-think it. I'll find a way. We will. We'll come out ahead. We'll win. That's what winners do – they find a way. They want the ball in their hands at the game's end. They score. We'll win. I think.*

PPCM had been a long-term Wall Street money-making powerhouse, and it certainly was not ordinary for their firm to be in this type of a bind. This meant that they, too, were now losing their investors' money. And in terms of a top trading house losing money, the equation was billions upon billions of dollars. Any pathologically competitive trading house would attest that the challenge had never been more intense to stand out from the crowd.

Back to doubt: *Nothing's working right now.* Schizophrenia was the new normal in the investment community.

Jacob knew this about investing strategies: How you got here, isn't how you'll get there. Money, the ultimate scorekeeper, was always in a transitioning phase. He repeated it to himself and his trading team often to affirm the message. *How you got here, isn't how you'll get there.* There was quite simply, a better place. Better thinking. Better actions. Better results.

The media sometimes had a way of making bad news seem worse than it really was. They were also generally aloof as to how money traded hands at the top. And it was precious to the top money managers and investment firms that they were unaware. It provided time to utilize information. Regulation would likely capture a victim, but the gears of the SEC often operated relatively slow. Time was money.

Retail investors were not PPCM's client base. Jacob and his team went after the big fish. Their target group was the top of the asset classes. High net worth individual investors and the businesses that they lead. The firm, specifically Jacob, had a longstanding track record of beating the street. Had. But not now.

He looked around the streetscape. People were walking briskly in their black coats and black shoes. As a clumsy generalization, Jacob thought that their attitudes recently were as dark. *Manhattan it seems is suddenly full of broken people. Bent, beat, busted. Low on hope and filled with doubt, they weren't always that way. They weren't that way just a short time ago.*

Nothing was working for the majority of the traders over these past three quarters. Nothing was working. Nothing. No-known money management group was posting uplifting results to take marketshare from another. The Dow was down and out, the Nasdaq as bad, the foreign bourses were now worse. Commodities had an impressive run last year yet were resetting to five year lows. The Forex was completely unpredictable. T-bills had an inverted curve which signaled a recession. A long and lucrative bull market was in for a long-term correction. The investment community was temporarily fucked.

He contemplated articulating the bad news that this quarter was likely to produce, and how it would sound to the top investors at PPCM. *Ladies and Gentlemen, it's more of the same. The overall market continues to be challenging and depressed. However... However what? I can't lie to them anymore. Ladies and Gentlemen, it's like this: we're in a period of wholesale wealth destruction. We'll get through it. Can't tell you what the other side's going to look like.*

The latest commercial real estate lending mess, similar to another subprime meltdown, was a longstanding center point of the blame casting. De-commits by long-favored regional banks continued to fester more bad news that just couldn't seem to self-correct. The federal government was making matters worse by generating additional multi-generational bailout packages, causing more of a manic-panic. The U.S. was approaching its third financial downgrade; a rendition of quantitative easing was in its fifth phase; another fiscal cliff was being discussed in congress. Several larger municipalities were discussing bankruptcy protection, requesting State intervention. *We're creating a larger economic crisis than the one we're attempting to fix.*

The pundits and talking heads on TV had been calling for the bottom week after week, using the word 'capitulation' indicative of massive and deep selling, and the thing that bothered investment bankers most: media analysts regurgitating lines cited from economic analysts about the state of current-day results as they compared to depressions, recessions and in general, other bear markets. He knew that this would pass. Bad news comes to an end. Eventually. Smart money steps in at the right moment. Meanwhile, there's today to deal with. He was thinking about leveraging the media's messaging and how it might sound coming out of his mouth for others to hear: *Generating fear would serve no purpose here...* Jacob thought about the constant data provided the fueled the selloffs, *...but someone will use the macro reporting to make money anyway. Markets go up, you make money. Markets go down; you get creative and find a way...*

His phone rang. As he retrieved it and looked at the caller, he rolled his eyes before his answered, "I sure hope you have good news." Moments of silence passed. Jacob tried to remain calm but could only contain so much. "We offered you a tremendous opportunity. It's disappointing to see that you're not living up to the candidate that we thought we were bringing on board. I've got to be honest here. When I picked up the phone, what I really wanted to say was...Jacob screamed into the phone: 'What now you fucking idiot!' ". A black woman in a parka passing by as he screamed jumped away wide-eyed, took several steps, looked back, then continued, walking faster.

"No, no, no, no, no, no, no....God no. Please. Help me here. You don't chase that logic. Fear is your friend; panic is your enemy." Jacob listened further, and cut the call short, "Call Vic, report the loss. Get back on the horse. You don't have too many rides left when you trade like that." He listened to an apology and interrupted one last time. "You're sorry. That's convenient. I'm sorry too. Sorry that you just lost your bonus for the quarter and lost the firm over a million dollars. You know, your client is going to love this. I'd love to hear that conversation. No fruitcake for you. I'm done. Talk to Vic."

Jacob paused. His face grimaced and he made a fist and held it in front of him for a moment. Taking a deep breath, he whispered to himself: "*We've never been here before. They're not afraid of failure, they're afraid of being afraid.*" Then he walked on.

The shooting pain returned. This time it was stronger. From his pinky to the top of his shoulder. Tingling pain. He took another breath. But it was short and harder to take. He stopped walking. Slowly, over a minute it was better. The pain was not gone. But he felt the difference between acute and dull ache. He took a few more steps to the corner and was again thinking about poor results and fowl moods, and at the moment, that there was no known escape from the broader financial debacle. His mind wandered for unfound relief.

He would have crossed. However, a uniformed police officer was at the other corner and the light was red. NYC had recently cracked down on J-walking. The fine was $400. *Fucking extortion*, he thought. This wasn't the real issue – but the bullshit that accompanied it was. Time was money, every single second counted.

Something beyond our control needs to change. His steps on the worn cement brought him to another intersection. He looked down at the pavement. When he was searching for answers and couldn't find them, he looked at the foundation of things. Broad and Beaver streets. The light remained red. The indicator was orange and counting down seconds with an LED display and accompanying sound beep: 12...11...10...9...

He looked up into the skyline, admiring the florescent lights burning brightly in the fifty, sixty, seventy story grey and glass buildings. He thought about Netherlands-based Phillips Electronics (PHG) which was listed as an ADR, and Honeywell (HON). *We aren't differentiating ourselves here, and that's been PPCM's mantra all along. There's always something out there that we don't know. Some useful piece of the puzzle that makes the overall picture clear or complete. Something that would lend itself to a resolution.*

He no longer saw the uniformed policeman but held his position clutching the briefcase.

Jacob was addicted to a search for arcane data, erroneous bits and bytes of information that would produce results beyond the peer group of other investment firms. . *Something or someone's got to save the damned day: What will today bring?* 4...3...2...1...

At 5:37am, on a chilly morning in Manhattan, directly in the middle of the crosswalk on his way to work, forty-nine-year-old Jacob Paisley hit the pavement. He fell to one knee first, dropped his attaché which caused it to spring open sending a few confidential papers to drift into the December breeze. The famous investment manager of Paisley & Pierce Capital Management landed on the shoulder that had tingled with a shooting pain moments ago. His head hit the asphalt street with a thunk. He was laying on his side, noticing the plumes of vehicle exhaust. Clutching the pain deep in his chest and disoriented, he attempted to focus. Oddly, the earpiece began playing the music which he had earlier paused to talk with Danny...*Madness.*

He watched the tangelo roll underneath a black limo nearby. The towncar looked just like the one dropping him off just two blocks away. For a minute he thought he had been struck by a reckless taxicab driver. And as he lay there, he realized he had instead been struck by a form of fate. The volume on the ear buds increased...*Madness...*

He first realized that his thoughts were not collected, organized, calibrated. Something within this predictable space of a business morning was out of place. His head wasn't working quite right, he panicked. An intensifying and alarming pain continued within his chest. He did not think of tickers at this moment but did realize that his own ticker wasn't functioning. His heart just didn't have the heart to take him all the way into the financial offices of Paisley & Pierce Capital Management today. No buzzing computer workstations blinking, streaming data, and churning out millions of pixels of information today. Like recent results toward missed quarterly expectations, he fell short.

There he was, now flat on his back, all things now in slow motion. Jacob looked up into the still dark morning that wasn't his to manage to.

His head then rolled to his side. He lay in a supine position, clutching his chest in the middle of the street. The cell phone was vibrating again in his pocket. Jacob couldn't answer the iPhone's neediness. He lay still, absorbing the intensity of this moment.

He turned his head to watch the Minneola come to a rolling halt directly under the axle of the shiny black chariot which had a momentary pause in its progress. At street level, even with the limited lighting, he could see its bright orange color. And as his eyelids became heavy, he considered results from previous trades made in the orange juice commodities market: Ticker FCOJ-A.

The music was so loud now it buzzed in his ears. He felt himself floating above his body. Rising higher and higher. Looking down at his image, further and further away. Sprawled out fashionably in the middle of the crosswalk, white and black lines on the asphalt surrounding his image. *Madness.*

2

The Opening Bell

He woke for just a minute to see a black man, presumably in his fifties or sixties, who Jacob seemed to think might be his doctor. The man was dressed out in light blue medical smocks with the surgical head dressing already covering the top of his head. His hands were held up in the air, just scrubbed and he was waiting for surgical gloves from a nurse unwrapping them from a sterile packaging wrapper. He looked at Jacob and was saying something. "Don't know if it's the devil's choice or if it's God's choice that we're going to save your sorry ass." The surgeon gave him a wink and turned away.

Jacob was foggy. *Did a trade go south?* He tried to say this but could not. Even in the frenzied state, he sensed a frantic situation in the operating room. He gave one more look at the surgeon walking away. Jacob was attempting to process. He was usually capable of tasking more than what he was comprehending at the moment. He thought: *Pain... in my chest. Shock. I must be in shock. Drugs. I had a heart attack. Doctor. EMT... Resemblance to the paramedic... The doctor was the paramedic? Drugs. Where am I? This isn't a hospital; this is the cab of an ambulance. We're en route. No. We just arrived. I'm confused. Timeline...sequence is off. Confusing.* The emergency medical technician was bagging Jacob. The medicated air filled his lungs with a hissing sound.

He closed his eyes. Hospitals, health centers, doctors, pharmaceuticals, medical products and equipment. Jacob thought the healthcare industry was deeply loaded with public and private investment opportunities. He was fading in and out. *Has the market opened? Did I miss any breaking news?* Tickers crazily drifted across his thoughts. He was in a hotbed of investment opportunity and had mental rationalization for each pick: *Medtronic (MDT), an industry stalwart, a price to earnings ratio of 15. Love it. A triple buy. Stryker (SYK), annual earnings per share of $4.45. Solid cash position. Boston Scientific (BSX), never should have acquired Guidant. It's killing them. Baxter International (BAX), next year's forward earnings should be $5.50 per share. Gave it a price target of $282. Can't get enough. Pain. Heart attack. Shock. Tangerines. Danny Fiannaca. Yachts. Black topcoats. Concrete. Asphalt. My head hurts.*

He heard distant voices. Three, four, five people were speaking. Men. Strange sounds accompanied. A heartbeat. It echoed. Two heartbeats. Water. Waves? No...whispers. Men talking, women whispering. Conversations about something unfamiliar. But, he didn't recognize what appeared to be two men talking. Deep tones. Serious. One was asking questions, another attempting to answer. This was not a medical conversation. It was something else. "What...?" One man asked the other, "What's his weapon of choice?" There was no answer. Silence.

Jacob couldn't open his eyes as much as he tried. But, he could hear the voices continuing. They appeared more distant, muted, difficult to comprehend and he was having trouble understanding the purpose of the dialogue. "His warship is the crusade of his words."

"I'm fuckin' hallucinating," drifting in and out of consciousness, Jacob was able to say this out loud.

Where's my fucking doctor? UnitedHealth Group (UNH), that analyst that I hate loves it. I told him to back off. He didn't listen. I was right. Wellpoint. My head. Wellpoint. My chest, Heart attack. Wellpoint. Doctor dressed in sky-blue scrubs. Wellpoint. What's the fucking ticker for Wellpoint?

He heard conversations about CABG. They were calling it cabbage. Technicians were talking in muted tones about ischemic results, risk adjustment, and performance obstructions. He couldn't hear, wasn't sure if they were talking about the trading day or medicine. In this drugged state, they were the same. Thoughts were now fleeting his capacity: *Take it all in, make sense of it, develop a strategy, and produce results.* He was out.

Jacob's mental market was now closed.

Beyond the miracles performed each day within the Mount Sinai Heart Hospital in Manhattan, the Dow Jones Industrial Average rose nearly 600 points. The S&P was up 1.8%. The Nasdaq listed advancers over decliners five-to-one. Pacific Rim markets followed suit, supporting the financial capital of the world. The price of gold was up $12 per troy ounce. Even the orange juice futures and commodities markets rallied. FCOJ-A contracts touched their $142 ceiling at the nearby New York Board of Trade.

As long as his memory served, Jacob believed that he was in control. He had his own hands on the wheel, navigating the course. Managing the micro and macro factors, he had deep rooted beliefs in his management of capitalism. The results were his. He used most of his resources most of the time to produce amazing results.

Moneyman, Jacob Columbus Paisley, was under the wheels of change. And he was not outpacing it. About to experience the velocity of the twists and turns that life can bring, and the momentum of that change, Jacob was in for one wild ride.

*****

She heard the bell from the microwave chime a 'ding'. Turning in the direction of the greasy fingerprint smudged appliance, as she attempted to open the door, he slammed it shut abruptly.

"You don't do it right!" he barked at her. His wife-beater tank top featured five varieties of stains, smears, and other-than-white blemishes. His long greasy and thinning blondish hair wasn't parted in the middle of his head but wasn't parted on the side either.

She said sheepishly, "I'm sorry, Cutter. You want it in longer?"

His angry reply was met with a furled brow and squinted eyes, "Make it hot, not lukewarm! Jesus, do I have to do everything? Get it right! Not wrong! Jesus." By nearly everyone's opinion, he should have shaved the scraggly attempt at a mustache hanging under his big and skinny nose.

"No, I'll do it good. I'll put it in for another minute and check it for you." She cowered at his disappointment in her and feared another fiery outburst. Who knew oatmeal could be so confrontational?

Turning away, he clapped back at her, "Kerri - you can't cook for shit."

In a raspy and vulnerable voice she answered, "You'll see..." she tried to be playful, pointing her finger to the direction of the dirty appliance. Confidence was depleted through their competitiveness – where he always seemed to win.

"No, you cannot. Never have been able to." His scowl endured as he collapsed on the couch covered with a sleeping bag and dirty laundry. Fumbling with the remote for the TV, he lit a cigarette and took a long draw. He exhaled in her direction while shaking his head in disgust at her.

He had a name: Jimmy "Cutter" Jude. The name, 'Jimmy Jude', was the only thing given to him by his parents before he was dropped off at an orphanage as an infant. Written on the back of a McDonald's fries' wrapper in a red magic marker, 'Jimmy Jude', was his first label. What followed was his doing. Perhaps it was for the purpose, by his mother or father or both, of someday reconnecting with him. That someday never came. The moniker: "Cutter" came later and for several reasons.

She was staring out the one grimy window in their sketchy efficiency apartment into a city where anywhere else would be a better elsewhere. She had a name too. It came without a French fry wrapper as a name badge. Kerri Latch came from a good home accompanied by a loving family, fine schooling, friends, and a bright future. As a teen in a well-respected grooming school, she had all the potential for a life which many would envy. Neighbors found her cheery; her teachers found her filled with a passion for curiosity and exploration; and her weekends found her helping family and friends. Unfortunately, methamphetamine found her too. Its grip pried her from her possibilities and that budding future found in the best storybooks of a charmed life.

Kerri Latch was skinny, dishwater-blond haired and hazel-eyed. She had the fleeting appearance of someone who was once head-turning beautiful. She remained pretty enough – but the drug abuse had clearly taken a toll. Cutter was her dealer.

Her likeness, if she had one, was Jennifer Lawrence. When she was younger, as in just a few years ago, several people said she resembled the actress. Kerri thought of her occasionally, seeing some similarities, and did so now in her reflection on the face of the microwave, between the fingerprints. The dark circles under her eyes made her think of a saddened Katniss – one who had been crying.

"Are you deaf too? Dammit woman...DING!" He pointed from the couch to the kitchen. He dropped ashes into his lap. "Damn it!" he wailed. He brushed the ember from his jeans onto the floor.

Her gaze out the window returned to the TV diner in the microwave. This wasn't cooking. She came from a home where food prep, the art of dining cuisine, and both elegantly and simply enjoying the meal together was a thing. That yesteryear thought was far away from this current moment. The bell rang and as she opened the door, she retrieved Cutter's chicken pot pie from the nasty food zapper which was covered with spills and a yellow sludge which was possibly mustard.

As she handed him the smoking dish, she looked at the tracks on her arms and thought about it again. She wanted a fix. She needed a fix. Cutter would help her if she was a good girl. "Be good," she whispered to herself.

"I know what you're thinking." It was a deep whisper, intended to be intimidating. He was right behind her, listening to her whisper.

She jumped in shock. "Oh...God... You surprised me!" Her hand touched her heart.

"Not God, baby. Just little ole' Cutter here. Ya know that you've gotta' give yourself a break from the product, Kerri." He was on his seventh beer and began slurring his words. A creepy smile found its way to his face, and he shook his head slightly, "You'll end up like some of my clients." He paused, raising his eyebrows. "That's dead, sweetheart." He took another drag from the cigarette and blow the smoke out of the side of his mouth in the direction of the stove which had a pizza box on the burners. When she turned toward the mess, he grabbed her ass and squeezed it. She tensed. It didn't excite her to have his hands on her, but she tolerated it. A means to an end, sex for drugs, was their arrangement.

Cutter's roster of 'clients' ranged from bankers and brokers to doctors and lawyers, to the everyday blue collar worker seeking pain relief. He dealt meth, cocaine, heroin, and pills of the rainbow – all the colors and to anyone with money. And for the name 'Cutter'...he cut class in school until he dropped out, picking up the moniker from an Assistant Principal who was unsuccessful in disciplining the young Jimmy Jude. Then, it stuck as he chased down money for a dealer, leaving his trademark: a cut, upon each victim his gang of thugs chased down. Finally, 'Cutter' followed him into this current profession as a Manhattan dealer – cutting the coke to extend the profits. His cutting agent of choice was a combination of creatine and laundry detergent. The late-night check-out clerk at Duane Reade wondered why the creatine wasn't helping the scrawny man who bought a 12-ounce container every so often.

She felt the need to get high and looked past everything else. The shitty living conditions, the lack of food in the fridge, how cold it was in their disgusting apartment because the radiator wasn't working properly. How her life had plummeted into the poor state that it was, and she especially looked past uncomely Cutter. Because he was her solution. She'd kill him...with kindness. He'd cave. This was how she did it. How she got her drugs, her fix, her place of relief, her reaching the coordinates of her destination - which was her known and unknown hell.

3

After Hours

People that give death a pause don't generally call it overtime, as they do in sports. They're offered an opportunity, precious moments, and with soulful acceptance they're grateful for what they've been given. They look forward to the next moment with bright eyes and a new perspective. Their faith firms, their vantage point is often higher, they have realized that conclusion gives each next moment a rare form of value. And they're often better people with their new leases on life than they'd be without it. Not always, but often.

Jacob heard the distant conversation again. Now, it was clearer. Two men talking. One asked questions, the other answered. Though his eyes were closed, he sensed a hazy and soft white light like a cloud. The voices felt as if they were in front of him and behind him at the same time. There were a series of questions, a pause, contemplation, and an answer provided.

The first asked, "What will keep him company?" It was a man's voice like Jacob's, but not his own.

The other answered, "It is what insulates him and acts as his companion. Chance."

The first voice said, "We'd favor that he loses his way." After some apparent contemplation, "Will he?"

The other answered, "We'll see to it."

The first asked, "And the sense of himself?"

After a lengthy pause, "Yes. That will be necessary."

A third voice spoke softly, "You're hearing this to know what lies ahead."

A still quiet lasted.

I must be dreaming, Jacob thought.

Jacob Paisley was waking up from open heart surgery in Mount Sinai's Cardiology Recovery center. He felt cold. When he opened his eyes, his first thought wasn't of tickers, or markets, or currency exchange rates or any of those things. He looked at the ceiling tiles. The metal cross bars reminded him of longitude and latitude bars on a map or a globe.

Longitudes and latitudes. Holding dozens of white ceiling tiles neatly in place. Longitudes and latitudes, the bar markers that make some sense of navigating our way throughout the world were the single component that put Garmin on the financial map. *Garmin (GRMN). Where am I? Heart attack. Drugs. Bed. Hospital. Surgery. Cold.* A vibration was felt in the bed. His ankles were being squeezed slightly for a few seconds. A compression device of some sort then slowly relaxed the pressure.

Jacob Columbus Paisley was born in Columbus, Ohio. He was J.C. for 20 years. As he charted his career course toward money management, he decided that J.C. raised the question as to what was behind the name, and he sought transparency. And he was concerned about the identity of his moniker being compared to the once-favored retailer. It wasn't material until he considered that it could in some small way inhibit being taken seriously as a stockbroker. Was J.C. Penney a name that could draw a legit financial audience? Maybe not. *Not the powerful assimilation I'm going to project*, he decided.

He changed one of the first things in his life that he was given, his name. J.C. became Jacob. It was easy to control things. Even simple matters like name changes. Most people didn't dare. Jacob dared, and found that it was his nature to control, and change, and dare.

Garmin (GRMN). Trades on the Nasdaq. Strong PE ratio. Hefty dividend. It's a buy, even when the market's soft. Drugs. Pain. Hospital. Who do I know that sits on the Board of Directors here? Surgery. Cold.

He fell asleep. A visiting nurse saw that his eyes were open for a short time and that he was moving. There was no one there for him when he woke. So, the order was placed to temporarily move him to ICU for observation, and then to his private room.

A short time later, the receptionists and operators began receiving numerous calls expressing a wide variety of interests in a man brought in to their emergency room several hours ago: a Jacob Paisley. The receptionists had no idea of who he was at the beginning of their shift. But they knew him well enough in its end. On that Monday morning, calls were carefully diverted, as gatekeepers had instructions. And by the afternoon, Mount Sinai's Hospital Administrator crafted a HIPAA-authorized press release that was to be the boilerplate response for anyone expressing interest in the moneyman in the ICU.

By the evening shift, flowers, balloons, cards and several baskets of well-wishes what-not began arriving. With no room assignment, they were diverted to a holding closet.

At 5:30pm, after the market had closed. Jacob's Administrative Assistant, Adele Kirby arrived. She was dressed in her usual dark skirt, light blouse, and scarf. Shoes from Macy's, a hand-me-down designer bag from one of her rich friends or occasionally, an ascending trader at the firm. The phones were beyond chaotic at PPCM that day. It was a day like no other. She wore a worried look as an accessory to her attire.

As a result of the extraordinarily unusual bustle, before making her way to the hospital, she quickly stopped off at Bobby Van's to have just one sparkling martini that their favorite bartender, Billy, suggested. "Best medicine I can prescribe for an ailment like this," he'd have told her. She drank fast, and it went straight to her head.

They, Adele, and Jacob, both admired Billy's ability to shine within gloom. His elixirs were remedies to the recently wild swooning Dow

Jones Industrial Average closes. Lately, Billy was their Bob Cratchit to the Ebenezer Scrooge of the market. She wouldn't normally drink on a weeknight. This was no ordinary Monday and she felt that she needed a moment to think things through. A familiar place that she sometimes shared with Jacob after hours felt right.

Her thought process was that she needed to think things through. Therefore, she turned down the idea of taking the company car. Instead, she chose a neon green cab. She had provided enough "*don't know what we don't know*" chit-chat and explaining today and wished to go solo in her thoughts. Even the driver would ask too many questions about Jacob. *Enough*, she thought. The cab took Church Street and the Avenue of the Americas to 11th, where Adele ordered the cabby to drop her off, stating she could take it from there. Truth be told, she felt that she might have wanted to stay for another drink, knowing it would be a long night. She would certainly manage much curiosity over the next several days, and it wasn't as if her day job went away. It would be a tough period to manage. The assistant needed an assistant.

Her cell phone rang. Looking at the illuminated face, she saw her son's name. "Hi Tim...yes, I'm almost there now..." She listened intently. "No. I can't. I've got a lot of work to do. Thank you though...I have...I need to..." The cell phone reception was generally good in this area, but the call was breaking up. "I'm sorry. I couldn't hear you...you were saying?"

Adele listened to her son justify a similar point and felt compelled to interrupt him, "No, Tim...stop right there. He's the one that put you through college. Mr. Paisley is the one that pays me a very fair wage. I can't have you say those things." More of a mother's patience was given before she cut into what he was saying "Tim, you got to stop it right there. He's a pillar of giving in the New York community. He doesn't run me ragged. I'm going to the hospital because I want to go, not because I'm on his clock. He's given so much to..."

The call was breaking up. Adele wanted to get off of the call with her son, because this sort of conflict drained her. "Honey, we can discuss this...again...later. I got to go. No, I don't. Yes, I do. No, I need to go. OK? OK. Will do. Maybe tomorrow. Love you too."

She began walking toward Mount Sinai to be more productive with her time. Her heels clicked on the sidewalk. Ending her call, "Give my babies kisses...alright, you too." She clicked the phone's keyboard. Taking a deep breath, she assured herself that her son was jealous that she enjoyed her work, believed in what she did, and deeply honored her boss.

Jacob had paid for Tim's tuition at New York University. His benevolence was why Tim was afforded the opportunity to attend NYU. Grades certainly wouldn't have paved the way. She believed that her son's formula for criticism was completely unfounded.

After 8pm, long after the domestic markets had closed, and after a wide variety of adult beverages were consumed at local bars and fine eating establishments such as Bobby Van's, several PPCM teammates and few other investment professionals arrived occasionally at the nurse's station. Jacob's whereabouts were not public knowledge. The *private room* and *Healthcare Professional ONLY* observation meant that their visits were to be brief.

The rising star trader, Daniel Fiannaca came to visit, staying a little longer than two others. To Adele, the junior trader replayed the brief morning conversation that he had with Jacob moments before the Paisley's misfortune. Then, Daniel answered several phone calls and disappeared.

By 11pm things were silent within the Mount Sinai Fuster Heart Hospital. However, the Asian-Pacific markets were open, the Shanghai Stock Exchange was piling on to the up-markets in the Americas, currency exchanges were 24/7 – the traders had some catching up to do from last week's shellacking that had taken place.

Nothing brings purpose to trading stocks, options, and futures like getting your portfolio's ass kicked the week prior. They got dusted last week, and Monday was an emotional day for the traders of PPCM. But the show must go on. The ailing boss would expect them to keep the foot on the gas and break all of the speed limits.

Adele was about to call it a night. She had arranged for a concierge to arrive in the morning, had returned twenty-seven voice messages from her cell, talked with several doctors and nurses, and was allowed in Jacob's room for a short time. Her work here was done. She had worked for the man the past seven years, knowing Jacob wasn't into hand holding, compassion, and tender moments. He'd want to know that things were better off without his presence than with it. That was the mark of leadership he'd want and expect. Adele would do her very best to *deliver the difference* that Jacob so fondly and often spoke about.

She left a voice message for another administrative assistant at the firm that she was leaving Mount Sinai, that Jacob was resting, that she thought things went very well, and that she would be in early to tackle the growing workload.

Her imagination wandered toward tomorrow when Jacob, through some twist of fate might possibly discover that Adele alone stayed late into the evening for him. Her imagination led her to a familiar place, a softer place than New York's cement pillars, a place where she was more than an Administrative Assistant at PPCM. A place where they had more in common than performance ratios and investor conferences. She thought of his blue eyes and tanned skin drawing close to hers as they boarded the corporate jet. He would say something like; *Adele – this time it's just about you. It's just about us. I've been thinking about you.* This was not a fantasy place of sex and reckless abandon. It was a green and blue space...a place of wholesome friendship...of being with a good human as a good human. Warm, but with a breeze blowing and kindness in the air. It was a place far from where they were right now.

She jerked in her chair. *Crazy*, she thought. *I - dozed off.* She sat up straight and looked around the waiting area on the eleventh floor.

A tall black man with big brown eyes and a few freckles on his cheeks just under his eyes approached her. His hair was cut short and had flecks of grey salted through it. He was dressed out in light blue smocks and was carrying the surgical headdress, or it could have been the disposable polypropylene shoe coverings – she wasn't sure. He tossed them in the trash can at the end of the nurses' station. Offering a gentle smile and nodding his head as he looked at her, "Good evening."

Adele didn't recognize him as any of the doctors on the rotation she'd picked up on, mulling from room to room – and she did not see him advising any of the nurses about patient treatments as the other medical staff had been. But the first shift had become the second had become the third. Her conclusion was that this handsome black man must work nights. She was comfortable with him right away but wasn't sure why.

Smiling, she replied with an exhausted and passive, "Hello." Her phone buzzed in her pocket. After fiddling with it, she looked up and he was gone. Adele looked around, arousing one of the nurses at the cluster of computers.

"You've been here all evening, haven't you?" a young Hispanic nurse asked in a soft voice. She had her dark hair pulled back into a ponytail. "He's not going to be awake until tomorrow. We've got it from here if you want to go get some rest. You look tired, sweetheart."

Her voice was groggy, but she needed to know and asked the question, "Why here? Why was he brought all the way here when he could have been taken to NYP?"

"What's that?" The nurse was recording numbers in a small handheld computer.

"New York-Presbyterian in Lower Manhattan. Sure seems like the natural choice for..."

"Contracts, honey. It's all about who got the contracts for care."

Discouraged, Adele admitted, "Of course...contracts." Under her breath she added, '*we tend to know contracts...*'

She wiggled in her seat a little and even though she hoped Jacob would know tonight that she was there for him, she was exhausted and seeking her cue to leave had found it. Her things were all around her: an iPad, phone charger, water bottle from the vending machine, and bag with countless other save-the-day items.

She said I look tired... Why does that always seem to be one of the things you don't want to hear - whether you're tired or not? Adele thought to herself.

The nurse had been thinking about her choice of words too. "Sorry, I hate that when someone says I look tired." It was as if she were reading Adele's thoughts. "We have your number, right?" The nurse had a radio clipped onto her shirtsleeve. Her scrubs were light blue like the color of her eyes which was striking with her dark hair. A static voice asked her to update the new ERP software system and to call down to the pharmacy.

Adele just nodded and thanked her. *What will tomorrow bring,* she wondered. She questioned her own thoughts about spending time with him outside of their frenzied workplace. She was just plain and simple. Adele, Jacob Paisley's admin. The thought of 'more' was a place she liked to frequent. There was a point in time a few years ago where an after-hours locker room conversation made its way on to the late-in-the-day traders and about the dozen Admins and support staff at PPCM. It was a group of the younger men traders, gathered in their open collar and loosened tie pinstripes, or shirtsleeves rolled up, or wearing vests with no tie. This boy talk was about the physical appearance of the women at the firm. Jacob was in his office out of earshot. Their chuckles became laughter and ribbing on each other.

Adele was still in the office but was in the documents room filing 10-Q's and 10-Ks. They didn't notice her presence. The door to the Doc Room was ajar so that she could hear everything being said. Even the low-voiced whispers were audible.

"How about that new hottie in Enterprise?" one trader chimed in. It was met with a rousing ranking system of "10 out of 10" or "Solid 9" or "Hot 9" followed by "Yeah's" or chuckles from the others.

"How about Kelsey in Finance?" another trader would coax feedback from his limited audience.

The guys paused. "She looks like your sister, what do you think?" one trader teased.

"I heard she likes it rough," another lied.

"She's actually not – that - into – gentlemen. Sorry, guys," another informed with an *I-might-know-something* smirk on his face. It was followed by rapid-fire questions, and comments of "knew it" or "I thought so" or "I'm still givin' her a big ole eight, fellas – if you know what I mean?". He was sitting in a chair, spread his legs, and pointed at his crotch. Laughter broke out.

Adele was uncomfortable with the conversation but remained silent, clutching a stack of papers, listening to the ruckus. She took off her heels and stretched her toes on the industrial carpeting of the floor. Florescent lighting flickered above. This was the one room in the office one didn't want to be in for hours. How long are they going to roast the 'Women of PPCM' Adele wondered?

Not knowing of Jacob's presence: dressed to go, overcoat on, attaché in hand, standing outside his office undetected yet listening the man-banter, the question launched: "How about Adele?"

Quickly, the most vociferous trader chimed in, "Yeah, if you're into Mothers and I'm into Mommy's...."

"Vanilla." Another trader chimed in.

"Nope." Jacob was loud, firm, and looking directly into the face of each of his treasured staff members. "Not Adele. She's off limits here." He paused for effect and made the point to look into each of their eyes. "Only if 'vanilla' means the highest level of respect and admiration."

Squinting through the crack in the door, Adele could see the stance Jacob took: guarded, a sentinel, the sentry of her protection. The interruption prevented them from what? Hurting her feelings? Showcased him as the custodian of her well-being? She wondered where the conversation might have led, as much as she was grateful for his appearance and re-direction. Her curiosity was high.

"Adele is a large part of the heart and soul of this organization." He spoke slowly and was stern in his command. "Not appropriate here, guys." His pause was pregnant, "Let's move on, please." He made his way to the plate glass door exit bearing the Copperplate font name of the firm.

The next day, while dropping off a file about a pending deal which Jacob was brokering, she dropped her physical proximity confession and added, "Thanks for always having my back."

His smile was slow, warm, and authentic, "We're a team, you and me. I got you." He looked out his office window into the New York skyline without really seeing it, speaking toward the window, "Things turn out best for the people who make the best of the way things turn out."

"Who said that?" she asked.

"I think it was John Wooden" he said, "But it's about you. The coach thought it was about the Bruins, but it was about anyone anywhere who is as amazing as you are. You Adele, you make it all work. You make the work go away and you make what is difficult - all - worthwhile."

She grinned and to hide it looked down at her heels, crossing one leg over the other.

He continued, reaching for her embarrassment as a target, "I think that not everyone sees you. And those which do might not see you as you really are."

Adele hung onto each word.

"You touch some of us in mystifying ways, and others in impactful ways, and others in ways we might not understand."

"That's the way that it is with everyone..."

"Not everyone," he interrupted. "You're very special, Adele. You're a good human. A beautiful soul that I'm fortunate to have in my orbit. I'm grateful for you. I mean that. And you're a beautiful woman." With that, he made her blush – for the win. Catching the radiance of his words for her, he smiled.

As Adele Kirby departed for the bank of elevators at the hospital, the black man resembling a surgeon reappeared. Still dressed in smocks, carrying a stethoscope and a clipboard, he paused looking in the direction of Adele's departure. He looked down at the empty and silent hall for a half a minute, studying the vertical and horizontal patterns of the floor tiles, and then slipped into Jacob's room undetected.

Longitudes and latitudes may assist us in navigating our distances. But they are merely the unwavering lines we use as tools to draw closer to where we may wish to go – to get lost or to find our way. Each person's perspective aligns the course for their own way forward.

Jacob always thought that how one approaches a situation determines, to a great degree, the direction, and the distance of the outcome. He also believed that in the situation of survival, the adaptive strategy worked best. Evolve when you need to evolve. Evolution was greater than extinction. But he wasn't about to follow his own advice.

*****

Her words were soft and spoken from her heart, "Listen, you know how this goes because you've heard it from me *hundreds* of times: You can take the boy off the island but can't take the island out of the boy. Go. Go see your Autie and Uncle. They'll be so happy to see you." She shook her head slightly as she described his ohana, his family on the island with the tagline: The Gathering Place.

"I'll bet Nanakuli has changed a little since you've last been." She wasn't trying to be convincing. The sleepy town didn't change much, and was somewhat opposite to the bustling Honolulu – which some tourists would describe as Hawaii. Nanakuli was complete with culture, rich storytelling of heritage, meanings and teachings of the original island kingdom, and a deep sense of *ho'omau* – which was the

Hawaiian word for preservation – or carrying on. In other words, it didn't change much or quickly.

"Go see your cousin. Go see Leilani."

Her hand brushed an eyelash from his cheek as they stood face to face, sharing a breath of life. Their kitchen was filled with smells of sugar cookies and lemon. Sunlight filtered through the blinds to warm the moment. The coffeepot had just started perking, toasted coconut – their favorite.

Brian Kekahanamanui was Hawaiian. Or part Hawaiian as the family, their ohana, would describe the 'Kekahanamanui' ancestry. Scattered across the island, he had Aunties and Uncles in Nanakuli, up in Makakilo, over on the windward side in the beach town of Waimanalo, and up in Makaha. Nanakuli, where he grew up, was a coastal town on the leeward side of Oahu at a point where the Farrington Highway turned north up the west side of the island.

Densely populated kama'aina and kanaka lived here. There was a difference between the two. Kama'aina simply meant that one was from Hawaii. Anyone. Kanaka meant more. It implied that one was of the Hawaiian people. For Brian's family, part kanaka anyway, like many of these 'locals' they were blended. Part Hawaiian, part Pilipino, part Portuguese, part Samoan. Depending upon the moment, pick your part. They laughed about that as they'd get together for kanikapila – which was the gathering of family and friends and anyone wishing to share their aloha – for island song and storytelling.

Kanikapila was Hawaiian music in an impromptu gathering, a jam session, a gathering taking place nearly anywhere. This sharing of song and often hula was an important part of Brian's upbringing. All of his cousins, Aunties and Uncles took part with ukuleles, guitars, and a pakini bass. Their sessions could last for hours or occasionally on a holiday weekend they'd migrate from venue to venue to venue, beach to homes to a nearby Burger King, covering all of the meals: breakfasts, lunches, and dinners. Brian's fingertips were sometimes blistered by the weekend's end. He was always richer in knowledge and his brown face would hurt from laughing so much.

She was right. He needed to get away - to see family, his Oahu ohana. It had been nearly four years. But he couldn't. They were facing the end of the quarter and were falling short of budget. She continued to try to sell it – a getaway for him, just him – back to Oahu.

"Baby, I can't," shaking his head 'no, he stood close to her, already dressed for work in a mayan blue dress shirt, navy sport coat, jeans and brown Olu Kai's on his feet. She pulled on the lapels of his jacket, drawing him closer for a deep kiss.

"Listen to me mister," she kissed him again. Her dark long hair was shiny, and her big brown eyes were upon him. She tried to talk tough, "I don't need to remind you of how important family is." Her smile was bright, but she tried to conceal it. Forcing a fake frown, her concentration was faltering. "Go to Hawaii, you hear me." Her gruff tone wasn't selling him on the point. They both broke out in giggles.

"I do need to call Leilani. She's left me a couple calls that I haven't returned."

"See. She misses you." Brian's wife of five years was the cliché: the love of his life. Laki, no middle name, Kekahanamanui was as blended as he. However, she lacked the family understanding of what was behind her name. Prior to her North American family, adopted as an American Samoan – she came with a name but no story. Laki meant "lucky" in Samoan. This was her depth of Pacific Islander knowledge. Her parents in San Diego were loving and did all things they could to provide for Laki as she came to live with them at age five. They and Southern California were all she knew. Money was tight, travel was limited, but love was an anchor which held them safe and tethered to each other.

As a petite, chestnut haired, umber-eyed, girl growing up in southern California, she was the crowd pleaser. Fun, spirited, friendly, smart, popular, and along with these strong qualities: incomplete. Brian completed her sense of self. They were meant for each other.

And they were deeply in love. Not at first sight, but quickly and over little time – they became friends in their first semester at San Diego State, then friendly, then something more, and then inseparable as they grew together.

As a Sophomore in High School, she asked her parents to complete a 23andMe ancestry service test kit. Following some mild debate they agreed. It came back somewhat as expected: she was Polynesian – without any surprises. The numbers of percentages were split between several South Pacific nations and equaled 100%. Her Polynesian features in her appearance were as evident as the quotients on the test results yet were lacking the narrative behind them.

There was a slight diversion in their upbringing...and at the same time, something else which they had in common. Laki had loving parents. Brian's parents passed away in an automobile accident when they were apart from him visiting the mainland, the 9th Hawaiian island: Las Vegas. He was a young child, experiencing much of what leeward side nine-year-olds forged through: maturing emotionally, learning to multiply in Math class, trying out for Little League, jamming on his ukulele, and adored as an only child by his loving Hawaiian mother and father. It was abrupt – when he learned of his loss and how his life must change. Without consideration, his Nanakuli Autie and Uncle immediately brought him into their family and raised him as their own.

He stood a head taller than she. Placing his hands on her waist he explained his condition further. "Listen, seriously...my district is the best of the worst. The numbers for the region are off. Tony is under the gun." He was describing his boss, his Regional Vice President, Anthony Carmetti – also known as Testy Tony, because he didn't wear stress or scrutiny well. Ever, including the competitive good times and persecuting bad. Tony was the founder's nephew. This came with additional awareness and expectations to perform well and his region was not. The need to generate competitive year-over-year increases in their comparable stores was exceedingly important. Brian's district was struggling to attain mid-single digit improvements and out of six district's it was the strongest performance the region could produce.

"Should we be worried?" her smile migrated to a concern.

"You should not." He knew how to quell her distress. "After the quarter closes we have a DM meeting in Colorado. We'll reset and have bigger targets to chase, but it'll be fresh metrics and include the comp offsets." This was retail jargon short in code: DM meant District Manager which Brian was for Southern California. Colorado was where their company, Janus One, was located. The targets always included aggressive growth budgets and the 'comp offsets' referred to comparable revenue numbers from the year prior – the holy grail for any retailer to achieve.

Her toes unfurled as she tiptoed to steal another kiss. "Okay BK-12, I won't worry." It was that simple.

"Let's not call ourselves that." He was referring to the nickname: BK12. It was code for his name.

She held her hand to his cheek and stroked his chin, smiling. As their embrace continued, she tried pulling him closer for one last kiss, but stopped short and whispered to him, parsing her words: "Shush..." Cocking her head to the side, with a wide-side-eyed look toward the hallway, "The – monsters...they – are – awake." They stood there in a frozen state, listening.

Rustling noises from the bedrooms made way to the small, cozy kitchen. Their 3-year-old son and 4-year-old daughter, who looked exactly like each of them made small steps in the direction of the white kitchen table with a butcher block top.

"We want pancakes", the little girl said.

"Pancakes," the little boy repeated. He rubbed crust from his eyes and carried a small stuff bear.

"And...we're off," she gave him a pat on the butt as she approached the children. "Of course you do, Lovelies." She spoke sweetly, giving each a small kiss on the check as she ruffled their bedheads.

As Brian turned away from Laki, his ankle twisted enough to cause him to wince. *Not today*, he thought.

Their daughter asked if it was Saturday, because Daddy could stay home on Saturdays and their small son repeated everything she inquired with fewer words. Brian briefly explained that it was a Monday and that he'd need to go to work today. He was filling his travel mug with coffee and looked at the new logo: *Janus One - Sports and More.* It still wasn't comfortable. He was trying to like it though.

His organization, Janus Team Gear, had merged with One Victory Sports. Janus was heavy on the soft goods: apparel and sneakers. One Victory was legacy sporting goods based, featuring sporting hardware over the jerseys and shoes. Over the past several years they were integrating brands and aligning strategy. The water cooler talk was that a sale was on the block. Their prospectus was on ten CEOs desks for consideration. "Out for bid" – the soul of their company wasn't what the DMs wanted to think about, let alone have happen. But this was corporate America. Every company has a price – publicly or in Private Equity. Janus One - Sports and More was their branding transition. Without the merger, they were 85 stores strong in the Pacific West. They were now boasting 190 stores nationally with a premier footprint on the east coast from the merger with One Victory, which was formerly based in Atlanta. Denver or Chicago were the considerations for the new home office. Brian was happy when the decision landed with Colorado's capital.

Janus was the ancient Roman and religious God of transitions, beginnings, featured by doorways to elsewhere's, and depicted as having two faces. Brian took a small sip from the hot coffee, running his thumb across the white logo on the admiral blue tumbler. Maybe it was the add-on "Sports and More" that didn't thrill him.

His ankle didn't' hurt enough this morning to take any pain medicine. He paused to think about it. No. There was the slightest limp which came and went. *No... Well... No.*

When he opened the door, he could feel the brisk air and saw a light breeze blowing on the eucalyptus treetops in park at the end of the street. Light green leaves rustled with a gust of wind. The lock on the ash-gray back door of their small home clicked shut as he closed it.

Outfitted with a backpack, a wad of keys in one hand, a bill for the mailbox, and the roasted brew, he approached their aging but mostly reliable minivan in the driveway. The commute down the San Diego Freeway to SAN would be congested.

As he drove off from their small home, he remembered how he first got tagged as BK12. It was when he arrived at a Regional District Manager meeting as the new San Diego DM. There they were: gathered around a large conference table. They were some of his managerial icons as a store manager. Now they'd become his peers. It was a point he'd have to prove himself all over again. The roster included a young black man leading the L.A. district, a former utility player for the Angels; two women who were former soccer stars representing the Bay Area and Pacific Northwest markets; from Denver and the rocky mountain region, a once-celebrated point guard with the Nuggets; a Mexican American covering the Phoenix and desert west markets.

Then there was Hank Purdy, a former lineman and Longhorn. He had red hair, was barrel chested, bowling ball shoulders and was the biggest personality in any room, describing his results or whatever it was that he was attempting as "Purdy-damned-awesome!" *Huge ego, that one*...Brian remembered their first meeting. Gruff, but at the same time, somewhat charming. Somewhat.

Each of the diverse staff of District Managers had a background in sports. Each had fallen from their grace of fame or their pinnacle of performance. Each brought something to the table for now Janus One – Sports and More.

Representing Texas, of course, because anyone outside of Texas needed the reminder that everything was bigger and sometimes better in Texas – Hank asked Brian to pronounce his name.

"Kekahanamanui. I'm Hawaiian," Brian rattled it off quickly the first time and could see that it'd take a moment or two to sink in. The other DMs simply saw a long last name filled with K's and A's and several other consonants and vowels and didn't know they'd have to pronounce it. Brian repeated the last name slowly, twice, "Kay-kah-hah-nah-mah-new-ee."

"Naw, son," spoke the big Texan, Hank, "Yer gonna need to white board that one fer me, please."

Brian chuckled and obliged with a dry erase marker. Spelling it out with spaces: K E K A H A N A M A N U I.

"But it's pronounced 'diffent than spelt'?" the Texan looked puzzled still. Brian read the room. They were already propping open laptops and checking their phones. Only Hank and his neighboring DM up in L.A. were still interested.

"Yeah, the pronunciation is a little different in the Hawaiian language." Brian was hoping that he was convincing, but quickly deduced what he was working with.

"Ah hell son, that's a lot of letters there. OK if I just call ya' BK 12? Brian and K-something, followed by twelve more letters?"

Tony, his new RVP had snuck in the room and took the helm of the conference table, "Sorry I'm late, was on the phone with corporate. The first item on the agenda was to introduce you to Brian. But it looks like you all have already met BK12."

There were a few laughs and then they took the time to explain their backgrounds and tenure – pre-Janus. Brian knew much of what they were telling him and made some new discoveries.

'BK 12' – the DM introduction - it wasn't how he pictured it in his head, but he too was an athlete and knew that rolling with the game time conditions was what collaboration for the win was about. He accepted the abbreviation. Hank's background in college football already provided common ground with his new peer.

The minivan accelerated up the exit ramp to the highway and into rolling congestion. They said they lived in San Diego. Yet if someone really knew San Diego and the coastal towns along the shores, they'd let them know it was Oceanside – which was a good 40 minutes from San Diego city center. Oceanside and south - good enough to call it San Diego. San Clemente and north – good enough to call it Los Angeles.

They felt lucky to be qualified for their $725,000, 3 bed - 2 bath home of nearly 1,600 square feet. "Maybe they made a mistake?" - they said of the bank which approved their home loan. It was followed by another question, "How are we really going to afford it?" Housing prices were only higher the closer to San Diego. Oceanside, east of the 5 was the best they could do with the schools they wanted. So, it wasn't actually nested up to the ocean, but a short 10-minute drive did the trick.

Brian turned on the radio. Laki had the volume turned up and tuned in to classic rock which they both enjoyed. A song, *Moving In Stereo* by The Cars had just begun playing. It reminded him of Fast Times at Ridgemont High. He joked with the traffic, only speaking to himself and rhetorically: *"Okay Drivers - How many of you are listening to this and thinking about Phoebe Cates right now?"* Punching buttons on the screen to a neighboring station, he landed on "I Love Rock 'N Roll, by Joan Jett & the Blackhearts. He caught the chorus. "One for two," he said to himself referring to how many songs he could catch the title and chorus on. He listened to some of it, then tapped the screen again. Stevie Nicks of Fleetwood Mac sang the ballad, *Landslide*, but it wasn't being sung from the chorus, so he'd have to settle for one for three today. The rest of the song was meaningful, and Brian knew it because he attempted to pick it on his ukulele. He saw himself doing that as a teen in high school back on Oahu. It was a song about growing up and the passing of time.

He then reached for a saved channel on Spotify: KINE, an FM channel out of Honolulu. He dialed down the volume. Softer island music played. A slack key guitar picked and strummed, and a woman's voice sang in Hawaiian tongue. He listened as he daydreamed, rolling along with the traffic.

Remembering his arrival at SDSU, which was what eventually led him along into his current position, he backtracked to a conversation which took place a dozen years ago: a smile came to his face. He remembered it well...

The college football coaches were seated in the head coach's office, flanking a wooden desk with two landline phones, a couple framed pictures and a stack of manila files upon it. Wearing team-colored polo's of red, black, and white, they were in conversation about a player when Brian walked into the room. The chair they wanted him to sit in was directly in front of the head coach.

"Have a seat, Brian." The eighteen-year-old looked around the room at the men in their thirties, forties, fifties. Their experience was intimidating to him, but he brought courage with him to the meeting.

"How was your flight in?" The head coach was reading through his high school transcripts and skimming some papers within the file. He thought it was his. It may have been something else.

"It was great, thank you sir," He paused briefly, then quickly added, cocking his head to the side in a deep voice, "I mean, Coach. I truly appreciate this opportunity to come and meet with you, and to let you see me in action, and to prove I can help this team win." He hesitated to tell them it was only the fourth time he'd been up in the air, on an airplane to the mainland. The third was when he came for the full equipment four-day session three weeks ago.

Another coach off to the side of the head coach, the Offensive Coordinator spoke, "Brian, there's a bit of a problem..."

The Defensive Coordinator was seated on the other side of the head coach and jumped in on the conversation, "As I'm sure you know, we've been looking at a number of candidates for your position. And we've identified some good players who can help us win."

A long and uncomfortable pause took place. The coach and the coordinators and a couple other trainers in the office exchanged glances.

Brian didn't know whether they were going to ask him to pack his bags and head back to the terminal or let him know he would be playing for the team.

"We're not going to be bringing you on as a Wide Receiver, Brian. There's a lot of talent out there. Sorry." The Offensive Coordinator was the most physically fit in the room. He looked at Brian when he spoke and then looked at the Head Coach.

Brian sat in disappointment. His shoulders slumped in a reaction to the letdown.

"But...there's a hole in our player lineup." The Head Coach seated at the desk spoke, "When we brought you in for a look a few weeks ago, we liked the moxie you brought to the show, your quickness, eagerness... Brian, we saw something we liked." The coach was making circling motions with his hand to help explain some form of enlightenment.

Brian shook his head 'yes' slightly and slowly. There was a glint of hope here. He heard one of the trainers from the back of the office cough. It was a nerve-wracking moment of silence.

"Brian, we'd like you to play Corner for us. Preferable Left Corner." This time it was the Defensive Coordinator speaking. To Brian, it felt like an offer. But it was now his turn to play coy. He hesitated.

"I've...I've only played Wide Out or Tight End. I've never been in the Cornerback position."

They pounced on that comment, "This isn't High School football on the west side of Oahu, son. This is collegiate, Mountain West. Your speed is an issue at Wide Receiver," one coach spoke with dismissal – waving his hand.

"And your size is a problem at TE," said another from the back of the office.

The Head Coaches turn came with the explanation and the strategy: "Brian, we want you on the other side of the ball and the other side of the line in the Mountain West Conference." He paused, checking Brian's reaction, then added shaking his head, "We've got a good shot at beating Boise State and UNLV with you in that position. And we got a great shot of beating UH. You know many of those players. Now, I cannot say you're going to start, that is up to you. But we'll have a number for you." The coach was referring to a jersey.

Brian understood some of their strategy and was thinking things through when the Defensive Coordinator jumped in, "Son, do you want to be an Aztec or not?"

"Growing up in Hawaii, I've always pictured myself as a football player for the Rainbow Warriors," delivering an extended pause, he sat there hoping that his teasing delivery would land well with the staff, "...that is until I met you fine gentlemen from SDSU – and learned of the great program here, off the rock. Now I see myself and my team beating Manoa." He smiled at seeing the Head Coach smile broadly, stand, and extend his hand to Brian.

"Welcome to San Diego State University, Brian." The Head Coach's handshake was aggressive and there were several chuckles in the coach's office. "Champions deliver championships. Let's go win."

He slow rolled down I-5 toward San Diego. Occasionally he'd see the waves of the other side of the Pacific curling against beaches in the distance. It was true what their real estate agent described when buying their home. Driving from Oceanside to the city: *It was one of the most beautiful commutes in the country. The view was mesmerizing. Who cared how long it might take?*

4

The Volatility Index

The flatline alarm at the nurse's station sounded a deafening squeal at 4:30am. The night shift sprinted to room 1154, where Jacob was sedated and peacefully sleeping. It had been a quiet night otherwise. But, the call to action turned out false. There was no explanation for the alert.

The ECG in the room was active and he was in a stable condition. The two nurses followed protocol, noting the disturbance. However with no cause for calling Jacob's doctors, the functional actions taken would be more of a technical system device issue than anything else. The RNs noted the medicinal application drip level in the IV, checked the catheter, monitored and registered vitals, and recorded statistics on shiny new tablet PCs.

The black man resembling the doctor that Adele noticed the night before emerged from Jacob's room at 5:30am, before the shifts changed. He was no longer dressed in the hospital smocks. His shoes were scuffed and worn, and his pants were dark brown and wrinkled. He was wearing a checkered flannel shirt that looked like it was a gift from many holidays ago, and he took a deep breath and looked in each direction. He had a dark jacket draped over his arm and was still drawing red suspenders up over his shoulders. First one arm, then the next.

He turned back around toward the door pausing to assess something and reached up to the room number plate on the wall, running his aging fingers across the number a couple times: 1154. Then, he reviewed the skin on the back of his hands, rubbing the wrists and knuckles. It was as if he'd been contemplating their work. There was an arcane rite within his actions. He yawned, turned, took tired steps down the hallway, finding his way to the staircase. The door closed quietly behind him. And he was gone.

At 5:40, one full day after Jacob's heart attack, again the flatlining electrocardiogram alarm sounded. This time, the alarm was valid. The ECG signaled that Jacob Paisley was crashing. His heart, carefully reconstructed a day earlier by New York's best cardiologists, was failing.

Four nurses in the area and two on-call doctors scrambled, frantically acting to administer Arginine Vasopressin, AVP. The peptide didn't produce the desired results within the two minute window. The defibrillator was charged, and with seconds counting, a doctor demanded that contact be cleared of the patient and shocked his heart with 1000-volt ZOLL paddles. The lime green neon beat-keeper responded immediately after the first attempt. The flatline was met with systolic and diastolic measurements of predictability. The outcome was favorable. Saved. The ECG alarm in Jacob's room triggered the alarm at the nurses' station, which was still squealing in a different octave than the one in the patient room, which stabilized. An oxygen mask was hissing on Jacob's face as the doctors and nurses attended to house-like speculation as to what could have caused the disruption. Acute myocardial infarction occurs when the blood supply is altered to the heart muscle. The circumspect doctors did everything possible to mitigate risk.

With sharp and rapid tones of diagnosis, their curiosity was somewhat solved when they threw back the sheets and found one black sock and one unlaced black dress shoe on Jacob's right foot.

But still...? Dressed to kill? How did the investment manager, wired to the cardiac monitoring devices, sporting a catheter, and heavily sedated manage to make it to a locked closet in his room and find the strength to slip on one sock and a fancy dress shoe before the alarm sounded alerting the nurses station?

After the doctors left the room, after Jacob was stabilized, two nurses were gossiping about Jacob's notorious wealth. "I'll bet he made more last week than I made last year," one said. Another slightly older nurse, with an uncle in the bond trading business, knowing the enormity of Wall Street capacity said "Honey, he's made more laying here, than you and I made this past decade."

"Yeah, well look who's on the table now, and who's standing. I'll bet he uses all the personal pronouns. I, me, my – all day long."

"Are you on that kick again? What you got against rich people?"

"Uh-huh. It's telling."

"You're something, you know that?"

"I don't' have nothin' against rich folks like this. But, five minutes into a conversation with one, I can tell you whether they really rich or not."

"Girl, I call BS on that." They giggled, traded barbs and chit chat about his condition as they quickly marked the medical charts. And before they left they were conciliatory in that they were in this together, caring for the rich and the poor, the forgotten and honored, neatly tucking him in and flattening sheets.

They later discovered that his cell phone had apparently bounced from the gurney and lay face down underneath the bed - the activity light blinking wildly.

No one knew that four outbound calls were made. No one suspected two trades from the European FTSE exchange. And no one, possibly other than a limo driver or Jacob's offshore cash manager conducting explicit wire transfers to a New Jersey checking account and well aware of a variety of indiscretions, would have known of returned text messages that evening to *Victoria*.

The one-shoe-on one-shoe-off story grew legs and ran as it made its way back to PPCM the next morning. The news of Jacob's quest to return to the offices of Paisley & Pierce Capital Management one day after a heart attack and repair surgery was magic material that quickly spread and was widely embellished as a call-to-action. *JP's will to win, his convictions and intentions, are second-to-none*...they said. If Jacob were there to adjust the collective observation of the team, he may have added that a team gathers their competencies in all forms of participation. The goal is usually toward points on a scoreboard. However, moving the chains toward a first down counted for something too. Anything to advance the cause mattered.

Jacob had a framed familiar African proverb quote propped up on a bookshelf in his office. The background pictured a lion, sitting in tall golden grass. The words were in black bold copperplate font and stated:

Every morning in Africa, a gazelle wakes up. It knows it must run faster than the fastest lion or it will be captured, killed, and eaten. Every morning a lion wakes up. It knows it must outrun the slowest gazelle or it will starve to death.

It doesn't matter whether you are a lion or gazelle... When the sun comes up, you'd better start running.

Like the lion, before the dawn, he was up and running so that he could eat. Like a gazelle, he was up and running so that he could prevent the experience of defeat – at the risk of all future success.

In 1989, Professors Menachem Brenner and Dan Galai published an academic article about volatility in the markets. Later, in 1992, the Chicago Board Options Exchange retained a Professor Robert Whaley to design an index based upon stock market volatility. It was referred to as the VIX. The VIX predicts movements, such as wild swings or stability, within the upcoming 30-day period.

The "fear index" as it's often referred to as, represented the lion and the gazelle. Running hard to eat, and running hard to avoid teeth – Jacob Paisley lived like the VIX. Leveraging bullish and bearish opportunities, writing contracts, aggregating the options, puts and calls – Jacob was running hard. He was moving a billion to make 10 million.

But, he wasn't running fast enough. And saw the gnash and felt the teeth.

His unanswered phone buzzed. Text messages accumulated. Email gathered. The activity light on the face continued to stroke red flashes.

It was early afternoon. The sun was shining brightly upon the New York skyline. Jacob looked out the window upon a hundred battleship-gray commercial buildings. Following Covid lockdowns, pandemic work-from-home hybrid agreements, each one had a partial workforce of people doing their in-office things-to-do, with or without purpose. Competing, teaming, operating autonomously or in synchronization toward a common cause. Their agendas were either aligned or disengaged. Thousands upon thousands of tiny little people with a hope of a better tomorrow.

He was thinking to himself and realized that it was more than thought. He was whispering: *That's why they would invest with an insurance company, or a financial advisor, or a money manager like PPCM. Investing is a down payment toward...*

"Hope," Jacob said it out loud as he daydreamed at the sky-scape, "Hope - is what they're really working for. It's what keeps them going back for more. Hope that tomorrow is...is better than today."

Adele, was stopped between the door and his bed. She had a small vase of Asian lilies in one hand and two contracts in another. "Should I come back at another time?" she asked.

He looked at her and smiled. "Hey, there she is." He wondered what he might look like to her. She'd never seen him vulnerable in this sort of a way. "No, come on in. I'm just... Just, nothing."

She approached the bed cautiously and set the contracts on a bedside stand, then took the glass vase over to a credenza. Her white blouse had a dusting of pollen from the pink flowers.

"I'm not used to seeing you..." she stopped short.

He looked down at himself, wearing the hospital gown and a sheet covering his legs.

She approached him and in a rare form of intimacy ran her fingers through his hair. He assumed he was mussed and appeared a little less than his primped norm.

"So...how bad was it?" His voice was course. Jacob was referring to the day.

"One drubbing was enough. Right? Isn't that what you always say to the Traders?" She was intentionally avoiding the question.

"That's for them, not for us." He had a way of mitigating bad news with the salespeople. When the day was worthy of distress, you'd have to say to yourself, 'Once was enough', and avoid the replay. As Jacob would explain in a sports analogy, people loved to rewind a bad day and play the highlight reel of the fumbles, and the bad passes, and the missed tackles. Jacob would tell his Traders that they should review the mistakes once, learn from them and move on. But, a good day? Revel within its greatness.

She looked at him staring into the distance, looking off into the corner of the room. "I hate to do this, but you'd kill me if I didn't. So, in the spirit of expediting, here are two contracts that I'll drop off for your signatures. In short, you got what we wanted on both. The Kingsley Foods deal, and," she looked at the second to remember it, "Jefferson County." Legal and the underwriters agreed to strike out your suggested redlines.

It was a new look for her. Jacob teased her about the readers. She was wearing black rimmed eyewear which he called the sexy librarian look.

"Seriously?" He said it with skepticism and relief at the same time, knowing that she was guarding him against stress. "What else?" He was prying.

"No. Not going to do it. Only simple stuff today." Adele was fidgeting with her phone to recant all of the bullshit that she dealt with earlier in the day. Shaking her head, dismissing hundreds of items that might have raised his blood pressure, "Nothing much here really. How should I adjust your schedule for January?"

He looked at his phone quickly and shook his head slightly, "No changes. San Francisco the first week, Miami and Chicago the tail end of the second, and London from the 29th though Feb 2nd. I'll only want the Gulfstream for the Bay Area trip. Business class is good enough for London, but I'll stretch it to include Zurich this time. Outbound, the afternoon of the first and returning with a red-eye on the second through JFK."

She was taking notes and also shook her head and said, "We'll talk about that later. Your voice sounds dry. Can I get you some water?"

Jacob was still looking at the schedule on his phone, then looked up at her and sighed. "What would I do without you?" he asked.

She smiled, and assured him, "You'd get by just fine without me. Who knows..." She looked at the IV with plastic tubing connecting the back of his wrist to the liquid back on a hook.

Jacob looked in her direction and spoke slower. "You're the one who's always watching what I eat; competing with me on steps; calming the frenzy; tossing buckets of water on my fires...", his voice trailed off and he looked back out the windows into New York's sunny skyline.

"Someone's got to take care of the company," she shot back. What do they say? - If you don't want someone to drive you crazy, then don't give them the keys to your sanity. Years ago... You gave me *all* the keys." They both giggled as her phone rang. Holding a single finger up, she motioned for Jacob that she'd just be a minute and stepped out the door. He felt tired. Too tired.

He was happy she came to visit. Givers, they were the 'honey' people. Takers – they were the 'vinegar' people. Adele was pure honey.

Adele added, "Has the doctor been in recently?"

"Nah – just the fucking nurses and vampires."

Farsighted, she dropped her chin to her chest so that she could look at him over the top of her thick framed glasses. A curious look was upon her face.

"You know, the Phlebotomists."

"Ah...yes, the vampires."

Just then the door opened, and a black nurse came in with a gray tray, carrying small white paper cup and a clear plastic cup of water. Handing it to Jacob, he observed a few pastel-colored pills, didn't question anything and swallowed them.

Nearsighted, she slipped on a pair of glasses from her smock's pocket and looked across Jacob toward Adele. "And I'd be the fucking nurse..." She offered a perturbed smirk.

Jacob placed the cup back on the tray, smiled, and offered a depthless, "Thank you for your care."

She retreated, insulted, the same way she came.

Adele shook her head, smiling at him without words. Knowing all of their moments were as measurable as they were immeasurable – she kicked off her heals and curled up on the couch in his room. Silence was sometimes the best medicine.

He closed his eyes, thinking that he'd sign the contracts after he rested his eyes...if just for a minute. Adele...she always had his back... He should have listened to her...taken better care of himself long ago...

Drifting off...it felt so foreign, yet so peaceful - to be temporarily out of the serial hectic moments that was the life of Jacob Paisley. As if he were floating above Adele and him in this moment, he was asleep.

Jacob placed a phone call to David Ripley. Too much to text. Ripley, an outsourced security specialist that PPCM used on occasion. Trust was the omni-ingredient in his business. Paisley and Ripley worked closely together on several projects years ago, and recently PPCM retained the consultant through a contract. He could trust Ripley.

He pictured Ripley taking his call, in his uptown apartment, regardless of the weather, inside at home, watching TV, eating a grilled cheese sandwich, and drinking a cold cup of coffee - whatever: wearing an old trench coat from Macy's circa 1995. Ripley had a distinct voice: croaky. Ripley called it vocal fry.

Jacob explained his condition and asked if any advice would be relevant.

After listening, the security consultant quickly offered an opinion. "A few things here, Jacob," Ripley began, "As you know, more so than anyone, my role exists due to secrets. Intellectual Property; patents; NDAs; contract violations; lies; misappropriations; insider-trading; indiscretions, and so on. Basically, what you know, what you tell me, what you haven't told me yet, and what you're not willing to tell me."

"Sounds familiar. With this, you know it all."

"So, no pre-existing conditions? As in, no prescription overdose? No substance abuse? No booze? No..."

"Nothing. None of that," Jacob interrupted.

"You're fine," Ripley replied. "Boring. But, there's no risk to administer to. Listen, in our line of work, it happens. There's fuck-ton of stress and heart attacks will happen. When you act or provide malicious conduct in a manner to create risk within a client's financial portfolio, you might have to manage to the behavior."

"Sounds like you've encountered this before?" Jacob asked.

"You have no damage control to grapple with here."

"And the Board?" Jacob asked. He was referring to a conversation to apprise his Board of Directors. There were several members which he had crossed recently.

"Fuck. The. Board of Directors", Ripley shot back. "None of their damned business at this point. You're not public, thank God. This is why I only work with Private Equity. You heard me, right? Fuck the Board."

"Thanks David, and...yes, fuck the bee-oh-dee." Jacob was genuinely appreciative that he took the call but didn't actually take the time to thank him with David's interruption.

"I gotta' be honest with you, Jacob. I thought we were going to have a different conversation. About...you know. Maybe Victoria."

Jacob listened carefully but said nothing.

"See...you're not saying anything. That tells me I might have my finger on your trigger."

"Let's leave Victoria out of it," Jacob thought of his siren-song.

"It's the abundance that usually does us in. Too much stuff, you're a hoarder. Too much speed – you wreck. Too much sunshine – skin cancer. Too much booze – you're an alcoholic. Too many drugs – you're an addict."

"Can we let this go today? I've had too much..."

"Ha! I see what you did there." Ripley's voice was extra-gravelly, "I'll go easy on you. But pump those brakes dude. I need you as a source of income."

"By the way, that trader that left you guys last week did end up with Goldman."

Jacob was perturbed. "Shit. I knew it."

"He's been in their Jersey City building and in the tower. Not sure which side of the Hudson he'll land on. From his email, phone and files, I couldn't find a hint of do-not-compete violations. He's clean and GS wouldn't let him leverage his IP inappropriately anyway."

"Yeah, I know. I liked him – he had the potential. Hate to see the kid go."

Ripley used a line he'd recited before about the Goliath competitor: "It's an army of scary-smart inmates over there. Thirty thousand of them.

"It's culture. I've lost four traders to their allure in the past year. There are less than a thousand of us. The juggernaut is attractive in several ways."

"Well, compressed workweeks and job-sharing might be important to some. But, not him. He left for the comp plan. From what I've gathered, he wants an eighty-something percent lift in compensation. Culture eats strategy...or strategy eats culture...or some bullshit. This kid is all about speed -to-dollars."

"...for breakfast, as they say." Jacob finished Ripley's thought. "Thanks for the update. I just hate to be a training station for any of the houses. Disappointing, but good to tie out on that one."

"Hey Paisley, I've got another call coming in. Can we break?"

"We're good here David, thank you."

"Anytime. Gotta' go. Late."

Jacob heard the beep, beep, beep which terminated the call.

After waking up and late into the evening he was at it again, coaching of his traders, "Work with the value bands to determine the averages. Measure the primary tendencies. And mitigate the risk through the Fin-Four stress assessment tool. Substantiate the lift with dollar-cost averaging, sector deviations and earnings projections. Get it on a GANNT chart and don't forget to run the capitalization ratios against the hypothetical over's and under's." He spoke in an industry code. Jargon woven into his instructions with metonyms, oxymoron and metaphors tumbled across his tongue into the cell phone. It felt comfortable. "I'd like you to run the prelim modeling with Danny."

Silence surrounded him while he listened to the voice on the other end of the line. "No, not really, he's a comer and I want to give him a few projects." A nurse walked in on the conversation to measure the drip from his IV bag hanging above his head. She checked his wrist, marked on a silver tablet from her smock pocket, gave him a quick smile and retreated to the hallway.

Adele had left the hospital room shortly after he awoke. The lights on the medical monitoring dashboard above his bed were blue, green and red numbers. Bleeps, blips, and numbers in a variety of fonts filled the screen. Paisley listened to some mild rebuttal on the phone. "There's no split of commission. I just like the kid and that'll have to be good enough." He felt the stitches with this free hand and grimaced at some discomfort from the incision.

"Alright, we're good then. Good job. Keep me apprised." The call ended and he looked up at the ceiling. It wasn't a prayer, but he spoke out loud while staring at the white tiles, *I need a nice surprise here. How about a little help. Please?* He looked at a clock on the wall. 1:25am. Jacob closed his eyes and fell into a deep sleep.

5

Uninvited

Cutter was abrupt with his reply to Kerri, "I didn't...I didn't invite you back you know. Just to be clear... You! You, were the one that wanted to come back!" It was a senseless argument and happened often because he could not control his emotions.

She had been pleading for him to pick up a Gatorade at Duane Reade since he was making the run for more creatine. Their exchange was about the imbalance of favors.

"Draining me dry, woman. God! I can't stand you sometimes. Shit!" He acted like he was smothering from accommodating her requests when she purposefully limited her asks, banking them for what she wanted most: drugs, a peg, to get razed.

This was dire though. Her throat was burning. She needed a drink. And a score from the beast. "Please, just help me..." she croaked as she spoke.

She lay on the sleeping bag on the grimy couch. Not moving much, she over-extended her reach onto a glass coffee table for Skittles. It was dinner tonight.

Drugs. This would mean that Kerri had to find the side of herself that she loathed. Her darkness. A passenger that was hidden within – and only came out when asked to. Her darkness came out to play when it was time. When it crawled back into hiding, it left a mess.

Kerri would have to piece things together and clean up the after mass. It was coming. The time was growing closer.

Crazy Kerri was the name of her dark passenger. She knew this routine too well because as her need for a syringe of heroine became uncontrollable and relentless, this would happen: Crazy Kerri would come out of hiding, reaching into a black duffel bag tucked away in the back of the small bedroom closet. Within it were unusual items. A black leather whip, a corset, handcuffs, a plum sparkly mask matching a bra and panties that looked like they were worn in a Mardi Gras parade or naughty costume party.

Kerri spoke of her altered self as a third person. 'Crazy Kerri' was who she'd reference when she needed her levity, supplied from Cutter.

"Maybe there's something I have that you might want." She tried in her best effort to sound seductive.

Cutter shot a glance her way, "Maybe there is." He smiled a beige-toothed smile through thin lips. "What flavor?"

She liked *Frost* the best. And after he was gone, she went there – knowing that when he returned with some sharps and the Wicked Witch, she'd need to pay her taxes. It was drug jargon for their exchange.

The acts in their '*play, then party*' exchange followed a pattern. Crazy Kerri would reach into her bag of tricks, sorting through what Kerri might have acquired, to gather a smile-maker or two for Cutter. Nothing was forbidden here, and Crazy Kerri liked the exotic darkness surprise. She'd shower and put on makeup, then slip into lingerie of lace, satin, mesh, or leather. Her sensuality grew as she gently touched perfume in tender parts of her body, lathering them with lotions. A moan would escape her throat as she knew their time together was growing closer – as was her hard candy, her heroine.

Cutter would be wearing a towel, laying on the bed. She'd tell him to remove it and "Put these on instead," while handing him handcuffs, or handing him a leather whip. He didn't know how to use it. It was more of a thrashing than a sexual prop, but a means to an end. She usually would endure a spanking which would hurt his hand more than her ass. But she could take it. The jack-up was worth it.

Their love making was all of fifteen minutes.

Kerri would spit - at her own image in the mirror with disgust for herself.

Crazy Kerri swallowed - the moment whole, enjoying the erotic action and the outcome. She'd do anything to generate a thrill which led to her side of their arrangement. When the rotation was for her pleasure, it wasn't for sexual reciprocation. But rather the process which followed their sexual deal: a point and a tie, the slam, the rocket fuel, and a parachute ride. Her drug nod was her end of their deal.

It wasn't an intimate sexual swap – it was commutation, a twisted trade, quid-pro-quo bartering. Their love making was a wicked transaction.

*****

"Well, you're not dead yet. Apparently, you're still workin' on it." The black man was flipping through some pages in a small red book he appeared to be reading or editing. "Unfinished business." He had glasses low on his nose, and looked over the top of the frames at Jacob. He was wearing a checkered shirt and had red suspenders hanging loosely over his shoulders while sitting in a chair in the corner of the hospital room.

"Who the hell are you?" Jacob asked in a groggy voice while still waking up. He wanted to rub his eyes but couldn't.

There wasn't an immediate answer.

Jacob spoke again, "You look like Morgan Freeman's younger brother."

"Younger? Small step, right direction. I don't know that Ellis Boyd Redding had younger siblings."

"Son." Even though he was recovering, he still had his wits. "Younger son. Much." He also knew that this was a foreign and vulnerable moment for him.

"Name's Gabe Hollins. Some folks call me Ruby."

After a breath, and a pause, Jacob sorted out the past couple days. It had been about as active as he could make it. But the handsome elderly black man didn't fit in anywhere.

Clearing his throat, to insert any amount of authority into this apparent lack of control, Jacob asked, "So...why do they call you Ruby if your name is Gabe Hollins? And *really*...who the hell *are* you?" Jacob tried to lift his arms. Things were still sore. Not an acute pain, but a dull ache. No better than yesterday.

"I am who I am. Already told ya that. Gabriel Ruben Hollins. Ruby for short." He marked the place in the small leather bound book and folded his glasses into his shirt pocket. "You're probably looking for a title, or my place in your life. See if I fit in correctly. Somethin' like that." The freckled gentleman seemed cheery. He also had a disposition of a playful presence. It was like he'd been waiting for this minute, for this conversation. The corners of his mouth were ready to smile. His cheeks were high and his eyes were wide.

Jacob still felt a twinge of conflict, but it wasn't in the inflection of the stranger.

"Well, why *are* you here? And... And that's what I'd like to know. Why are *you* here? And how'd you get past my security?"

"Your security?" he chuckled. "Hospital volunteer. I'm sort of a bridge to what's next. But, let's stick with hospital volunteer for now."

"What? Hospital volunteer?" Jacob repeated, "For what?"

"That depends."

"Depends on what?"

The black man smiled now, "On - what needs fixed?" He spoke slowly and calmly.

"Fixed?" Jacob was growing impatient and pressed for command of the conversation. "Listen, I don't *know* you. And I'm pretty sure you shouldn't be in here. And I probably don't *need* you because nothing needs *fixed* right now. I had a heart condition, and that's been taken care of. Everything here has been fixed. So, if you would be kind enough to go *volunteer* somewhere else..."

Ruby interrupted, looking directly into Jacob's piercing blue eyes with a coded message of purpose, "Dakota."

Jacob hesitated, and then added, "Dakota? Dakota... what?"

"Your cardiologist, his name's Dr. Dakota. He fixed your heart, but there's more fixin' to do."

"Fixing?" It was then that Jacob immediately recognized him. "You. You were in the ambulance on the way to the hospital...and. And you were washing your hands before surgery. You said something to me. And... I've seen you before. Wait. I don't know where I know you from, but you are familiar. What's happening here?" He looked around the room for answers. There were none. He looked at the floor for a foundation of meaning. Just clean polished white tiles.

Over the hospitals intercom, a soft classic melody played. A xylophone played a lullaby. Jacob listened for a moment and asked his visitor, "What the hell is that?"

The black man named Ruby was smiling and when the short stanza ended, he answered. "Newborn. Nursery music. A baby was just born. You know, a lullaby. Brahms lullaby." And after looking at Jacob the smile on Ruby's face diminished. "You don't...do you?"

Jacob looked past Ruby blankly. He shook his head slowly, thoughts elsewhere, and as if he were answering the wall, "No." Then he added, is the fucking maternity ward?"

"They say when something needs fixed, God sends a baby to do the job."

"What?"

"You're out of your zone, aren't you Jacob Paisley?"

Jacob was confused, uncomfortable and reached for the bedside control.

"It's as if you're swimming upstream, right?"

"I swim like a stone." He said this as he pushed the red HELP button at the top of the control panel.

Ruby took a moment to consider what had just happened and finally responded, "That's good to know." He took another glance at Jacob as he gathered the sections of a newspaper and folded them neatly to tuck under his arm. He paused and as if he were placing the final pieces of a puzzle together smiled at the result and said, "That's it then."

"You should go." Jacob demanded.

"And as far as who I am. Well, we have met before. I gave you resuscitation and chest compressions on Beaver Street until someone finally called 911. But, more about that some other time. Perhaps. Right now you've got Dr. Dakota coming in to see you." He slipped a brown jacket on, and gathered his things. "Jacob Columbus Paisley. Born on a Sunday. Lived on a Monday. Puts himself first. Makes the rules as he goes." Ruby mocked Jacob's false threat, "...How'd you get past my security..." He chuckled again. "This is gonna be good." The door was opened and the he was gone before Jacob could ring the call button again.

Jacob was considering that he had been given medicine that caused a hallucination. *Maybe they mixed it up. You hear occasionally that that sort of thing happens.* He was fine the last two days. Lots of sleep, some limited communication with senior traders at PPCM, Adele had visited three times on Tuesday and twice yesterday.

The concierge that the firm had sent was set up in the next room and was operating upon calls, email, and errands. And more importantly...he had exchanged a dozen naughty text messages with Victoria. Victoria. Oh...Victoria.

Puzzled, things were not fitting. He didn't care for or agree with what had just been said. And as it settled, the incongruous comments from the black man implied that knowledge was one-sided. In the world of high-stakes money management: this was dangerous. *How did he know I was born on a Sunday?*

He felt his chest. The incisions were much smaller than he thought they would be. The burns on his ribs from the defibrillator itched. It was now three days later, he was calibrating what had transpired over the past ninety six hours.

In walked a tall thin Caucasian man in a physician's jacket. A nametag, DR. DAKOTA, was clipped onto the pocket. Dark curly hair and stylish rectangular horn-rimmed glasses, this must be the same cardiologist that he had talked to the past two days, but for some mysterious reason he had little association with.

Something wasn't fitting. Something wasn't processing quite right. Jacob thought that sedation was the culprit. Dr. Dakota said nothing just yet, as he traced a stylus over the screen of a tablet computer.

From the adjoining room, Shelby, the PPCM concierge walked in and asked, "Sir – everything alright?" She was blond, petite, athletic looking. Dressed in a low cut white blouse and a navy skirt she said, "It sounded like you talking, but there didn't seem to be anyone in here. And I have your phone, registering calls. Everything good?" She glanced in the direction of Jacob, and the doctor.

Confused, Jacob faked it, "Good." He looked at Shelby and dismissed her and squinted at Dr. Dakota. Bewildered, Paisley questioned his own logic and reconsidered the past two days lying in the hospital: *Ruby. Gabriel Ruben Hollins. A client? A competitor? It's the first time I've seen him? How can that be? Drugs.* But, he disqualified that because Tuesday and Wednesday were somewhat productive, and he remembered the interaction with a wide variety of specialists in and out of the room, educating him on terminology and recovery plans and setting expectations. Most of it fell upon deaf ears.

He saw tickers again within products and people's actions. The hospital had CNBC, MSNBC, Bloomberg TV and Fox New Business. Some things appeared normal, and some things were *off.*

Dr. Dakota finally asked, after a lengthy review of the charts, "And how are we feeling today?"

At first, silence was Jacob's answer. And then for the second time within two minutes, he faked an answer, "Much better. Am I on any - juice – you know hallucinogens?"

The doctor looked at the chart on the PC, "Ahh...no. Nothing that you've been given should alter your mental state other than sleepiness, grogginess, sedation. You know, pain relief." He looked at the charts from the tablet personal computer again, "No. No changes made. The antibiotic topical may have changed. That's all. Why? Is there a problem?"

"Not at all. I'm curious what I'm on."

The doctor smiled and pointed at the three IV drips hanging above Jacobs head and said, "Well, that is a little more than just Kool-Aid. But, we will probably have you off of that in a couple days. There's an anticoagulant called Dalteparin and a Beta Blocker call Ziac. That's it's short name. Want to know it's long name?

"Sure." Jacob was wondering which drug house carried the patents and what the pipeline looked like. He was wondering about the fair-market-value of the brand and whether protection was being contested by any of the healthcare industry lawyers that he knew in the Princeton area where many of the drug firms were located. He heard the doctor talking, but was not listening. *Focus*, he thought.

"...prolol hydrochlorothiazide. We just call it Biso-25 for short. I'll have the nurse bring you the actual scripts and the side-effect detail. Your charts don't indicate any allergies, are there..."

"No, no allergies. I was curious, that's all."

Dr. Dakota scrolled a few more notes on the computer screen. After a familiar nurse joined Dakota, they teamed together to poke and prod at Jacob, registering stats and logging his conditions diligently in a notebook PC.

Jacob asked, "Is there a black man, a hospital volunteer that is supposed to visit with me?"

They briefly looked at each other, knowing that there were no visitors that had been hanging around this private room. The private clientele rooms were closely monitored.

"An older gentleman named Ruby?"

"No – don't know of a Ruby," the middle aged doctor replied.

"How about Gabe? Or Gabriel Hollins."

The nurse was certain. She flipped bangs from her forehead and replied. "No sir. I've been providing care on this floor for a few years now. We have no one here by that name."

Jacob described him to her, and to the doctor with no more progress. "Look him up in the directory, would you please?"

The nurse said that she'd check it out. The doctor made a few more notes in his log, grabbed Paisley by the ankle on his way out the door and said, "Be well. The hard part's over. Time to rest," and with no more bedside manner, was gone.

The nurse changed the top sheet, and carefully laid a heated blanket over Paisley's legs. It felt nice. He reached for his personal phone on the bedside table. A notification push message came through.

Victoria text messaged Jacob: *naughty pic? Make u feel better?!*

He texted back: *that'd be nice, but the real thing will cure my ills!*

She forwarded a link to private room chat session on an app she loaded on his phone for him..

Jacob texted: *u'r a very combustible force / u know that - right?*

His phone blinked red indicating that a file had been transferred. He was about to open it when Shelby walked back into Jacob's room from her assigned makeshift business center in the adjoining room next door. She had a small stack of documents with her, clutching them with both hands. Her legs crossed while she was standing at his bedside.

When Jacob saw her, he barked the command for her to check on a Gabiel Hollins as well – perhaps Ruby. She dropped off the papers on a bedside rolling desk and replied, "Certainly sir. Right away." She rushed off without actually knowing what her directive really was.

Then, a social worker, a grey-haired woman about his age visited Jacob and provided some more advice and precautions pertaining to Jacob's tender state and advised him of the pressure of his work, how a heart attack could have been brought on by a sum of years of stress, and that he probably wouldn't be himself for a couple weeks. She mentioned that the hospital could provide a number of forms of counseling, and he adamantly rejected the offer.

Jacob said to her, "Listen, therapy like that is for someone who remotely wants to get better. It's not for someone who wants to stay the same. I'm not mentally desperate. Not looking for psychological support. Allow yourself to consider that. It isn't for me."

Thinking that the job didn't afford him a couple weeks to recover, Jacob contemplated the immediate urgency in the market and the potential of another gyration, this time in the form of a quick recovery. When bear markets bounced, the gains were often captured within days. Buy and hold was a thin slice of the diversification of a capital management firm these days.

She said he'd need bed rest for two weeks. He found himself in a rose garden, with a thorny dilemma.

The counselor added, "Listen, it's the advice you need – perhaps not the consultation you want. Your mind just happens to be outpacing your body to the point that your body is rejecting the pressure, the lifestyle, the choices that you're making. You're not exercising as much as you..."

"Outpacing?"

"You're lucky. Your condition is a result of your workload and could directly be due to stress. Listen, you've got to take it easy. A toe-tag in the basement isn't as far away as you might think."

"We'll talk later." The unconvincing counselor shook her head, scribbled a few notes on a clipboard, and left. With a wince, he reached to the bedside table for three prospectuses on the bedside table. *Fucking LBO bastards*, he thought, as he read through the redlining on the leveraged buyout contract agreements.

The counselor was pressing her luck, "We haven't even discussed Dietician benefits for your cholesterol and high blood pr..."

"We – will – fucking – talk – later. Or we will not." Jacob barked at her.

Her head down, out the door she darted, avoiding further conflict.

Shelby came back into Jacob's room. She dropped her pen, and bent over revealing too much cleavage. "Mr. Paisley, there's no one by the name of Gabe, Gabriel, Hollins or Rooney at this hospital."

"I didn't say Rooney. I said Ruby. Jesus. Get it right, would you?"

"Right away, sir. Sorry about that." She tossed hair off her shoulder and retreated to the adjoining room. The flirtatious concierge left the private room, but the scent of her remained. Jacob attempted to identify the perfume which briefly made him think of Victoria again. But, he needed to focus.

He dug into the papers, reading emails, signing off on a few agreements, initialing that they had been read or authorized in some form. If he could go to the offices of PPCM, the offices could come to him. Adele's workload was extreme. He needed her there. And this concierge would have to serve a purpose for now other than making dinner arrangements for the traders. Setting up cocktail meetings, personal shopping, and slipping fine details into client events was all good. Times like these called for unusual actions. PPCM was going to Deliver The Difference to the investment community.

The hospital originally said that there wasn't a chance. However, when the PPCM Charitable Trust cut a sizable check, the patient in the next room was moved so that the concierge, Shelby, could move in. A $100,000 donation was a decisive motivator in tough economic times. For the hospital record, Shelby was admitted to follow policy.

She came back into his room. "Mr. Paisley, I'm sorry about that. They stated that there is no one by the name Ruby either. I asked them to keep checking until they found someone by that name."

He was over it. "No worries." He looked at her slipping the tip of a Monte Blanc pen through her lips into her mouth. In and out. "Ah...sorry? Are we good here?"

She appeared understanding, but offered a blank stare. An uncomfortable pause of silence finally gave way to a small smile from the woman and she tilted her head to one side. She moved over to the bed. One knee was up on the corner of the bed. The slit in her skirt had shifted revealing her toned thigh. Shelby leaned over Jacob pointing out a dinner arrangement contract that he was looking at for a client appreciation event.

"Sir, they've countered your offer with..."

"I've got it, thanks. I kind of know what I'm doing here." He found the intimacy threatening. Even in his fragile state, he wanted nothing to do with comfort from her. It made him want Victoria all the more.

She backed away, rejected. Not asking if there would be anything else, with her heels clicking on the floor, she retreated to the adjoining room.

His phone rang. It was another trader seeking guidance. After indicating that it was fine to call and in doing his best to bring a sense of normal, he reassured the steps that the trader was taking with a seventeen-million-dollar trade.

When he realized that he'd have to sell what he already sold, he attempted to give a pep talk, "It's gutsy, but you're dialed in. You're hotter than hot. Listen to me John. Are you listening? Are you listening to me? Good, because I thought you were talking instead of listening..." He found himself losing his cool, and tempered the delivery.

Some silence passed as the trader expressed respect. Jacob jumped back into his new role of sideline coaching, "I told you - smoldering. This is your trade, your move. Hot, man, hot. Gold melts at nineteen hundred degrees. Titanium melts at three thousand degrees. Your blood – your blood - doesn't even come to a boil until four thousand degrees. Don't let the little things get you all hot and bothered."

Jacob listened to hesitancy and began questioning why he was talking the gutless trader into making money. "John, it's just seventeen million. It's not like you're going to get *fired* over this." The other end of the conversation became animated, and Jacob assured him to proceed, "Just kidding...I was on a heated theme. Got to go. Make it happen. Don't fuck it up. Use the collars and limits. Nothing at market. Hear me again, nothing at market pricing. You're white-hot John. Gotta' go now." Hanging up the PPCM trader, he tossed the phone onto the tray table.

Jacob was suddenly tired of inactivity. So tired of lying and sitting on his butt, he was able to manage to sit on the edge of the bed and stand. A little dizzy, but good enough to move around. It felt better. Not having the catheter in offered more freedom. Still wired to the ECG and an IV drip, he couldn't go far without wheeling the machine along. The power cord was his short leash.

After a half dozen short steps, he sat back down.

Shelby came in after hearing some movement and helped tuck him back in. Even though she was on *his* payroll, and she had to do what *he* wanted, he toned down his harshness, and even thanked her.

As she flattened the white sheets she asked him about a conference call scheduled for the next morning, "Chinese? Have you worked with this translator before?"

"Justin Chen. He's translated for me on several occasions. Let's get him on the line fifteen minutes prior to call start.

"I provided the dial in, and will email him and call him to confirm today sir."

"Mandarin." Paisley tried to smile. It was more of a wince.

"What's that, sir?"

"He translates Mandarin."

She opened her mouth to say something, but paused knowing he'd just think that she knew less than before with the pleasantries. Shelby decided to play defense. As soon as she crossed the threshold of the neighboring room, she exhaled and fanned her face in relief.

He was becoming restless and began to daydream. The conversation between the two voices in his dream while in recovery provided company to the moment of inactivity...

The first man asked, "What will keep him company?"

The other answered, "What insulates him and acts as his companion. Chance."

The first man provided a suggestion, "We'd favor that he lose his way." And after some contemplation, asked, "Will he?"

The other answered, "We'll see to it."

The first asked, "And the sense of himself?"

After a lengthy pause, in a soft voice, the second man replied, "Yes."

A third voice spoke softly, "You're hearing this to know what lies ahead."

His cell vibrated and he took the call: "Hey - how you doin', you crudgy bastard?!" It was Noah Pierce, his former partner. Pierce's voice was slower than the New York hustle, and the gentleman originally from South Carolina always seemed to calm Jacob.

"Hey part-timer. How's the retired life treating you.?"

"Jacob, it's plain borin' some of the time. But, wonderful most of the time."

"What hole are you on right now?"

"I'm at Safeway, pickin' up some kabobs for a barbeque tonight. Judith is makin' potato salad and that four-bean salad ya say ya like so much. What hole are you on or should I say whose hole are you on?"

Jacob ignored the jib, "I'm fine, really. Mild pain, but it isn't much once you're out of the shock of it. As far as business is concerned, it's just a speedbump. I spoke with Adele and a few members. The Board is moving forward as usual and it's all good. We've prepared for this sort of risk and all systems are a go. Your legacy is looking like it's still intact." Jacob listened for a long time. And through a series of nods, agreed to join a formal call with Noah and the Board of Directors to instill additional confidence and provide timely updates.

"Jacob..." there was a deep pause, "this here is life sendin' you a message...lettin' you know that you've been runnin' too hard, son. An' too fast an' for too long."

Paisley just groaned. *You too*, he thought.

Pierce went on, "How many eighty-hour work weeks have you stretched together?"

Jacob thought about Pierce's question. He multiplied 80 as in hours per week by 52 weeks in a year by 15 years and came up with 62,400 hours. "I take vacations," he attempted to argue.

"Your vacations are usually of the type where you're seekin' a play, makin' a move or a buck or two. And the women and the booze and the adrenaline seekin' stuff you do... Son, there's only so much you can cram into a week. You get a normal persons workweek in by Tuesday afta'noon. Whatcha outta' do is come on down to Carolina and have some lemonade on the porch and go fishin' with me. And think 'bout nothin' for a little while. Forget that place. Whatcha' say about that?"

Pierce was right. *He was always right* which is why Jacob enjoyed his conversations. He offered balance with the intelligence. But, he wanted nothing to do with slowing down. "I'm needed here. And if I need to downshift, you know I will."

"Nah. Can't say that I do know that. But, think about it, will ya'? Seriously."

"I will."

"Yeah, I've heard you say that before."

"I will Noah."

Jacob ended the brief call with several performance stats and clandestine reasons why business continued to suffer and coded causes for the diminished financial outcome. He assured Noah Pierce that he'd think about some time off and a visit to South Carolina. It was what he had to say at times to get him off the phone. There was no consideration for time off. None. The call concluded and he was left with nothing other than silence and a scowl. A reassurance that he secretly wanted wasn't really delivered. And for the first time, he wondered if this is how he would spend his golden years – managing his company and its results remotely.

He picked up the phone again to call into the office. After he asked to be patched through to an unknown recipient he listened for a while then began: "I think you might be on to something. But, you've got to bake it. Take all of the health factors into consideration. Develop the product through logic, that's the only way it'll get around any legislation. And be careful of HIPPA." Silence swallowed a minute, then Jacob jumped back in, "The healthcare industry will love to challenge if it attacks margin. Use the body mass index stats, blood pressure, cholesterol counts, smoker, non-smoker, wellbeing statistics, industry employment rankings, racial and proximity profiling can only align as the insurance companies' disciple their actuary tables."

He listened intently, then barked out an order, "Listen, there are too many people talking over each other. I've got to jump, but hear this. After we take it to market, we'll create instruments like the banks did with housing, and we'll insure the chaos." Jacob Paisley needed a new product, and desperate to generate a new bubble.

He listened further then concluded the call, with "Hey – good job here. I'm a fan. Boys step back, the men step forward. Let's circle back next week. Send me an invite for 15 to 20 minutes for an update. I'm out." He punched a button on his phone dropping from the conference call.

Making money off of the baby-boomers transfer of wealth and Affordable Care legislature revisions would be second only to the western hemisphere's transfer of wealth to the east for oil. Blood was in the water.

"*A shark does what a shark has to do*," in nearly a whisper, Paișley spoke the words, quietly to himself. It was a phrase that he used often. It defined necessity.

Shelby entered his room again to drop off three small packages. "These arrived yesterday afternoon, sir. One says urgent, the others were sent Fedex overnight. Adele is managing email and postal correspondences unless they indicate personal and confidential as these do. She just wanted me to remind you."

He nodded. A small package from Arizona captured his attention first. He unwrapped it. The glass globe paperweight was a token of appreciation from the Thunderbird School of Global Management. It had country etchings on the solid glass ball which filled his palm. A banner of appreciation circled the equator stating: *PPCM and Thunderbird: A Partnership To Enhance Leadership Throughout Our World.*

As he looked through the clear Thunderbird glass globe rereading the etched impression, Rick Santelli on CNBC absorbed his attention. Santelli was a longstanding on-air commentator that had recently agreed with the Fed's decision to pause interest rates. Now he was on a rant about anemic interest rates in the European Union compared to domestic rates. Rick commonly brought commodities into play. And this was why Paisley was interested and suddenly became angered.

PPCM had a play upon silver, iron ore and grain from South America to China. Locked interest rates wouldn't allow them to float paper against contracts and absorb the differences. Jacob clenched his jaw tightly and felt the rush of heat course through his veins. They were betting on rate fluctuations. This could mean millions in losses to bottom-line earnings. Santelli was pounding his fist on a desk in the pit of the Chicago Board of Trade.

Jacob did the same, grabbed the glass globe, and without thinking heaved it at the television. Sparks flew from behind the wall mounted TV, and the screen immediately went dark. The glass ball bounced loudly from the crash and ricocheted off of the walls.

Shelby ran into the room to have the globe roll to her feet. She picked it up and gently handed it to Jacob. "Everything alright sir?"

"Fucking – fuckers." He was shocked at his own reaction. It was a loss of control and stability. Passion wasn't a bad thing. An uncontrolled outburst causing physical damage wouldn't score comfort or confidence with anyone. The emotive response wasn't an evolved reaction. A civilized business leader just didn't acknowledge relevant information with an echo of runaway restraint. But it felt good.

He looked at the globe. The etchings of the continents and the oceans were easily identifiable. The Pacific had a rainbow colored chip, like a windshield's mosquito crack, from impact. Just north of the equator, it sparkled.

He sat it down gently, and tenderly this time, assured her, "I'm fine. Thank you." Looking at the floor, white tiles running parallel and perpendicular. The foundation always offered a simple form of logic.

*****

Brian was returning home following an abbreviated day of blitz visits, completing the afternoon at a free-standing unit inland off Interstate 8, near La Mesa. Occasionally he'd trek home on the Escondido Freeway. Today, he completed his store visits sooner than he'd expected. Since there weren't issues, he was rewarding himself with the slow roll on the seaside northbound 5. He exited the highway, making his way to the 101 with sunshine in his eyes. The only shadows touching the pavement were from the overpasses and green and reflective white highway signs stretching over the roadways. Now heading west, he slipped on a pair of Maui Jim sunglasses to minimize the glare.

This is what he came to see, what his long-way-home detour provided: a big wave swell was in. Surf was up. Double overhead curls rewarded the brave-the-cold-water surfers with a treat. Black's Beach was his destination.

These breaks weren't for the faint of heart. Some of San Diego's best surfing was here, especially in the winter. Parking his car, he'd have a short hike to get to where the blue on blue met the bluffs. Bordering the ocean's edge, these chiffon rounded cliffs were spotted with shrubs. Overhead, colorful hang gliders or flocks' seagulls would catch the wind gusts and float effortlessly. Golden sand. Majestic cliffs. The bluest water in southern California.

In the summertime, occasionally, nude sunbathers would get their vitamin D here. Surfers referred to them as 'nukes'. This wasn't why Brian liked Black's. When it was on, these slow curling barrels reminded him of Oahu's north shore – where he would sit on the berm and watch famed professionals carve at the mavericks for prize money. His playground during the winter sessions growing up was on the west side, Makaha – and not during the shootouts or Surf Series. School was in session during those challenges.

Here there were surprisingly only a dozen surfers, covered in neck to toe in wet suits. This time of the year, San Diego water temps were unbearable to an island boy – even while wearing the neoprene suits. It appeared to be a killer riptide causing the longboard big wave riders to paddle especially hard. He sat on a large flat rock, high above the beach to observe the barrels, breaks, and backwash. The sets were lining up, with a few bombs on the horizon. There were a few surfers which appeared to be charging the largest in the big wave lineup. Others appeared to be spent or waiting for a distinctive clean ride avoiding the crashing close outs.

To accomplish the other reason of his homebound deviation, Brian reached into his pocket to call his cousin, Leilani.

She picked up immediately, "Hey Cuz!"

"Who dis?" he teased.

"You called me, nerd!" They both giggled and started ribbing each other immediately. As an only child, Leilani leaned on Brian for much when they were kids. Brian taught her to ride a bike, play her first ukulele, and in the calmer waters of Pokai Bay Beach Park, to stand up paddle. In school – he helper know she could stand up for herself, oversaw much of her homework, and through middle school, to fend off the boys. Her hula girl beauty was irresistible to the west side boys. Leilani's cocoa skin, moon-sized dark brown eyes, and chocolate-pecan hair which flowed the full length of her spine screamed

Pacific Islander. But it was her vibrant and stirring personage which drew people to her. She lived Aloha.

They were close. They kept in touch. Leilani was attending University of Hawai'i - West Oahu while working at the local luaus as a dancer - and things were busy for them both. She had new news.

"I met someone special, Cuz," she was excited to share. He could tell she was smiling while she spoke. "We haven't said it yet, but we're in love."

He was a protective cousin, listening to her joy, "Wow, Cuz. Ku'uipo? Tell me about him." Ku'uipo held the Hawaiian meaning for sweetheart. Brian thought he knew every boy, or their family, or could find out about them if they were from the leeward side. She was not short on words and did all the talking. Brian was watching the rolling surf and wincing at wipeouts while Leilani shared with him, things they did together, places they went for dates, and how he spoiled her. She also said that he was *very* attentive.

This was what Brian felt a need to delve into, "How so?..." He listened to 'ore one-sided conversation. "And what do your Aunties and Uncles have to say?"

"They haven't met just yet. We tried a couple times, but he was called in to work. He's a financial analyst – works downtown."

Brian wasn't sure why she wasn't convincing him of that point. He wasn't going to press at this time and paused the interrogation for now – knowing he'd have to check the dude out. What was best for Leilani was what he wanted.

"What's this lucky guy's name?"

"Yancy."

"Yancy?"

"Yeah, cuz, Yancy. Tall, dark, and handsome – just like you know I like 'em." Her Hawaiian pidgin was slipping through again.

"Island boy?"

"Uh huh."

Now Brian's pidgin was called upon, "More island boy than me?"

"Ah cuz, you mainlander haole boy now. You go San Diego and get all vanilla on us," she teased playfully.

"Well, I can't wait to meet him, Mr. Mocha Frappuccino."

They giggled and shared the latest happenings about what they cared for most – family. Eventually Leilani asked what the kids wanted for Christmas and what kind of macadamia nut cookies and banana bread Brian wanted sent for Christmas.

"Ono grindz..." Leilani taunted the fiftieth state's eats he was missing out on. Brian was dreamy at the thought of his Aunties banana bread.

When they finally hung up and Brian finished the commute heading north up to Oceanside, he cranked KINE – and sang his island tunes loudly and proudly.

He would need to dial up the 808 local gossip exchange to see if anyone had intel on Yancy.

*****

Jacob's mind again wandered off into the delicious direction of Victoria, and he found a moment of happiness. He remembered their getaway to Jade Mountain in Saint Lucia. In the distance were white powdery sand coastlines, coconut fronds catching the breezy trade winds, bungalows lining the shore with wooden docks to dive into the lapis blue waters. Towering lush mountains with exotic foliage hosted similar resorts with brightly colored Caribbean umbrellas to protect the sunbathers from too much sunlight and venturing eyes toward occasional topless tourists.

But closer to him, and more importantly, it was her. Studying her mannerisms for years, he knew each of her movements, and his heart warmed seeing her from across their suite, encouraging him to come closer. Drawing him into her dreamy eyes. Yes, Victoria. She motioned for him to follow her. He could make out that she was smiling and playful, moving slowly and seductively. Her shoulder length brunette hair was irresistible and was flowing in the ocean breeze. The white swimsuit cover up was stark contrast to her dark suntan. He followed. She removed the cover and bare her slender waist and bare breasts. Wrapping herself around him, he remembered her warmth.

Realizing that he was daydreaming of another time, and far from this moment, he managed to control his mind's narrative over the next moments and the love-making that lasted for hours.

In a suite above all others at the boujee resort, Victoria would look away from Jacob to the ocean's ship-less curved horizon. He joined her, wrapping his arms around her as they would look off into the distance together. Together, he thought. Still looking off into the sunrise, she reached her soft cool hand to his face and embraced his cheek as they'd marvel at the bright colors where the morning sky would meet the sea. And she repeated what she liked to say to him, "Listen, you've got to understand this – with you, it's about so much more than I thought was possible."

Jacob would think that the slight arc of the ocean's distance offered up unfound opportunities ahead. It was an explorer's purpose. It was a risk-takers mission. It had the potential to lead anywhere and everywhere and nowhere at the same time. It was the snake in the garden offering knowledge, tempting with gain. Opportunity. Victoria.

In the terms of a Wall Street investment manager, the earth's horizon - at the point where the sky meets the sea, was a beautiful forward-looking statement, something that resembles hope. And hope was one of the best of all things. He realized that he was recycling in his daydream and hoped that it wouldn't end. But it did. The present moment always called for a curtain-close to fond memories.

*****

They were waiting for Cutter's supplier. It was a 6 o'clock appointment "I'm thinkin' 'bout expanding my franchise." Cutter looked across the Empire State Trail and past the cross traffic at the taillights of the taxis on W 10th Street as they crept into West Village. An occasional horn blew as the lights turned from red to green. The city noise was vibrant as the Manhattan sunlight careened casting steel-colored shadows against down

He said it again. "Are you hearing me, woman?" He grabbed the lapel of her jacket. It was cold and she was using the collar to cover her ears from the wind.

Kerri apologized meekly, "I'm sorry. What's that?" Her eyes were watering from the bluster. They were sitting on top of a wooden picnic table between Piers 45 and 46. The Waterfront of New Jersey was to the west where the horizon's color was just beginning to collect. Most of the glass-faced buildings now had a reflection of color upon them. She remembered sitting near this spot with her mother when she was a child. *It was cold sun today*, she thought.

"I said...I said I'm thinking about expanding my franchise." He repeated himself. "Just need to learn to cook."

"What... What...franchise...?" She frowned and squinted and asked with rare skepticism.

He was caught off guard by her scrutiny of his trade. "My business. My craft." As if he thought dealing was a legitimate career or that he was bigger at it than he was, he repeated himself, "My franchise. I'm gonna' build it up. Me and Boomer. I just need to go to cooking school."

Boomer was his supplier. They split the proceeds of the drug deals 60-40. Cutter was on the lesser end of the arrangement.

She questioned him sternly, "You're expanding? And going into the restaurant business."

He raised his hand as if to strike, "Woman..." He feigned the slap with the back of his open hand.

She whimpered and winced away from him - feeling that there always might be a first time for a blow. "Don't," she whimpered.

"Don't make me want to do it. I will if I need to..." He already bullied her emotionally and psychologically. When would it lead to physical abuse or something worse?

Her torso rocked forward and back as he recoiled. This relentless craving was a soulful piercing pain which needed to go away. Crazy Kerri would need to make another appearance soon.

"There's my man. My partner. Right on time." Cutter jumped from the table and walked toward a large leafless tree in the Hudson River Park. Their clandestine meeting and exchange was never anything that she was a part of. She saw some form of a 'bro shake' and looked away toward red brick buildings aligning West Street.

A mother pushed a baby stroller on the walkway close by. Kerri knew that now was not the time. It couldn't be. But she wanted to be a mother someday. Perhaps when she could control herself. It would require a sacrifice she couldn't control at this time. *But things can change...for the better,* she thought. The mother and the navy stroller turned and were careening in her direction now. Kerri saw the little boy or assumed it was a boy with the cadet blue blanket swaddling the infant.

Without gloves, her hands were curled up inside her jacket to keep them warm. Kerri was close enough to wave toward the child and the mother with her arm sleeves as they wheeled by, but she was ignored.

Crazy Kerri wanted no part of what was happening. Crazy Kerri knew she was on deck, being called upon the play her part. Crazy Kerri saw Cutter returning from the meeting with Boomer and with product.

Kerri helplessly felt that she needed to get zonked. She needed the good lick, a bingo, the antifreeze. Her graduation from a jolly pop to the gutter junkie who would do anything at this point was the high-speed train, derailed. The tracks on her arms proved it.

*****

Once he awoke, he thought more of Victoria. He allowed himself to think of her touch. Seductive, sensitive, knowing just what to say and do, she aroused him like no other woman. In the spirit of the season, she was naughty and nice.

He remembered a Friday night in October, taking HeliFlight's Sikorsky from Manhattan to Boston for appetizers and a wild night of sex. A smirk touched his face as he thought of warming the bottle of Krug, popping the cork, pouring the sparkling champagne from the gentle smoky mouth of the bottle over her naked body and slowly licking it from her skin. She wiggled and giggled underneath him. Her heels were at the foot of the bed, her black dress was tossed on a credenza. She wore nothing else. His hands held on to her hips and in rhythm they moved back and forth with pants of excitement.

The door to the room opened. He was alarmed and focused.

"How we feelin'?" A nurse had a plastic sleeve and a vial in her hand. "I'm going to draw some blood." She moved to the right side of the bed since the IV was on the left. After a pinch and after the empty vial filled with his blood, she said, "Good boy. Want a sucker?"

Answering the first question, "I'm good," then the second question, "OK."

She placed a piece of gauze over the red drop left behind on his forearm and quickly wrapped it with purple tape. "Leave that on for 20 minutes, OK?" Then, reaching into the pocket of her smock, she grabbed a tootie-fruitie Dum Dum and gave it to him. No smile was on her businesslike face.

As the door swung shut, the daydreaming resumed and he thought about the return trip from Boston with Victoria. It was the next evening. They got into an argument about living arrangements. He wanted her to move in. She wasn't ready.

Victoria was quiet and distant, fiddling with her phone, most of the trip back to Manhattan. When they touched down on the heliport she said, "Listen, I've got a girlfriend picking me up. We're going out for drinks."

She reached up, grabbing his scarf, drawing him in close for a soft kiss followed by a smile, "We're good." Pearls dangled from her neck, she lifted the strand and bit them with her teeth, tipping her head to the side. Her teeth were bright white as she held the pearls in her mouth. She dropped them and the smile and said, "Call me." Walking away, her heels clicked on the concrete. Always leaving him wanting just a little more, she didn't turn to look back.

6

What's Your Story?

"What's my story?" Jacob thought about that for a second and repeated, "What's my story? What's your story?"

Ruby had asked the question while Jacob was waking up. Snapping the paper, the black man looked over the horn-rimmed cheaters he was wearing.

"Well?"

A conversation was ignited. Surprisingly, there was much to be said between the two. They discussed money, net worth, statistics, and benchmarks. Ruby crafted an argument for each point of Jacob's articulation with a counterpoint of emotional balance, or values, or human kindness and the power of the imagination, or the substance of reality.

When Jacob felt a corner coming, he'd would turn his thesis to simply state that Ruby didn't understand how money transitioned from dock to destination. Jacob knew the intricacies of global financial markets as well as anyone, and the edification of lay people was only entertaining to a point. Ruby would summarize that we've all tread a road of gain that each man benefits from one man's advance.

Jacob participated in the conversation since it was refreshing to talk with someone much different than the riddelers, swindlers and bribe-takers he often dealt with. He described that money was a primary measurement of a man's success. His outlook on life, his eternal optimism would equate in some small way to his financial gain.

Ruby would have a manly deep-in-the-chest chuckle, and reply, "The Dow Jones Industrial Average cannot remotely measure the pulse of the human soul."

"Well Ruby, every cause has its charisma," Jacob was assessing the healthcare equipment attached to the wall behind his bed. He was reciting mantra from a distant conversation while auditing wires and digital blipping screens from twelve inch beige boxes. "You see, in the world I live in, it's about differentiating oneself. It's about differentiating predictability of the course that money may take. Are you overly bullish, or overly bearish? Something's going to resonate with somebody in their pursuit of the attraction of gain. There are those of us that forecast for the near-term, analysts that cover opportunities in industry specifics as well as those that can call for cyclical headwinds. And then there are those that assume that the markets will move sideways and encourage you to trade on volatility. It isn't as much about what really happens as it is delivering a unique message that attracts what is at hand."

His new acquaintance sat quietly. Ruby simply shrugged his shoulders.

The capital-manager, Jacob then continued, "Money. Power, Leadership. It's – just - a - game. You convince, and you live off of the herd's mentality. *Very nicely*. Trading today's money for tomorrow's is more about the derivatives made off of volume, than the actual product. It's about attraction. It's about a convincing story. And it's very much about being first. The old proverb is proven time after time: What a wise man does in the beginning, the fool does in the end." And then he was quiet.

Ruby pretended to listen intently, but changed course and asked, "Do you believe that our lives can be backwards compatible?"

"What the hell are you talking about?" Jacob answered with a question.

"Nothin', pay no attention. Really. I'm just an old man thinking out loud." He reached for a little red padfolio and jotted down a note in it.

Jacob felt the tape and gauze dressing covering the incision on his chest with his fingertips. "I believe that ideas and their values have more than intrinsic income. A trader, for example, proposes their idea for a financial vehicle and assigns a value to its worth. Say two hundred fifty million dollars or maybe half a billion. How far can we run with that idea – if it launches? How many people benefit from its run? Could be millions."

"Isn't someone on the other side of that exchange?"

"Someone who didn't do their homework *may* be on the wrong side of that trade, and someone who *predicted correctly* or *just got lucky* is on the right side."

Ruby scratched his chin and slowly asked the question, "When does it all end?"

"Never. It's a perpetual system. Companies will come and go. Ideas, trends, values. But, it's cold hard math. It's capitalism. There is no final trade."

Ruby was taking a note in his red book, which Jacob found slightly distracting. "What was that last part?"

"Finance, values, trading. It's all about supply and de..."

"Nah, the last thing you said."

"There is no final trade."

Ruby stopped writing. He looked at Jacob and smiled. "There it is then." He stood, slipped the slumping red suspenders back over his shoulders, held on to his red notebook tightly, said nothing else and shuffled out of Jacob's room.

*****

"Oh, I called Leilani." Laying on the couch with the remote in his hand, the volume was turned down low. The kids were in bed, sleeping. With the lights dim, they were channel surfing and nothing was landing.

Brian looked at his beautiful wife. Laki's long hair was tied into a ponytail. She was wearing her pajamas red and black checkered pajama bottoms with a polar fleece top.

Her head was against his shoulder until she reacted. "Oh yeah, what did she have to say?"

"She met a guy. An island boy."

"That's great. She called you to share her good news. See...she misses you, Brian. She misses her cousin." Her arm was wrapped around his. When she glanced up to see his face, she paused. "What? What is it?" One side of his was scrunched and she knew there was something else.

"It was - the way - she said something."

"What?"

"She was saying he was *very* attentive. He liked to take control. That he didn't like her spending as much time with her friends as she did because then they weren't together and that she never had anyone pay as much attention to her as he did."

"Hmm..."

"Yeah. It just came through her lips awkwardly. And maybe I'm reading into it wrongly. But..."

"You know her," she interrupted him waffling in his thoughts. "Stay close."

They landed on a football movie which they had watched together a dozen times before.

"Ugh," she huffed. "I'm getting us a bowl of popcorn."

Brian's thoughts returned to his ankle, his years playing football, the end of his burgeoning sports career as a player, its sudden ending. The play by play was repeated in his mind countless times. Those voices which spoke over each other from a variety of people in his life: "*You'll never play again, but football can still be part of your life. - Why don't you come home, Brian? - We don't see any other option, Brian – I'm sorry it had to end this way. - Brah, can you still surf? -That rerun will make kids not want to play football. - Dude, you got tore up. -SDSU will honor the remainder of your scholarship, Brian. - It isn't responding like we had hoped. - Your ankle is a mishmash of bone and cartilage and tendon that doesn't resemble what an ankle is supposed to resemble and do - Maybe, with time and much luck you'll be of some value in another capacity - At least you'll get a solid education which you can do anything with.....*"

These were the voices of his family and his friends, his coaches, the doctors, the specialist, the rehabilitation coordinators. Men, women, the young, the old, the wise, the hopeful voices, and the realistic voices – mostly acknowledging that it was time to move on to something else. Something other than pro sports and what meant most to Brian then – the game of football.

"You're thinking about it, aren't you?" Laki was looking at him as she was tossing kernels into her mouth.

He changed the channel.

*****

Hours later, Jacob was again shouting wildly into his cell: "Christmas season?!!! Christmas season?! I don't give a fuck. Six weeks from now it'll be earnings season and that's more important. There's no room for sub-par performances on my trading desks! You got that?!"

There's was some animated gibberish that Jacob listened to for a few seconds, then interrupted: "You don't have a lot of options here. I'll expect to see the delta corrected and a solid recovery plan for the miss. Get it together." He hung up abruptly.

Thoughts he could not capture merely a day ago were seized. Words that he could not find were illuminated for his arsenal of personal assaults toward underperformances and disliking.

It was late Thursday afternoon. The sun was beginning to slide down the southwestern side of the lapis blue sky. Jacob dialed into one of his bank accounts. Listening to the woman's voice providing voice prompts "Password?"

"Fourteen ninety two."

"Next password?"

"Columbus. One – four – nine – two."

As the woman's voice proceeded into the pallet of options, he interrupted.

"Balance," he barked.

"Your portfolio balance is...", there was a pause, "twenty three million, nine hundred eighty seven thousand, six hundred seven dollars and thirty five cents."

Disappointed in the result, "End call." Jacob returned his thoughts to the prospectuses on the bedside table. He reached for a red pen lying next to them and picked up the first file for review. Pausing, he glanced off into the distance without focusing on anything. He grabbed the cell phone, punched a button on the glass screen and began speaking while looking at the white sheet of paper with fine black print. "Supplement. Quote: 'The fun is not intended as a vehicle for trading in the futures, commodity options or swaps markets. With respect to the Fund, the investment management group, operating within the rights and conditions of authority, are currently underwriting revised conditions of Commodity Pool Operator exchange mechanisms, and, therefore, are not subject to CFTC registration or regulation. In addition, in relying upon related exclusions from the definition of Commodity Trading Advisors..." He looked up, and stopped.

He was back. Jacob was alarmed to see him sitting on the chair in the corner. He appeared from nowhere.

"Was that English?" He smiled at Jacob. "Adele was here while you were sleeping. And that bell on your phone rang a few times." Ruby was apparently keeping score.

The past four days were surreal. He was surprised and wasn't surprised at the same time. Ruby had found a way to make himself welcomed into Jacob's affairs. "From a man that doesn't exist, you sure find your way into the moment, don't you. No one has heard of you, Mr. Hospital Volunteer."

Ruby smiled, and looking at the business section, turned the page of the newspaper. "It's tough out there. Don't you think?"

"Really? You don't want to know." Jacob was on familiar ground again.

"Try me."

"The shortest foot notes version. Eighties – pharmaceuticals and bonds. Nineties – information technology and remarkable volatility. New millennium – here comes, as an acquaintance of mine refers to it as, *the extension of credit by instrument.* The housing and commodities bubbles, governmental recovery through printing money and more volatility index trading. Quantitative easing. Recoveries and setbacks. Fiscal cliffs and unexplained momentum surges. Decade one – here we are with the growing demographic separation. There has nearly always been the capacity for diffidence, doubt and uncertainty that reveals itself as time marches on. Quantitative tightening. Covid-19. Crypto. AI. And so it goes..."

Ruby interrupted the rant, "Sounds like you've lived it?"

"Not done. Bull market – one of the best we've experienced. And then the house of cards comes crashing down hard and fast. The moment is defined as sputtering. It isn't where you make buckets of cash. Jacob dipped his head to one side, "Indeed. I've been enabled to be right all along." He paused for a while. "Until now. Back to figuring out what's next while being vilified, resorting to creative instruments and shadow banking to move forward and get ahead."

Ruby spoke as if he wasn't listening to any of the words. Changing the direction of the conversation, "Adele seems like a real nice lady. It seems as if she's been working with you a long time." He had obviously helped himself to matters that didn't concern him, and it annoyed Jacob.

Jacob's attention turned to his cell phone, focusing on streaming content of financial headline news.

Ruby was talking about people needing help, and the family members he met, about caring for others, and what a benefit he found in listening to the stories that patients in the hospital told. He focused on his memory, and squinted as if he was inspecting detail within the words.

As if he heard a foreign language, Jacob asked, "What?"

Ruby just smiled, closing the newspaper, "Never mind. I'm an old man, and sometimes we just like to ramble on and listen to ourselves speak."

"Do you smell that?" Jacob asked.

"Can't smell," Ruby replied.

"You...cannot...smell?"

Ruby pointed to the back of his head, "Fell of a tractor on my granddad's farm when I was a kid. Hit a fence post right about here." He pointed at his temple. "Couldn't smell from that day on. What a rotten piece of bad luck that was."

"So you could smell? I mean you were old enough to remember and to know what things smelled like, and after the fall you just stopped being able to smell?"

"Exactly." Ruby asked, "What is it you smell?"

"Popcorn. I'm sorry, but it really smells good. I didn't think I'd smell popcorn in a hospital."

"I miss smellin' popcorn."

Jacob took a deep breath and asked, "What do you miss smelling most?"

"Fresh cut grass, ball glove leather, fried chicken." He thought about it and added to his list, "orange peel, gasoline, tulips, my mother's perfume."

Jacob thought about Victoria's perfume. His thoughts were of her straddling him, naked on his penthouse bed. She'd say, *"Oh yeah? You like this smell? Does it make you want me? Do you want to be inside me when*

I wear this perfume?" She kissed his chest and worked her way down his torso with her lips. A smile returned to his face as he returned to the present moment there with Ruby.

"Tulips? Tulips don't have much of a smell, do they?"

He contemplated the flower: "Maybe it was daffodils. My mother had flower beds filled with yellow flowers that bloomed in May." Ruby was looking out the window as he spoke.

Those are the smells of a twelve-year-old boy, Jacob thought. Then, he spoke, "Smell is our most common sense."

"Common sense?", Ruby questioned.

"The smell we share most as a common like or dislike. One that we can relate to most. Or, so say scientists or research or whatever... College Bio 101, maybe."

"Well, I suppose so." Ruby mumbled a bit and leaned back in his chair.

Jacob thought of her scent. He closed his eyes and thought about how Victoria smelled when they meet at the airport, or go out to dinner, or make love. He drifted off to sleep.

When he woke up a short time later they discussed the market close. Ruby was reciting several fearful articles that he read in the New York Times. Jacob corrected much of what was said, provided a long soliloquy of his version of the truths, and provided an edification of creative instruments and empirical data that supported the fact that the fast money just never sleeps. Jacob explained that just a few basis points could equate to billions of dollars exchanging hands. Ruby asked basic questions that were indicative of his not really paying attention, or not really caring.

Their conversation meandered. It was all about Paisley. So, it stayed active. Jacob interrupted himself when the cell rang. It was Adele. He asked, "Top trade of the day?" Looking off at Ruby he smiled, then reached for a pen to stroke a few notes. "Rorschach?! You've got to be kidding me?" He listened for a few seconds, "And overall?" A few seconds of silence passed. "It's a god-damned Christmas miracle. Looks like team Jenga is making a comeback."

Ruby listened to the one-sided conversation while making busywork in the red notebook.

Paisley continued, "Let's call it this: Q1 – Winners Take All. Then list the top ten prizes. I like the G6 lease, you win and fly ten of your best clients to a Lakers game, stopover in Vegas to tie one on, and cruise back to the east coast or wherever over the weekend. That one made the list. The Round The World Twice trip is good, but I don't like the traders to be off the floor that long. Their backup teams aren't as effective, so let's table it for now. The Breitling timepieces have been done. We won't do that again. The Virgin Galactic Charter to Space is outrageous. If they want to discount the experience fifty thousand, maybe. The ten-million Bonvoy points is alright. But I'm pissed off at MAR right now. HLT is squeezing me too. I'm giving lodging a pause." In Jacob's ticker-speak, he was referring to Marriott and Hilton. He paused for less than a minute, listening. "Let's look ahead and come up with a few more. Email me detail when it boils." He looked at the list in his hands again, "A driving experience with Danica Patrick? And a trip to her winery in Napa for wine tasting – what's it called, *Somnium Vineyard?* - I like that one...correction...*love it*...she's full of drive. See what I did there? Only if she makes a speaker appearance and revs up the winners."

He looked at his cell phone and interrupted himself. "Adele, got another call. I'll give you a shout later." Jacob attempted to catch the other call, but it slipped to voice mail. After looking at caller-ID, he laid the phone down and looked at Ruby.

"Rorschach?"

"You know, like the Rorschach tests. This guy plays racquetball with us at the men's club. He's good. But he sweats. So he wears a grey tee-shirt. That's all we let him wear. When he sweats, it's on his chest and stomach and looks like that Rorschach inkblot test. You know, the one's that look like butterflies and bats and woodland creatures.

When a junior trader is invited to play with an executive, we invite Rorschach to play and after the game, we ask the junior trader to identify the sweat spots on Rorschach's tee-shirt. The juniors are politically correct and the answers are all the same: animal hide, moth, two human heads, elephant, bear, crab. But, when a trader has been around for a while and is seasoned, the answers are much different and usually take on some form of sexuality: I see a big ball sack, a vagina, two women getting it on, a butterfly with a huge cock. And so on. That's generally the difference between a junior and a senior trader: Rorschach."

Ruby didn't know what to make of the answer, so he shook his head in agreement and offered an, "Ahh."

Paisley supported his point, "It's actually pretty accurate." He sorted through other papers on the rolling bed stand hovering his bed for a specific paper. His cell rang again, and he leapt into an arsenal of criticism with the unfortunate caller on the other end of the line.

Ruby winced at the language and listened intently. The call ended with "...there aren't enough explanations for the holes in your thesis! When you screw it up like that, you really need to ask yourself – is this the right thing for me." Paisley tossed the phone on the bed.

A long pause of silence was broken by, "Three words to describe yourself..." Ruby challenged Jacob.

Jacob paused to carefully consider the challenge. Rubbing a yellow crust from his eyes, he thought about it – he had just attended a management consulting seminar in the third quarter and the descriptive words that he self-identified were fresh. He picked three of his favorites: "Competitive... Creative... and...and...Influential."

"Hmm...power words." Jacob was pleased with Ruby's summation. "Does 'Creative' have anything to do with the financial instruments your company dreams up and sells?" And then he wasn't as pleased and slightly disappointed in the crass dismissal of the work behind the *instruments.* He sought no rebuttal.

"How about you?" Jacob was remotely curious what might come out of Ruby's mouth. From the naïve questions that Ruby asked about finance, words such as 'sophisticated, calculating and insightful' were far from what was expected.

"I love that question. My dad always used to ask me that." Ruby looked off into the distance to remember. Jacob did the same, assuming his memories of his father were not as fond. He quickly thought about himself and didn't ask the question again.

"You favor your father."

"Well..." Ruby curled up one side of his mouth. "There's a story there, but we can't get into it right now. My father was a jeweler."

Jacob reciprocated with, "And mine sold fire escapes." Neither of these statements were true. They looked at each other with blank stares.

"There are two important points to make here. Will you remember this?" Ruby asked.

Jacob considered the request, and finally replied, "What is it?"

"Our beliefs and how we tend to see things – perspective. These are two pillars that expand or contract us. I need you to think about this as you recover. Faith and introspect. Word it how you wish – these are cornerstones we build from. Will you remember?"

"I can do that. Beliefs and perspective. Widely different man-to-man. We don't go toe-to-toe on common ground, but I certainly don't disagree."

"Good stuff. Thanks." Ruby took a breath and offered a long pause, then spoke, "Say here's something I'd like to ask since I've never sat on a Board of Directors like you do."

Paisley thought about the numerous BoD's where he had his hand in their pockets, and then of those he officially sat on, "Go ahead, ask."

"Well, what's your relationship like with all of those folks? You all want the same things or is it always a battle of some sort?"

Jacob opened his mouth to answer, and uncharacteristically paused, "We're frenemies most of the time. Friends and enemies, a blend. It's different on any given Board. We want the same things, but not in the same way. Why do you ask?"

"Just curious. That's all."

Jacob wiggled in his bed. His butt was sore. His incision itched. "I miss my routine."

Ruby itched his ear some, and replied, "Oh yeah? Can you tell me about it?"

"It's just the sizzle. You know? The hard press of the moment. It's been a companion of mine for a long time."

"Chances are rest is doing you some good."

"Yeah, I get it. But, the lifestyle..." Jacob raised his eyebrows and elaborated, "The lifestyle is pretty seductive. I'm supposed to be in Switzerland here pretty soon for an annual conference. The Federal Treasurer wanted to meet with Wall Street types, including myself to get my thoughts. And...by - the -way, it happens to be the end of the fucking quarter..."

Jacob looked up from his rant to an empty seat. Ruby was not in the room. A nurse with a tray of hospital food looked at him with disbelief that he was talking to himself. She asked, "Everything alright here?"

"Just leave it." He pointed at a table next to the window, "Over there. I'm not hungry right now."

"As you wish." She dropped off the plastic tray with a beige colored plastic dome. The aroma crept out from under, and Jacob thought that it stunk. She left the room with white sneakers occasionally squeaking as she walked. Paisley thought of NKE, Nike – trading at 19 times projected earnings. He closed his eyes and thought more about the affluent lifestyle that he was eager to return to.

*****

With Cutter, there was no need to boost and shoot. Drug slang was like a language of its own. Kerri did not need to steal to support her habit. She had a reliable source of her junk. Along with a sustainable supply, came an awareness that she needed to control the lack of control. If she might ever have a baby – there would be no way she could consume any substance. She swallowed the small white birth control pill and slipped the pink dial container back into her dresser drawer.

Groggy, as she was recovering from her *'out'*, she fell back into bed and picked up the book on the nightstand about managing her bad habit. She wasn't treating this knowledge as an addiction cure – she was just feeding her illusion. For now, this was phantasm. Delirium came and went. Seventeen pages in, she was too tired to read any further. Drowsiness was in charge here. Uncontrolled muscle spasms in her shoulders frightened her. They had begun two weeks ago. It wasn't a good sign. Her nails and lips were a bluish color. The book called it *cyanosis.*

Daydreaming of baby names: Bobby, Danny, Luke, Mark. Emma, Mia, Ellie, Chloe.

The paperback fell within the bed to chapter seven: the CDC stats on heroin overdoses which caused deaths over the years. The numbers dramatically grew year after year. It spooked her. No Sophie, no Noah, no Luna, no Luca, no Ava, no Asher.

No drugs. No need for Crazy Kerri.

Cutter was clattering dishes in the kitchen. "Where the fuck is the ketchup?" he clamored while banging cupboards.

She croaked out, "There's packets in the drawer."

He complained continually while making himself a sandwich. "You eat all the chips?"

He's helpless... Really. She thought to herself while hearing him bitch about having to serve himself. Crawling off of the mattress, she walked to the small dinette table, stopping once to balance herself. She saw him in a grey flannel shirt he lifted from a department store near Times Square. Their one-bedroom Hell's Kitchen apartment was an easy walk. He hadn't buttoned it yet and his trademark white tank was underneath.

"It's getting cold again."

"If you were a career girl, that might not be a problem." He was quick to reply and constantly reminded her that the small monthly trust money she contributed wasn't enough to cover their rent. He had to contribute with his business earnings.

She wouldn't remind him again that he didn't run a business. The last time he pulled her hair at the base of her neck so tight that strands came away in his grip.

Cutter's ability to accept criticism led to his rage and wrath which never ended well for Kerri. Perhaps confident and crafty Crazy Kerri could navigate it, but Kerri was much too submissive for the conflict. Her passive behavior was dishonest to herself and only fed the Hazel hell beast, her hero of the underworld, which violated her respect and dignity.

It was Crazy Kerri which caused the honeymoon, which was known as the early stages of drug use before addiction and dependency, to happen. She was the feeder, the catalyst, the vehicle of necessitation. Crazy Kerri was the wild and daring woman which Cutter could never have had. Crazy Kerri's servility of sex for drugs was growing in presence.

Kerri knew an intervention was outstanding. It would be tough. She returned to her names list not knowing why she desired to be a mother: Lily, Layla, Riley, Aiden, Dylan, Jayden, Gabriel. Gabriel for a boy. She liked it: *Gabriel.*

*****

When he opened his eyes, he realized he had fallen asleep again. Ruby was back in the room.

"And now..."

"Now what?"

"Now a couple questions I've been dying to ask you." A topic off limits was approaching. Their relationship was heading toward a wall.

"If you don't mind me asking...who is she?" Ruby's forehead wrinkled as he asked the question to Jacob.

"Who's who?"

"The text messaging you've been getting. Ruby waited for a few seconds and without looking at Jacob pressed, "Pretty?"

He told some version of a lie each day, but couldn't say that it was no one. That wouldn't be believable to him. Victoria meant many things. Jacob replied with a firm parameter, "Pretty, yes, but enough. Not going to go to that point." His brow furrowed. "Listen, I don't truly know you. Don't mind you being in here for some conversation. Don't mind sharing a few stock picks that I'd share with anyone. There's no proprietary information trading hands here. But, you can't go there."

"Seems I struck a nerve." Ruby's appeared happy that Jacob became defensive and his charming smile was shining. "Call girl? Hooker? Don't want the Board to know how you dabble – Hell, how you navigate the sex trade?" Ruby's volume intensified.

Jacob's phone chimed with an incoming text message. It was her. He hesitated before laying it carefully down on the bedside desk. "Listen, I know little about you. You seem to know more about me. Let's agree to..."

"What, I live in the big garden down the street. Have a bunch of neighbors that are millionaires. What more to know than I'm simple compared to you."

"You mean Central Park?"

Not answering the question, Ruby mastered the obvious, "You live in one of them big fancy condos. One of the fanciest. Probably paid five thousand dollars a square foot..."

"It was closer to six. Years ago. You mean to tell me you're homeless?"

"No Jacob, I'd say you were more homeless than an old weathered fellow like myself. But just like you, here and in life – I'm just passin' through." Ruby's comments were all pointed now, with an intent, and quick.

"I liked you so much better about 30 minutes ago. Before you opened your mouth. Before you said what you said. Listen pal, you're time here is about to come to a close. ."

"Sure, it is." He paused, "But, have you ever considered that a high roller like you might be more homeless than an old man, all worn down, little to show for a long road...like *me*?" Ruby appeared to be dusting crumbs off his trousers, and stood surveying his immediate area of few things he had with him. The small leather red book was lying on the chair.

Not exactly sure where this was going or certain what to do, Jacob was calibrating his next step. He reached for the call button and clicked it twice. "Did you Google me?"

"Huh?"

"To gather information. To know where I live, what I do, what my background looks like, did you Google me? Did you look up my address somehow, and then go to an MLS? What else do you know? What digital dirt did you dig up? I'll bet you work in the industry. What firm? Whose payroll are you on?" Jacob was relentless.

A shark's going to do what a shark does; it attacks when it senses prey. Seasoned in financial inquisitions, he quickly fired one after another. "Is this another media stunt? Let's get in the head of the finance guys since they've pummeled returns? Are you wired?" The relationship was already strange, but was venturing to an edge.

Ruby smiled and moved toward the door. Reaching into his jacket pocket he pulled out a bright orange Minneola. "I almost forgot. This was yours." He tossed it into the air and it landed in Jacob's lap. Confused, not sure where anything was leading, Jacob gave an unusual blank stare.

One of the last things that he said before he departed Jacob's room was at the moment, meaningless: "Get out of your own head." There was a pregnant pause. "Maybe...all of us...all of us, need to know ourselves a little better." He looked at Jacob and winked. "There it is, then. Smells like trouble and I can't smell, so I'll be moving on." He was gone.

It was a stale moment. The hospital room was empty. There was an exchange of verbal volleyball moments before. Now, it was completely silent. The motors from the machines didn't hum. The ECG display didn't tick. The fluorescent light didn't buzz. Nothing.

"What the fuck was that?!" Jacob asked himself aloud.

The leather red book remained behind.

A new nurse wearing light blue smocks, one that Jacob didn't recognize walked in. She seemed to be disturbed, bothered that she was interrupted from another task. "Did you ring us?"

"Yeah, a long time ago."

"A long time?" She looked at a white smartphone on her wrist, "Like less than two minutes ago?"

"Exactly."

"Give me that red book."

She put her hands on her hips, thinking that this rich boy had a secretary in the other room and she was fetching his personal items. Under her breath she said that she didn't go to nursing school for crap like this. Jacob didn't hear a thing, and wouldn't have cared anyway. He heard silence, for the first time in a long time.

She gave it to him. It was small, red, leather cover, and appeared to have no markings on the leather cover to indicate what it was. Assuming it was a journal, she handed it to him perturbed. "Where I come from we ask politely, and say please." Refraining from conflict any more than that, she asked, "Anything else?"

"No. You can go now."

"Gladly." If the door slammed, it would have. The hydraulic sleeve brought it to a gentle close.

Jacob held the little red journal in both hands. *What do we have here*? Curiously, he opened the worn soft leather cover.

This Journal Belongs To: G. Ruben Hollins. 'We're getting somewhere', Jacob he said out loud, but quietly. He turned a next page, worn and dog-eared.

He read the few notes taken, and saw the photograph taped to the page. Immediately, he was alarmed and without any hesitation reached for his iPhone to call his Ripley.

His company's organizational safety had been breached. It was his responsibility as the key co-founding executive and chairman of PPCM to avoid any encroachment of client or company confidentiality. And he was clearly in the position to seek guidance in managing this variety of risk.

7

Matters of the Heart

There's a delicious irony in those that break the laws of the land, asking for protection from those serving the laws of the land. He felt somewhat compromised in this situation.

Jacob didn't believe that just any love was good love. Peril could always follow carelessness. His prior relationships had turned out to be costly. Love, his version of it, was a guarded commodity that moderately fluctuated in its value and net-worth. Similar to investing, in love there was a place for a buy and hold strategy. There was also a more lucrative place for a trade.

The world of high-end prostitution was filled with risk. Considering the varieties of Manhattan call girl options, the high-end was actually the most risk adverse. At that end of the market, an extravagant experience wasn't filled with an hour of splitting the sheets. A true girlfriend experience took place.

Uncomplicated emotional needs were fulfilled at a fifteen hundred dollar an hour price tag. The sex work industry and investment trading, similar in supply and demand, were a fit.

Prostitution consists of three basic classes: hookers that perform sex by act, escorts that offered sex by experience, and the high end. Sex work had many distinctions that were separated and dictated by price. However, one similarity in all of the classes: as the hours racked up, the discounting would begin. An escort's weekend could go for $25,000, a week for $40,000. Rules and risks would vary dramatically from call girl to call girl.

On the highest end of the spectrum, the price tag could go ridiculously beyond all reason. This ridiculous and unreasonable region was where Victoria resided.

Jacob had three calls to make: one to Victoria: one to Adele; and one to Ripley, the security consultant.

The call to Victoria would be so much more sensitive, as personal interest had ventured into professional. Both his and her secret was out.

A call to Adele, would be a call of groundwork.

The call to Ripley, the securities-community strong-arm investigator, would be a call that he would never have wanted to make. *Which order, and how much information needed to be divulged?*

The call to Adele was factual, and he elaborated with more detail than he thought he would. He knew that Adele was disappointed and potentially heartbroken. He felt ashamed. But, logic quickly replaced feelings, as he recited to himself that a deeper form of trust could be built in such ways.

His call to Ripley was quick and easy. He fessed up, and provided all of the necessary information to David. Jacob felt much better after talking with the investigator, receiving a template of action items and a very structured response of denial if any questions surfaced. He thought after speaking with Ripley that it was a non-issue.

Now...Victoria. "Hey, it's okay. Some things are something. And some things are nothing," she said. She always left an indelible imprint in his heart. After explaining what he found in Ruby's red book and apologizing, she replied, "Listen, it goes with the territory. I knew what I was getting myself into, and it's probably just another stalker. Don't worry about it sweetheart." She called him that often.

"I think there's more to it. I don't know. I just..." he trailed off.

"Baby, it's nothing. If you're concerned about your company, I understand. But, you know I can take care of myself and I'm not worried...at all." Her voice was soft and convincing.

"That's what my security detail told me – he said it was basically a non-issue for the moment, but to pay attention, to take note of anything else. And then he gave me some template to follow if I was asked anything."

"See – there you go. It's a non-issue. Listen to him."

"I'm checking myself out tomorrow. I have private care from home. A nurse."

"Is she a naughty nurse?" Her voice teased and giggled.

"Stop it." A smile was caught in his voice. "Listen, I'd love to have you here. Will you..."

Victoria interrupted him, "Absolutely. I can't wait to see you. I'm looking at a picture of us right now, the weekend you flew us to Monte Carlo on the GulfStream for that fundraiser."

"I miss you," he said.

"I miss you, too." She was teasing again, "You know. You might need some additional nurturing from a naughty nurse after all. Are you going to...you know..."

"Am I going to..."

"Well, when can we...you know," she paused. Finally, since he didn't reply, she whispered, "have sex again?"

"I don't know. I'll ask the doctor. Soon, I hope. Very soon."

"Me too."

"Listen, I'll let you go. Again, I'm sorry." Jacob had something to look forward to, seeing Victoria tomorrow, and his spirit was much brighter after talking with her.

"See you tomorrow. Hugs and kisses." She waited.

He didn't want to hang up. "Wear that perfume I like? I want to see you, give you a squeeze, and smell you."

"Of course. Now, get some rest." She held on for a few seconds, then hung up.

I can - never - get enough of her.

*****

They were playing Chorus, Chorus, Chorus. It was a game Laki harkened back to playing with her friends during their freshman year of SDSU. They could only play every 3 to 4 minutes, the duration of an average song across a half dozen channels. Pop and Rock were easiest, Country was not as familiar but was fair game for the channel surfing competition.

Scoring was simple: Five points for all three songs where each had the title of the song, in the chorus being sung, as the song was dialed into. One point for one song, or two points for two. Zero, if you couldn't catch a break.

They were heading to a casual dinner party in Rancho Santa Fe which wasn't too far away. It was a friend of a friend of Laki's who begged her to join.

Maybe, just maybe they could squeeze in 4 or 5 rounds, depending on the traffic. It was now Brian's turn. They had the volume on the radio cranked. "Okay, okay – it's been about four. Here we go. You ready for this?"

"Go!" Laki shouted. The kids were in the back seat mimicking her.

He drew the first station; *Party in the U.S.A.* blasted their speakers. "Yes! Brian laughed, "Knew I could count on you Miley Cyrus! One for one." He cracked his knuckles and changed to Rock N Ride, 1980's Rock. *Sweet Child O' Mine* from Guns N' Roses, played but it was Slash's guitar solo a few minutes in. No chorus. "Awe..." he shouted with disappointment.

"One for two! Not the champion." Laki teased. "And for song number three?"

He punched in Spotify and caught AC/DC's, *You Shook Me All Night Long.* "Yes, two for three." He clenched his fist and calibrated points on their notepad tucked in the dash. "Plus-two for the good guy equals one hundred eight seven."

"And how about the reigning champion?" she inquired, knowing that she was miles ahead.

"Her hotness now has two hundred forty-one." He threw an index finger in Laki's direction and added, "You, my love, are a radio terrorist."

She had one hand on the steering wheel and raised the other, fist to the roof of the car – pumping it in a victorious fashion. It was a game, months in the making, which made commuting a little less tedious.

"I think I'd do better with KINE," he teased, referring to the Honolulu station he listened to constantly.

"Yer killin' me there, BK," she glanced at her phone for directions.

"On another note, bonuses are hitting next Friday." He knew she had a garage door opener and a recliner on the short list.

"Short list bonus, or long list bonus?"

Probably short list, but we'll see how profitability came in. That's always the wild card."

"Nice." She added and glanced over at him. "That's nice," she reaffirmed by nodding her head 'yes' and softly smiled at her husband.

"And on another note, I was able to go a mile on the treadmill today – hard. Without pain."

She took a deep breath. Letting it out, "Oh, that is good news." It was Laki which rode the regret train with Brian as he transitioned from promising athlete to college student, to retail store manager, to district manager. She was in the train's passenger car which experienced it all. From her best friend to her husband, she cheered him on through all of it – the athletic brilliance and the setbacks. The pain was managed with time and strength conditioning, but the hope and disappointment took much longer to heal. Her hand reached over the console to his and she squeezed it tightly. "I'm so proud of you." His good news made her think, *maybe it's - finally time to disembark.*

Brian looked at Laki, admiring her cocoa beauty. *Man, I married a hottie.*

"Are you? Are you looking at my ears again?" Her self-conscious tone was evident. Laki thought her ears were too small.

"Exactly. Definitely. Tiny ears. Too little for your head. What am I going to do with you?" Brian teased her, then changed the subject and added, "What are we bringing?"

"Butterscotch Blondies and coconut brownies." She paused and added, "You know...from us brownies." They both smiled.

It isn't so bad being a Pacific Islander, Brian thought. Looking at her again. Her olive skin was lighter than his. "I'm more...brown than you are..."

She interrupted, "Did you bring beer."

"Got it. The good stuff, Kona Longboard."

She sucked in air through her puckered lips, "I wonder - if they're like, fine wine people?" Laki looked over at Brian, "What do ya' think, Mr. Traveler?"

"We'll find out."

The further they drove, the larger and more established the homes became. Many had gates or small guard houses at the entrances.

"God, I'd love to live here." Laki was driving slower looking at street addresses and for the prescribed lengthy driveway to their destination.

Brian leaned over to kiss her cheek as she turned right. He leaned back in the passenger seat and started scrolling through his phone and chuckled to himself, admiring the zip code's star-power of residents. He read the roster to her as he scrolled though the list: "Phil Mickelson, Jenny Craig, Drew Brees...Bill Murray."

"The Ghostbuster?"

"Yeah..." Brian smiled, thinking that Dr. Peter Venkman was how she related to Carl, the Groundskeeper of Caddyshack – which was how he saw Bill.

"Troy Polamalu."

"Who?" Laki had a crush on him, so Brian knew she was joking.

"Ahnald. Da Govna'! Schwarzenegger has a vacation home here. Tiger Woods, vacation home. Oh, and a little riffraff here: Bill Gates."

"Let's go there..." Laki was squinting, looking for the turn. "But I don't think I have Mr. Softy's gate code."

Aligned with turquoise blue agave, a fortress of a mailbox, and security posts at the gate, she asked, "Ready for this? A dozen screaming kids?"

"This belongs on the long list."

"What?"

"Bonus." He said, smiling at the up-classing they were about to experience.

"Oh yeah, I know, right?" She added, "We might be the poorest people at the party."

Jacob reconsidered how they were dressed and looked at his attire: dress jeans, a long-sleeved Aloha shirt featuring navy tapa print, Olu Kai's. Then, he looked over at Laki. He thought that she was always charming: tight fitting jeans and a cotton sapphire pullover with a small eggshell-white pineapple stitched on the upper left chest.

She did the same, checking her dress – then peered over to Brian.

Then, they shrugged their shoulders at the same time.

Her thumb left the steering wheel pointing toward the back seat, "They're adorable. They look like you."

"Pretty sure - they're wine people. Fine wine," Brian acknowledged as they made their way down the sculpted curving asphalt driveway aligned with well-maintained landscaping, featuring neatly trimmed bushes and brightly colored flowers and large granite boulders dotting the flora in what appeared to be a Morse code-like pattern leading to a mansion of a home.

Preemptively, and defensively attempting Parents of the Year, they threatened the kids to be good - or else Santa Clause wasn't coming.

8

Capitulation

The market was ten minutes away from opening when Jacob was wheeled out to the limo. The shiny black Mercedes was waiting to pull up under the hospital canopy. Another car was without it's driver, so the limo couldn't move forward. His driver offered a smile and nodded his head to Paisley when their eyes met, but no words were exchanged.

Adele and the concierge, Shelby, were walking along the hospital orderly pushing the wheelchair. Their collective work chatter was a small step toward normalcy as they reviewed several orders of business which they would regularly apprise Jacob of, and they shared some small-talk water cooler gossip of the traders' at PPCM.

They reached the curb, painted a fresh coat of glossy red, the same time the driver opened the back door to the car.

The sun was shining bright into the crisp Manhattan morning. The reflections from windows and passing vehicles caught Jacob's attention for just a second. He briefly thought about the nature of reaction from action. And it was then that he found his groove. FSLR – First Solar. How had it performed this week? Tickers felt natural again. HE – Hawaiian Electric had just contracted new solar farms on Maui and Oahu to build upon their decarbonization initiative. The HE press release stated that the island's additional green energy would produce an estimation savings equivalent to eliminating 850 cars off of highways over the next ten years.

It's so easy, he thought, *new competition will encroach on this category as the need to wean off of foreign oil progresses. And every mega AI chip maker has expressed deep commitments to filling the photo voltaic pipeline.* INTC (Intel), AMD (Advanced Micro Devices), (NVDA) Nvidia – the tickers were alive. And he was too. A Democrat will be voted out next year. A Republican will fill their void – and we're back in the fossil fuel business. *God, I love this game.*

An 'ever' moment was approaching.

This would be the first time that Jacob would be together with Victoria and Adele at the same time. Ever. A first time 'ever'. Suddenly, he realized that there was an unidentifiable tension potentially in the air. He wondered briefly why he didn't anticipate this.

Shelby said her goodbyes as the orderly offered to help Jacob out of the chair.

"Where's she off to?" Jacob asked Adele. She stood next to him in an usual alabaster blouse and black skirt. Her coat was draped over one arm with a black bag big enough for files on her shoulder.

"She has a dentist appointment." Adele answered, looking at the young woman leaving them to return to the lobby.

"Pretty smile," Jacob continued with the small talk. Here was the moment which he felt might be tricky. He decided to go with the flow.

"Would you like to sit in the middle? I can help you." Adele asked and offered.

"Yeah, no - I'll be okay. I can slide" wondering if he really could slide over, "I think."

The driver had exited the limo and opened the back door where the three of them would meet for a first encounter. There she was – Victoria, stunning, sitting on the far side of the bench back seat.

"Hey there." Jacob's heart warmed and ignited when he saw her. This was a perfect place to bring her together with Adele.

They'd have to put on a bit of a performance. A degree of acting was required. He only mentioned his romantic interests with Victoria to Adele. The details, and the volume of lust, and inappropriateness was avoided, even though he thought Adele knew.

Here they were together: a celestial human, innocent in all her actions, virtuous to others, pure in heart - Adele.

A full force of guilty pleasures, scandalous and sinful, and occasionally immoral – yet irresistible: Victoria.

"Awe. It's so good to see you. Come here," she said. Victoria was wearing a soft red cashmere sweater and jeans. Jacob couldn't remember the last time he saw her in jeans. And then he did remember. They had cost him nearly $800 on a long weekend shopping trip they took the December before. She convinced him that they were the best, and such a good deal. Her brunette hair hung against her sweater, brushing her breasts.

"I don't want to hurt you," she said as she hugged him. It was a long hug and they held each other tightly.

He breathed her in as they hugged, and secretly whispered – "Mmm... that's nice." Then he let go and sat upright looking mostly at her and then at a dark TV monitor on the back of the driver's and passenger's front seats.

"I'm good, really," he lied. "You look beautiful. It's so very good to see you too." They looked deeply into each other's eyes. Not saying anything for a few seconds, yet sharing volumes of feelings and secrets. There was a playful sense of contemplation between the two of them. Jacob felt good to be back.

He said it with an animation, "God, it's good to be with you, and back outside, and...and alive!" Jacob felt much more joyful than usual and smiled brightly. Victoria hugged him again, harder, and longer, kissing him on the cheek.

"Yes," she said, "it's good to be alive, and well, and to always have things to look forward to." Their eyes met again and romantic moments were rekindled. And then Jacob remembered to finally introduce Adele.

Jacob looked at Adele, holding her jacket and her leather portfolio, sliding in next to him. But, something was vaguely different. She had a strange look on her face. Uncomfortable? Awkward? He didn't understand Adele's withdrawn position.

Scooting back toward the door the driver was closing, she was somewhat nervous. The moment felt something like judgment and it was unlike her.

Victoria identified the jealousy immediately. The best high-end call girls knew human behaviors masterfully and navigated appropriately. Holding out her hand, she took control. "Adele, it's so very nice to finally meet you. I'm Victoria Santori. Jacob has said so many wonderful things about you." She was sure to use Adele's, Jacob's and her name in her greeting in an attempt to create a unit.

Adele's interpretation was that Jacob was talking about Adele with Victoria, and was not talking about Victoria with her. Retrenching her intuition, she squinted, and shook Victoria's hand. "Nice to meet you. Is it bright out here, or what?" She faked a smile in Victoria's direction. "I need my sunglasses." She reached inside her purse. Adele's squint had nothing to do with the sun, and Victoria knew so.

She gave the man dressed in a black suit a dead glance as he clicked the door shut. Adele sat on the driver's side left. Jacob was in the middle, between the two. Victoria was to his right.

Victoria reached over to hold Jacob's hand. To distract them from doing that and to occupy Jacob, Adele handed him a thin manila stack of files and a blue takeover prospectus to review. She reached for the remote to turn to Bloomberg, knowing Jacob's attention would be split. A non-profit charity was ringing the opening bell on the NASDAQ. The talking heads were counting down the open, explaining the extreme gravity of the futures. All the arrows were red deltas pointing down. Forces were at work, creating pre-panic. Paisley didn't think too much of it, but did wonder about his team's preparation to work with and against the Volatility Indexes to leverage the news properly. Nevertheless, like anyone in the business, he was curious why the pre-market open pointed to a two-hundred-point drop.

He handed the short stack of work-to-do back to Adele and reached for Victoria's hand again. It felt warm, and soft, and real. Yet, he knew that 9:30 meant business and he looked to Adele. She seemed perturbed.

Jacob absorbed the moment and assessed the situation: How did he get here? He looked for the foundation, toward his black dress shoes, at the floorboard of the limo to capture the week's events. Monday: heart attack. Tuesday: unconscious most of the day. Wednesday: some interaction with Adele and Shelby and that black man, the corporate spy – Ruby. Thursday: Ruby, again. *Disgust.* And Adele, and Shelby and visitors, and the incident with Ruby, and more disgust. The call to alert David Ripley. This moment: sitting in between the two closest women in his life, anticipating the day, the market's open, the opportunities that any given day could bring. That was how he landed in this moment from the surface.

Underlying circumstances were always more sophisticated. But...he was alive, and would charge ahead even, if need be, from his penthouse. Anticipation was at play. He had a business day to look forward to, and was excited with an opportunity to raid the indexes, bark trading orders again, counsel the attainment of capital, and to attack the benchmarks with a voracious appetite. His home office, a byproduct of the pandemic lockouts, was more hybrid than many. He had more screens at home than at HQ. Anticipation lingered.

Showtime. He was immediately disappointed as the bell rang and the Dow was down 450 points. The S&P - equally off, 1.5%. His driver, rolled the interior cabin window down and informed him that the car wasn't starting. He apologized and said he'd have a look at the engine, and left the window down between the front seat and sitting area in the back of the limo back exposing their privacy to an empty cab. Jacob was thoughtless about the issue, instead fixated upon the tickers paying little attention to anything else. Victoria and Adele had drawn their phones from their bags and were nose down, between taking glances at Jacob – fixated on the screen in the car.

Dow down 615. Dow down 886. S&P off 2.1%. The Nasdaq was getting dusted too, slipping 1.9%.

The three of them saw the tickers sliding across the streamers on the screen of the TV, a sea of red.

Adele recognized his concern, knowing he'd prefer to be in front of several screens at home - and asked Jacob if he wanted her to call for another limo, but he didn't answer.

"That doesn't look good," Victoria chimed in.

He ignored her comment too.

Concentrating on the tickers but paying little attention to anything else. The decko on the monitor now displayed the Dow down 975. Dow down 1,095. Dow down 1,108. What had he missed? Where had a selloff like this been hiding?

The capital markets were like a theater that was filled to capacity with high net worth investors, deep pools of public and dark pools of private equity. Someone had just run to the front and yelled 'FIRE!' And in a manic panic, every source had to sell before it fled.

A sell off like this was hard to miss. *Fuck, fuck, and fuck. What the hell. How would we have missed this?* He reached for his cell phone. The hood of the car clicked shut.

Victoria spoke softly and seductively. It was above a whisper and mostly to herself to hear, but it was intentioned for Adele to hear as well: "Men. Men and their money. And men and their fast cars and their big boats and their exotic properties and tropical vacations to sneaky places." She glanced at Jacob, not paying attention to her. "Men and dollars and numbers and their big watches and expensive suits. Men and their hobbies. And men and sex. Men and sex, and sex and men and their women..." They were posturing.

"Can you please be quiet?" Adele was abrupt. She lowered her sunglasses to wince at Victoria, who immediately stopped speaking.

Jacob, in a trance, turned his head slowly looking away from the seat back monitor to Adele. Then, a small smile found its place on his face before he looked back to the freefall.

Victoria, upset, looked out the window to the New York streetscape.

Dow down 1,267. Dow down 1,523. Dow down 1,895. Dow down 2,244.

Capitulation. It was the term for frantic selloffs.

Capitulation. Equities dumping, capital descent, a thorough market plummet. A correction beyond a dive. Complete cratering.

Capitulation. A description reserved for 'nowhere to run, get - out - now'. The S&P was plummeting even faster now. Stock market capitulation was underway. The Dow was down more than 2,400 points. The Nasdaq was in freefall, down three and a half percent. Dow down 2,597. The S&P was now down four-plus percent. The exogenous shocks to the market were in charge.

Capitulation identified the "Back Monday" flash crash in October of 1987 and was captured several times within the manic panic of the 1929 market collapse. It was most recently felt in the subprime meltdown in October of 2008 – and in the Covid-19 pandemic lockdown in March of 2020.

These drops were primarily silent. Impacting net worth, and financial statements, and impacting jobs or business investments. They had trickle repercussions which impacted the economy; would appear in countless articles and fill headlines for years to come. Their crash residual and would be talked about for years.

What happened next was a different kind of a drop...

WHOMP!!!

The crash was a thunderous...*SMASH!* The windshield splintered into a million checkered squares but held together. The car sank at the impact, with the undercarriage bumping against the asphalt, the frame bottoming out. The clangorous thump was startling. It was darker in the car now, with something covering the windshield. They weren't sure what it was.

"What the hell is he doing out there?" Victoria spoke first in a bewildered tone, assuming that the driver was checking under the hood again.

Nine seconds passed by. Then, Adele, Victoria and Jacob realized something completely different had just happened. A small stream of blood trickled onto the evenly crackled spider web glass. A body lay on the windshield motionless.

After realizing what had happened, in the flash of a moment Victoria was out the door darting twenty feet away from the scene. She ran in her red sweater, brunette hair floating behind her sprint. Jacob realized her instant departure. She was out for number one. Victoria was seeking Victoria's safety.

Adele reached for Jacob's hand to assure his safety. Speechless, she opened the door and carefully helped him out of the car, ushering him to the sidewalk. Both were backing away from the limo, holding each other.

Jacob watched Victoria, arms crossed, continuing to backpedal away from the car, assessing the body lying on the cracked windshield. For a moment, he thought that she was considering potential exit strategies. *Is she going to run away?*

Adele finally asked, "Are you alright?"

"Yes...I...you?"

"What just happened?"

"I don't know. It's a body. A suicide?" He was confused but trying to solve the moment's puzzle. "What do you think?"

"I think...I think that was a deafening crash." Adele still clutched his arm and he clutched hers as they stood still trying to understand the gravity of the moment. "You're sure you're alright?" Her concern was not for herself, it was for Jacob's safety.

The limo driver looked at Adele and Jacob in disbelief and said, "He just - fell - out of the sky."

Jacob, noticing that it was a tall black man lying on the windshield, slowly walked to the crushed hood. He noticed the familiarity. Red suspenders. A plaid shirt. The same trousers that he'd seen before on the same man. *Could it be? It appeared to be - Ruby.*

Jacob was attempting to absorb the surreal magnitude of Gabriel Ruben Hollins lying motionless. Eyes closed. Peaceful. His face not disfigured from the fall. One arm at his side, the other under his back against the windshield. Jacob moved in for a closer look, and to see if he was breathing. He reached his hand out with the intention to check for a pulse, but before he could an emergency technician burst through the doors rushing to the body.

What appeared to be a long and uninterrupted moment of stillness was suddenly filled with commotion, and noise, and a buzzing swirl of nursing attendants rushing to the body, and a surge in the hysteria of all of it.

From a crystal clear, deep blue sky, the light of day was shining on Ruby's body. Three of the hospital staff were looking at each other, shaking their heads in disbelief. One orderly looked up to a point where the man's body may have jumped from. A stretcher was being wheeled out. A fire alarm must have been pulled or sounded as a siren started to sound...

It's a mystery how the mind wanders aimlessly and articulately at the same time, Jacob thought. He reviewed a challenge Ruby had served him with over the past few days, and repeated it for no comprehensible reason under his breath: "Three words to describe yourself."

Jacob Paisley smelled what Ruby could not – gasoline trickling from the fuel line. The master of money quickly recapped his interaction with the man lying motionless on the windshield of the limo. Bridging from one conversation with Ruby to the next, desperately seeking a connection for action like this, he found nothing. There was no beacon as his guide. There was no explanation. There were no more tickers lighting up his thoughts.

The alarm went silent – and so too did Jacob's ability to reason.

Together, they were. He held Adele's arm tightly. They reached to hug one another. In doing so, he looked across the pavilion to see Victoria standing with her hand over her mouth, isolated and perhaps baffled as well. Alone.

*****

Kerri was wandering through midtown. She had no specific mission. Her motive was to not think about the beast. It was her intention to isolate Crazy Kerri from Cutter.

What started as a long walk from Hell's Kitchen through Times Square to Bryant Park – led to stretching her legs further to the 102-story Empire State Building and another eleven-block stroll to Madison Square Park and the triangular Flatiron Building. At one point she began counting baby buggies and was approaching her count of seventy-two.

Walking past a dozen drug stores along the way, she stopped in front of one near Union Square. A commotion was taking place at a hospital across the street. She looked in the direction of what appeared to be doctors and nurses attending to a body on the windshield of a fancy black car. But her stare and focus were hollow. A pretty, dark-haired woman in a bright red sweater stood watching.

"*I was pretty once,*" Kerri said. She realized she said this to herself quietly but that someone walking by in the opposite direction had heard and looked back at her with a frown after they passed. Her paranoia was strong, and she cowered from the judgment, looking back toward the scene near the hospital's entrance.

A couple standing on the curb held each tightly, observing the calamity. Other people began gathering around the stir.

Kerri had walked thirty-seven blocks, experiencing twenty-three red lights, passing eight McDonalds and fourteen Starbucks, stopping to rest three times, and said nothing to no one - to reach this point.

She stopped watching the scene and walked into the store, meandering her way to the childcare isle. Carefully categorized by feeding, swaddles, burping cloths, diapering, bath time, play time, sleep, health and safety, clothing and health and safety – she stopped at the baby toys. Handheld rattles, bright colored teething pieces, and soft plush stuffed animals consumed a section of the isle.

Kerri found a fuzzy and soft caramel colored teddy bear. It was holding a baseball bat, wearing a pinstripe jersey, and matching pinstripe hat - with a twist turn dial on its back. Winding the musical crank, in the chimes of a xylophone, it gently and slowly played *Take Me Out to The Ballgame.* She listened at first, then quietly sang along with the tune, "Take me out to the ballgame, take me out with the crowd; Buy me some peanuts and Cracker Jack, I don't care..." The music advanced, but her words from her lips didn't.

She thought about what a tragedy her life had become..."if - I - ever get back..." Her eyes rolled into the back of her head.

Her knees collapsed first, and she fell into the metal shelving, dropping the stuffed animal. The gentle chime from the bear continued to play.

Crashing onto the floor, she lay in isle seven unattended for nearly a minute until a pharmacist in a sterile white jacket came to her side, calling out loud for other workers in the store to assist her.

Kerri's eyes were closed, her arms were extended outward, away from her body. One hand was open toward the heavens, the other, palm down. Several tendrils from her dishwater blonde hair crossed her face.

She lay alone, peacefully on the cool white tile – far away from her unappeasable necessities, her dark and raven needs, here in this staidness – free, at the moment, from the relentless dominion of her other self.

PART TWO:

THE LIGHT OF DAY - A REFRACTION

CURRENT DAY...

9

Liquid Diversions

He wasn't dead yet. He was still trying. It was just a matter of time.

Jacob clutched the brass handle at Bobby Vans. He had opened this door more than a thousand times to celebrate great achievements as well as to drown the down days at PPCM. There was a chance...that this would be his final visit.

The aromas inside didn't yet smell of a wide variety of grain fed steaks, or roasted garlic mashed potatoes, or rosemary encrusted chicken. Those smells weren't far off. It was five o'clock. The market's close would give way to the weekend, and at Bobby Vans that meant premium steaks and seafood, masterfully crafted cocktails, schmoozing galore. Paisley wasn't there for the fine-dining tonight. His purpose was liquid. He was going to get drunk beyond repair.

The bar stools were evenly lined up at the oak bar awaiting the frustrated, the enlightened, the exhausted, the determined, the thirsty, and most appropriately - the thank-God-it's-Friday-let's-get-freaking-smashed customers.

Jacob looked for a few familiar faces he would recognize behind the bar and nodded his head as they dutifully shined wine and cocktail glasses and prepared for the evening. The crystal-clear glasses clinked as they were neatly stacked.

The bartenders were all men, wearing white serving jackets, neatly pressed, black pants and shiny black dress shoes. Their hair was cut short and each looked as if they may have just been photographed for Details magazine. They wore brushed nickel name tags with just first names engraved. Paisley never paid attention before, but did tonight as they passed by: Brian. David. Sebastian. Marcus.

Friday's were the peak night at Bobby Vans as many of the rich and famous would make their way back to their family homes in Connecticut for the weekend to get out of the city. The commute out of Manhattan could be grueling. Five-to-nine PM was always lively as the financial fish stories would either grow or get away while large amounts of alcohol were consumed. It was largely assumed that this was one of the places where more insider trading tool place than anywhere else. A few too many and something was inappropriately whispered. It happened all the time.

Jacob had just been fired.

The Board of Directors, his own hand-picked Board, ran him from his very own company: Paisley Pierce Capital Management. The Board of Directors, or as Paisley recently called it, *the fucking B of D*, believed that separation was the only way to salvage what remained. To retain client interest, provide value, and someday soon sell PPCM, there was no option - the CEO had to go.

Jacob Columbus Paisley was on the outside looking in. *It's business*, he thought. *Logic. Emotion-free zone. Capitalism. It was never supposed to be anything more than business.*

Sitting still and alone in his thoughts, recanting the Board moving forward with his termination, he summoned the words used in a final review. Sitting around a large mahogany table in the PPCM boardroom, he recalled the review - the recant of his dismissal.

Seated at the table were his hand-picked Board members. This was a gathering of wisdom, experience, and ultimately business success. Custom suits from Hall Madden. Crisply pressed white dress shirts with ties and matching handkerchiefs. Dresses from Bergdorf

Goodman. Shoes shined weekly at Cobbler's. The gang of exclusive and expensive luxury brands ineluded Hermes, Versace, Fendi, Armani, Baneciaga and more. Ivy League educations; homes in the Hapton's; super yachts tethered to slips at Miamarina Bayside. There was no shortage of confidence, nor was there a need to score keep within this team he had assembled throughout the years. This was a group of white and gray-haired tenured captains of their industries. And they were the kings of their kingdoms. Lions, with the scars from their decades of battles, gathered here to judge.

They lined up around the table: Jim, Claire, Brian, Santosh, Anita and Bruce. Their strong sense of personal ownership was doubtless. Now they were gathered here, his sapiential circle, but without his awareness, to take action.

A 4:05pm Board meeting, unanimously called for, on a triple-witching Friday - a day of enormous trading volume - due to the expiration of stock options, index futures, and index options contracts simultaneously coming due. It happened four times each year; once each quarter. Unusual pricing sways created risky value changes in the assets.

But he knew - he knew a while ago that this moment was conceivably coming. Inevitably, he was steeled for this conversation.

One board member, Dr. Brian Baker, a tall man with short white hair and who always wore a bow tie nearly shouted, "Jacob, it's as if you moved from being stable and predictable - to - operating upon second guesses, wild hunches - and chances." He was first to assess and was less-than gentle with the delivery of his words and criticism. "You migrated from springboards of financial platforms, industry leading bright ideas, really good shit, to..." he shook his head in search of the right words, "grasping at anything to do something. Damn it. I hate this." He motioned to a short blond-haired woman in her sixties that he was seated next to.

Next to him was Claire Dainsley; a former CEO of a personal healthcare organization. Usually appearing in a parchment of pearl white blouse with a black or navy skirt, today she wore a dark checkered print dress. Her hair too, was short. She was less dramatic in here depiction and brief, "You just lost your way, that's all. The confidence is gone." She cupped her chin in her hands for a moment, then finished while looking away. "You used to have it all figured out, and that momentum led the organization. But, like I said, you just...lost your way." She shook her head and finished, "I don't know what to say. I don't have anything else to add." Her eyes were filled with tears but they didn't spill over on to her cheeks. "I hate this."

Next to her was Jim Byrd. Jim was a short man, balding, bitter, and dissatisfied with nearly *everything.* Jacob wasn't sure which of his personality attributes was a leading way to describe him - and often questioned himself about why he thought he was a good fit for *his* Board. *He was what? A whiner? A griper? A squawker?* A squawker, that was it. That was his leading peculiarity.

It must have been the divorce. Jim Byrd's wife took him to the cleaners, and perhaps that was the reason he had turned so ugly. Jacob didn't care for his demeanor over the past several quarters. And with the curt and acrid assessment of Paisley's performance, quarter after quarter, Jacob liked him less and less. It led to his wondering what he saw in Jim Byrd, sitting in *his* seat at the head of the table. *What's with this posturing?*

Byrd was much more abrupt, "No." disagreeing with Claire and attacking, "It's as if you went fucking nuts!" Jim Byrd moved his head back and forth, from side to side, and raised his elbows up and down to mimic a contortion of some sort, "Fucking nuts, Paisley. You lost a sense of yourself." Jacob remembered squinting at the comment. Jim continued, "What's with all of your squeamish hand-wringing lately? We don't want you to share the same fears of the markets. We're in a game where the only difference, the only difference, is when the odds are stacked in our favor. And you, Jacob, can no longer do that for the firm that bears your name. You've become the Cliff Clavin of..."

"Stop it!" Claire interrupted. "Enough of that." It was unusual for her to lose her cool. The boardroom was silent.

"But I must..." he continued. And Jim Byrd did extend his long-drawn-out exhortation, looking at each of the other Board members in the effort to sell his point, "His gibberish from the last twenty years has been replaced by AI. Everyone can be a Jacob Paisley with artificial intelligence." He was moving his elbows together in an awkward display of body language. then, Jim Byrd looked at Jacob with his beady hazel and blood shot eyes and continued, "You did not transition. Digital innovation transformation is what you convinced us all of executing to." The mean-spirited man circled his finger in the air indicating everyone in the boardroom.

"Can you give me an example of where you think I fell short of...?"

"Sure, let me bring it to the ground for you," he loudly and rudely interrupted Jacob. "Work is about what you do. Not about where you work, not a place you go. You didn't deliver upon the hybrid model attracting the best talent. Your talent is working professionals in greater New York. Your talent pool has shrunk. *Our competitors*...have the A-Team across the country and globally. *Your* B-Team is made of locals."

Jacob sat, listening and observing Jim Byrd's face becoming an indescribable shade of pink. *What color is that exactly?* Jacob thought, *bubblegum? Flamingo? Punch? Valentine?* The short, bald, bitter man's temples bulged indicative of his passion to fire Paisley. *But oh no, you could never shut up, could you?* Jacob thought, listening to the rant continue.

"CNBC only calls for a soundbite from you when someone else cancels or when they can't find anyone else..."

"Jim! Enough!" Claire began, and other Board members also asked him to quell the tirade.

"Almost done here," Jim went on without any additional pause, "Champions are recognized with medals. Champions are made and built with actions. In your last year, client count shrunk 32%, that's thirty-two percent! Confidence has plummeted. Our NPS scores have fallen from 48% to 22%, that's twenty-two percent. Worst - ever. People don't want to work here any longer. Your team has migrated from a form of change management fatigue to a comatose state. PPCM's services numbers are down, our consulting practice numbers are half, our trading platform is, well you know how shitty those numbers are - you won't delegate them away, so they're your numbers. Most important of all, your 'Customers for Life' campaign...was a big swing and a miss."

"Well, there are some factors here: The FED went fucking hawkish. Everyone on Broad and Wall took a 20% haircut this past year. It was a December to remember. If you want to know why, it's..."

Jim interrupted his rebuttal, "No! No! We don't want to know why today. Today is too late for us to know why - from you." The veins in the maniacal board members' forehead were bright with rage. "By the way, what the hell is a leap and a stretch? Some creative instrument of leverage? That alone juiced numbers as we did our own stress test on your cooked books." He was shouting now.

"It's what many of the top houses do. They can do it. It's legal because of the deregulation..."

Jim interrupted Jacob again, "I really don't want to hear you speak any longer. Ashamed! I'm ashamed that I am connected to you in any manner. this is not going to go well when it breaks. Listen, it's this. The Board of Directors has met, Jacob. We've got a unanimous no vote of confidence. You're out!" He paused and finally looked at Jacob, "I'll yield the floor to the rest of the Board." Jim finally shut up.

I'm out? Jacob sat there, silent, and somewhat stunned at hearing that flow through Jim Byrd's lips the way that it did: sour.

Then, as a course of due process required, the others followed with less fiery judgements.

To Jacob, something about the first three meant the most. He sat silent throughout all of it, listening carefully to the words used in his demise. For the most part, they were like lyrics in a somber ballad or bad country song.

Jacob spoke following the reviews, "It's all bullshit. And you know it. We're in a position of ascendancy, then and now. You just don't see it. The fundamentals are there for growth in the future. When things make sense, whether known or unknown, they tend to crawl - to - the - surface. This doesn't." He looked to the faces of each member of the table. "Look, we're in a period of amassing enormous amounts of data to support the outcome-based decisions..."

"Would you like to talk about the woman?" Dr. Brian Baker interrupted, "Would you like that to crawl - to - the - surface?" He raised his eyebrows indicating unsaid words to Jacob. the silence did the speaking: *Unfortunately, good sir, we've got you in a position you likely do not want to be in.*

Claire Dainsley brushed something from her sleeve, and added, "Jacob, let's not do this. It's over. Get off the horse. Take the money and run."

Jim Byrd spoke once more and delivered an evil grin, "Yeah, let's talk about the woman. Let's get Ripley to talk it through. Let's talk about the fucking millions in T&E that landed on that line item of the ledgers." He was excited of the prospect of bringing someone down. It made him feel bigger. The short balding man looked at the door, around the boardroom table seeking agreement, but only found the other members with their heads down looking into their hands. He continued in his rant, "For shareholders and clients and your team to understand that a hooker was on the payroll would..."

"No!" Claire spoke quickly, we agreed! We're not going to do that!" She was diverting their attack. She reached for a tissue from her purse to blot her eyes.

Jacob saw int he corner of the room, seated next to a Ficus tree, David Ripley. He hadn't noticed him when he walked in. Ripley sat there swaddled in his trench coat, not making eye contact with Jacob - instead looking down to the industrial charcoal collared carpeting.

Betrayal. A disloyalty. *Someone got to him. What a sellout.* Trust had been broken. So much for secrecy and the bond of discretion the two had pledged years prior.

Jacob felt dispirited. Ice water coursed through his body.

This was the crestfallen moment to accept defeat. *Finally.* Jacob realized that there were assumptions made and knowledge gained that hadn't been shared with him. In one swift moment, he felt like a victim of his own doing. Hope instantly transitioned to guilt. Fight became flight.

"Your personal diminished value has harmed the company..." Jacob was somewhere else in his head but also listening to the voice in the room. He wasn't sure who it was, speaking, a man at the other end of the boardroom table. His focus wasn't on the additional commentary any longer.

"It's as though you gave up your peripheral vision," was mumbled by someone. But at this point, Jacob was outside of his conscious mind. Like in a state of listening to voices without people behind the words, he studied the grain of the wood in the boardroom table. *Complexity sometimes favors the unconscious mind. It's where we occasionally go to solve,* he thought. This was a moment void of color. All things were now black and white and shades of gray.

"The anointed one's reign is over," he heard this muttered, but wasn't certain who said it. It stung. *The anointed one's reign is over.*

Jacob reached for the separation contract, thumbed through the thirty pages, flipping it to the back page. It would no longer matter what any of it said. What's the number?

He reached for his Mont Blanc, a gift from Victoria. It was missing. When was the last time he used it? Did he leave it on his desk? He was going through the moments that had led to its use. *Where the fuck is my pen?* he thought. It disturbed him as he fumbled from pocket to pocket. Maybe Adele would retrieve it and give it to him later.

Without saying anything, Claire stood and reached across the table offering hers.

He didn't say anything for a minute, just looking at his release statement. It felt like an hour of solitude. Intending to sign, he paused again - and made a request, "I want Adele to be taken care of." The room was silent. "It's the only request I'll make. One year's salary as a guarantee, including the firm's annual performance bonus - and if that's a no-go for her to continue as is - a two-year payout."

The Board members all looked at each other and shook their heads in a quick nod. They had fired the founder.

"Done," Jim Byrd squawked his elbows again as if trying to lift off. "I'll act as interim CEO while we conduct a search, considering internal and external candidates."

"Oh, they'll just love that," he muttered quickly to himself. Jacob was referring to his team and considered their oncoming anguish with Jim Byrd stepping in to the day-to-day action.

Claire reached her hand under the table and produced another piece of previously printed white paper from nowhere and said to him lowly, "Jacob, we anticipated that. We have a three-year separation agreement pre-written for Adele. More than fair. We thought you'd ask for more."

He sat there at the corner of the boardroom table where the CEO and Chairman doesn't routinely sit - in a somber state, and signed the contract's back page looking at the title on the cover:

Termination Agreement
Jacob C. Paisley, *"former"* CEO PPCM, LLC
Attorney Client Privilege
Do Not Compete Clause and Discourse
Severance Package Acknoledgment
Contractual Separation Addendum

Former. He stared at the work in a state of silence and thought deeply: *This too, was always - always intended to be temporary. Like a trade, we make our money through the money leveraged from others. What screws us up most in our lives is the picture in our heads of how it's all supposed to be.*

Where was the mea culpa? There wasn't anything that Americans couldn't forgive and forget. Pete Rose, Martha Stewart, Arnold Swarzenegger, Michael Vick, Charlie Sheen, Bill Clinton. Depending upon how you viewed it - there were numerous mistakes made and forgiven. Fame restored or enhanced as a result of the turnaround. Paisley's contrition was a conversation away from the long leash that the BoD had been granting him. It led to scrutiny and his unfavorable outcome.

He replayed that dismissal in his mind one more time, remembering something else: Jim Byrd tucking in the comment, "...the seeds of your destruction were planted long ago..." *What the hell did he mean by that?* Jacob wondered. He thought about his final moments in the Board Room, sitting there, helpless, feeling like a caged animal with minutes left to live. He was particularly disappointed in one phrase used to describe his conduct in the separation package that was drawn up against his contract: *...Due to executive leadership negligence and actions taken that acted against the well-being of the organization...* Nevertheless, he was a professional, and shook each hand as he departed, unescorted.

Jacob's final moments, leaving the boardroom and walking through an empty PPCM lobby, were deathly silent. He was alone. He opened one side of the tall thick glass double doors, walked through, and turned to watch the whisper spring hinge automatically close the door behind him. Jacob took one step and stopped. He turned to see the copperplate logo etched upon the glass entrances - and in this case, his exit- the font read:

PAISLEY PIERCE CAPITAL MANAGEMENT, LLC

He ran his fingertips across the logo and title, feeling the inscribing. No one watched the departure. It was his moment. Speaking slowly and soulfully, "It was a good run. But...but it's time we break up. No hard feelings? No hard feelings, I hope. I just don't love you like I loved your yesterday."

In slow motion, he walked away from PPCM, the company which he had built, toward the elevator bank to punch the down button one last time. Once down to the lobby and outside, in the crisp December air, he strode a block away to Bobby Vans - thinking of a song from his treadmill playlist. His stride matched the rhythm of the beat from My Chemical Romance's rock ballad, *I Don't Love You.*

*****

Brian was alone in their home office, away from the ladies beginning to gather and chatter. For research and a reference point in an e-mail he was writing, he needed to retrieve a merchandising report for his stores from a couple years ago. He slid open the closet door where a battleship gray filing cabinet stored reams of paper reports.

Above the filing cabinet on a shelf was a cardboard box which had all capital letters written with a bold black Sharpie: THIS WAS THEN. It was a purposeful message he wrote for himself. An ego check. A reminder to live in the now, not the past - was the intent. He couldn't help himself, as he longed for a trip back to Nanakuli to see his island family. It was heavy and he grunted lifting it from the shelf to the top of the metal cabinet where he could sort through the contents.

Inside the box were several trophies in the shapes of football players running with the ball. One was like a Heisman, but silver instead of bronze. Its placard stated: ALL-STATE WIDE RECEIVER. Several were metal footballs attached to the tops of small granite blocks in a variety of colors and each had an engraved metal plate on the front - a distinction of Brian's accomplishments or school records. Another was a large gold cup which declared on the engraving: HAWAIIAN OFFENSIVE PLAYER OF THE YEAR. He lifted it, holding it the longest and remembered the conversation he had with the coach of a neighboring team as if it were yesterday:

"Brian, we'd love to have you come play with us in Waianae." The coach was a big man, taller than Brian was at six feet. The conversation took place in his sophomore year of High School. "We have a way around the jurisdiction of living locations that the state mandates..."

"No disrespect intended Coach, but I'm a Golden Hawk. Nanakuli is home. I have family and a community that I'm playing for too. It's not just me."

The coach looked at him and smiled. "You have an opportunity to play for a winning team and gain a lot of awareness here, Brian." He held his big paw of a hand on Brian's shoulder, "Are you sure this is what you're willing to turn down, son?"

Brian thought about his Aunties and Uncles, his cousins, and friends in the Nanakuli valley. Playing as a Searider would be a no-brainer for almost every other player. D-1, the highest distinction in High School football. "There may be regret later, but the Golden Hawks need me, Coach. Got to do what I think is right, for now, for them, for my team."

"Your decision, Brian...it's just another example or what a very special player you are, what a remarkable young man you're becoming. I'll enjoy watching your success - on and off the field. A lot of people will."

There was no regret in sticking with the hometown team.

Brian reached into the box further to a scrapbook his Auntie had put together for him. It featured all of the Honolulu Star headlines and the articles of the young Brian Kekahanamanui player, ascending to the top of Hawaiian Islands stardom. He turned the pages which had yellowed long ago. They now smelled musty. The cellophane page protector crinkled as he flipped through the scrapbook. Briefly reading each headline:

Young Nanakuli Receiver Carries Team to The Endzone for Win

Golden Hawks Win Again with Kekahanamanui's Four TDs

Hawks Soar High in Dramatic Westside Win

QB and Receiver Duo Score 36 Points

Friday Night Lights Burn Bright for Nanakuli's Hawks and Receiver

He stopped flipping through the scrapbook when he approached the next article and paused to read it:

The Story of Brian Kekahanamanui and His Nanakuli Golden Hawks

It described Brian's conduct on and off the field. His service within the community and working as a volunteer for the Hawaii FoodBank, his stellar grades in class, his love of the ukulele and how he loved *kanikapila*, jamming the old island tunes. His favorite artist: Israel Kamakawiwo'ole, of course. Brian was quoted in the article, "I love IZ. He's everything the west side represents, the voice of Hawaii."

The purpose for the article was to point out Brian's losses and hardships, overcoming adversity to rise within Oahu's sports scene.

Within the article was what the coach of Waianae, who tried to recruit him early in Brian's high school years, said, "This young man turned me down to represent Nanakuli. His allegiance to his community, believing in rising up with others on his back is pure Brian. I wish more players in Hawaii football were as considerate of others and put people first. A class act. Keep your eyes on him. yes, he'll score points and win games, but as a man - as a great human - he'll be one to watch. Obviously, I'm a Brian Kekahanamanui fan."

That was nice, Brian thought. He flipped to a page which showcased the Nanakuli Golden Hawks schedule and statistics:

@ Farrington, Won: 40 - 14

Home versus Campbell, Won: 42 - 21

@ Kahuku, Won: 56 - 28

Home versus Moanalua, OT Won: 36 - 30

Home versus Aiea, Won: 29 - 14

@Kamehameha, Won: 48 - 30

Home versus Damien, Won: 37 - 32

@ Leilehua, Won: 48 - 28

@ Punahou, Won: 28 - 16

Home versus Mililani, Won: 45 - 10

Regardless of who was at the quarterback position, he made them look good. The season leading scoring, passing, rushing, and receiving stats were posted below the roster and schedule. His name was featured throughout as the force in football to reckon with.

He reviewed his crossing into the end zone with each game. Then, Brian though of the hits. The crucial part of the play - when he was brought down. Being pummeled into the hard field of the play - and popping back up for more.

The final pag3 from the Star was an opposing coach and his own coach being interviewed about Brian. *"He's one of the toughest I've seen. Teflon. Kevlar. Steel-belted radial. I don't know what the kid is made of but he takes it and gets back up for more. You can't teach that; you cannot coach to that in High School football or sports in general."*

His coach agreed and added: *"It isn't just on the field of play either coach, it's in everything he does. I like the way you said that - Teflon, Kevlar, steel-belted radial. I'd add - this young man appears bulletproof. Really looking forward to seeing what he does on the mainland. Too bad UH couldn't tackle him, but that's just Brian working his way down the field. The Aztecs have a great player heading their way."*

He retrieved a black neoprene pouch of DVDs from the bottom of the box. Each shiny disc had been carefully cataloged by the game date and opponent. It was tribute to his contributions as a courtesy of the Golden Hawks AV department. It was intended to be a surprise at the end of his senior season, but Brian knew the audio-visual te3am was working on the project for an assignment. At the end of the ten discs was an interview between two high school coaches. it was a regular piece on one of the local station, KHNL, to bring in two different coaches each week and discuss the potential that players had as they were being considered for college ball.

Brian knew the newsreel well. He had watched it a hundred times before. A local TV personality, Billie V, was interviewing his coach and an opposing teams' coach about another player...and about Brian.

"Coach," the broadcaster asked, "as you know, on this segment, we like to find out a little more about players - perhaps off the field." His voice was deep and commanding, "Brian's grades, good - could improve? - tell us about his scholastic aptitude." It was a staged question.

"Listen, if Brian wasn't playing ball, he'd be writing code, or building rockets, or running a company. You know he takes his studies seriously." The coaches smiled and Billie V cut in with another question.

"Yeah, that was a bit of a layup. How about his favorite gridz?" Billie asked.

"He's a Nanakuli boy. I've watched him devour poke. Foodland, of course. Mac salad kind of guy..."

"Foodland...so ono..." the other coach added.

"How about a girlfriend? Does Brian have a girlfriend you know of?"

"You know he's got a fan following and I'm not talking just west side girls."

Billie moved the handheld microphone to the opposing coach who added, "We should call him up and ask him - don't you guys think?"

The morning newsman moved the microphone back to his mouth and added, "That's a great idea, coach."

As Brian's coach retrieved his cell from his pocket, he muttered, "He better be on his way to class right now, let's see..."

The competitive coach had already reached into his pocket and dialed Brian, "It's okay Coach Iona - I've got him on speed dial..." to which they all laughed and Brian's coach added, "Hey - you recrutin' my star player?"

The opposing and teasing coach hung up, and said, "Knowing the character of Brian Kekahanamanui - he wouldn't take my call anyway."

Once Brian was reached by Coach Iona, the question was asked by his coach: "Brian, good morning - listen, you're on the morning news here with a couple Oahu coaches and Billie V and a question was asked I'm not sure I can answer..."

"Oh, wow - hey Coach."

"Brian, we want to know if you have a girlfriend?"

A few seconds of consideration were met with Brian answering while smiling, "Hmm...just one? There's a lot of great wahine here on the west side, Coach."

The coaches and the TV personality all laughed.

Brian continued, "No, no girlfriend right now Coach. That's for the post season."

"Good answer," his coach added. "I shared with Billie and Coach Boz that you're considering a number of schools to continue your player experience with and that SDSU is the top consideration for now."

"That's right, Coach."

"Well, if that's the way it goes maybe there's an Aztec girl out there for you."

"Maybe. We'll see, Coach."

Brian though of Laki. Meeting her. Falling in love with her. His coconut Queen. He marveled at what they had built together. Their mainland family, their warm home, his promising sporting goods retail career - all forge3d from a foundation of good values from family in Nanakuli. And his thoughts returned to one of the loadstones for all of it: football. The plays, the snap of the ball, and the action. The hits. Those bruising tackles. That ground-pounding pain. They would leave stories that weren't written in the Honolulu Star of any of the local papers. Memories for Brian for a lifetime. He remembered the ankle turning crush which ended it all. The stretcher. The ambulance ride to the hospital. The football ending diagnosis. The regret was the story that was written - but for Brian to remember as unfinished business.

He carefully placed Auntie's scrapbook back and the sleeve of DVDs in the brown box, laid the trophies carefully on top and shut the lid of the box. He returned to the chair at the desk, and when he sat, wiggled his ankle around.

Brian was feverishly clicking at keys on his laptop when she walked in.

"Be careful there. You might hurt yourself." Laki was in the home office to retrieve some additional wine glasses from a closet. She was hosting a neighborhood woman's book club and didn't realize today was a day-drinking opportunity. Mimosas were on deck.

"What did we ever do without data?" Brian asked no one in particular but said it out loud. Sever of the early arrivers were chattering in their living room which was a couple rooms away. He couldn't hear their conversation but knew that a few women were talking.

"Quarter shaping up?"

"Yeah, it is." Not mentioning his trip down memory lane, he looked at a spreadsheet next to an e-mail, and added, focusing on today instead of yesterday and answering her question, "Maybe up 25% for the district, year over year, and plus 15% over budget."

"Rancho Santa Fe, here we come," said Laki, "But the kids - they'd still have to go to a community college, right?"

He smiled, "Right - and you'll still have to clip coupons for Albertson's forever."

"Deal." They were joking.

The kids ran down the hallway. It sounded like a herd, because there were five of them. Their two and three others from the book club moms.

"Who's minding the rug..."

"Don't you worry, we got this." She cut him off, and he knew they leveraged an older sibling to babysit while they gossiped and drank the fruity bubbly drinks.

Laki leaned over to kiss the top of Brian's head as he pounded away at the e-mail which he was crafting. Software had not only enabled the managers of the stores and the district managers leading them to communicate with efficiency opportunities unique to their markets, it rewarded the early adapter with a commanding lead which could position them for the annual President's Club trip. This year's venue: Cancun. Brian was more interested in winning and rewarding Laki with a six-day, five-night stay at an all-inclusive resort then he was in taking time off and being away from the kids. In total, fifty of the greatest Q4 performers and their plus-ones would beach it up for a long President's Day weekend getaway. Brian and Laki had won twice before. Janus One spared no expense, lavishly rewarding their best of the best. The trips were always exquisite.

He closed the laptop and trekked into the kitchen to refill his glass of water. Four purple-foil bottles of Proseco were flanked by mango, orange, and pineapple juices. One Minute Maid quart of Hawaiian POG was off to its side. *That's got to be Laki's*, Brian said to himself.

Not wanting to embarrass Laki with his appearance, he looked down at his sweatpants and tight tee shirt and muttered to himself, *good enough*. He wanted to hit the gym and get in a run before he needed to head out for the rest of the day - and would want to check in with her.

The clucking and the clattering of the women stopped when he walked into the living room where they were gathered. He froze, looking at the seven of them looking back at him. *Oh brother, I did something bad*, he thought.

"You had me at hello," Laki said compassionately.

Brian didn't know what to say. He stood, sizing up the group of eyes upon him. Then, one of the moms broke her deadpan silence with a giggle and the rest of them laughed.

"What? You went Jerry Maguire on me?" he finally questioned the group, looking at Laki. Smiling, he turned to walk away, and then turned back to Laki and the other moms, "That was an ambush, Laki."

"Hey," she shouted back, "Did you want something?"

"Oh - yeah," he dropped the smile, "Other than, 'you complete me,' I'm heading to the gym before my trip. You OK with that? Need anything?"

The moms had already begun chatting about other things and paid no attention to the secretive exchange taking place between Laki and Brian. She fanned her face which was code for, *I think you're smokin' hot.*

He smiled at her and mouthed her favorite words into the air without saying a word for the group to hear: *I Love You...*

With a glass of water in his hand, he retreated to the office and noticed a call had come through his cell phone lying next to the laptop on the desk. It read, *Missed Call: Leilani.*

*****

Well...fuck. Now what? Jacob thought to himself. He hadn't had a concrete backup plan in a long time. Ten years ago, maybe. *Why not?* he wondered. CEOs get fired all the time. Poor performances, check. Loss of confidence, check. Ethical misconduct, check. Double check. Reckless guidance. Maybe. Failure to adapt to change. Well... Personal conflicts of interest... Yeah, that one too. He'd hit most of the landmines for dismissal. It was a real wonder he still had his legs. Jacob thought about the lamest excuse of all and worn-out pitch job which Board of Directors would state: *to spend personal time with family.* Fired, for sure.

The severance was nearly fifteen million. He sat unattended at the Bobby Vans bar, reached in his pocket for his phone, punching a speed-dial button to hear a female voice prompt.

"Password?"

"Fourteen ninety two."

"Next password?"

"Columbus. One - four - nine - two."

A woman's voice proceeded into the familiar prompt options; he prematurely interrupted the automated voice. Glasses clinked in the background.

She spoke: "I'm sorry, please repeat your request."

He spoke loudly, "Balance."

"Your portfolio balance is..." there was a pause, "forty-two million, one hundred twelve thousand, two hundred six dollars and twenty-four cents."

"End call." He closed the application on the screen, logging off of the call and slipped the phone into his dress slacks. No one was around. He smirked to himself and said out loud, "Big fucking deal...I got fired today and made fifteen million by doing so." Then, in some strange form of disbelief he found humor in it all and chuckled for a few seconds.

"How'd that happen, if you don't mind me asking?"

Jacob was surprised to hear a reply to his self talk. He swung around on the stool and was startled. Thinking he was alone, he just looked at the black bartender standing with a tray in one hand, and a clean white pressed towel hanging over his forearm.

"Hello old friend." It was Ruby. Smiling, holding a glass of water and sliding it toward Jacob.

"I have a strong opinion about everything. So, most things don't leave me speechless. This does." Paisley said no more words for the startling moment.

He didn't have one of the brushed nickel name tags on his lapel like the other bartenders did. "My name's Ruby. I'll be taking care of you tonight. Can I start you off with a beverage?"

Jacob just looked at him. He looked at least ten years older. Ruby, or the Ruby lookalike, with graying hair and a few more wrinkles than Jacob remembered stood ready to serve.

A pregnant pause of silence took place. To Jacob, that was an eternity. Finally, with a dry reply, he spoke. "The top shelf Scotch. Lots of Scotch tonight. I'm drinking my dinner."

10

Random Acts of Blindness

The bright light from the physician passed left to right in Kerri eye. First one, then the other. He finally asked her, "Any more fainting?"

She murmured, "No sir," and shook her head slightly. Adding to her response, "I mean, no Doctor."

"Light headedness?"

"Mmm, no," she contemplated each question carefully.

"You hesitated," the doctor moved the bright light shining on her pupils back to the original.

"Just thinking..." she replied.

"Nausea? Have you been following the Dietitian's advice?"

"No. No to nausea. Yes. Yes, to following her advice." Kerri was dressed in a gown, sitting on crisp white paper at an examination table. Every time she moved; the paper rustled its crinkly noise with her.

"Is that your boyfriend out there?"

Kerri leaned in toward the man in the white lab coat, whispering to the doctor, "I'm not really sure what we are, but we're together."

The doctor smiled and took notes in her chart. He then proceeded to poke and prod and take more notes in the file, asking her about aches, pains, menstruation, exercise, and any other medications she'd been taking. For some unknown reason – lifestyle choices didn't make the list of queries – perhaps because the doctor knew and for whatever reason did not pursue what was obvious. Her arms no longer were black and blue from tracks, but several small scars remained near her veins.

She was trying to get healthy. She was fending off the call of the hard candy beast. Her strength against jacking up had improved and she had more than a doctor's bright light shining in her eyes. She had a beacon of hope for wellbeing.

Our eyes are the windows to our bodies. Many diseases and markers can be seen with by a trained medical professional. The hope that shone from Kerri's eyes was the first aspirational purpose she held in span of several years. But she saw something else too.

Outside in a hallway makeshift waiting area, next to the scale and a blood pressure monitor, Cutter scrolled through his cell phone. His long hair was now pulled back into a ponytail wrapped with a black band. It wasn't as thin and stringy anymore. He still wore a wife beater tank top underneath his jacket, but it was clean as were his jeans and boots. No longer did he sport the scraggly mustache on his upper lip and two weeks' worth of scruff on his cheeks and chin, not filling in. He was clean shaven.

If he were to be without the jacket, one could tell that he'd been working out. Little guns were beginning to appear as his biceps were taking on muscular definition and his triceps were beginning to resemble a horseshoe. His six pack on his torso was taking shape from the training and exercise.

Even though his appearance had improved, Cutter was in no way the man a woman would want to bring home to meet her father. *Daddy, meet Jimmy "Cutter" Jude. He's the man of my dreams!* – would never be said.

When Kerri dressed and left the examination room, Cutter was waiting for her and asked, "Ya gonna' live?"

She kept walking toward the exit.

He made certain that the PA or no nurse watched as he grabbed a fist full of hair from the back of her head, "I said...are you okay?"

She was soft in what she said next, her head was still tilted back as his fist held her tight, "That was a question, not a statement. And I didn't hear you. But, yes – I think so."

He let go.

Kerri knew that there wasn't much curb appeal from Cutter. But he could pass off as better than he was a year ago with the diet and exercise. Crazy Kerri was on an extended leave and who knew...Cutter had probably found himself something else for his sexual needs.

Her concern was increasing that his strength was becoming more of an issue and that she couldn't fend for herself if there was to be a conflict. On one hand, she was happy for him that the proteins he would cut the cocaine with finally had benefits to his own health and vitality. On the other hand, her concern grew that his newfound power and muscle were going to be her peril to manage.

*****

Laki walked into the office after checking on the children. She saw Brian sitting in his office chair next to the desk with his head in his hands. He was decidedly emotionally upset.

She rushed to the floor, kneeling in front of him, "Baby, what is it?" Her soft hands surrounded one of his.

He held his face lower so she couldn't see the worry and concern. His eyes were teary.

"Tell me..." she whispered, stroking his hair. Her thoughts darted to his family – their family in Hawaii. They were aging and his uncle had a doctor's visit scheduled for a small pain in his back, "Are your Auntie and Uncle alright?

Brian shook his head in the direction of 'yes', then summoned the courage to meet her eyes with his. "It's Leilani – she's..." He dug deep for the right words, "She's been... She's been...hurt."

He thought about what he just said - and then sorted through the emotion and communication required to tell it like it really was. With settled words and some resolution, he told her: "She's in The Queen's Medical Center – West Oahu. She was beaten."

"Oh...God...no...no..." Laki reached out to her husband to hug him.

He continued with what he knew, "She has a broken nose. And cuts on her face..." He cried and motioned to his own face, pausing for a few seconds, continuing, "And bruised ribs. Some internal bleeding maybe."

"What the hell?" Lake was shocked. "How?..." "Who?..." She stopped herself short of seeking an answer with her own reply. "Yancy."

Brian shook his head in the direction of 'yes'.

Yancy.

Yancy – they both thought of how happy she was just a year ago. What did they miss? How could they have better protected Brian's cousin? What more should they have done? *He checked out.* They sought the 411 on him and the closest they got to a red flag was that someone said he seemed protective. But a couple calls should have led to a couple more and perhaps a couple more. His parents worked in data security for a Bay Area company. It seemed to be going well when they called – that is, until it wasn't. Something changed. A switch was flipped which quickly made a good relationship a bad relationship. It was within a couple calls. Then there was the breakup and the cold calm of nothingness. *Then, what...this? Why?*

Sweet Leilani.

They held each other for a minute with Laki breaking their embrace and the silence. "Where is that scumbag now? Halawa?" She referred to the correctional facility which was the state prison for the city and county of Honolulu.

He shook his head 'no'. "They can't find him." Brian said this with an unlit conviction.

Silence loitered in the moment. They listened to each other breathing as they looked to each other for answers and an understanding.

"It's an island, Brian." She sought assurance that he wasn't thinking about a vigilante manhunt for the purpose of vindication, "He can't slip through. When the west side community finds out what happened, he'll be had. Nanakuli strong, you know." Laki reached her arms around his broad shoulders again and considered the disturbing thoughts of Leilani being harmed going through his thoughts.

Laki was thinking, as she held her husband tightly, the chances were rock solid this situation might not go well. He loved his childhood cousin and served as her big brother, protecting her. She was worried for him and it showed.

*****

Since it was the final day of the quarter's accounting period, Jacob had assumed that there was some potential for an after-hours get together, but only listed tentative in the office happy-hour invite. And it certainly wasn't for Bobby Van's. It was a swanky new location in Midtown.

Here he sat all alone.

His best customized suit from Watson Ellis was wrapped around him, a dove gray English tweed. An azure blue Stefano Ricci micro medallion silk necktie was loosened some, but still hung around his neck. A matching scarf neatly arranged in the suit's breast pocket. A starched white dress shirt shielded him from the soft silk pants and jacket linings. To say that his shoes were eight hundred dollars would be telling half the truth. They were eight hundred dollars per shoe. *All dressed up with no place to go*, he thought.

The bartender listened to him tell the cliff-notes version of his afternoon.

"Sometimes things happen for a reason," Ruby was trying to be consoling as a bartender sometimes is. Listen much, offer whispers of wisdom and encouragement.

"I still don't believe in that." Jacob was of Team Logic. He added, "I believe that things happen *because* of reasons. *Because of*... Randomness rules our lives. We're really just lucky to be alive floating between moments. There is no pre-written agenda. What happens falls into place, or it doesn't. Sure, you've got experiences, and your intellect, and talent that persuades the outcome. But, timing and general output is much more out of control, than in control."

"You will." Ruby smiled, paused for a minute, then added, "Look at me, look at you. Something from nothing – or meant to be?"

"Something from nothing. Never loses its charm." Jacob thought of Jim Cramer and looked around to see if he made an appearance. *Still early,* he thought.

"Nothing quite like discovering what you've lost, right?"

"I don't know think I know what you mean by that. But, I've never bought into the notion that life is like a puzzle. The pieces snap into place by design? Hardly." Paisley was shaking his head.

"Lots of folks do. They think differently than you do. Less logic, more faith..." Ruby was polishing glasses with a white linen cloth. The warm tumblers squeaked against the damp washcloth in his hands.

Paisley interrupted again, "They want to believe in something, because they seek an easier solution than having to create, or execute, or implement and then redirect when their plans fail. That takes work. Hard work. They solve problems with hope, or ignorance, or by some form of blindness." He didn't know why he remained passionate – or why he was opinionated – or even interested.

He was here to let it all go, to allow the moment to overtake him and to slip away.

"Well, we all think differently, and that commotion of diversity makes..."

"You know, Ruby, I spent six hours at the New York Metro precinct explaining my assumed interaction with you after you mysteriously landed on my windshield. The police finally determined that you were terminal, dying of some incurable disease and released me. I had my private doctor visit me at the station for a checkup since I didn't return to my co-op after being released from Mount Sinai. Six hours with NYPD, then six months assuring my board I was stable and competent to resume duties, followed by six months of dodging allegations of misconduct and the scrutiny of internal investigations, and then six fleeting minutes to sign my golden parachute release agreement as my own Board of Directors ran me out of my company." Jacob gripped the glass and swirled the ice cubes.

He drank the goblet dry and motioned with his fingers for another. When Ruby returned, Jacob added: "You know what the weirdest thing of all was?"

"What was it, friend?"

"Please don't try to be pleasant. I'm making a point. The point is about you. The detective working on your suicide case botched it all up. A body out of the morgue falls from the ninth floor of Mount Sinai. End point. The body was a cadaver and names didn't sync. End point. That red book with all of your notes about me ends up having no print in it at all. End point. It all unraveled."

"Was it ever really wound?"

Paisley just looked back without reply. After a long pause, he said, "You asked me a year ago, '*What's Your Story?*' and we spoke. So, I ask you, Ruby...what's *your* story?"

Ruby wasn't telling his story, just yet. "My case wasn't made. That's interesting. Look at you – a man once at the top of his game, sitting here confused, looking for an answer in a glass of scotch."

"Classic diversion," Jacob muttered.

"Remember what I said about defining what you *believe* and challenging your *perspectives*?"

"I remember your small sermon. Beliefs and Perspectives. You asked me not to forget that. Did you first hear of that in a pew somewhere?"

"Something like that," Ruby added: "You might want to embrace divine intervention."

"I don't go for that, I..."

Ruby interrupted. "It can be a very real thing with faith and a belief in the imperfect good."

"Imperfect good."

"Victory might not come from a zero-zero score in the market, but compromise moves us all along. Believing that it isn't all about man-made machine parts grinding together for an outcome."

"Doesn't sound like capitalism at all."

"Better off without me?" Ruby asked.

"What?"

"Think things would be better for you if I didn't stumble over you in the intersection? There was no gain other than the gain of a man's life out there in the street. Divine intervention. Give it a chance." The old man smiled while moving on to polishing wine glasses.

Jacob just looked into Ruby's brown eyes, seeking something to say, but coming up short on words. His perspective was changed.

"My father tried to kill me once. Or I think he did. It's said, he said rather, that he pulled the trigger - just once. The gun didn't go off. Lots of things can always turn out different than they do. That's the capacity for change. Crazy, huh?" As if Ruby was the only voice in the bar, Jacob was listening only to his voice. The white noise and clatter in the background was muted.

"Your father tried to shoot you? He actually pulled the trigger. Why?" Jacob looked for Ruby's vulnerability but found none.

"Well..." He paused, placing both his hands on the bar in front of Jacob, catching his breath. "He made a split-second decision, an assumption that it must have been very difficult – a tragedy maybe, being Ruby, being me. How about that?"

Jacob contemplated what had just been said.

"My family never had guns in the home." As a kid, Jacob was exposed to boring afternoons at the Country Club, enduring piano lessons, and trips to a few and distant relatives over holiday breaks. Since he was an only child, it was always all about Jacob.

"He didn't take a second shot. The next time he pulled the trigger was his last, or so I'm told." Silence consumed a brief moment. "Without so much as a word, I forgave him."

They both saw the events as they happened in their own mind's eyes. Jacob saw a version of disastrous misfortune. Misdirected anger – a father with a desire to take the life of his own blood. He saw a unexplained challenge of some sort met with an emotive conclusion.

Ruby saw something completely different, in Jacob's eyes, and he smiled.

"Take it easy on yourself," Ruby's smile snapped Jacob out of the moment and a frown. "It wasn't quite like what you're thinking."

"How do you know what I'm thinking?"

"What's that?" Ruby asked again.

"I said, how - do - you - know - what - I'm - thinking?"

"You asked, and - I don't."

"Another."

"You sure?"

"Make it a double."

"What's that?"

"Double." Jacob held up two fingers.

He looked at the iPhone. It would be turned off soon. It was surprising it was still on. He'd be labeled INACTIVE in the PPCM associate lookup tool. His email would be redirected in the directory and the firm's assigned executive admin, or Shelby *somebody*, would reroute assignments. It was over. Jacob noticed several text messages:

WTF?

Tell us why when it's good for you to tell us why, please...

No Jacob, no Danny!

I'm out!

Whisky Tango Foxtrot!!! Fuck that place!

Haters gonna hate. They'll get theirs.

He didn't know if the troops might rally and that meant a night out on the town, or if it might mean nothing. An emotive moment from some of the favorites that didn't have forty million cash in a high yield savings account.

Ruby returned with another. The amber contents in the glass had three crystal clear ice cubes floating. Jacob raised the glass to Ruby.

"Here alone?"

"Again." Jacob knew that his limited social circle in personal matters was already identified. He looked down at the floor to avoid Ruby's stare.

"Hmmm? What's that?" Ruby held his hand to his ear as a gesture of not capturing what was said.

"I said, *again.* As in - here alone, *again.*" Jacob pronounced clearly and tried to be more articulate.

Ruby folded the white linen and draped it back over his forearm. "Our friends tend to identify us, don't they?"

"You could say that." Paisley looked at the floor of the bar, away from Ruby's question. He found safety in the foundation. It was where he was comfortable and could navigate from.

"Do you have difficulty hearing?"

"What's that?"

"Do – you – have – difficulty – hearing?"

"Oh. Uh, yes. Can't pass a hearing test anymore. Legally deaf. But, I can make out what you're saying between what I can hear and reading your lips."

"I thought bartenders were supposed to be good listeners?"

"We are." Ruby chuckled. "But you know..." he paused, "I'm no bartender." He winked, turned and was off to another customer at the other end of the bar.

Jacob swirled the ice cubes in the tumbler. *Fucking code. The guy speaks in fucking ciphers half the time.* There was no sense he could make of Ruby, then or now. And it didn't really bother him that logic was displaced with unexplainable moments. There was a curiosity that needed to be solved. A mystery that felt comfortable and thrilling as much as a risk that he normally would take.

Ruby returned and asked, "So, what's it feel like being fired? By your own Board, I'm assuming?"

Jacob looked up to Ruby, glanced at a hanging chandelier in the main dining area for the right words, and an answer, "Actually, somewhat liberating. I think I was in the game too long."

"We do tend to hold on, don't we?"

"Indeed. It's as if we don't – "

"What's that?"

Jacob continued slowly and retraced his thoughts, "...it's as if we don't or aren't willing to trade what we want for what we have." And as he said it, he dated himself back to when he got in the business, long ago.

And as if Ruby was reading his mind, asked, "So how'd you originally get in the money management business?" He reached to his earlobe, rubbed his fingers on it, and stamped his thumbprint on a glass of water he sat down in front of Jacob.

Paisley stared at the thumbprint and thought of the answer to the question. His memories traced back to the time that he was a junior trader, nearly twenty five years ago. He was in a meeting room with a half dozen of his peers for a quarterly business review. Several of the firm's executives were grinding and driving for answers to understand a lackluster performance. They were in there for over two hours and the emotion was intense due to a timid response. Only Jacob had any acceptable answers to offer. Only Jacob was doing any talking. Only Jacob was delivering his numbers, exceeding the quota. Only Jacob was providing the competitiveness and determination that the executives sought. Jacob was trying to distinguish his performance from the competition to climb in the organization and had strung together several decent team-leading quarters.

A black man came into the room to replenish the water pitchers. He stood next to a young Jacob Paisley and did the same thing. Rubbed his thumb on his earlobe for oil to leave a thumbprint.

Jacob remembered the moment. He looked up at the black man pouring a glass, which was unusual because they normally just left the pitchers on the table. Paisley looked at the thumbprint and frowned. He looked at the disrespect of the dirty glass and frowned, looking up at the black man. The man winked and disappeared behind him.

"What would you have done, JP?" The executive at the head of the table asked the question, but Jacob stood up to look for the black man. His chair rolled back to the glass window of the 35th floor of the Manhattan tower. He spun around and there was no one behind him. The concierge had vanished.

Paisley had a frown on his face, and blurted out, "What the hell? Don't fuck with me. I'm going to kick your ass!" When he said this, it was as if he was in sync with the conversation of the table and making a statement.

The executive pointed at Paisley and declared, "You see team, that's the passion, that's the fire we're talking about here!"

It was nothing more than an oily thumbprint on a water glass that caused the separation.

He looked at the waiter Ruby, and remembered the hospital volunteer Ruby. He vaguely recalled the doctor and the EMT Ruby. And now ventured into his past to find the water boy-concierge Ruby.

"It was you." Jacob found disbelief in the thought of it. At the very same time he discovered a moment of authentic wonder, something that had escaped him over the years. "Was that divine intervention?"

"No, it was not." Ruby offered a broad smile and wiped the thumbprint from the water glass. "Mr. Paisley, in the hospital I had but one point to deliver which was to get you to this moment."

For Jacob – the question *'Was that divine intervention?'* meandered in his head. It was as if an unconsidered opportunity had just opened. A new adventure. It resembled a sexy financial trade, but it had no apparent outcome. There wasn't the anticipation of the risk or reward. He sat alone in his thoughts at the bar because Ruby had walked away to attend to another customer.

Jacob squinted to see across the restaurant at the small gathering in a booth. It was no one he recognized. *Bet that conversation isn't as weird as what's going through my mind right about now. When you're down and out – they tend to let you wallow for a while.*

Bobby Van's in the Financial District had some history. Not only was it in the old JP Morgan building, but some of the walls were lined with old depository boxes and the vault led to a private room which could be rented. Following Covid-19 lockdowns for restaurants, the company walked away from this location to focus their interests on the Midtown venues. Then when it was right, they returned to the popular destination on Broad Street. Wall Street legends like the highly acknowledged Art Cashin of UBS; the silver fox correspondent Bob Pisani; and *Money Honey* Maria Bartiromo, and other Bloomberg or CNBC personnel frequented Bobby Van's – gathering in a corner booth. It was roped off with a plum velvet and brass fitting stanchion. He couldn't think of MaBaMo without also thinking of Sophia Loren. The resemblance between the business journalist and the actress was striking. So long financial reporting...hello politics. He was walking down Memory Lane. It felt lonely.

There were no prominent figures from Wall Street there, as the booth sat empty and void of an occasional request for a photo, marinading ice cubes, or storytelling.

*****

"Where are we going? Our apartment is that way." Kerri pointed meekly with one finger, trying to indicate behind them as she nonetheless followed Cutter. Walking two steps ahead, not with, he wasn't looking at her. They were walking south on 9th Avenue, toward the sun that now had more clouds hiding it than clear skies for it to shine and warm them. Since it was a one-way, all she saw in the street were taillights from the hundreds if not thousands of yellow taxis and other cars which were outnumbered. In between the buildings which were hiding the sun, and when the clouds blew by quickly, she'd look up to the sunshine to warm her cheeks if just for a few seconds.

His ponytail was tucked in a light jacket he was wearing. It wasn't new, but it wasn't what he usually wore this time of the year, which was a sable black nylon parka. She thought that he must be cold too.

The aroma of hot dogs was in the air. A cart was across the street and Kerri was hungry. Her appetite was back.

"That smells good. Are you hungry?" she prompted, making it about him and his needs. Crazy Kerri usually did that. Crazy Kerri had been vacant while Kerri summoned all of her might to manage the beast. The beast's appetite for the brown sugar was absent. Temporarily. That meant hot dogs were the focus, not this field trip.

"C'mon. Hurry up. We gotta' meet up with Boomer." Cutter said nothing else. Walking faster now.

She walked behind him, wishing she had a dog with all the fixings: mustard, relish, onion...

Hooonk! A taxicab blew its horn, scaring Kerri. Her heart raced. A red illuminated hand was held up in front of her. She'd taken her eye off of the crosswalk clock and scurried to the safety of the corner leaving the ambiance of street vendor hot dogs behind them.

Cutter looked back and shook his head, acknowledging her poor choice and hindrance to his pace. He didn't reach out to hold her hand but did grab her jacket sleeve to boost her pace.

Eventually 9th Avenue turned slightly and changed its street name to Hudson Street. The brownstones were nicer. Bikes were locked to the glossy black painted rod iron at the steps of each building. Trees began lining the street and the zoning changed from *'anything goes'* to areas featuring shops and those of homes and apartments. Gardens were tucked in between some of the brownstones and features of art were found within the parks. Glossy freshly painted fire escapes were on some of the buildings but many of the homes and apartments of red brick with black or white trimmed windows had none, instead having a small garden in front of them, aligning the street.

They turned the corner where a deli had some street seating. There were two elderly couples seating, sharing coffees with a small terrier at their feet watching each passing walker. She waved at it as their brick pace slowed somewhat. They were facing the traffic now. There wasn't much. The further they walked, the nicer the area became. A small pizzeria door opened as a customer was leaving. Again, she breathed in deeply the smells of the sauces, the cheeses, the oregano, and the toasted pepperoni.

Kerri thought that it was odd that Cutter hadn't said anything for nearly a dozen city blocks.

The leaves from the trees aligning the street had fallen off months ago, but the shrubbery still gave a warmth that the climate did not offer. White twinkly Christmas lights would have glowed from some of these four and five story buildings if it were dark, but they were not.

He stopped in front of the nicest red brick building on the block. A combination of round arched windows on the lower floor and rectangular windows with their trim painted black was where Cutter looked. Ivy grew in flower boxes outside of the windows, dangling in the slight breeze. The front door was taller than most and appeared quite stately. The shiny brass latch handle with a matching brass lock was about as opposite to their apartment, chipped painted round handle back in Hell's Kitchen.

It suddenly made sense to her. Why they walked all the way to the pier from where they lived to retrieve a small duffel from Boomer weekly. Cutter and Boomer weren't partners at all. Cutter worked for Boomer. Boomer was his drug lord.

"Special delivery," Cutter said to Boomer as the door opened. Kerri didn't know that he had knocked. The two of them shook hands in the code they usually did. They walked in. It was a home – nothing like where they lived. Wooden floors, area rugs, glossy leaved dark green plants, a bookcase filled with books of all colors, shiny see-through windows that looked out upon something rather than the side of another building. As Kerri looked around, taking it all in and warming from the cold walk, more was apparent: peace, a sense of order, organization, a place for everything – everything nice or new or treasured.

Soft Jazz music was playing on a large stereo system. A piano and a saxophone were joined by a snare and a bass. It was so quiet that it was difficult to hear it.

They immediately walked into another room, to discuss what appeared to be an important matter. She could hear them talking quietly but could not understand what it was they were saying as their tone was low and calm.

Something delicious was cooking in a Crockpot in the well adorned kitchen. Kerri didn't know what it was, but she knew she could dive right in with a spoon or a fork or her bare hands. Boomer took their coats and hung them in a closet near the door. Inviting them to have a seat on an oyster gray couch, he fluffed some pillows for her to collapse on. She exhaled as she sat and took another deep breath of the kitchen's cooking goodness.

Kerri immediately felt at home. She felt at ease, comforted, and safe, despite knowing that it was all likely purchased illegally. Continuing to look around this living room area – she careened her neck to see into another room which seemed to have more of the same, comfortable furniture surrounding a large TV hanging on the wall. Off to the side – this was where Boomer and Cutter were now whispering.

Romanticism artwork was found on walls where there were no dark painted bookshelves or TVs. Gaudy antiqued gold painted frames showcased the paintings of angels, fairies, horses, nature scenes, wartime battles, and naked women. Some of them expressed debate and a sense of intense conflict. Others were of peace and stirred feelings of love.

She looked at Boomer speaking softly with Cutter. He was a black man. All the paintings were of white people. The floating angels, curious ferries, triumphant soldiers, and beautiful women seating with their breasts exposed and their hips covered with sheets – they were all Caucasian. Why?

They returned. It was Cutter who finally looked at her and spoke. "I've been telling you that me and Boomer," he looked at the black man, "we're going in business..." He cut himself off. The lie wasn't consistent. "We have a project together." Cutter looked back at Kerri, but it was more through her than in her eyes. "I'm going to take a trip, to set up shop."

Pausing for a minute, sizing up both of them, she asked, "Where are you going?"

"I can't discuss that with anyone right now,"

She felt he was scripted and saying what Boomer asked him to say or to not say.

"To anyone? Or just to me?"

"You're doin' real good Kerri. You're getting off the sauce. Boomer's going to help you. He had someone he knows OD and knows what to do to help you get sober." Cutter motioned toward Boomer for an assist, but the black gentleman remained silent, allowing the two of them to move further into their discussion about his absence.

"Well... Well, how long are you going to be gone?" She held her arms over her small breasts and brought her finger to her mouth to chew on her fingernails as a sense of nervousness encroached the moment.

"Maybe couple weeks, maybe longer. If things go as planned, I might need to bounce between here and there for a while."

"Well, maybe I should go..."

"Kerri, we think it's best for you to stay here for the time being." It was the depth of his tone she felt comforting. Cutter rarely used her name unless it was *Kerri, get me my dinner.* Or *Kerri, you're a useless bitch sometimes.* Or *Kerri, what the hell makes you think somethin' stupid like that?*

She wasn't sure. She didn't really know Boomer. This felt like a good moment, but good moments turned. Kerri became Crazy Kerri – or used to – quickly. What if Crazy Kerri could not be maintained. Where there drugs here in Boomer's place. She could not be around Dr. H. Not if she ever wanted to be a mother. Looking at Boomer, she just stared while wondering these things.

"Say somethin'." Cutter had a way with words. Curt, gruff, brusque. Boomer was quite nearly an opposite.

"You'll be safe here and I promise that I'll take good care of you while Cutter is away."

It was the surest thing to how she felt as a girl so many years ago – someone willing to take care of her. Or at least, to say so.

"Well, what if I need something?"

"Then we'll get it for you...as long as it's something you don't need." Boomer had moved his pawn, and the game was on.

"You don't have any shit here, do you? I'm trying, I'm trying so hard to get off the skid so I can..." her eyes filled with tears. It was not completely from Cutter leaving. It was a fear of herself and the unknown. But Cutter was her unstable consistency.

Cutter, he was nice once when they first met. He didn't beat her, but he bullied her – pulling her hair, smacking her ass, twisting her wrists until they hurt. No bruises or contusions – but a different kind of injury – to her self-esteem. And then there was the greatest suffering of all: his supply of the junk in exchange with Crazy Kerri. They're sex for drugs arrangement where Kerri would get down on her knees, between his, and beg for anything. Cutter could turn. He might strike her. And Boomer might have a dark side too. She was uneasy.

"There's no skag here, Kerri. Never has been, never will be."

"Well..." she was considering what might happen if Crazy Kerri came out – and could not have her wishes met. Might she turn elsewhere to get sprung? She was shaking her head and rocking. Standing to pace, tears ran down her cheeks thinking of returning to the bad place – the place where Cutter liked her to ride. A place where the sexual transaction was always met with a dose of the beast.

"What if..."

"This is a place for your wellness. Not the turf for your relapse." Boomer looked into her eyes as he tried to console her concern with his comforting words. It helped some.

"Looks like you kids are gonna' get along great." Cutter was less than concerned about her or the exchange between them. It was as if he was already gone. "We good?" he asked Boomer.

Boomer shook his head in the direction of 'yes' as he watched Kerri continue to pace, chewing her fingernails.

And without a hug or more words for Kerri, Cutter grabbed a backpack that he hadn't been carrying with him before from Boomer's closet. He looked back at both of them and said, "Aloha bitches," and he walked out the door.

A long silence passed between them. Kerri didn't know what was expected of her. She stood Boomer, not pacing any longer, and asked him, "What do you want from me?"

He carefully considered his answer. The jazz music was still playing softly in the background. "I want you to be happy. Comfortable. Feel safe. To know that things will be alright for you. And that I'll do you no harm."

She wiped the water from her eyes and gave him a slight and quick nervous smile. No, he's no Cutter, she thought. But she didn't know what she didn't know and it was take time to build trust.

"How about some chicken soup? Been stewing in the crockpot for hours. I'll put some biscuits in the oven too. What would you like to drink. I have some eggnog, but no sauce to go in it." He was referring to alcohol. "Red wine drinker, here."

She thought, *That's it. That's the goodness I smell. Chicken soup. Just like Grandma made...*

There's TV in the other room if you want to watch something. Hallmark channel always sucks me in. Or maybe some Christmas music. I can turn off this babel." He motioned to the stereo. "I prefer the oldies. You know Bing Crosby, Frank Sinatra, Ella Fitzgerald..." Boomer paused. "Lady Gaga."

Kerri slowly turned her head toward Boomer for a sanity check.

He had a deadpan look in her direction for a few seconds. Boomer acknowledged her ornamental curiosity.

She smiled, knowing he was teasing.

"There it is," he said, smiling too. "You can sit here and make yourself at home or help me in the kitchen. Might be nice to get to know each other a little better." A moment later, the Christmas music was summoned and she was listening to Karen Carpenter's voice wishing them to have a little Merry Christmas.

She was not allowing herself to be fooled. Guarding herself from the fast track to recklessness, she was cautious with Boomer. But for the first time in a very long time, there was a 'better elsewhere' that had crept into her thoughts. It resembled what colored C7 holiday lights shone on a cold December night: a cheerfulness of idealism and brightness. In her heart was a credence called hope.

"I don't even know your last name," Kerri spoke softly, "What is it?"

"Hollins," Boomer replied, "Boomer Hollins. Nice to meet you Kerri Latch." He extended both of his hands to shake hers. They were as warm and as welcoming as he was being, acting as her host.

*****

When Ruby returned to attend to Paisley, he asked, "So, what's next?"

Jacob paused in his thoughts and words, considering them, then offered what he was thinking about most over the past week, "I've got a guy I ran money with at the Morgan Stanley desk a long time ago that's been asking me to visit him in Cupertino. Works on Sand Hill Road, where many of the venture capitalist and PE firms are."

"Venture capitalists? PE?"

"Correct. The valley's where much of the new money originates from. It's not the Roman Empire of capitalism like this place, but it's a fresh start. That's what I'm going to need to do." Then he added, "PE – that's private equity."

"When you say it, you believe differently, don't you?"

"What's that?"

"Huh?"

"What do you mean by that?"

Ruby flipped the damp towel into a bin and reached for a dry linen from under the bar. "It sounds different coming from your head through your lips."

Jacob looked at the diminishing effervescence found in the glass, and felt the buzz in his head from the drinks. *I suppose that's so*, he said to himself.

He walked away for a moment to attend to another customer at a nearby barstool and returned to make a suggestion. "Say, why don't you get away from all of this concrete once and for all? You know, something really different. Buy a dog, set sail, live on the edge. Be part of something bigger than yourself." He chuckled.

"Bigger than myself. That's what *I did*." Jacob was muttering.

"How about going out a little further? You've been a trader for a long time, right? I think you're on to something. Trade the Atlantic for the Pacific maybe. You know...if you leave the shore behind and go out beyond where you can touch what you've already touched – you just might surprise yourself."

Ruby reached for a cocktail napkin and a pen from the register area. "This is the way they do it in Silicon Valley, right?" He jotted a few numbers together in poor handwriting.

This must be a crazy encryption for something. Man, this guy's a nutjob. Jacob looked at the number, smiling. "What the hell is this? A code of some sort?" He held it up in the light to see it better. It was nothing unusual, just a simple five digit number on a Bobby Van cocktail napkin. "Five digits. Nine, six, seven, zero..."

A loud crash came from the kitchen that likened the sound of glasses and dishes. And as often happens, after several bewildered patron looks, a small awkward applause was given. It was the interpreted gesture of, "Oops!" And of, "It's alright, we all make mistakes," by the customers. In the meantime, the immediate scurrying of the waitstaff meant that someone's dinner was being rushed. Jacob stuffed the napkin in his jacket pocket.

When Ruby returned, it was with a question, "Victoria. So how did you come to meet up with that girlfriend of yours, anyway?"

"Irresistible Victoria," Jacob said it was a sigh, looking into the glass of scotch. "Really want to know? I'll tell you.

"Really." Ruby acted as if he had all the time in the world and leaned on the bar next to Jacob.

Jacob paused. *Victoria.* Time stopped to catch up with the moment when he first saw her.

Victoria.

"Pierce was in the business, Pierce – my business partner. We were a small shop with the Midas touch. We had this absolutely-killer-of-a-quarter, and the team went out for a celebratory night out to, you know, fund New York. The night lingered on, and we ended up at an after-evening bar for another drink. This is not unusual – after a blow out, we call it a Day of Decadence. Then, there were fewer of us, maybe a dirty dozen. But it's only nine o'clock. And we were hammered and one of the traders suggested a new strip club...."

Jacob recalled detail, the music playing, the colors, the women. "We walked into this upscale club and the greeter suggests that we...I don't know – maybe by the looks of us, we go into the VIP Rooms. The guy I'm with had been there, and asks for the Private Clients Room. The greeter said he'd have to go get the manager..."

The moment was vivid in Jacob's mind's eye: "A handsome black man comes out of a back room and guides us to an upstairs area. They buzz us in. I'm not feeling comfortable – I look at the manager and ask why the additional security...and he...he..." Jacob looked at Ruby.

Ruby replies, "Handsome? I'll take that, coming from you."

"It was you." Paisley stalls, "You were the manager."

"Why don't you go on? The woman. Tell me about Victoria."

"But, you'd already know about her,"

"I wouldn't know what you know about that young lady."

"I don't believe it. You. You introduced me to Victoria." He shook his head in disbelief. "*Why not?*" he said to himself.

Victoria.

Jacob recanted the experience. He replayed it again, as he'd done many times:

There they all were. They climbed from two stretches into the club. You could hear the music from the street. ZZ Top's, She's Got Legs was playing loudly. Choice tables were instantly cleared for the group. The most beautiful women in the club suddenly multiplied in number and surrounded our well-dressed suited men. The traders showered the strippers in tips of twenties, fifties, and hundreds. The stunning women seemed to instantly pool around us - and a carnival atmosphere was produced. Several other provocative rock songs blared. Drinks were poured, consumed, poured again.

"Time to dance," a junior trader shouted. Tears for Fears, *Sowing the Seeds of Love,* began playing louder than loud. He championed the stage with his fellow traders joining in immediately, dancing on the stage with these strippers. Man, woman, man, woman, man, woman – hip thrusting each other in a line dance. As their hips pumped forward, their shoes would jump a few inches. Neckties were taken by the strippers, with the exception of a curly haired trader that resembled a Saturday Night Live cast member. Everyone called him Bobby even though his name was Chuck. He retained his tie, wearing it tight over his dark curls as a headband. The *Sowing the Seeds of Love* song continued playing in Jacob's memory as he remembered *'Bobby'* shouting, *"I fucking LOVE this!"*

A redheaded stripper clutching his waist behind the young trader as they move to the beat of the music shouts back, "Love is how we pay the rent, baby!" And they all laugh.

He continued to remember that night, not realizing that Ruby had departed. "So many shenanigans," Jacob said. Once he realized that the old man had ventured away, he continued with the smile-inducing remembrance of the tomfoolery-filled night...

He sat down with the traders being pampered by the provocative entertainers. They were talking about their momentous year-end bonuses for like a New York second, the music was loud, they ordered more top-shelf drinks – the best that the strip club offered. Then something whimsical happened. The bass of the beat vibrated the drinks on a table between them. The club's two most beautiful women with long legs, one wearing flowing fuchsia lingerie and the other in a black corset with a garter and stockings, walked into their private area. They smelled delicious. It wasn't the sweet and cheap perfume, but something unusually exotic, sensual, intoxicating.

Victoria, wearing black, sat herself next to Jacob. Her mascara was smokey and her eyeliner was shadowy making the whites of her eyes bright. Her friend, a cute short-wavy-haired blond in fuchsia was sitting next to the other trader, playing with his sideburns.

"You're the boss." Victoria looked at his tie, felt the lapel of his jacket, and glanced into his eyes. "I can always tell."

"I'm just one of the Portfolio Managers..."

She interrupted him, "You're not a PM."

"Okay, you're right, I'm a Senior Manager of Financial Accounting..."

"You're not a quant and you're not a PM."

How could she have known. And she cut to the quick with the acronyms and the industry jargon. Of course, this was the Financial District and she did her homework on the shoptalk and idioms.

"I can see the way they look up to you, the way they coddle...how they seek your attention... It's like you've got nine nurses, just waiting for you to get sick."

He was here, in this one black leather seat – with the most beautiful woman he had ever met, her flirting with him, running her slender fingers around the collar of his suitcoat, gently touching the back of his neck, telling him that she could spot the leader of the pack. What wasn't to like?

Finally, "Yes, I'm the boss."

"Yes, you, are."

After a minute of lust-filled pleasantries, Victoria says to her blond stripper of a partner: *'Hey Missy - handsome men and their new money. Meet the rising stars of PPCM.'* and the blond said something like, *'Giddy up. I like their momentum, let's show them a good time!'*

How did they know so much in such a short amount of time?

The place, Jacob thought, was famous for a reason. He was in total recall, sipping the scotch at Bobby Vans - while drinking in his meeting Victoria for the first time.

He remembered the tantalizing moment clearly - she had a chocolate-brown haired shoulder length bob with bangs. Her locks were healthy and full and hung down to her bare collar bones. Her smile was bright even within the dim lighting of the strip club. She was wearing crimson shimmery lipstick which slightly sparkled when the neon lights from the club or the reflection from the chandelier would reflect the stage lights on her face. She looked rich. Her confidence was strong, but not overbearing.

Ruby returned and was drying a glass and smiling, "Go on."

Jacob squints into the glass he's cradling with both hands, warming the booze within, and in an effort to put together each specific detail, continues telling Ruby, "The dark-haired brunette leans over me, placing her hand on my thigh. She's close to me and whispers something. 'You smell nice,' she says. 'I like your...' She looked down at my pants, and added, '*pants*'. She leaned back - and it felt - to me - like we're the only people in the private room. I say, 'I like your...' and I looked, *shame on me*, right at her breasts in her black sequin corset, and said, '...*pearls*.' She had this long dark Tahitian strand of pearls laying on her chest. Her bright white teeth nibbled on them."

"Then she looks at me and says, 'And I like your...slowly looking at me from head to toe...*shoes*.' But she has these stacked shoes that are Lucite. I didn't really like them, but I was just saying it like she did. 'And I like *your* shoes.'"

"She looks down at my shoes and says, and I like your...*pants*. I said something like, 'You already said that.' Her hand slips inside my leg up to my groin and I'm looking at my trader-pal and the blond sitting next to him and they're already making out. I didn't..."

As Paisley looks up, he finds Ruby gone - again. He made his point to the old black man, his pseudo-bartender, Jacob decided. *That guy is ubiquitous*. He continued to think back on that first evening which became a night to remember.

The black leather seats, smell of cigars from a smoking section that did not contain the belvederes, the neon purple figures of scantily clad women holding on to a pole, and the naughty off-the-stage and in the dark corner topless dances taking place were not uncommon evenings for Jacob's crowd.

This night, however, has some special scorch to it.

A small blond waitress with small breasts wearing an electric blue corset, panties, and stacked matching dance shoes carried a silver tray. Upon it were stacks of wrapped bills. Tens and twenties. It was above her head as she approached the bar, buzzing with several bartenders trying to keep up with demand. She paused in a visible spot between where the drinks were being served and the main stage and shouted, "Ten thousand dollars – a round for the bar!" Everyone cheered loudly.

He recalled Victoria seductively and silently approaching him. She was the most beautiful of all the irresistible women in the club. Taking him by the hand, leading him to a private stairway, she said smiling,

"C'mon. Come with me, we'll have some fun," and lured Jacob into a private room at the top of the stairs. They were alone.

"Don't you have to be on stage...?"

"Oh, baby..." she paused looking back, "I don't dance." She cut him off and smiled. Jacob assumed she was a hooker. Then, she reached into his pants retrieving his wallet for his AMEX.

"Hey..." he protested slightly.

"I just need to borrow this for a moment. Promise to give it back." She winked and turned, disappearing for a minute, returning with his American Express platinum card, and a small round mirror hosting and reflecting four lines of powdery white cocaine.

"I didn't know that I snagged the founder." She was referring to his credit card which called out his name followed by the full title of the LLC: Paisey & Pierce, Capital Management.

He tucked the shiny card back into his wallet.

"Blow?"

Jacob shook his head.

"You sure? It's the good stuff."

"I don't...."

"I do."

He shook his head 'no' again. Handing him back his platinum card which merely paid for their private room, she took the round mirror and placed it on his lap, over his crotch. She knelt over the mirror and leaned her elbows on his thighs. Victoria looked at him for a few seconds, smiling some and said softly, "Hey there, try not to rock my nose candy." She was referring to his arousal. He couldn't help himself and she looked up into his eyes as the mirror jostled and tilted. Jacob thought that she was like no one he had ever met. Victoria was the Forbidden Fruit. She snorted softly and slowly, and then with a white frosty nostril, looked to him, leaning over, whispering in his ear, "We need to play."

That was it. That was when he first knew there would be stories to tell. A *'something'* would become a *'something else'*. It was a night like no other.

"So..." she teased, "you don't smoke, you don't sniff...what's your thing?" She looked up at him and they locked eyes for an elongated moment.

He said nothing.

Breaking into a smile, she slowly added, "Yeah, me too..."

Jacob knew...*'there's something there'*, then – at that moment.

Victoria wrapped a fluffy black boa around the two of them and they talked about anything which came to their flickery minds and upswept delusions. She dialed into him and asked him for his advice on investing. They traded thoughts on stock picking, their S&P projections for the year ahead, which companies might be next to seek and an IPO and buying on margin.

Eventually she asked him if he was hungry. Since many of the traders from the firm had just devoured steak and lobster, he thought about it. *Not really...* When he didn't reply immediately, she asked, "You want some sushi?"

"At a strip club? Sushi?" he winced at the thought of the pairing.

"They'll get us whatever we want. Might take a while. You're not going anywhere; I'm not allowing it."

"I mean, sushi...here with strippers...just seems..."

She raised her eyebrows, "Got texture issues?"

"No. No thank you on the sushi."

Deeper into the night, she took off his tie and said that she was going to keep it as a souvenir – and that he'd have to ask her out to get it back. She slowly unbuttoned his crisp white starched dress shirt revealing his bare chest.

"This is a man's chest." Her smile faded into a look of admiration as she said it, running her fingers and palms over his torso. Unexpectedly, she unbuttoned her own corset and bared her breasts. He looked at her, then into her eyes. "I don't do this with just anyone. I don't strip." Victoria leaned against him, chest to chest.

"It's a strip club."

"I entertain," she said. "It's not just a strip club."

"You're entertaining alright." Jacob held her, and covered as much of her as he could with his jacket to keep her warm. They intentionally kept it cool in the clubs. For nearly an hour it was their cocoon.

They talked about anything that might keep their lips moving and their eyes intertwining.

At one point Jacob asked her who she had worked for. He was thinking that there had to be a broker or bourse or trading platform she was connected to. When she replied nonchalantly, '*it was a while ago, for Nicky at Mastro's*', Jacob chuckled. Her long tenure as the hostess at one of the most expensive steak and seafood restaurants made her no vixen of finance. She was, however, an irresistible maven of mischief in Manhattan,

Her fingernails ran up and down Jacob's thigh as they snuggled in this private room. Her head snuggled next to his chest while he talked to her about money making and the fine art of capitalism.

"Is it really art...or sport?"

He hesitated and in a softer voice than he normally projected, "Why not both?" Looking into her eyes, he saw a depth of mystery. His intrigue with her was quenchless.

"What are you wearing?" he asked as she cuddled to him, nearly naked.

"Not much, can you..."

"Perfume..."

"Oh, something one of the girls gave me. Do you like it?"

"It smells like springtime in the French Riviera. Grasse, perfume capital of the world. I like that."

"Never been," she added lightly touching his chest with her fingertips.

"It's a bit of a playground..." he didn't finish his sentence but was thinking...*for the wealthy.*

"Hey," she said playfully. Drawing the collar of his shirt with her fists closer to her, and as if she were telling him what would happen next, she asked, "You want to get out of here?"

He felt a seductive puff of her breath and the question from her lips upon his lips. Curiosity filled his forehead and he asked, "What do you have in mind?" Thinking that maybe he'd misjudged her throughout the evening and that this was when she'd lay out her offer a vice, she said mischievously, "I don't know – maybe I don't want this night to end right now. Let's go kill something."

"Kill something?"

She was reading him. Looking for a playful partner to make a moment with, "You know, the rest of the night...or the morning...or a bottle of old Rip Van Winkle."

"Bourbon drinker too? My oh my, am I in trouble or what?"

Slipping her top back on to cover herself, she grabbed him by the hand, "C'mon, let's go. I'll get my coat."

"Okay," he mumbled. And he thought to himself, *the exchanges won't be open for trading for another five hours. I got this. Moment maker here.*

She stood close to him, tiptoeing to whisper into his ear, "You better be here when I get back. I'm not done with you yet..."

"I will, I promise. Maybe we're just getting started."

He went to take a piss and returned a few minutes later. When he did, she did too. "Did you pee?"

It was an unusual conversation for a fairly new acquaintance. "Yeah..."

"Me too." She smiled. "God, I had to go so bad, but didn't want to leave your arms."

Jacob looked at the change in her attire. From a risqué up-classed playmate appearance to a distinguished woman which could fill a boardroom seat. Her dress was cocktail professional. She had slipped on an overcoat which you'd find a classy Carnegie Hill woman shopping at Bloomingdales or Barney's and on her way to have Capuchino's with her longtime ivy league college girlfriends, he asked – "Are you sure you don't trade over at Goldman Sachs?"

"No," she smiled.

"Schwab?"

"No..." she giggled this time.

"Fortress,"

"No..." she laughed sweetly. "But I think I like it that you think I might."

"JP Morgan?"

"You got me," she teased. She caressed the dimple in his chin with her finger. Victoria grabbed his hand, "C'mon money man. Let's go kill something."

They departed the swanky club and ran across the street and without the intersection light to guide them after a taxi passed by and no others were close. Soon the bars would be closing. It was late.

The orchid purple neon sign from the strip club was fading behind them as they ran like children with a reckless abandon toward their next adventure.

It was warm for a night in Manhattan in December. They were several blocks away from the Diamond District, running toward Bryant Park. And then she got serious for a minute and looked at me behind her, and asked me, "Do you think I'm pretty?"

"She's this mystic goddess," Jacob said to Ruby who was back polishing whiskey sniffers this time around. "And she did something I wasn't expecting, she gives me a quick kiss on the lips and says, '*I like you, you're fun.*'" She grabs my hand and says, '*Let's take a shortcut to the park.*' At that point I probably would have followed her anywhere."

"We did something you should never do in New York. We walked through an alley where there was something illicit taking place. A drug deal – something we weren't supposed to see, some sort of a crime – or just got caught in the wrong place at the wrong time, but this young guy in his twenties starts chasing after us, shouting for us to come back to the dumpster he was hiding behind. She's wearing heels and running away faster than I am, but he continues to chase us. We might be a half a block in front of him, then all of a sudden, he's hit by a passenger car. His body goes flying as the car's tires screech to stop. The guy had run out in front of a sedan, and he got ...clocked."

Ruby was curious and had paused the buffing of the glass.

"Victoria says, *'let's keep going.'* She reaches for my hand, and I hesitate. It's the scene of a crime, and I told her we should go back." Jacob remembers Victoria reaching out to his hand tugging it in her direction slightly.

"*'I think I'm still high,'* she says softly while looking up to me, *'I can't be here right now.'*"

"We held hands for a few blocks, exchanged contact info before I slipped a limo driver a couple hundred bucks and asked him to get her home safely. Would call it a first date, but it was shortly after that that she told me that she had no idea that something like that would happen when she said, *'let's go kill something.'* She gave me a hug, climbed in the car and looked back at me with her smoky eyes and asked me to call her."

The memory made him wince as he sat there. He very well knew how to manage momentum. And in terms of money, he knew how to manage a loss. But he had not mastered the management of an idle feeling, unresolved and unanswered. The vacancy he felt inside was as warm as it was cold. The lack of definition was the loss he was left with. *So maybe that's it*, Jacob thought to himself. *Perhaps that's what a broken heart really feels like.* He reached in his shirt once again to feel the scar running up the middle of his torso.

Ruby returned shortly. "How about when you really get to know her?"

Jacob frowned, and contemplated what it was that Ruby was fishing for,

"What are you searching for...physically or – "

"Like – your first date, let's say."

"Well...we... So, we want to see each other right away, after that first crazy night together. The chemistry was strong. I thought that it was anyway. And it wasn't just the attraction. I don't think that it was. I asked her later and she said it wasn't just the physical attraction, it was the confidence, the maturity, the conversation. Anyway... Coffee houses were springing up all over New York She asked me to meet her at a Dean and Deluca. Prince Street. SoHo. Between Central Park and the Financial District. She writes the address on a notecard and kisses it in red lipstick."

Paisley, stops and smiles off into the distance. He's looking out the window, yet at nothing. He thought of her. How she behaved: playfully. How she smelled: like flowers. How she paid attention to him: undivided between nothing else. How she looked: heaven-sent. They arrived for coffee at the same time.

He remembered her image, how she looked. She was wearing a short skirt, so short, a V-neck navy cashmere sweater top that came to a stop at her midriff, revealing some of her tight stomach. The black watch plaid pleated mini, deep green and navy, blew in the light breeze. She wore black leather boots just shy of touching her knees, and carried a tiny black purse that must have held a credit card and a cell phone, not much else.

"So, I have my driver drop me off and I'll call him when I need to be picked up. She was walking up at the same time. A beautiful relatively unknown but irresistible woman, soon to become my angel. We order at the coffee bar and go to sit down; the place is packed – and I ask if she's comfortable if I buy out someone's seat."

"She's always...always the prettiest, the most sensual, most exotic woman in a sea of women. But something was different in her appearance, so I ask, 'Where are those bangs?'" Her hair was pulled back, but brunette tendrils were dangling. It was a much different look than in the club, and in some ways even better. The light of day illuminated her beauty."

"Victoria replied, so cutely, 'The clip ins? My fringies? That's a club thing. Why? You like them?' And like a nervous little schoolboy, I told her that I liked everything. We didn't talk about her curves, her rack, her favorite types of men, or favorite other-stripper type things. It was a normal conversation. We spoke of first date stuff. Movies, music, current affairs, sports – Yankees, not Mets and Giants, not Jets - and all of the other ice-breaker topics. We agreed on or agreed to disagree on – everything. It was a four-hour three cups of coffee first date."

Jacob remembered that their coffee became cold and neither of them wanted to part the discussion, so they continued to drink cold coffee in sips until they mutually were ready for another cup.

"She asked me if I was happy...doing what I do. I said I was meant for it." His *memory of their talk lingered.*

"Kids?" Jacob asked.

"Oh God no!" Victoria was quick with the response.

"So that's a 'no' then?"

"It's not my thing."

Three times she adjusted her bra straps, pulling the light cashmere sweater off to one side of her shoulders, revealing a satin plum brassiere underneath. It reminded him of what she was wearing in the strip club. She made sure that he noticed.

Jacob asked how long she had been stripping or dancing or whatever entertainment she provided. Her response was that she'd been at it for ten years or so.

"Always in New York?"

Her response wasn't what he anticipated. *"Miami...Miami is where I got into it. Dallas, Vegas, of course, then L.A., and up to the Bay Area. And now New York."*

"Wow, worked your way across the country."

"It's good money."

"And what's your definition of good money? What would it take to make you say, 'Enough of the night life', or what would be your buy-out number? You make what one-hundred grand a year?"

"More."

"Two?"

"More."

"Damn. Three?" he was surprised.

"Close enough. I'd kiss it for three," she looked longingly at Jacob and from her smokey mascara eyes, batted them at him. "Got a girlfriend? A steady thing? Or do you just pick up us club girls and play with us for a while?"

He looked at her, assessing that she was dreamy. An aspiration. Someone missing in his daily and quarterly quests for the almighty dollar, someone that he yearned for.

"No, no girlfriend." Jacob hesitated, when hesitation wasn't his thing, and reciprocated, *"You?""*

"There was a guy. In Miami. He owned a club. I was young..."

"You're young now." Jacob interrupted her.

"How young am I?"

He looked at her face for wrinkles and couldn't find one. *"Twenty-eight."*

"You're sweet."

"Okay...let's try this again, twenty-nine?"

She blew him a kiss.

"Thirty - "

"Two. Thirty-two," she interrupted.

"Let's do the math. Fifty, cut in half is twenty-five. Add seven and you arrive at thirty-two."

"Younger woman math? Really? Age is just a number."

"So where did you spend your twenties?"

"Back to Miami," Victoria took a breath, looked off into the distance but didn't say anything else. Finally, she said, *"It's complex..."*

Jacob paused, *"Complex or complicated?"*

She asked, *"What's the difference?"*

"Complex involves behaviors that are not reducible to basic elements. Complicated means that unnecessary processes or elements can be simplified or removed." She looked at me like no one had ever looked at me before.

As if she admired me. "*We don't need to talk about Miami...*" Jacob added, "*There's always more to the story.*"

"*He wasn't nice to me in the end, so I made a tough decision...and had a high-school friend who moved to Dallas, and she asked me to come for a visit.*" She stopped herself, telling the story while staring at her cup of coffee cradled by both hands to warm them. Then she continued: "*You're right. There's always more to the story.*"

He pictured something especially dark and chose not to continue with the inquiry about that topic.

Jacob continued thinking about that first real conversation outside of the club situation. He thought about her asking him why there was no steady woman in his life. She asked if there had been many. And he answered that work was his mistress.

"Work?" Victoria adjusted herself in the wooden seat, "Would she go down on you?"

He froze and looked around to see if anyone was as interested in this conversation with her as he was. No one seemed as attentive to the words spilling through her pink lips as he was. She was his, exclusively.

"Work..." Victoria continued, "Does she ride you until she's raw...down there?" Her eye contact was direct and deep. "I'm not buying it. There's something you're not telling me. A man like you...without a woman like me?"

He said nothing.

"Like you said. There's always more to the story. You'll tell me. Somehow...some way...I'll work it out of you." Tipping her chin down to her chest, she smiled a naughty look while maintaining eye contact. "You'll tell me about all of your dream girls, Jacob Paisley."

This wasn't his imagination conjuring her. It happened.

The replay in his mind concluded when Ruby set an empty wine glass down and picked up another to remove spotting. He asks, "Run that by me again. At the beginning...you were going to pay someone to leave?"

"Well, I didn't want to be rude. Strange how I can recant each detail. This gentleman taps me on the shoulder and says that we can have his table. He was leaving...and..." Jacob stopped talking.

Ruby looks at him and the empty drink, and motions toward the tumbler, "Still at it, or does this one do it?"

"It was you. Once more...it was you. You offered your seat to us, for a price, you provided the table. But, you looked a little...different. Each time I've met you, you're just a version of yourself." Jacob sat dumbfounded. Confused at how it happened. "You keep cycling through my life. I didn't recognize the pattern until just now."

Jacob Paisley was amazed at something more than numbers, and financial statements, and balance sheets and restructuring corporate debt. He wasn't focused on a creative swaps vehicle or foreign currency hedging mechanism. It was a pattern within his past. A surreal moment...that captured all of his attention.

He thought about how the butane fueling his memories went with Victoria, seeking Ruby somewhere else within the detail, but found none other than the seating. Then Jacob paused, and separated himself from his memories. It was a fleeting moment of transformation. He looked into Ruby's eyes and saw something familiar, a connection of some kind.

Ruby placed both hands on the bar squarely in front of Jacob. "Remember the two pillars of potential we spoke of? Beliefs and perceptions?"

"I do. Beliefs, yes. Perceptions, yes."

"Add two more: feelings and thoughts. Feelings. Thoughts. This is the important exchange between the internal process and the external. It's where many people break down, it might be what stops them, the rejection and how they handle it. The difficulty planning the transition between what they think and what they say. That remote control on the couch or internet or good book to read is easier than reachin' out to touch someone. What you think is really who you are. Tough showing your colors if you don't have any – some folks try to do that.

Tough to make your point if you don't have the right audience to accept it – some folks try to do that too. After all, the system's only going to deliver what it can."

"Again, you're wordy and preachy. Was your father also a preacher, or street poet, or something?"

He chuckled, "I'm just an old man making a stand. Remember this. Feelings..." he pointed to his heart. "And thoughts..." he pointed to his temple. Two more pillars of human potential. "But, you already know that. Right?" Ruby smiled. "You're a wise man. You've been in leadership and sales, and that's a transference of emotion. How you feel about your company, your product, you clients, and ultimately yourself. Confidence is the catalyst of making the point come across. Progress is the product."

Ruby was staring into Jacob's eyes, wiping a glass clean with a linen dish towel, while delivering a monologue. One of the managers came over and touched Ruby's forearm, and he spun off in toward the direction of the kitchen.

Jacob slammed the rest of the drink. The memories, pieced together with a new context of information, were familiar and foreign.

He slipped his fingers inside his shirt to feel the scar on his chest. The scar was now faint but the memory was fresh. His heart hurt in a different way. Victoria was clearly focused upon the money, the experiences, the game. She was dangerously convincing in expressing her feelings for Jacob and mastered the girlfriend experience. He felt hallow. A vacancy existed inside his chest where she once inhabited. *Why would he allow himself to afford her residency in his heart? How did it come to that?* Thinking about her, the moments shared and the words exchanged. Fake. Real to Jacob when it was convenient to fool himself...a charade to Victoria. He thought about the deception. *Perhaps it wasn't always deception, but when did it change? Stop this*, he thought. *Just...stop. This is toxic.*

Jacob couldn't help himself. He thought about her again. That first date at the coffee shop. Her schoolgirl looks in the pleated green and navy checkered short skirt, showing off her belly button and tight waist, the sultry conversation.

Before they departed the Dean & DeLuca, and prior to giving up their table, she mentioned that she'd be right back. He thought she needed to use the restroom and perhaps she did. But he looked over his shoulder to see her in a short line, ordering. At that moment, it was odd. She disappeared for a minute and then went back to pick him up at their table for their exit. They left the coffee shop to return to the bustle of the New York city streets. The small white cup with its white lid was held to her breasts closely. He thought she was keeping warm with it.

"Here, I got you one for the road." Victoria handed him the cup. "It's time for me to vanish for a little while. I'm a working girl tonight." She gave him a soft kiss on his cheek. "Now that I have your attention, or at least some of it, we'll be in touch, right? Call me?"

He knew that he needed to play it cool, and replied simply, "I'll call you." Really, his thought of her at the club with other men created an unexpected surging jealousy. He wanted her.

Her heels struck the concrete sidewalk with a confident stride as she began to walk away.

The cup was light. It didn't appear to have liquid within it, but something was there. He opened it as she was walking away. She had removed her panties and tucked them inside. Plum, like her bra straps. The satin purple undergarments were neatly folded into the cup.

He looked up to see her look back once. She paused for a couple seconds, turned to face him looking into the cup he held in his left hand, the lid in the right. Then he looked back up at here. He smiled and spoke, "What, no napkin?"

Victoria said nothing, instead, she placed one hand on one hip and rocked it while smiling at him playfully. The short skirt wafted with the movement. Only the two of them knew that she had nothing on underneath it. Then she spun back around and disappeared into a crowd. Continuing to look for her, he realized with some sadness that she was gone - wearing a little less than when she had arrived. Now he had a souvenir too. The trade was a tie for underwear. It was a fair exchange.

As many times through that afternoon they agreed, *there's more to the story*, he knew at that point, occasionally there was less. He stuffed her plum and shimmering panties into his suit coat pocket.

His memory was vivid, recalling the way she looked at him at just the right time, how she worked his vocabulary into their conversations, the use of her hands as she spoke to make an agreeable point, and the compatibility she engendered with him.

The first law of attraction. Physical proximity. The second law of attraction: congeniality. The third law of attraction: allowing.

"I could have a girlfriend," he allowed himself to think. He felt her panties buried in his pocket once a block as he walked without a sense of direction between the towering Manhattan buildings.

That was then, at the beginning of them.

He reached into his jacket pocket to retrieve the cocktail napkin with the number. He looked at it again as Ruby returned.

"When and if I ever do this, this...little thing you think I should do...all of this becomes real. You provide a bit of explanation. Deal?" He didn't know why he was even entertaining the thought of Ruby's challenge – but he did.

Ruby chuckled in the direction of Jacob, and nodded his head, "Okay - as you wish. Deal."

11

A Twist

Brian's Auntie and Uncle in Nanakuli had not convinced him not to make the trek to Oahu. He was determined. '*Why don't you come when she really needs you, not now when she did not,*' they told him. He had looked for flights on Hawaiian Air earlier in the day but didn't book the flight. Earlier in the day he was looking for the lightest task and workload days in the busy week ahead, wondering if it were possible for him to get away.

He made several calls to better understand the status of his cousin. Calling friends and speaking with family several times, he was assured Leilani was healing. Still in some pain, but more embarrassed in her judge of character. Her bruising had already migrated from red and purple to greens and yellows on the parameters. It was a good sign. Her nose was reset and still looked twice the size that it once was. His Uncle said, "Her nose was cute. Now it looks like a big honker." They tried not to giggle, but it was the way he said it, with Pidgin, that made Brian miss home, his island home, all the more. It sounded something like: *"Nah she got beeeg honka. Butchoo no worry, she got coco in her blood. She Havai'ian strong you know."*

He felt a heavy and pulling need to be there but was also immediately relieved when they told him that Yancy was in custody, in pretrial detention, under remand. No bail would be set.

Yancy – incarcerated. Justice would be served. Vindication would endure. *Lock him up, throw away the key.*

Domestic abuse detainees were held in separate locations in the rock prisons – as island-girl domestic abuse was usually seen as heinous, even to convicts. Word wasn't contained there. Everyone knew everyone. And everyone knew what Yancy did. Brian thought that he would get what he deserved – and was likely backpedaling to avoid his certain upcoming castigations.

Brian knew a thing or two about backpedaling... It wasn't the easiest thing to do – and there could be consequences. He revisited the transition to Defensive Back position at SDSU.

"Son, we've got two things to do here. One...is to teach you to run backwards. The other...is to teach you to hit." His defensive coordinator coached him, "Off of the line, across from the Receiver, when the ball is snapped, you backpedal, backpedal, backpedal, turn in the direction and run in parity without penalty." He thought that the message was simple until he had to do it with something faster than he was and bigger. "The next thing is to hit. Hit hard enough to slow the momentum. At the hips, around the knees, on the ankles. Slow the forward progress."

The drill was morning, afternoon, and night in its messaging recurrence. Game tape after game tape. Which players did it well, which players did not. He heard the coaches indelible mark in his head repeat, "Backpedal, backpedal, backpedal, turn, hit. Backpedal, backpedal, backpedal, turn, hit."

The hits. One after another after another and after another. He was becoming more proficient at his new position each week. Freshmen aren't often offered starting positions. However, when the score was favorable, in the fourth quarter, they would seen playing time in the grooming effort for perhaps year two, or three, or for their senior season. In the meantime, they bulked up and evolved from high school boys into manly men.

As luck would have it, Brian's varsity protégé was injured early in the season which meant that Brian and his equal level playing teammate split squad the left side DB position.

It was the sixth game of the season in the third quarter when he was covering someone in the Receiver position which had 30 pounds on Brian. But Brian was keeping up with him. The opposing player was a senior and was notorious in his playmaker position, but he wasn't a target. Brian was like a pesky flee on defense. Raid couldn't kill him. Coverage was strong.

That's when the ball was snapped. Backpedal, backpedal, backpedal, turn. It was all of four seconds which changed Brian's young career in football.

The Receiver came directly at him. They were ensnared with a Tight End and another lineman. The Tight End was the target. The ball came loose. He heard bones crunch, but in the state of play, didn't realize it was him. *A fumble!* Three big guys and Brian, with Brian at the bottom of the dogpile. The scramble for the ball left nearly 700 pounds leaping on Brian's lower torso and pulverizing his bones at the bottom of the tackle.

It was his ankle which was twisted backwards – in the direction that ankles aren't made to assume. He was in shock. The stretcher was brought onto the field and the reply was featured on SportsCenter as the "Big Hurt" of the week. The announcer acknowledged Brian's career "ender" like this: *The Aztecs bright season dimmed this Saturday against Boise State with Brian 'Kay-kah-hah-nah-mah-new-ee', yes, I needed some help with that and practiced it a dozen times – taking a major 'Ouchy' in this play. I don't think ankles should look like that. Maybe it's me, but I just don't. Our thoughts go out for Brian K of SDSU and his family. Speedy recoveries...if there is a recovery after something like that.*

Yancy. He had something like that to look forward to – a well-deserved big hurt, without the continuance of the full-ride honored scholarship.

Brian pictured Yancy holding a football, standing midfield. He only had Facebook and Instagram to reference but didn't picture Yancy as the athletic type. A spoiled little rich kid with a chip on his shoulder was what Brian imagined. Brian other the other hand was a former athlete, who fell short of something special. He was fantasy-strong in thought: dressed out, full equipment, running toward Yancy – just standing there holding a football that he didn't deserve to hold. Leilani. He was going to take him out, running toward Yancy for a big hit.

*****

Jacob was thinking about the final Board meeting again.

"So what was it really?" Ruby asked. "What was the problem that caused your kerfuffle with your Board?"

Jacob thought to himself. *Oh, I don't know dude, maybe at least $350,000 per year, divided by four quarters, resulting in $87,500 per quarter so that it wouldn't flag an internal audit? Oh...and that action - multiplied over several years?* The answer was *a line-item expense that he hid on the financial income statement.* He said nothing.

Since there wasn't a drop-down box in the PPCM ledger for *'girl-friend experience'*, they agreed to list it under T&E. Travel and Expenses – within the Sales, General and Administrative header. Ripley advised him. Turned out, it was bad advice.

It all led to an 'end of payroll experience' for Victoria. He shook his head in disbelief and perhaps at his own lapse in judgment. Did the elimination of funding cause her disappearance? She told him numerous times that their relationship was not about the generous benefits. Or perhaps it was an intervention from Ripley which led to Victoria suddenly ghosting Jacob. They were close. Too close. An external force caused her to cut and run.

That hurt. It stung. He was managing to more lust-loss than he had ever dealt with. *Why?* He just wanted to hear from her to understand what caused her to flee. It wasn't like her. Of the dozens of text messages he sent her: *I want to see you, can we meet?* only one was returned:

Let's do that. I need a little time away, but soon.

He was left to determine her new definition of 'soon' - and to pseudo-stalk her. She wasn't at her Lenox Hill apartment which wasn't far from his Upper East Side penthouse on Park Avenue.

Who got to her? Who had something threatening to share with her that he couldn't make melt away. Someone. Unless...unless there was something about her which she kept hidden. A secret that she never shared with him. It was this fantasy he felt a need to clutch onto. Nothing else made sense.

Jacob looked up at Ruby and shook his head slightly, then tapped the bar, "I'll have another." It was his sixth or seventh. He was losing count.

"Don't you think you've had enough?" Ruby turned his head to one side to question judgment.

"Trust me, I'm just getting started. You're not much of a bartender if you're counting me out. That can't be good for business." Jacob looked around the bar, now nearly filled. He estimated that there were sixty to seventy people within the cramped space.

"Where are your friends?" Ruby asked Jacob.

Jacob tried to ignore him, but couldn't help himself, "They're in a better place tonight. I wouldn't want my friends to share this moment with me. Bottoms up, please." He pointed across the bar at the colorful presentation of liquor and was referring to the bottles of booze.

"Mixed signals," Ruby spoke to himself as much as to Jacob, "that's the language that the subconscious mind understands and speaks. I'm afraid you're playing with fire, child." Ruby looked down at the bar top, then up at Jacob, "As you wish." Another drink was mixed and poured. "Here you go."

"I'm buying a round for everyone." Jacob challenged Ruby's rigid discernment. He had been hardened with years of celebrating accomplishments and drowning anguish with alcohol. *How could this moment be any different?*

Ruby gave him a blank stare.

"Did you hear me? For everyone."

"For everyone what?"

"I'm buying a round for everyone. For everyone." Jacob motioned his fingers in a circle while holding up his amber beverage. The ice cubes clinked in the glass.

"I'll get the word out."

"And I thought bartenders were supposed to be good listeners." Paisley said, mostly to himself. He looked around to see if he recognized anyone, but didn't. No one was present to raise a glass to his leadership, or extend a hand of appreciation for employment, or express sincerity toward his own Board running him.

Ruby quickly approached the other bartenders. Immediately they worked the crowd, first seeking out anyone with less than half of a drink in their hands. The bartenders knew that the word that a free round was heading their way would spark interest, make the volume increase, and generally create a more profitable evening.

As loud as he could declare it: *"Round for the bar!"* Jacob shouted. "That should do the trick. Now I have friends." He looked directly at Ruby as cheers exhumed.

Within a minute several of the bar's patrons gave Jacob a pat on the back, briefly thanking him for the kind gesture. Several minutes after that and as if his announcement were self-serving and intentional attention, like a magnet, two stunning women in strapless black dresses straddled the chair Jacob had claimed. A blond with long curly hair was caressing his upper arm, and an auburn redhead was touching his forearm with light strokes of affection. Flanking him, they took turns whispering into his ears. Jacob was amused with the attention but didn't allow himself to be easily persuaded. He made eye contact with Ruby, mentioning his drink was low - again.

Excusing himself from the two, he made his way to the men's room. The tile floor was of black and white checks. He spent a minute staring at the painting above the urinal. It read:

Stand A Little Closer Please – It's Not as Big as You Think

Now... that's funny. I've either seen it a dozen times before - or it's new. How would you know? He tucked himself in and zipped up. I'm getting righteously hammered, he thought to himself. The stall flushed as he walked away.

Shrugging his shoulders, he washed his hands, reached for soap – it smelled like eucalyptus mint. He liked it. He stopped when he saw his face in the mirror. It was a day to remember and one to forget. His face had a deep healthy color. It was as if he'd been to one of his favorite getaway destinations - sailing in the Caribbean or to his favorite sneak-away spot in St. Lucia. "That's the alcohol." He said it out loud, but there was no one else in the restroom.

12

Mishury Loves Curmpany

Instead of paying attention to time, he was counting drinks. Two more had passed.

They were laughing now. An adorable young blond had latched on to him. Perhaps it was the free drinks. He didn't care. Finally, he wasn't wallowing in loneliness – reproducing layers of pity and sympathy for himself. He had taken care of Adele in his separation agreement. Now he wouldn't allow himself to be alone – without Victoria while he dialed up commiseration.

"What?!" Jacob shouted above the noise in the bar, leaning into the blond sitting on the neighboring stool to his right. His hand found a place on her tight left thigh. His fingers were inside the hem of her little size two red dress.

"Austentatious the vodka!" she screamed with a bright smile on her face. Her cheeks were pink. But she would have said *'her pinks were cheek'.* She bit her lip and crossed her leg over his fingers. She looked at him smiling, quickly turned away, then slowly looked back at him. Squeezing her legs around his fingers, she reached for the glass to toss back a deeper swig.

"What?!" Jacob still didn't understand. He attempted to repeat what he heard her say, "Austentacious?!"

"Huh?" She opened her legs and grabbed his hand, motioning it a little further up her leg, "What'd you just say?!"

He looked off in the distance to determine how hammered he had become without food. "What's austen...whatever...mean?" Having to focus on syllable, he made it sound intelligible.

She giggled, tilting her head toward him. Her forehead landed on his shoulder while she worked up the reply, "I said..." She was slow and batting her eyes with drunkenness, "All - I - can - taste is...the vodka!" He felt her breath on his ear. Cute, spunky, careless. It was what he needed for the moment – some levity.

"Oh – 'all-I-can-taste-is...I thought you said something...way beyond my vocabulary. Some sophisticated word...like austentatious – I didn't know what the hell that meant. Obviously, I too...have been drinking!" They giggled and continued talking. Her hair was a bright blond, her teeth were a bright white, and her eyes were big and bright blue. She was nothing like the seductive and sensual Victoria. Her vivaciousness was a good fit for the spunky moment.

Jacob decided that much change would come his way.

The evening had stretched into night. She said that business talk was off limits, because it wasn't sexy talk. He provided a couple highlights about how bad things had become, and how they could get worse. The blond replied, slurring some of her words, "Well, you know what their say. They." She had her finger on his nipple. "Your know what they say." She giggled more and loudly. "What they say...is... mishury loves curmpany. Mishery. "

"Misery?"

"Yeah. That." She placed her index finger on his chest. "Loves company."

They talked, sometimes in mumbled speech, about sex, fashion, favorite travel spots, and for some peculiar reason: sushi. But, mostly about sex. They laughed and kept the cocktails coming in consistent succession. Several more rounds of drinks had come and gone.

Finally, she confessed and quipped that she was there looking for a sugar-daddy. Her trust fund would soon be expiring – and her disapproving mother would not tolerate her feckless public behavior. So, she was out on the town to drive her mother mad. Or to make her reconsider the trust's monthly stipend.

Jacob wanted nothing to do with that drama. He was however drawn to the minor amount of attention from her which he was receiving on what should have been a big-deal kind of night.

"On a scale of one ten, ten...one to ten...turn, I mean...ten bein' you're black out drunk...how...where are you...where are you at?"

"I'm at 'yes'". She swallowed, looked at him, steadied herself, stood, and moved closer. Jacob wasn't quite sure what she was doing. His right thigh felt warm. She had subtly lifted her skirt and with little friction, was riding his leg, appearing to hug him. It was purely an uncouth view from anyone glancing their way. A classless exchange in a public setting was nothing Victoria would have done. His leg felt damp.

"Oops...I got a built-in waterfall. Hot men do it to me," she teased. Backing off of his leg, he looked down to see her wet spot left on his custom and tailored suit.

Surprised, Jacob said nothing. This wasn't it. This was not what he came here for and wouldn't let the churlish moment progress to the next. *I'm at yes. Get a grip, Paisley.*

"I gotta pee'," she quickly added, "that's not pee - on your leg. Can you take me to the men's room?"

"What?"

"I wanna' to pee in the men's room. I've never peed in the men's room before. All my friends have. Will your 'scort me. Escort me?"

Jacob thought of a couple courses that this could lead, but looked around the crowded bar once again. "No. You gonna have to...going to have to go to the ladies." He pronounced what he could, realizing he got the message across.

"Oh...okay...poo," she pouted, and stumbled around the stool. She reached down to take off her shoes, reached for her small matching purse, and gave him a soft kiss on the neck.

"Beer here when I beeter get back!"

He stood to see her off and to assess whether he could stand.

"You bet-ter beer here when I come back," she made an attempt at the correction. Placing one hand on his shoulder, and another on her chest as she belched. Giggling, "Excuse please." She turned and wobbled through the crowd in the direction of the restrooms.

Paisley checked his watch out of habit. Eleven thirty. Time didn't matter right now. He had plenty of it. Jacob didn't need the timepiece, and since he was drunk, slipped it off his wrist and held it in his hand, then slipped it in his pocket. He was going to give it to Ruby. He didn't know why he felt the way that he did. But, it just felt right. Time to lighten his load? Time to simplify? The physical proximity of this moment favored the mysterious old black man named Gabriel Ruben Hollins. He knew why he wanted to give Ruby the watch. He wondered...and he even predicted that they just might meet again. *I'll get it back...someday. He's just going to borrow it...*

After a minute passed, Ruby made eye contact with Jacob. Paisley motioned for the check. He was officially trashed, yet had enough wit left to know that anything more would lead to some form of regret.

When Ruby brought the tape of the evening over, the evening staff manager accompanied the five-foot receipt. "Mr. Paisley, we thank you so much for your patronage over the years."

Jacob had never seen him before. Looking at the bill, "Nearly nine thousand – not'll that bad. In the past it's burn more." He focused on speaking as clearly as possible. Jacob tried to add twenty percent in his head, but the former money-manager just couldn't do it. He printed twelve-thousand dollars as a total, skipping the tip line. "If this isn't er-nough, let me know." Paisley handed the receipt to the manager.

Ruby and the manager stood with Jacob, and the manager spoke, "Thank you so much for your generosity, Mr. Paisley. And...I'm sorry to hear what happened..."

Jacob walked off mid-sentence toward the men's room. And then he stopped. He turned to see Ruby directly behind him, looking back with a blank stare. "Usually...it's the women...that go to the restroom...together." Jacob spoke slowly to enunciate. He reached for Ruby's hand to gesture a handshake, and wrapped the fourteen thousand dollar timepiece onto his wrist. "Until we meet again, sir."

"Man, you're one tough needle to thread," Ruby replied.

Another loud crash came from the direction Jacob was heading. He turned to see the pretty blond being ushered toward the entrance, out of the restaurant and bar. She was wearing a man's jacket, covering her red dress. Her head was down, in shame.

Two women were gossipingly splashy with their comments about the vomit in the bathroom. Rolling their eyes wide one of them said to two men they were with, "She got sick, like...*real* sick."

"Yeah, like all over the place way sick," the other added.

Her shoes remained at the bar, under the empty seat. *Not a Cinderella story here*, Jacob thought.

Haven't you had enough? echoed in Jacob's ear. He'd overdone it as well. He looked at the floor – to the foundation - for meaning. *Ground yourself.* Again, he tried his technique to control the moment: *Ground yourself.* It wasn't working. The floor. It spun. And all he saw were black and white tiles evenly arranged to form beautiful patterns of nothingness on the floor of the bar. Walking away from Ruby, he forgot about the watch.

After he made his way to the men's room without Ruby as a chaperon, he hunched over the stall propping one hand one the wall to prevent the restroom from spinning. It helped. He relieved himself and washed his hands. Again, smelling the soap. It was time to go. He needed fresh air in a big way.

His iPhone was blinking. Text messages had arrived. One from his bank – about a deposit. One from his AMEX about an unusual charge, seeking affirmation that it was not fraud. And one was from one of his favorite Junior Traders if not the favorite, Daniel Fianacca. It read: *JP: BoD & new mgmnt are torturing us. Had 2 wrk late. Team is burnt + we're all heading out of the city for w/e. We"ll catch up w/ u later. Plz keep N touch.*

That was it. That was the extent of a CEO being terminated for several reasons. That silence was uncomfortable. He said out loud for no one to hear him, "Get used to it."

Paisley slid the cell into his jacket pocket. And he felt more alone than ever before. Looking around the restaurant and bar one last time: no Victoria, no Adele, no friends, no acquaintances.

He was in a crowd of people, yet alone.

As he reached for the handle of the door to exit, he remembered walking in. This was likely his last night at Bobby Van's in the near term and definitely in the capacity to drown sorrows or celebrate victories. It had grown to be a centerpiece place of triumph and defeat; productivity and contemplation. He came to this favored watering hole to mark moments.

He looked around one more time, and his eyes settled on Ruby, wiping down the place where Jacob sat for the last six hours.

Ruby looked in the direction of Jacob, expressionless. They stared at each other. Jacob turned to leave. He didn't give more thought to the unexplained situation of Ruby's reappearance. It couldn't be solved at this moment, he considered. *Let it be.*

He took a moment to reflect: Bobby Van's had been the establishment that led to many experiences with varieties of people over the years. But, there were no Victoria or Adele tonight. Two very different, yet equally important women to him. A pair of invitations that he had hoped would be accepted generated no-shows. He hoped in a way that one of the two would help put his tenure at PPCM behind him tonight. And at the same time hoped that they would not both show up. He didn't know why he invited one, but knew exactly why he invited the other. Adele was his vault. As it turned out, he was going out 'solo' and that ended up being the appropriate fit. He was left to relinquish memories by himself, and to drink with strangers. And he wondered if this was a sign of things to come.

The outside air was cold. Immediately, he felt less hammered. The red-dressed, blond-haired, blue-eyed, bright white smile blond was nowhere to be found.

Jacob walked around the block, past the building lobby entrance to good old PPCM. He thought nothing of it, as if he didn't know what the consonants stood for. *Four right turns*, he thought. *Start there.*

There were no cars on this stretch of Broad Street. Nor were there any on New Street, a section of Wall, or much of Exchange Place. These honed cobblestone streets were more pedestrian pass-throughs than for deliveries. It was an area free of taxis, passenger vehicles and traffic controls. Only emergency vehicles had pass through rights. The smell of Manhattan exhaust still managed to find a way here though.

Four right turns. Jacob took a right at Exchange Place past the green painted railing to the subway. One. The December breeze was at his back. He raised his overcoat collar. A short block, William Street, had one way traffic and he was walking close to the buildings as the sidewalk was tight and there was scaffolding work being done on the tower above. Two. Another right onto Beaver Street had him walking with the traffic. There was little at this time of night. Three. Returning to Bobby Van's entrance, he stepped back admiring the old bank building. Four.

The rich detail, columns, finials, gargoyles, and architecture in general was deep in historical significance. *There's a reason why this place is as magnificent as it is.*

I do feel better. Surprising how little effort it takes to begin to feel control again. As he left Bobby Van's, the sodium street light bulb burned out.

He saw in the distance, further down Broad – the flowing in the breeze American flags showcasing the American way, freedoms bounty, and of course - a nod to capitalism. The lighting on the columns of the Exchange was commanding and glorious. It resembled a Roman temple. The grand entrance colonnade, detailing the pediment was built in 1908, reconditioned several times, and was brightly lit. At 100 feet tall, the figures represented in the pediment were eleven in total – were symbolic and representative of commerce and industry. The bronze Fearless Girl statue who had once faced the charging bull, stood, facing the Exchange, with her hands on her hips - sporting a ponytail and a look of determination on her face.

Something caught his eye.

A man fell to one knee on the other side of the street. Then to the pavement with both knees before he collapsed, face down. The body lay motionless twenty feet away. It took several seconds for it to happen. However, it was as if Jacob watched it for minutes in slow motion.

Out of the corner of his eye he saw a man run across the street in Paisley's direction from the other side of the street. Then racing past Jacob down Broad. *What had just happened?*

In a flurry of response, several men rushed to the motionless man, one assessing that medical attention was required and began shouting for someone to call 911.

A uniformed delivery driver in the area frantically used his hands to express what he saw and that the man had been stabbed.

Jacob noticed the door to Bobby Van's opened and two men ran out the door. One in a white apron and the other, which appeared to be the manager of the restaurant. They ran toward the motionless body. He heard sirens in the far distance. Then, he realized the man in the apron was Ruby. *Of course. You're not done with me yet, are you?*

Here they were, less than two blocks from where Jacob collapsed one year ago. He took small steps toward the scene to be closer and to determine if any other help was needed.

In the darkness he couldn't pay attention. It was clearly Ruby. Ruby was on his knees in the middle of the street at the victim's side. He took off his white linen apron and used it to brace the man's neck and head from turning. Another bartender appeared and the now-turned-medic man took his apron off and handed it to Ruby.

"Will be alright..." Jacob heard Ruby talking in low tones, but didn't hear everything he said. Ruby held his ear down to the victims mouth. It was moving, but no words were said. Ruby looked up to Jacob, directly into his eyes. A blank expression that said more than Jacob wanted it to.

Of course, it had to be Ruby – to make the night all the more interesting. What else could happen?

Sometimes things happen for a reason, and sometimes things happen because of reasons. You choose.

As the EMTs arrived on this street with little traffic other than pedestrians, the growing crowd was cleared back, and the sense of more sophisticated medical attention was quickly determined. Ruby gave his name to an officer taking notes. The loading of the victim happened quickly. And as quickly as it all happened, it all began to dissolve. Ruby, the other bartender, the manager of Bobby Van's and the crowd of looky-loos, the intrusively late-night curious onlookers broke up.

Is he dead? Jacob asked himself.

From somewhere in the disseminating crowd of now fifteen people: "I think he's dead", a woman's voice said it first. And she began to sob.

Several NYPD Officers were now asking questions to anyone still willing to make statements, but the comments overheard were the same: *it was dark; he appeared out of nowhere; the runner didn't appear to be walking with the victim; the victim was dressed darker than the night; there wasn't an altercation that could be seen.*

It was midnight.

He took small steps away from the scene, away from the attention, away from anything which might connect him further to a parallel event. Again. His thoughts of a similar situation, the situation with

Victoria and their first night together - occupied the real estate in his head.

"The needle in your mind is wearing out that vinyl, Jacob. Ground yourself," he said, realizing he'd regained control of his vocabulary.

Time to cut and run. Get out, now. Now. But he did not run, he walked. Jacob decided to go to Battery Park. It was away from the moment and would serve as an opportunity to sober up. He could look out at Lady Liberty in the Hudson. The recent reconditioning was complete. She'd be an illuminated turquoise beacon facing southeast and most likely hard to see clearly, but the resemblance of what she stood for would shine across the river. She'd have to serve as his soulful companionship for what might remain of this night. No Victoria. No Adele.

With several blocks yet to go, replaying the previous baffling moments, he listened to the sound of his pricey shoes striking the concrete sidewalks as he moved toward the river. It was getting colder. Again, he raised his overcoat's collar to protect his hat less head from the breeze. Again, he'd find a minute to reconstruct some sanity. Again, he'd sink into a trench of disappointment – only to find a way to dig himself out of it. Again, he'd need to fabricate a plan for his 'what's next?' as he had done thousands of times before. He felt Ruby's cocktail napkin with its five-digit code in his suit pocket. Again, *Madness.*

13

Metal, Muscle and Merry

"Oh-for-three!" Laki teased, "Again. C'mon, let me see it, let me see your Oh face," she looked at Brian and giggled.

He shook his head. You've got three or four minutes – get ready. We'll see how you do."

Chorus, Chorus, Chorus was 'on'.

"What's this?" he pointed at her glass of red on the counter, "and where's mine?"

"It's wine. The red kind. And it was sooo good, so good. But now it's gone. Open another bottle?" She looked at him and winked.

Brian reached above the refrigerator into the cabinet for a bottle of cab. "This work?"

"Yeah, I think it'll do the trick."

"What trick is that?"

The kids were gone. Laki fibbed to her parents that they had a Christmas party thing that they had to attend, for Brian's work. What really happened was that they bailed on a neighborhood holiday hayride to spend some time together, alone. The *alone time* ended up as Brian leaving work early to get new tires for the minivan; Laki helping with an upcoming craft fair at preschool; Brian cleaning out the garage; Laki doing the laundry; Brian secretly shopping online for Laki's Christmas present: and Laki preparing dinner.

He looked at the refrigerator. A stick figure crayon drawing of their family, their home, and a purple tree – all under a rainbow was showcased on top of the other fridge-worthy masterpieces.

"What's with the purple tree?" Jacob asked. "And she thinks we have a fireplace in our humble home?"

"Hey there, Mr. Art Critic...she's trying. Santa's got to have an entry point, right? Tis the season."

He looked at the arc of the rainbow. "She nailed the colors of the rainbow. Good girl."

"What's that?"

"ROY G BIV"

"Huh?"

"Red, orange, yellow, green, blue, indigo, violet. She has them in the correct order - with red at the top."

Laki looked at the rainbow hovering at the top of the drawing. "Either that's the way the crayons fell out of the box, or she takes after her mother and has an eye for the detail. Maybe she'll be a da Vinci, or a van Gogh, or a Picasso."

Briance winced, "Well, they're all men so...no. You missed that little detail." He looked in her direction and smiled, but she was stirring something on the stove.

With a hand on one hip, the spoon in the other, circling nothing in midair, while looking off into no particular direction, she finally came up with a name, "Georgia O'Keeffe."

"If you say so."

"She did say red, yellow, and blue were the 'Mary' colors."

"*Mary* as in a woman's name or *'merry'* as in Christmas?"

"Neither...she meant *primary*. Oceanside, California public school system at work there. Kindergarten at work. I didn't teach her that."

Brian chuckled as he walked up behind her, "Smells good, what's cookin' good lookin'?"

She retrieved two eggs from behind the future masterpiece on the fridge, making eye contact with her husband, "It's a surprise. Been a rough week. You're getting the special treatment tonight..."

"Smells like...awe, you do love me. Loco Moco! I'm gonna' have a kanak attack!" A *kanak attack* was Hawaiian code for eating so much you get an intense feeling of laziness.

"You could...but the kids are spending the night at my parents." She gave him a longing glance and then returned to stir the gravy and rice.

Brian hugged her from behind as she turned down a dial on the stove, eventually squeezing her small breasts. Her broke from the embrace, "Okay, that should do it."

"That should do what?...You were just getting started."

He punched a button on the stereo summoning the first station, Radiohead's hit, *Creep,* was just beginning to play. "Oh-for-one!" he proclaimed proudly.

"Tough one. Love that song," Laki said, singing alongside.

"Tough one. But you are special, though." He referred to the lyrics without reciting them. "Ready for round two?"

"Bring it, music man."

Brian punched another button, for a different station arriving at *Hey Jealousy*, by the Gin Blossoms. Unfortunately for Laki, and fortunately for Brian, she was on the Oh-for-Two side of the scorecard.

"Damn. I'm getting shut out tonight," she huffed.

"Maybe not." Their sexual innuendos always grew stronger as the evenings advanced, with and without the Cabernet Sauvignons. Brian's undertones weren't as edgy as Laki's. He was trying to keep up. "And for round three..." Another button on the stereo was tapped, and he teased, "Classic rock – do your thing."

AC/DC's, *You Shook Me All Night Long*, saved the day – for Brian. The song was in the middle of Angus Young's guitar solo.

Laki shook her head slightly while smiling at Brian. A spoon in her hand shook in his direction. "Next time, island boy. That's foreshadowing you know..." she was referring to the lyrics.

"Oh-fer-Three!" He was excited not to be the only one skunked tonight. "C'mon, let me see it. Let me see your Oh face."

She turned down the stove, licked the spoon clean and sang the next verse, using the spoon as her microphone. Reaching into the utensil drawer, another stainless-steel spoon was drawn and handed off to Brian. While looking at each other, attempting not to laugh, they collectively sang what lyrics they knew – although they were few other than the refrain.

Sexual playfulness quickly advanced from frolicsome to fiery - before the song was over, and since just the two of them were alone for the night, Laki began moaning. Her 'Oh' face was suggestive. Brian thought that Laki's version of Meg Ryan's character, Sally Albright, was causing his version of Billy Cristal's character, Harry Burns, to look around the diner. Without an audience, he drew her close to him as the song concluded and kissed her deeply.

Lifting her off of her feet, and holding her in his arms, he carried her down the hallway toward their bedroom. She giggled, wiggled her toes in the air holding onto his broad shoulders and neck with both arms, and moaned some more without the spoon in hand.

As peculiar as the gift of love can be - they realized that chance meetings, physical proximity, common denominators, shared values, dreams, lust-filled moments, and the widely defined definition of love - were all just components and fractions toward what Brian and Laki Kekahanamanui held most tightly as their treasure - unworthy of any surrender.

His regret, a short-lived college football career, was a low raised ridge across a roadway. It would not leave his thoughts but was a lingering speed bump. Her love, an accelerant toward all things good, brought forth something better than what he wanted most: a treasure he adored and prized so much more than the trophies and memories found in the cardboard box on the top shelf of the office. With time, Brian now realized that the person you'll talk with most in life – is yourself. So, you better be saying the right things.

Laki was in his head and in his heart as much as he was in hers. The companionship of the two was thriving and unremitting. Like the rainbow masterpiece on the refrigerator – the arc encompassed them.

The reach, Brian's love for his wife, like a boat at sea on a journey toward the horizon – to arc the flatline – was becoming the adventure which he would not trade for anything.

*****

As Jacob walked away from Bobby Van's and when his favored establishment was out of sight, Adele turned the corner heading toward the restaurant and bar. It was later than late, but she couldn't help herself. She sat home alone, stewing for hours, waiting for something to happen. When it didn't, she ventured out – seeking a chance encounter.

The establishment was the attraction for countless all-important moments with Jacob: the distinguished and the elite celebrations, as well as the challenging and the arduous. It had never been for a consequential juncture. This was a turning point.

They were two blocks from each other. She was walking toward their often-visited location all while he moved away, heading to the water.

She walked briskly toward the entrance. This institution was a part of PPCM's and their soul and they always felt invited. Once she was inside, Adele slowly walked through the eatery by day, drinkery by night, hoping to find Jacob. But, he was nowhere to be found. After repeating her steps, her shoulders dropped in disappointment that she missed him. She reached for her phone to text him but froze – reminding herself that he just might want time alone.

Even Adele could retreat. She needed time alone too. Time away. With a three-year severance, perhaps this was the sign she was seeking. The uncertainty of no longer working with Jacob was a form of torture. The change, she knew, would ultimately do her good. And yet, she felt that she needed to be near Jacob.

In a moment of peculiarity, *'Some things happen for a reason. Team Hope, here.'*, Adele would quip.

'Some things happen because of reasons. Team Logic, here.', Jacob would rebuttal. They'd always have that.

A black man, working at Bobby Van's, wearing a white cotton apron was at the counter and looked her way. It was a stare more than a glance. She couldn't place the face but he did look familiar but not connected to this place, and he wasn't a familiar longtime staff member. What she did notice was a pair of red heels under an empty seat at the bar. Adele headed in that direction.

The speculation toward what Jacob had up his sleeve was eating at her. Adele would give him a day. Maybe she'd reach out tomorrow or the day after. She thought again about his frame of mind. Yes, perhaps he just wanted to be alone at this moment. But here, at this place which they often frequented, just felt right. It was later than late for Adele. Maybe, she would have just one drink. *Not like I need to be at work bright and early tomorrow...* She felt glum for having to think of it.

"There is a pair of heels under that chair," Adele mentioned to the bartender.

"Well, you've heard of knock your socks off? We have knock-your-socks-and- shoes-off drinks here." He was attempting to be charming.

Adele accommodated with a slight smile, "Cheesy. I'll have..."

"You want what he was having...right?" He paused to make a point, "What Jacob...what Jacob Paisley was having?" The black man's glance was intended to be penetrating and intentional.

As if a trance, she replied, "Sure...that'll do." Her stare was bewildered. Not knowing what might happen next, she sat quietly awaiting instructions or a course to follow. She looked around. No one was jumping out to surprise her. It was no punking. It was just her, and the know-something-she-did-not black man at the ready to pour whatever Jacob was drinking – likely the best scotch they served. "I'll have that," she added.

Ruby retreated to a plethora of colored bottles, mixers and ice, crystal clear glasses he'd been polishing throughout the night, and bartender chatter to mix her libation. He returned quickly, "Drink for the lady...Adele."

She slowly cocked her head to the side and frowned an *'I'm going to learn something here, aren't I?'* kind of frown, thinking that an interesting discussion or some comprehension or perhaps an explanation of a series of events might be approaching.

He tossed the white towel to the side and placed both hands on the bar in front of Adele, leaning toward her. Giving her all his attention, it was as if she were the only patron and as if he had the remainder of the night and a secret to share with her. His understanding and wisdom were at first hidden by a blank look which evolved into a small smile.

Walking away from Bobby Van's - he wanted anything but that...solitude. It was awful. Jacob walked toward the bronze Charging Bull at the Bowling Green triangle. The cold air nipped at his ears, nose and chin. His eyes watered with the wind when rounding a corner. Loneliness, it hurt.

Before he reached the US Bankruptcy Court, passing an alley and from behind a dumpster's edge, a twenty-something looking thin man appeared. He was the same height as Jacob. The first things Paisley noticed was that he had long greasy hair, unkempt, a scruffy beard, and a long overcoat which didn't look like it was really his.

Then, it appeared. The luminous intruder. It glistened in the city light which came from the office towers above. A shiny handgun pointed in Jacob's direction immediately swallowed all of his attention.

"Hand's up mu-thu-fuck-a." When the young gunman said it he pointed the revolver directly at Paisley and gave a crooked-toothed grin.

Perhaps because he was buzzed, or perhaps because he was attempting to process, or perhaps because it had already been on hell of a day...Jacob just froze and looked into the man's eyes. With little lighting in this spot, he couldn't see them well, but did notice that they were darting around. Perhaps he was nervous and anticipated conflict.

"Did you hear me, rich boy?"

"Do I know you?"

"You gonna' know a slug if you don't give me what I want."

"Alright, alright," Jacob said. "I'm reaching for my wallet."

"That's right, mu-thu-fuck-a." The young man turned the gun sideways, and straightened out his arm directly at Jacob. He offered a crooked-toothy grin. *Something was missing*, Jacob thought. *Confidence? Confidence.* The grin was fake. It was classic misdirection. There was no confidence in the gun-pointing youth.

He had too much to drink earlier, yes and was mending his judgment lapse, yes. But his disposition was remodeled, and he had reached a point of no longer wanting to be anyone's victim. Not tonight. No, not anymore. The Board of Directors had done more than it anticipated. Jacob lowered his left arm and no longer reached for his money inside his jacket pocket. He thought for a second, then found words.

"Listen, you don't want to do this. You see, I'm the wrong guy. At least for tonight I am. And this...this is the wrong time." There's an illuminating freedom that sometimes comes with having less to lose.

"Money - or else, bitch." The greasy assailant was befuddled.

"Else." Jacob had found his focus, his face found determination, and he added, "Bitch."

The gun cocked. The metal in the firing chamber sounded deeper than he thought it might. But he found uncommon courage himself. *This isn't it*, Jacob thought. *This isn't that defining moment.* He said it again. "Else, bitch."

Jacob reached out for the silver handgun. It gave a hollow metal click as the trigger was drawn. He held onto the barrel more than the mugger held onto the barrel as they struggled for control. Jacob easily took the gun from him, and used it to hit the skinny man in the forehead.

He stumbled backwards after being struck by Paisley and tripped backwards. When he fell his head hit the corner of the steel dumpster and he gave Jacob a dazed look of pain as he fell onto his ass. His forehead was split from the gun, and the back of his head was ruptured from the corner of the unforgiving metal. He reached his hand to the back of his head and saw that blood trickled onto his hand. He let out a shrill cry. Scrambling to get to his feet, he was off-balance and fell back onto the ground again.

It wasn't that much blood, Jacob thought. While shaking the gun at the attacker, "Bad timing. Mu-thu-fucka. I'm unpredictable tonight. You hear me? You hear me?!" He looked around for a witness, but found no one.

The once-gunman fell silent. He tried to stand once more and fell again, this time his head hitting the alley and turning his head to the side, eyes closed. Jacob slipped the gun into his jacket pocket and took a few seconds to capture the moment. He looked at the pavement. And again, looked at the knocked out hack lying flat on his back. Clammy perspiration, greasy hair, pimples on his cheeks. Jacob re-guessed his age as a late teen, early to mid-twenties punk.

Did that just happen? he asked himself. *That was too easy*, Jacob thought. *I need to get out of here...now.* He wanted no connection with this moment, and looked around and up for voyeur-like cameras which may have captured the reverse mugging. It was an alley. Seeing none, he walked away. He replayed the dubious situation in his head twice as he continued to make his way to the park. *Good for me, bad for him?* It was a moot question that became more ambiguous with each step away. Jacob kept looking over his shoulder a block away to ensure he wasn't being chased. He felt the gleaming, yet false, security of the gun in his coat pocket. '*Muth-a-fuck-a*' was recast several times.

Jacob continued his cadence at a quickened pace, listening to the strike of the expensive shoes on the cement. Now several blocks away, the need to canvass for safety was subsiding, but the Adrenalin remained heightened. He was no longer lost in thought about Victoria or Adele or PPCM or Ruby or the other side of his life. He was thinking about each step and how it distanced him from a potential outcome of dire consequences.

As he made his way on the sidewalk of Battery Place, walking briskly toward Pier A and Castle Clinton, there was what appeared to be homeless woman wrapped in dark blankets, sitting upright on a something dark that appeared to be another blanket. A cardboard box seemed to serve as a container for belongings. Homelessness was more than common throughout New York. It was a kingdom of panhandlers, mendicants, and beggars. But this felt unusual, out of place, for some reason - singular. She was the only indigent person anywhere in Jacob's course within the park.

Squinting, he could make out label on the brown cardboard box on its side: Pringles. As a result of his history in the market, Jacob thought about the Proctor & Gamble ticker: PG. *Give it a rest, Dude,* he shook his head. *Time out on the tickers...please.* Jacob hesitated to take another step and thought about walking across the lawn to avoid interaction but decided not to. He wasn't going to take shit from anyone tonight. The gun felt heavy in his pocket. He'd never carried one before. As he came closer, he noticed that she was pretty, thin, perhaps desolate as he approached closer. Her hair was ash blond in color but with only the city lights from the towers and yellow sodium park lighting, it was too dark to see clearly until he was closer. There was something else.

She had tear-stained cheeks. She had been crying. Her black wool coat was old and torn. She was sitting on a sleeping bag.. Jacob looked down at a cardboard sign with black handwritten marker in block lettering stated the obvious:

SOMETIMES THINGS
JUST DON'T TURN OUT
LIKE THEY WERE SUPPOSED TO

She made no eye contact. Jacob slowed down as he approached her. Out of the box crawled a little girl, apparently the woman's five- or six-year-old daughter...or sister...or someone. It wasn't a makeshift suitcase, or a place to house household items at all. It was something much more. It was her little girl's habitat – for tonight at least. Jacob, childless, wasn't a good judge of age. But, he noticed the similarities in their looks. The dirty blond hair, round blue eyes, high cheek bones, small nose. The little girl had a round rock in her right hand. She climbed onto apparently her mother's lap resting her head on the woman's shoulder.

He stopped walking. Had to. *No*, was the only thought that crept into his head. *No. No.* He looked up from the sidewalk to meet sad eyes looking back at him. The little girl rested her head onto the woman's breasts. The mother looked beyond Jacob with a blank stare. Drugs? Paisley wondered.

The woman then looked at Jacob, and said in a sweet soft voice, "Merry Christmas."

He tried to say the same thing, but his lips made no sound. He had to take a step away, and couldn't reply as he kept walking. He made it to the fourth section of sidewalk cracks beyond the woman and child and came to a stop. Snow began to fall. He turned around to walk back to the pair sitting on the blanket.

As he reached them, he knelled down next to the mother. "How can I help you?" he asked.

"Oh, thank you sir. If you have any pocket change, we could really use a meal. I promise you I won't use it for anything other than food." It was cold. Her reply was warm – which caused Jacob to think that it was especially unusual to find them at this hour, in this frigid weather, without shelter, without food, without hope.

This was a form of Paisley's definition of fate, not Ruby's. These two were here because things happened due to reasons. Bad luck. Not predestined despair.

Jacob reached into his pocket and gave her what he had. It was a little over four hundred dollars. She looked at the dollar bills with amazement. "Oh my. Sir, are you sure? This is too much."

"My name is Jacob. What's yours?"

"Mary. You are so kind. Thank you." She stuffed the bills in her pocket.

"And your little girl is?"

"Marcy. Just like Mary, but with a C. That way we'll always be close." She backed away.

Jacob knew in an instant that he must smell like booze, and to avoid creeping Mary out, backed away. He was standing while Mary sat. Marcy was standing in between them.

"Thank you. Merry Christmas to you and your little girl. You take care of yourselves."

Her eyes welled up with surprise, appreciation and disbelief, and she nodded her head gainfully. In a whisper, "Thank you so very much."

Paisley walked on, and nearly made it to the next street corner this time when he stopped and turned to return to the woman who had quickly stashed the cash and was reaching for the blanket.

"I'm sorry. Me again. Back for more. Help, that is. I want to help you. What happened here, if you don't mind me asking?"

She wiped her eyes and softly recited her story, "We were living with my father. He passed away last month. It was a freak accident just down the street. A taxicab hit him...."

Jacob looked up the empty streets, and pictured an accident. He saw several options. One, of Ruby comforting a victim – her father perhaps.

"...Unfortunately, the doctors couldn't save him." She lowered her head and became solemn. Jacob didn't need to hear the rest of the story. Her loss cascaded into the moment of this meeting. This was a moment where he could make a difference.

"Listen. You can't be here on the street. Whether it's mourning your father's loss. Or, money, Or, whatever has brought you here. We need to get your little girl in a safer and better place."

Mary shook her head slightly in the direction of 'yes', appearing to know that this was no place for her little girl, but deplete of resources. "You're right," she said softly, defeated, nodding her head. Mary repeated herself, again in a whisper, "You're right."

Jacob reached into his wallet for Adele's card. "Listen, here is the phone number for a woman I'd like you to call on Monday morning. She's a very good woman, the best I know. You tell her we spoke. I'll call her and talk about what we'd like to have happen. She'll help you get into a better place."

"Oh, sir. Thank you for your kindness."

Jacob stood up and walked with them to State Street where he could hail a taxi. Once there, he waved to an approaching taxi, with a light on top: AVAILABLE FOR HIRE.

Mary's daughter, Marcy reached up to Jacob's hand and held one of his fingers. She was cute. Her eyes were big for her face. He looked down at her not knowing what to say or do. All he could think was that it was an unfair situation.

"Mewy Chwismas," she said softly.

Jacob patted the top of her head gently acknowledging her as the yellow car slowed down. He gave the driver a hundred-dollar bill for the fare and instructed the cabbie to take them to the Marriott in lower Manhattan. They ditched the potato chip box. The woman had only one duffel saddled on her shoulder and was carrying her daughter wrapped in the blanket with both arms as she climbed into the yellow and black car.

"I'll call ahead, and make the hotel arrangements. You just make sure you call Adele on Monday." For the first time in a long time, he knew what needed to be done and felt good doing it. For the first time on this day, he did the right thing. For a small moment, a smile found its way to his face and warmed his heart. It was no longer cold.

The flurries became bigger flakes, and it quickly began to snow harder.

"Thank you. Jacob."

He closed the door behind them and waved slightly From inside the dark cab of the taxi, she briefly waved back, then turned away. The taxi drove off heading north into the city where something better awaited the two of them.

"It's unfair," Jacob said it for no one to hear and to the taillights of the cab as it accelerated away through an intersection and a yellow. *When things go south, you go north.* He thought about his world of unfairness and how he had done so well within its parameters. Not unfair in terms of how he was treated – perhaps his undoing was all in his own hands. But rather, how *unfair* had favored him for so very long. Unfair wins. Unfair survives. Unfair takes marketshare. Unfair identifies. Unfairness empowers and creates and evolves into a lotus land of more unfairness. He had tweaked the controls to know the balance of the overall performance of the machine called *Unfair.*

Jacob spared himself from any self-pity, thinking instead of how Mary had not prevailed over the world of unfairness as he navigated.

He had done good here.

On a day that he assumed would be anything but, he had helped someone beyond his pool of influence. His kindness felt like a new currency. And he felt like he had more of it to give.

Beliefs - and Perception. Feelings - and Thoughts. *WTF? What was up with all of that? Is he just...just so fucking full of himself? Or...or...is there something else there?* The two sermons of his acquaintance, Ruby, were what? Ramblings? Deliberations? Or were they a parley to something yet to be? His war ship for the last two decades was having the answers to the questions, both asked and unspoken. Now he was a captain without the boat.

I don't know. I just - don't - know...felt like an odd thought rattling around inside his head. A spare part in his mind that didn't grind well with the rest of the oiled and engaged gears.

The wind whipped and his eyes watered – but his heart was glowing. Jacob reached into his coat pocket for what Ruby gave him hours earlier. His fingers slipped past the handgun for the cocktail napkin containing the five-digit number: 9 – 6 – 7 – 0 – 7.

*****

Kerri Latch and Boomer Hollins were sitting in his living room looking out the front window into the street. Snow had begun to fall. Flurries at first, light and softly floating in mercurial directions. Then, as the wind increased, a light and steady blanket followed.

Inside, it was warm, cozy, a place she wanted to be – provided peace and comfort. She was lying on the couch under a beige fluffy blanket; he on a penny-brown big leather recliner – feet up, resting on a throw pillow.

She felt safe with her new acquaintance, Cutter's presumed partner. They had just finished watching *It's a Wonderful Life* in the neighboring room with the big television. It still smelled like buttered popcorn; Boomer popped for them.

They made chili together earlier in the day. He shared his secret to a killer five-way recipe, pulling a can of Skyline from the cupboard.

He spoke slowly and was comfortable with his pace of speech. It was nothing like Cutter's irrationality.

"Not really a secret, but with a slow cooker, kidney beans, onions... ground turkey, a couple jalapenos...and a can of Cincinnati's finest – it makes a mighty fine comfort food bowl of chili."

She helped him prep and cook, saying little, listening a lot.

"You like it four way - or five way?"

Her puzzled look made him explain Cincinnati chili basics. Spaghetti and cheddar cheese please, was Kerri's reply once she understood.

"The works it is...a.k.a. five-way."

It was late.

Kerri looked at the small four-foot artificial Christmas tree which Boomer had resurrected earlier in the day. Together they adorned it with a dozen ornaments and three strands of white twinkling lights. Then, when she was taking a bath, he snuck a small Christmas present under the tree. It was the size of a small shoe box, wrapped in red paper with a gold bow. To: Kerri, From: Boomer, Happy Christmas! She still had some time to reciprocate and get him something. It would mean another trip to the ATM. She had money – unless Cutter drained it from her account.

"Would you like to make a trip back to your place tomorrow to get a few things of your own?"

She contemplated what she needed but just looked over at him in the dim light and shook her head, 'yes'. Finally, she broke her stillness and reflective state.

"I don't even know where he is. Isn't that odd that I didn't care?"

"Well, about your caring – I can't speak to that. But, as for where is Cutter...and I cannot tell you exactly...but can say he's far from here on a project for the syndicate. He has asked for this project for a while now."

"Syndicate."

"That's what we call our organization. Our association. Our cartel."

There it is - Kerri thought. The acknowledgment of the illicit cabal – all cleaned up by Boomer. At least the words coming from this drug dealers' mouth were prettier than those that Cutter spewed. She compared Boomer's kindness and the respect granted toward her in their short time together to the hair pulling and uncompromising demands from Cutter and decided she didn't really care when he returned. But she didn't say that to Boomer. Not yet.

"What has Cutter told you about me? You two have worked together for a while, right?" She didn't expect the featureless reply.

"Nothing really. Nothing specific, I should say. He...he really kept you off to the side, apart from what we've worked on together. He said that you were trying to clean up and that you had nowhere to turn while he was away on the project. Once he had his buy-in for the syndicate, he asked me to...no disrespect intended here...to babysit for a couple weeks."

"Babysit?"

"Meeting you, getting to know you – that's not what I see."

She felt discarded by Cutter but did not really care. The nondescript explanation of their relationship to Boomer wasn't Boomers doing, it was Cutter's. He wanted Crazy Kerri all to himself.

"Buy-in. You said once he had his 'buy in' – what's that?" she asked why she propped herself up onto her elbows under the fluffy pillows.

"One hundred thousand dollars."

Kerri thought of, among other things, the grocery store pizzas; how she had to beg him to pick up something substandard or slight if he were already out or intending to go somewhere; about how he grumbled that she was such an *'anchor'* to him. She had a hard time picturing Cutter with money in the bank or under the mattress or wherever he had the hundred grand stashed.

She suspected that there was a price for everything. Her heroine needs were costly in ways she both understood and could not comprehend. The darkness of this night filled with gentle and feathery snowflakes would pass.

The other darkness, ruled by reckless desire alone, would weigh her downward. That was her gravity, not as Cutter's anchor, but as her own voluminous mooring. Begrudging and resenting her id...the Crazy Kerri...she had managed to chamber her away, for the time being.

Boomer's tone was low and almost a whisper, "What's your preference? White lights, or colored lights?"

"Umm...I don't know."

He waited a minute, and added, "Sure you do." His comforter was brown, and his toes stuck out at the end of it.

"Colored. Reminds me of when I was a little girl. My mom and dad had a few strands that we'd staple to the wood trim of our home."

"What's your favorite Christmas cookie?"

"Uh...I don't know." She had a different tone and was wondering what he was up to but was drowsy and barely had her eyes open. "Maybe..." she added, "those white almond balls with powdered sugar."

He answered slowly, and Kerri could tell that perhaps he had been dosing off, "Oh yeah, those are good."

"What do you like to do...on Christmas morning?" He yawned as he asked the question.

"Umm...I don't know..." she was stumped. "What is this...twenty questions?" Kerri tossed an available throw pillow at Boomer, giggling a little, hitting his groin with the loft. *All I know...is that there isn't anywhere I'd rather be right now, than here...*she thought to herself.

Boomer let the last question and the pillow toss go unchallenged as he closed his eyes.

Growing tired, contemplating his questions more, she snuggled back under the warm furry comforter on the couch. Not thinking of one hundred thousand dollar buy-ins for who-knows-what, her floaty and wafting thoughts like the gentle snow falling outside, were of baby names: *Lydia, Arden, Andy, Lucy, Cooper, Elliot, Asher, Gabriel.* Still the front runner for a boy's name: Gabriel. There it was - again. Odd that it too was a suggestion, from a good-looking elderly black gentleman, on a park bench. The day she took the long walk and then collapsed in the drug store near Union Square.

Why? Why was this longing so cogent? Why was a baby so compelling when self-preservation should be the most supreme ambition?

Kerri closed her eyes. She saw what she needed to see. Not as in a reflection in a mirror, where she looked undernourished or pale or scared. But as she hoped she could become. It had been missing, the sanguinity. A most favorable outcome, known as potential, hovered within her dreamy whims.

PART THREE:

THE BUSINESS OF LIFE

ONE YEAR LATER...

14

The Final Trade

He wasn't dead yet - but was marked for it. Time was approaching. Death would land, claim its victims, and in time, deliver a gift to those not chosen in the path of its arrival or in the wake of its departure. The gift would be a remembrance.

"Aloha Kito," proclaimed the sailor. His hair was long, touching his shoulders, deeply graying with random shots of dark color through it. He had several days of beard stubble, bright blue eyes, and a deep dark tropical suntan. He stopped at the bench where an elderly Japanese man sat carving the two inch thick sticks. He shared a bright smile. A yellow Labrador Retriever bounced behind the sailor carrying a stick in its mouth. Its' tail was wagging with a slow even cadence as it followed his every move.

"A-lo-ha, Kai Koa," a groveled voice answered. The Japanese man appeared excited to see his visitor, and provided a smile that would serve either as an orthodontist's dream-come-true or greatest-project-ever. They squared off, the taller sailor standing above the shorter hunched Japanese man sitting. Their chins lowered to their chests with eyes fixed to acknowledge each other respectfully.

The sailor was wearing a navy long-sleeved t-shirt that had a white copperplate logo on the left chest: Pau Kahana Cruise Company. He reached down to rub the dog behind the ears. After receiving the look of gratitude from the dog, he then reached into his baggy khaki board shorts to find a biscuit for his happy companion. The grateful dog crunched the small bone in a couple of chomps and sniffed his master's pocket for another. "Later," the sailor gave him a stroke of affection on top of the lab's head. The dog appeared to adore the affection, as his ears were scratched. If dogs could smile, it would have been a grin.

Kito was sitting on a green metal bench facing the marina's boats. His back was to the sun, which was just beginning its slow descent from the mostly sunny sky above toward the sea. The silver sparkles on the water from the reflection were still an hour away.

As an unusually short Japanese former fisherman, Kito was sea-worn and deeply tanned. He was a regular at the Marina, sitting in his favorite spot carving a hibiscus stick with a pocketknife. Taking the time to talk with anyone that would stop to ask him a question, he was friendly – but his second language, English, was difficult to understand as it was more Hawaiian pidgin than the actual language.

A typical Hawaiian evening like this would offer a spectacular sunset. Some storm cells gathering to the left and right would provide a dramatic difference of colors. The sky held more moisture than usual but the trades blowing helped tame the humidity. No gathering clouds yet touched the sea where the sun was likely to set. If the cloud banks at the ocean's edge cooperated, the sunset would be bright amber and red with flecks of yellow and purple in the thunderheads flanking the horizon.

They knew how sunsets at the several resorts up the coastline played out. Guests at the well-maintained hotels and timeshares flocked to the lagoons, many with a drink in hand, to capture the views, clicking portraits and selfies with their phones. Then, after the sun tucked itself below the horizon, the tourists would cut and run. The best colors were often yet to follow, and the brilliance of the contrasts continued for another half hour. It was often missed.

It was a master planned area, here. Several decades in development, things were on island time – meaning slow growth. Pumped in water fed the foliage here on the leeward side of Oahu. The bright green grassy lawns were dotted with coconut trees Deeper green palm fronds swayed in the evening breeze. Bougainvillea and hibiscus flowers were well manicured along the beach walk and brightened the seaside pathway. The Tiki torches were not yet lit. Their deep golden flames would be tickled by a gentle trade winds, and wiggle with delight at sunset.

The sailor ran his fingers through his long hair, pulling it back. He had a navy visor tucked in his back pocket with the identical logo as the shirt. Slipping the hat on, he asked, "Been meaning to ask you, what's with the sticks, Kito?"

"Dey use 'dees fo da Tues-day night luau," Kito replied. "Da Chief - he likes 'dis kind. I just carvin' dis small groove here so he can do da fire."

Together, they borrowed from the monologue of the high Chief at the luau from the closest resort and said together, "...you flick your bics, we rub our sticks." They both chuckled.

Kito stopped carving to look at the sailor's dog. He had a treat of his own in his pocket. He asked, pointing at the hopeful tail waggery, "Can me give Kolohe da snack?"

"Of course, but I think I'm going to have to take him for more walks since he's getting fat." He knelled down to be eye-level with the happy dog. "More walks or less treats, what'll it be boy?"

The dog stopped wagging its tail and cocked its head. Its eyebrows were raised as if it were asking: *Are you crazy? More walks, more walks. More treats and more walks too. Both please.*

"That's what I thought," said the sailor. His smile was white. "Can you say: 'Mahalo' to Kito?" The dog sat at Kito's feet and placed its chin on the old man's knee.

Kito scratched Kolohe's neck under the navy-blue color that had the same *Pau Kahana Cruise Company* block lettered logo. "Who? Who...out..out on boat to-night?" He stuttered some when he asked.

The sailor reached for a manifest in his hip pocket and read the print: "Looks like three Veterans and two from...Hoku Hope Foundation," he replied. He noticed a special note about the couple from the foundation. "An elderly blind man wants to see - the - sun - set." He shrugged his shoulders and stood up.

"Why not," Kito stated as he shrugged his shoulders too. "Dey say dat no see, no smell..." He was making motions with his hands about eyesight and the nose with the hand which held the knife. The sailor backed away. "No hear...no problem. Feel. Feel..." The knife wielding stick carver indicated from the heart that feeling the radiance of the moment was as significant. "You know...feel."

"Maybe. We'll see..." Understanding that the elderly blind man might not actually see, he added, "...or something like that." He thought that Kito would find no peculiarity in the comment anyway.

"By da way, dat mean *star*," He struggled to get the "s" in the word out and again pointed to the heavens above with the air wafting knife. "Star."

"What does?"

"Hoku...dat means 'star' in sky." He returned to the carving with the weathered blade.

"Cool. I'll get it eventually." He looked down at Kito carving at the sticks. You catch anything this morning."

"Naw, da fish fickle. Not even get bite." He paused and looked off into the Marina. "Some brah give me beeeg tip for catchin' Ulua. Go way out to-mor-row...to-mor-row morn-ing. Maui way." He looked at Jacob directly. "Dat da prize fish: Ulua. Bring Kito da big money. Fill Kito's tiny boat." He offered another toothy grin at the prospect.

"How big are they?"

"Eight-y, ninet-y, hun-dwed pounds! Big fish, you know. Big...like you." Kito dropped the stick and held his arms out to show size and Kolohe backed away from the knife's edge, ducked his head, and whined.

They chuckled at the bashful rescue. Kito smiled his genuinely happy-to- be-here-in-this-moment grin and they both looked toward the vessels rocking gently in the marina.

"What do you do if you catch one. A beeeg fish?" Jacob's attempt at Pidgin wasn't convincing. As he said it, he realized it sounded like a foreign language slipping across his tongue. "What do you have...a Louisville Slugger in your boat to..."

Kito looked at Jacob and said it as if it were a secret, leaning toward him, whispering, "Rum."

"What?"

The weathered Japanese fisherman said it louder, but as if there were other ears listening and there were none, "Rum. Like drink." His eyes grew as wide as he could make them, "Make fishes eyes go like dis. Den, knock 'em out." He held the big- and wide-eyed pose for another two seconds, then faked what death might look like as he dramatically tipped his head to the side, stuck his tongue out of the corner of his mouth and squeezed his eyes shut tight.

"Rum knocks them out?"

Kito opened his eyes again and shook his head yes. "No hit fish. Give dem drink. Make eyes go beeeg." He bent over to pick the knife back up from the ground, returning to his work before Jacob appeared.

The marina held slips for two hundred boats consisting of sailboats and trawlers. The commercial fishing boats and the premier power boats occupied the front dock. Lined up in their sixty-foot slips, the dominant color of the hulls was white, with an occasional boat showcasing a unique color. An occasional navy, turquoise, or a light gray boat broke up the long row of commercial crafts.

The sailboats were on the next dock back and throughout the half dozen docks beyond that one, numbering a hundred. Their tall white masts rocked gently with the surface ripple in the protected harbor. Mainsails, jibs, and mizzens found on the sailing boats wore covers of royal blue and navy. Two mega-yachts were safely leashed to several cleats on a separate dock, along a kukui and coconut trees lined peninsula at the marina's edge.

Then, there was Kito's boat. The smallest and most-in-need-of-a-makeover fishing boat, cleated near the end-tie of the C dock. The Japanese fisherman frequented the marina several times per week which was more than most. Some of the dinghies from the largest sailboats challenged it in bow-to-stern size. It cleared twenty feet and bound to a 30-foot slip. Somewhat an eye-sore when compared to the other shiny hulled sailboats and decked trawlers, it was also agile and easy to navigate through the gauntlet of docks to take out into the channel and open ocean.

Marina's occupancy throughout the year was sparse. There were few liveaboards. Many of the floating craft here were visited occasionally for maintenance; occasionally for sun and fun; and occasionally skippered for a peaceful getaway weekend. So, it was quiet.

"Listen, I got to get going, Kito. If I don't see you for a while, Mele Kalikimaka, my friend." The two bumped fists. Kolohe stood and held out his right paw to shake too. Kito reached over and shook Kolohe's paw, giving the dog a toothy smile.

The dog looked at Kito and barked once. It was uncommon for Kolohe to bark like that. Kito and the former money-manager turned power-boat Captain, Jacob Paisley, looked at each other and beamed.

The phone in Jacob's pocket rang as he and Kolohe walked toward the gated security entrance. Through the passage way, they slowed some as they made their way down the ramp to the front-facing dock and their boat.

Jacob could be heard, saying, "Well, that's unfortunate. What do you suggest we do?"

*****

Brian Kekahanamanui's flight on Hawaiian Air touched down in Honolulu at a quarter past two. After he rented a car at the airport, he accelerated on the westbound ramp of the H-1, heading to The Queen's Medical Center in Ewa Beach.

His Uncle's stroke tipped the scale. His Auntie said that *perhaps it was time* for him to visit. Their requests were minimal, so her subtle request had an emphasis. At home in California, Leilani's encouragement for him to visit was all the assurance he needed for this visit. It was not a favored time of the year for Brian to take time away from work and his mainland family. But there was a force multiplier to contend with. Yancy.

Yancy had a connection. Someone which he knew got him released from prison on a technicality. As part of parole, he was to make no contact with Leilani. That didn't happen, apparently. A phone call from a man to Leilani with the words spoken, "I know where you are," was all that was said. And all that was said was enough to cause a pause - a panic for Leilani who had learned a valuable lesson – a need to escalate broadly.

First things first. Second things, second. Uncle first. Yancy second.

Brian's called Laki at home to let her know he had landed and was on his way to the hospital to visit with Uncle. She had her hands full with the kids. While multitasking, small talk questions about the flight, a review of her morning household chores, and what the next couple days held in her schedule were the topics. He asked her no questions and agreed with everything she said. It was code for his mind being preoccupied. She knew him well and laid off the interrogation. It was Laki who booked his flight online, coaxing him to go. The call was brief.

It was his intention to drive to Nanakuli, home on this island, and plan his next move. Perhaps that would include involvement from some of his trusted friends. Or, perhaps going alone was the play. He thought he'd have a five-hour flight to develop his strategy, but he was only thinking of what must have been going through Leilani's mind. The scenario's consumed the time in the air. It seemed like the fastest flight from SAN to HNL ever.

He punched buttons on the radio screen to summon KINE, 105.1 FM, island music time. The Mana'o Company's, Drop Baby Drop, and as luck would have it – it was the chorus. He shrugged his shoulders. *Too bad, doesn't count.*

"Home away from home," he simply said to himself as the car sped past the Aiea and Waimalu exits. He sang along with the island tunes as he made the trek along the middle and west lochs of Pearl Harbor, noticing in the southern distance, above the agricultural fields below, the Skyline rail systems cars which appeared to be slowly and peacefully coasting on the tracks. "Island time," he muttered, acknowledging the costly and lengthy decade it took to bring the light rail into motion.

His phone dinged in his pocket indicating a text message, and even though he shouldn't he did. He reached for the device from his shorts and read the message as the music played and he drove toward the Kunia and Ewa exit ramps.

*****

Jacob was on the dock with his phone in his hand trying to cancel the remaining two reservations from the Hoku Hope Foundation. The vets needed to reschedule for next week. Without Adele, it didn't make sense anyway for a sunset cruise. And then there were the clouds gathering on the horizon anyway.

When he turned around, they were standing behind him, unexpectedly.

"What's the name of this boat?" the thin black man asked.

"The Final Trade," Jacob answered the short black woman as he examined her companion closely. *What's killing him? Paisley wondered.*

Jacob recently began working with a local charity: The Hoku Hope Foundation – as a result of benevolence requests and at the ask of another charter boat owner, a new acquaintance of his in the marina – a catamaran sailboat Captain who took Veterans and their ohana out for sunset sails as a charitable venture. Other charities were occasionally also part of the roster of souls on board.

The assumption: the new passenger was most likely experiencing his last days. And as a result of a life-limiting ailment that had spread to his brain, the deathly thin man had lost his sight. Jacob assumed he was in remission or having a good day, as he looked left of center, but in the direction of Jacob. He seemed chippy. Wearing an Angels ballcap, Ray-Ban sunglasses to hide his eyes, and clothes that were oversize, the man gripped the aluminum rail to balance.

"The Fin-al Trade," Dorothy said it slowly. "Oh, I like that. Not sure what it means exactly, but it sure sounds lovely. Bill, this is a beau-ti-ful boat. All shiny, white and navy blue. Real pretty. Teak woods and accents of brown leather everywhere. And this man keeps his boat clean. Real clean."

Appearing overdressed, or just seeking an opportunity to dress up, she wore a black pleated skirt which fell below her knees and a top which like a polo, beige and flowery print within the fabric.

They were both wearing shoes.

"We don't want to have anyone fall, let's leave our shoes in this box that I'll store under your seats here in the dodger. He pointed to the roof which covered most of the top deck. They both kicked off their slip-on footwear and the captain retrieved it for the Tupperware container.

"Is this a new boat?" she asked.

"As far as boats go, pretty much." Jacob liked her southern accent. It was warm and slow and comforting to listen to her speak. "Your accent. It's very charming. Where are you from, if I you don't mind me asking?"

"I don't mind at all, and thank you. Savannah, Georgia is hometown for me. Have a son that done real well in finance. Course, he wouldn't a wanted me to tell ya that. He'd a say he's just yer' average trader. Bought himself fancy condos all over the place. Live with him 'bout six months, and take care of one of his properties over here durin' the summah'. Work for the Hope Foundation when I can. That's where I met this handsome gentleman, Mr. William Fetch."

She was darling. Jacob steered clear of the comment on trading, but grimaced when she mentioned it. He assessed that she was probably in her sixties or seventies.

"It's so kind of you to offer your service and time to the foundation. They're fortunate to have your service." Jacob was calibrating his audience and thought that perhaps he should dial down on the corporate-like speaking. These seemed like authentic people well beyond caring about doing good for the appearance of doing good. It mattered to them, caring for others. They lived Aloha.

Then, Jacob looked closely at the old man. He was hunched over slightly and gripping the handrail and even though he could not see, appeared to be looking into the direction of the marina's water. He was clearly relying on her guidance for each move made. The old man took each small step with a frailty. Large, dark sunglasses covered his eyes and most of his face. On his head was a black Veteran's hat with stars and bars above the rim. It called out his service in Vietnam. He wore a light grey jacket and long pants that appeared baggy making him look thin and as if he had lost much weight in his sickness.

"Dorothy, William, it's nice to meet to you both."

Paisley looked at Dorothy holding the old man's forearm, guiding him on the ramp toward the yacht. William reached for her hand for reassurance. He smiled in a direction near where Jacob was, sensing direction.

Holding out his frail hand, "Pleased to meet you Captain. Bill. You can call me Bill."

Jacob shook his hand feeling paper thin skin. "Welcome aboard Bill."

"And I'm Dorothy Johnson. How do you do?"

They shook hands. "Dorothy."

He guided them the rest of the way across the ramp and into the craft.

"What else do you see Miss Dorothy?" Bill asked Dorothy.

"Well, lots of boats with masts, and ropes on the masts. A couple of them are taller than the other. One of them looks like it might be strung up with Christmas lights. This boat doesn't have a sail mast. So, no lights."

"This boat...is it a big boat or a little boat?" The old man had no idea what a treasured vessel it was. Any marina would be honored to host the appeal of the pristine yacht, tightly tethered to the dock cleats.

Slightly disappointed, but without any braggadocio tone in his tuck in comment, Jacob added, "It's a luxury power yacht. An Aicon Vivere, a 66-footer. Italian. Cruising speed of 36 knots. Twin inboard Cat engines. Four cabins, two baths. Over 300 gallons of freshwater capacity."

"Sure is pretty," Dorothy repeated. She asked, "What are those two big white bubbles on the top of your boat?"

"Satellites."

Jacob realized the technical specifications here likely meant nothing. So, he explained little in way of specs. "My first mate is not here. Her name is Adele. She is not going to be joining us tonight. She's en route to New York to be with her grand kids and her son for Christmas. It'll just be the four of us, if we are counting Kolohe. I assure you that you'll be in good hands. We'll keep you safe and provide you with an exceptional sunset tonight. Maybe. Looks like some storm clouds are forming. And of course, we have beer and wine, cheeses, fruits and desserts to enjoy on the way. If you don't tell anyone, we might have a Mai Tai drink make an appearance. First question I have for you is, are we off to a good start?"

They both smiled and shook their heads, and acknowledged that it sounded wonderful.

After settling them on a white padded seat facing the captain's seat, Jacob reviewed a few basics about moving around on the yacht, some housekeeping and safety rules. Adele normally explained these hosting functions.

"We will venture out a little less than a nautical mile out from the marina and then could decide whether we want to return or venture out a little further. This, by the way is the best dog on Oahu." He rubbed Kolohe behind the ears. The dog wagged his tail and sniffed Jacob's pocket for a treat. *Nothing. This time: skunked.*

Jacob stated what Kito had mentioned, that the sunset might be stunning this night, the trade winds were still gentle, and they might even see a few dolphins or if they were lucky, humpback whales.

As he said that, he looked at Bill and mentioned that they might even hear them spout as they breached the surface of the Pacific. Bill smiled and in a groveled voice said, "Well, that'd be something, wouldn't it?"

Dorothy looked around at the interior of the craft. "I'll bet this big boat cost you lots of money."

Jacob looked at the two of them and smiled. He flipped a toggle switch and Hawaiian music began to play. An ukulele, a slack-key guitar, a piano, and a soft melody sung by a woman singing about the *moana*, and the *aina*, and the *pikake* flowers. The Bose sound system was crystal clear in clarity. Dorothy smiled, sitting next to Bill, and held the old man's hand.

Kolohe sat panting, on the other side of Bill, looking up at the old man looking off into no particular direction.

"This time of year, we see them just about every day. Most of the snorkel companies and whale watching excursions guarantee it, or your money back. As you know, I don't accept money. So, no money back," Paisley smiled.

"Oh, I almost forgot," Dorothy reached into her purse pulling out a white unmarked envelope. "Captain Paisley, this is for you."

"What's this?"

"It's a tip."

"No. Please, I won't accep..."

She interrupted him and leaned forward to whisper in his ear, "It's a thank you note from Mr. Fetch."

He nodded his head and offered a slight smile, folded the envelope and stuffed it into his back pocket, "Dorothy, Bill. Let's go to sea." Kolohe nuzzled in and smelled the envelope before Jacob slipped it in his shorts.

Jacob, unhooked to bow and spring line clips, tossing them to the dock below. When he throttled the Aicon slowly forward, the craft moved gently from the port and carefully into the gentle waters, toward a green and red flashing beacon. The channel markers, red and green, were fixed into the seabed and didn't bob. Jacob waved to a sailing catamaran that was heading out to sea alongside them. A man and a woman were waving back. The cat revved it's engines and sped ahead of them faster.

Dorothy was the closest to Jacob and asked, "What kind of a boat is that with two bottoms?"

Before Jacob could answer, she was speaking to Bill, talking louder as the wind whipped, "Bill – that boat has two bottoms. It a pretty boat like this one. But, a lot smallah. They're all so pretty."

The double-hulled catamaran was picking up speed. Dorothy squinted to read the name on the back of the vessel. "Captain Paisley, what's the name of that boat?"

"Ho'ohuli."

"What's that mean? It's Hawaiian?"

Jacob had just ventured through the Bishop Museum earlier in the week with Adele. A large piece of artwork that represented Hawaiian culture was named Ho'olhuli, and he knew the answer. "To cause an overturning. A change."

"Oooo." Dorothy smiled in the direction of Bill. And nothing more was said as the distance between the two crafts widened.

As the Aicon broke free into the open waters of the Pacific, and away from the marina's channel markers, Jacob opened up the twin engines mildly causing the bow of the yacht to arc slightly upward. He kept checking on Bill to make sure he was hanging on. This was a new thing, but Paisley was excited to take one of the local charities out to sea to see, smell and experience the beauty beyond the shores of the local resorts.

His new passengers, Bill and Dorothy, were paying more attention to his yellow lab than anything on or outside of the yacht. Jacob frowned and thought that it was odd. But, Kolohe was pretty amazing and entertaining too.

The wind was in their faces. The sun was slipping toward the horizon as the yellow sky began its slow transition to orange. The navy and white yacht gently bounced them as they raced southward, away from the shores of Oahu.

Dorothy was the first to break into a giggle, then Bill, and finally Jacob. Israel Kamakawiwo'ole's *Somewhere Over The Rainbow* began to play on the ship's speakers. Kolohe was wagging his tail while raising his nose to sniff the salty sea air. Apparently the yellow lab was happy too. No matter how often he had taken the craft out to sea over the course of the past year – it was always Paisley's thrill to reach for the ocean's horizon.

As the yacht traveled further out, from 40 fathoms to 80 fathoms and deeper, the water changed color from light and inviting turquoise to deep and mysterious dark blue.

They listened to the Hawaiian songs and talked about the fading coastline of Oahu. Jacob was no expert on the culture or history of the leeward side, but he was trying to answer the few questions they had for him. The value he added to any of the occasional passengers he helped take to see was borrowed information that he tried to commit to memory.

After reaching one nautical mile, the boat turned heading northwest toward 305 degrees on the coordinates. To their southeast was Barber's Point, bearing an occasional flash from the light house. The landmark, named after the brig, *Arthur*, struck the coral reefs represented the southwest tip of Oahu. Their direction was up the leeward coastline, with the lush greenness of Nanakuli and Waianae valleys interrupted by Ma'ili Point, acting as another landmark for west coast traveler. In the distance, with some effort, the taillights from passenger cars slowly moving up Farrington Highway could be seen. They were making their way home to the beach towns on the west side. Bill, the old man saw none of it. He looked in the opposite direction and smiled.

Apart from two other vessels, they had this stretch of the mysterious Pacific to themselves.

Jacob offered them both a Kona beer and Maui-based wine – but they both opted for a water instead. When it came to the sea-friendly platter that Adele assembled, they declined the food as well. It was unusual since it was complimentary, and they were the first to decline. He thought that Bill might have a dietary restriction due to medicine and the Dorothy was too kind to eat without him.

While they were out, the thunderhead that he had occasionally been monitoring to the southwest had nearly doubled in size. He throttled the engines which were churning them forward at 12 knots down a little in their destination less cruise and in a moment of considering a next move, the smile faded away from his face. *Hmmm, don't like the looks of that*, Jacob thought to himself and winced at the thought of turning back so soon.

Kolohe who had been a little more attentive to the storm clouds rapidly gathering shifted his eyebrows to express a dog's sentiments of concern too.

Jacob brought the engines to a slow churn, to inform Dorothy and Bill that they might need to divert heading out further, and potentially cut the trip short. He'd state the obvious, that this storm blew in from nowhere, was extremely unusual, and that they could venture back out toward Honolulu if it looked like the weather would cooperate to the east. This was after they trekked back to the safety beacons of the channel.

When the hum from the engines quieted, the music could be heard again. A man's voice gently sang about the Aloha spirit and the beauty of the islands.

He turned around to find Bill and Kolohe looking pointlessly into the direction of where the sun would set if there were no threatening clouds, but there was no presence of Dorothy. It was as if the old man were enjoying the rock of the boat on the water, the wind picking up, and the music more than anything else.

"Did Miss Dorothy make her way to the head...to the ladies room?" he asked Bill.

"Who's Dorothy?" The fragile old-timer took his Veteran's hat off, and Jacob realized a familiarity. "Yes, she went into the cabin below, she whispered to me that she wasn't feeling one hundred percent."

Perhaps it was the trimmed hair hidden under the hat, perhaps it was the shape of his forehead, and perhaps it was putting the presence together. Then, he took off the sunglasses and his eyes were white with exceptionally small irises and pinpoint pupils. It was alarming and the old man's eyes were difficult to continue to look at.

What it wasn't was an old man named Bill Fetch after all.

Ruby smiled at Jacob and said, "My dad used to have that look on his face. Usually when I did something wrong. But, really, I cannot see. Truly. So, I'm just assuming you have that look."

"You're here under some false pretenses mister." Jacob looked at him closer. "You've lost, what, 30 pounds since I saw you last?"

"Something like that. Cancer can be a little bitch. But, let me fess up here. I'm not really blind." Ruby reached his thumb and index fingertip into his eyeballs to pinch and remove the contacts which presented the disquieting display. He tossed them overboard.

"That's much better," Ruby said as he stood up straight. The true whites of his eyes were pink and bothered from the contact distraction hidden behind the large glasses.

"A costume, of course. And...and...is that what it is? Cancer? To be candid, and since I like to believe that I know you... You look like shit."

No reply was immediately given. Soaking up a silent moment of Jacob's judgment, Ruby just smiled and rubbed the top of his head with both of his old hands. Then, finally said, "Well, I'm sorry about that."

"I'm not surprised to see you, you know. I've been wondering if and when, mostly when, we might meet again. So, there isn't a look of disbelief on my face like you might think."

"Alright then. Aloha – as they say."

"So, what'll it be this time? Another heart attack? Can't have a stabbing and run? What's the calamity encounter going to be this time? We're not going to sink, are we?"

"No, no, no...nothing like that, you just relax for a change, alright?"

"I have. I did just like you suggested. I found a zip code: 96707 that seemed to fit. I'm here because of you."

"Well..." Ruby looked in the direction of Jacob but added nothing else.

"Why me?" Jacob asked. Why do you think we met and what is it about me that you've focused upon? I feel like, I don't know, some sort of project."

Without any hesitation, Ruby replied, "Absorbtion."

"What?"

"You're exceptional at gathering the detail and processing it. You're a money-maker. You, you're best in class, sir. But you're still an underclassman. People are drawn to you, but they don't stick with you. Other than...well, we'll get to that."

Jacob looked at Ruby for more. "Can you say more? I'm having difficulty coming up with a conclusion from just that."

"There are lots of folks that float through a lifetime, like on a cloud. They make some difference. They add and subtract. But, they mostly just float." Ruby motioned his hand toward the sky. "You have a gift of influence. You can absorb something completely, interpret it, and make a change happen."

"When we met at that bar on Wall Street..." Jacob began but was cut short.

"Sure. You said if this happens, I'd owe you an explanation. And I'm giving it to you. But, it really is just that. You don't float. You have a way of grounding yourself and yielding differences. Few people really do. Think about it this way. History books are filled with people that have captured a moment or moments. They manipulated our course. There are a finite number of men and women that actually do that." Ruby paused before saying more, "This is your 'if'".

"Where is this coming from?" Jacob was puzzled by the surge of explanations from Ruby.

"I'm in a position to transition knowledge to you. You'll act as a sentinel and share it with others when the time is right. There aren't a vast number of us, but there are others that have the capacity to make a difference."

"That doesn't necessarily answer my question."

"Answers your question enough for now. I'll say it again. There are a finite number of people that can change the course of history. I was delivered to you for this very moment. Just as you'll move carefully from one point to the next to influence what may come."

Jacob didn't know what to say. The words stumbled out of his mouth, "Everyone...everybody matters...and every single person...makes a difference...in some sort of way."

"This is true. But, to discover – to sail to an unchartered territory – to deliver a difference, there aren't as many of us as you might think. And you didn't used to say those kinds of things, Mr. Paisley. You used to judge more, consider less, collaborate even less. It was purely more about you...than us. You've changed. And..."

"Are you describing the difference between being ordinary and being famous?"

Ruby stood to place his hand on Jacob's shoulder. "Listen, you're a smart guy. Just offhand, how many mathematicians can you think of?"

"Perhaps a dozen."

"OK, good. How about scientists?"

Jacob thought for a few seconds, "I'd say thirty or forty. More with more time to think about it."

"How many disciples did Jesus – "

"Twelve!"

"Nice. Number of canonized Catholic Saints?"

Jacob thought for a moment, "Uh, hell I don't know..."

"Okay," Ruby smiled and said, "Maybe we'll forget about that one for now. How many influential people in finance?"

Quick to reply, Jacob blurted out: "Hundreds! *Thousands!*"

"That was an easy one – that's your industry. How about US Presidents?"

"I know that there are forty-something. I could probably list thirty, maybe thirty five."

"That's not bad. You see my point. There are a limited number of people that are at the top of mind for true change."

Jacob had a puzzled look on his face. "But, you aren't page one news. I'm not trying to be disrespectful, but you might not even be page sixteen news – other than jumping out of hospital windows, landing on cars below." He smiled at the moment well behind him now, but quickly grimaced at the thought of Ruby lying on the hood. "You make change happen, yet you aren't..."

"Famous? Jacob, what I do...this...isn't about famous. Famous is for amateurs. This is about making a true and meaningful difference. Sometimes...much of the time...that happens behind the scenes. More than you think. The kind of change I'm talking about...it cannot be done by being well-known or famous." Ruby shook his head.

For the first time, Jacob began to understand that the product Ruby was selling wasn't something previously known. He needed to better understand.

"Sentinel? What's that?"

"Not the best word for it. But we'll get to that later. Let me continue. Here it is - take that number of people that you can remember for anything that they've done brilliant or otherwise. Add to it, the number of people you know. This is your lever of influence. What they've done, the good and the bad has left an impression on you. Now, add to that group of known or remembered people an equal number of influences that guided you to the point you're at today. These are your enablers. I connect the two. I'm playing a part of the thing in between, an agent of watching and an agent of change. A bridge - to connect the gaps in human potential. Like a said, there are a finite number of us."

"Ruby – this is way out there. I'm not as judgmental as you might think I am. But this is far-fetched..."

"It's not your place, it isn't our place to judge. It's important not to. What needs to happen will happen."

"And I need to accept a role? That I'm not willing or understanding the part I need to play – "

"Jacob, your choice to do the right thing isn't always yours. Sometimes it's just innate. You do it."

"What kind of knowledge did you – "

Ruby interrupted him again, "None. You'll know. It's in you already." He pointed in the direction of the dark clouds, "That way.."

"We're not going near the horizon; you whack doodle old man."

"Let's just sit and watch it for a while." Ruby patted to the seat next to him, for Jacob to come sit. "Please?"

"I need to check in on Dorothy – your co-conspirator who..."

"She'll be fine man. Give her a minute, I'm sure she'll be back up refreshed."

"The wallowing does tricky things to..."

"Sit down? Please."

Jacob looked around, anticipating an event. "We can do that." He turned off the slow-going humming engines. The boat wallowed more as the slow coast came to a complete stop. He steadied himself and sat next to Ruby.

Kolohe jumped on the cabin bench and sniffed his pocket for another treat.

The music continued to play. A woman sang about Haleakala, a man sang about a highway in the sun, and a pair of men sang a melody about Hawaiian eyes. Adele liked the melodies and made the mix for Jacob to play for the sunset excursions. The craft slowly rocked while they sat, saying nothing, listening to the island music looking toward the darkening colors where the deepening grey clouds in the skies met the mercury waters.

Ruby broke the silence. "Say, I've been listening to this Hawaiian music all week. It's good and all. I like it, but could we change the channel?"

Jacob tossed a remote on the bench next to Ruby. "What do you have in mind?" He looked at it and picked it up handing it back to Jacob.

"Don't know just something different. You pick it."

Jacob punched a couple buttons to summon an alternative rock station. A moment of silence was filled with the radio reverting to auxiliary play. The device clicked and Aerosmith's, *Living on The Edge,* played.

"That's odd", Jacob said out loud but to himself. He turned the unit off and back on and repeated the steps for the FM radio to play. But the same results were produced. The auxiliary play returned to the elder rockers singing about living on the edge. The device had a mind of its own. He turned down the volume.

The ocean's swell picked up and they were rocking more from the surf's energy.

Jacob flipped a toggle switch and the twin engines obeyed. The outer Pacific was still portside. They were slowly moving further up Oahu's western coast at a gentle pace, away from one of the approaching thunderheads. Jacob had become skilled at dodging what the locals called 'ili'i li'i'. Rain. The engines noise seemed to fall silent as the first pearl of lightning and delayed thunder rumbled from the direction of the growing storm clouds. One noise displaced another.

Kolohe tucked his tail between his legs, lowered his head, and whined.

Ruby reached down feeling his way to the lab and stroked the crown of his head. "You're a good boy. All will be alright."

The worried dog whined a little but seemed to be comfortable with the old man and licked his hand.

*****

Brian was pleasantly surprised and was excited to share the new news with Laki. A call to her was met with first her debriefing him on their little monster's behavior at the mall, then their meltdown at the grocery, followed by the spilled chocolate milkshake in the car.

"Just so you know...they're *never* getting another McDonald's milkshake in the drive through again," she spoke in a feisty manner.

"You're cute when you're mad, you know that?" he tried to calm her.

"I'm serious. They played me. They said they'd be careful. Those little liars. If they weren't so cute and looked like their father, I'd drop them off at the fire station."

"Why the fire station?"

"Safe-haven law. I can do that if I think it's for their safety, like me not wanting to kill them, and get away with it. Baby Moses laws. You know, they'll be wards of the great state of California."

Brian thought he knew his wife thoroughly and pictured her thinking of what to say next while twirling her long brunette locks of hair while lying on the couch in their tidy living room couch. He pictured her in a cute top, tight jean with her toes wiggling in the air...listening intently to his every word.

What she was doing was laying on the couch – only she had a bag of half-eaten salt and vinegar potato chips resting between her breasts. The house was in a state of unrecognition. She was sporting unmatching sweatpants. Her ponytail was tucked inside a hoodie. And the mute was on the TV, hiding Real Wives of Orange County from him while she ranted.

Almost the same.

"I'll sell their things, then we can move to Rancho Santa Fe..."

Brian interrupted her, "I have something to tell you. It's Yancy."

Laki stopped her tirade and asked seriously, "Yeah...go on..."

"There was a technicality. He got released and - there was a mistake of some sort, and it got sorted out...and now." Brian was choked up, saying the rest, composed, but emotional, "He's back in jail, Leilani is safe."

She held her hand to her chest and the bag of chips jostled, "Oh that is good news. Oh, thank God."

"He's not going to get to her."

"So, he made just that one phone call to intimidate her? No other threats?"

"Yeah, something like that."

"And your uncle, how's he?" she asked.

"He's doing better, regaining some of his strength. I saw him today and will go back tomorrow with Auntie and maybe Leilani."

"Oh, honey – that's such good news, so good."

"Still want to ditch the kids?"

"Naw, I'm over it. They'll get Cheerios in the morning instead of pancakes though."

"You're harsh. Poor little rugrats. Give them a hug from me when you see them tomorrow and tell them I'll bring them some malasadas from Leonard's when I come home."

"Oooo, and don't forget momma – your Polynesian sweetie wants a haupia."

He knew that the coconut filling was her favorite. "Of course. Couple more days here."

Laki wanted what was best for him. "Take as long as you need. But no longer than two days, or you'll return childless," she teased further. "What are you going to do tomorrow?"

Brian thought of the beach walk run he had been planning, "The surf is calling."

"Surfing?"

"No, a swell is coming in, but 'no' to surfing just yet. I'm just going to get a few miles in out at Ko Olina Beach Park."

"Love that place." Laki imagined them watching their keiki playing in the lagoon's sand while they propped up on a couple beach chairs in the shade.

"I'll get out early if I can. Looks like a huge storm is brewing right now though. It's dark out there, huge storm clouds. Small craft warnings were just issued. Looks like the weather person ambushed us. They were calling for partly cloudy, then mostly cloudy weather. No sunset tonight."

Laki didn't say anything as she listened to some rusting coming from the kids' rooms, "I hear a stirring in their zip code."

"Okay, baby. I'll call you tomorrow."

"Alright. Love you."

"Love you too, honey." Brian ended their call. He'd been away from home less than a day and missed his bride already. His thoughts transitioned to his current surroundings at his Uncle and Aunty' s place in Nanakuli, in the room he grew up in, and how dreams of playing football filled his dreams while lying in the bed he once again slept in that night. High school, collegiate, professional. The well-intended fantasies consumed the younger Brian's fancies, leading him from here to there to meet Laki and build a life and family of his own – and eventually back to this moment.

Leilani. He thought about the relief that his beloved cousin, Leilani, must have felt when she learned of Yancy's timely return to the slammer.

I get it, hitting someone in football. It's an aggressive game, a tough as nails bruising sport. But...but...how in the hell...creature to creature...do you harm someone so lovely, so sweet, so selfless, so giving? How would you...could you...do something like that to a girl, a woman so precious?

He imagined Yancy midfield and helpless - Brian geared up for aggression, game face on...coming at him full force...in a mad dash to hit, hurt, halt. That was it. Brian wanted to stop him from afflicting pain and distress ever again. *Creature to creature – why was hurting Leilani your option?*

Brian laid down on the bed where the dreams were forged, where the decisions of his 'better elsewhere' were pondered, where the thoughts of his potential were ruminated. While lofting the fiction of his yesteryear's across his rehearsed illusions, his eyes became heavy and he fell asleep dreaming only of flying with the wind.

15

Cooking Codes

Ruby was not as frail as when he walked onto the yacht. An act of deception. Academy award material with the hat and the glasses and the massive weight loss. He sat in a seat near Jacob as they were slowly cruising. "You've lived an imperial life, my friend. Sovereign, preeminent. Do you not think this?" He leaned closer to the now Captain and placed his hand on Jacob's shoulder.

"Is that what you'd call it?" Jacob closed his eyes for a brief moment. Dozens of thoughts about what he had done within the financial sector vividly appeared and vanished.

There were the Yankees games with the PPCM team. It consisted of a suite filled with young traders, still in their suit jackets, ties loosened. They were all accompanied by beautiful women on their arms. They were bragging about their performance bonuses while casually watching the games. Moments of forced smiles and artificial laughing at their own jokes or each other's misfortunate trades. Copious amounts of booze. Food, an abundant spread - too much food really. Jacob could see himself as the last one in the suite at one game, taking a cell phone call about a deal. Looking at the leftover food that would go to waste. He saw himself later walking out of the game to meet with Victoria for a nightcap.

Naughty Victoria. Back then, there were the private jet flights to Las Vegas. A nightclub or two. Night would become early morning, but before the clubs closed. Victoria, in a silver dress. Gold sparkly confetti falling from the ceiling, covering the two hundred young people on the dance floor. The music grinding a beat. Jacob sitting on a red and black velvet bench watching her dance with another woman provocatively while he was texting about an initial purchase offering. She would occasionally look over at him to make sure he was stimulated by her advances. Cards and roulette and craps. The gambling. The penthouse suite. The sex.

He thought then about the sex-filled trips with Victoria in the Caribbean. Then, the skiing at Beaver Creek. Sex in the limo. The lavish dinners at dozens of rooftop restaurants in dozens of cities. Seafood towers, limitless bottles of Cristal, making the most noise in any establishment they visited. He thought about business meetings in Hong Kong, Davos, London, Frankfurt, Paris, Dubai. He thought about how he was anticipated within each city. A concierge using his name at each hotel - *"Bonjour. Welcome back to the Four Seasons, Mr. Paisley. Your room is awaiting. Our finest, for you, of course."*

His thoughts drifted to his suits. His tailor at Barney's. The walk in closet for his suits. Neatly arranged, color coded. Victoria, naked, taking off his tie and undressing him in the closet.

Jacob was frowning. He thought of the Ferrari. Spotless black. The smell of the leather steering wheel in his hands. The way the engine purred. Teaching Victoria to drive it in the Connecticut countryside. Cringing at the gears grinding.

An imperial life, Ruby called it. Sovereign.

It wasn't better. It was just different from anyone else, from everyone else. It was different from the other ninety nine percent. *What gets compromised when we get conditioned?* Jacob reflected on that for a moment.

Then, he thought about Adele. And he smiled. He felt the muscles on his face shift. The next day – that conversation he had with her after meeting homeless Mary and her daughter homeless Marcy. That cold December night. The one where he began to change. The phone call to Adele to coordinate moving some of the money their way for the purpose of helping others. He thought about simpler things and found favor in them.

The guilty pleasures weren't completely behind him however. He also thought about picking out the yacht with Adele. As they were talking with the yacht broker, she said, "*It's one of the biggest boats in the marina, but that's never stopped you before. If you think that's what you need...*"

"*It isn't just for me, it's to share.*" She gave him a hug, and his heart warmed.

The thought about the evaluation of his life, and about how nothing was as it seemed when this man appeared, and about how things reached a disturbing conclusion frightened him.

"You went somewhere just there, didn't you?" Ruby asked.

Jacob snapped out of his trip down the lane of memory. "With the way you say it, you make it sound like it's over." A minute of silence passed by, "Silence?" He was seeking a reply with uneasiness.

"As they say, it is what it is," the man paused, "until, it isn't." He looked at his hands, rubbing them. In some strange way, to Jacob, it appeared he was admiring the work they had done in days past. "But, to answer, no. I don't think so. I believe it's just beginning."

"How do you mean?"

"At any point in our lives, what we do next is the most important thing. It's what we do first toward things that change our course as well as others. Perhaps that's why God so easily forgives us. Because there's an eternal line of "what's next" just a waiting for action."

Jacob thought for a minute and asked a question. "The first version of you couldn't smell. The next version of you couldn't hear so well. Now, played a part that you couldn't see. Does the pattern go on from here?"

"You gotta' ask yourself what senses *you're* missing?" Ruby was looking over Jacob's shoulder at the storm clouds on the horizon.

"I wouldn't say I'm missing too much."

"Maybe you're missing what you're missing. Perhaps your sense of wonder, what you are truly capable of with the life you have...perhaps that's missing right now. Have you ever thought that the process of thought that got you from one point to another, also led you away from where you could have gone?"

Jacob needed clarity, and deftly replied, "Say what? I don't fall for regret."

Ruby stood back up and looked into the direction of a blast of wind that just brushed across the water. "Of course you don't. Self-made man of money. What made you a brilliant businessman was enough, once upon a time, to make you a brilliant businessman. And at the same time, it set out to be your demise because it wasn't up to your potential. You're capable of much more."

"I disagree. I met the challenge. Finance was my fit, my destiny. I met the mark. I was successful, then I simply wasn't. End game."

Ruby smiled, "I disagree too, my friend..." Then, the smile melted from his face, and for the first time he frowned, "...with what you just shackled yourself with. Listen to yourself. And not in a one dimensional, methodical, linear way. Your limit is your imagination, and your effort to get you to wherever it is you want to go."

"Ruby, I am a retired capital asset manager. I made people money with money. And in a few cases..." he shrugged with one shoulder, "I helped them lose it. But I made many more very, very, *very* rich. It's over, and I'm stepping down from seeking my "potential" as you call it."

"Retired?" Ruby chuckled. "Guys like you, adrenaline junkies, you don't sunset yourselves. You take a little break and get back on a different bucking bronco."

"This is a form of retirement. It's not what I'm used to but, I am seeking a new line of work here. And I do have a sense of wonder. I took a zip code on a cocktail napkin from a bartender in Manhattan, and fell in love with this island in the middle of the Pacific. Logistically, Hawaii is one of the most isolated places in the world. I'd call that wonder."

"Wander. Not wonder."

"What?" Jacob didn't follow.

"If you're not wondering, you're wandering." Ruby was grinning again, and added, "I see we have a little more work to do here. Let's go out a little further."

Jacob looked in the direction of the increasing wind and clouds. More thunder and flashes of lightened threatened them. "Whatever. I think it's been quite a change in the last year. Two years actually. It's been a year since I've worked. In contemplation, I've remembered some of the things I'd forgotten." Jacob looked out at the sea, and was amazed to see the storm clouds forming heads larger than he'd ever seen. "I've remembered that there is always the element of luck to consider when evaluating one's own brilliance or accomplishments. We're really just lucky to be alive and in the moment which we're in. Or unlucky. Our results, my results were more random than I should take credit for." He spoke to hear the words over the gentle splashing of the waves, or the soft humming of the outboards, or silence.

"What else is it that you remember?" Ruby asked.

Jacob looked at his shipmate and took a step in his direction. "Well, I do believe you can say that delivering your very best, producing those pinnacle performances, occasionally serve as an inhibitor to a man's potential. Many would say that when I was in New York, I lived at the top, the very best that a man could live. But, most of the time I lost my way. Greed took a foothold. 'Wanting more of whatever I pursued.' was my lodestone. I wanted better. Better became an enemy to the wonderful life that I had."

Ruby chuckled and agreed that the imperial life, was a weigh-station to other moments such as this one with the sparkling sunset which he could not see but could feel. "Jacob, becoming less of who you were is becoming more of who you are. Remember that. You live through a lot of memory. You know, I heard once that ninety percent of what we think about is what we've thought about. That only leaves ten percent for new experiences. How 'bout that? We demonize ourselves when we are too focused on the past. The horizon on the sea, that flatline that lies ahead... That flatline that we don't explore often enough, that's just the beginning of our potential. There's an explorer in each of us. Perhaps we'll never fully achieve our potential. But, perhaps we don't really consider or care for discovering it. Think about potential this way – the moment you're born, you're a winner."

"Aren't you beating your borrowed point to death?" Jacob looked up at the rocking mast and then at the storm clouds.

"Let's just say that each life is a one in a million miracle that can go generate another million miracles."

"So, what's the real topic here?" Jacob asked.

"Each life, each one in a million outcomes, can deliver another million impressions.

"It's about derivatives."

"You could say that. It's all about the small basis-point transitions from one point to another," Ruby said. He went on, "Some folks say, 'things, they happen for a reason'. Well, perhaps it isn't as much about a predetermined purpose as it is that there's a reason things happen."

"Lots of little one-in-a-million occurrences, random factors, satisfied sense-of-wonder attainments, they led us to where we are, but are just a point along the way to where we can go," Jacob summed it up, while looking to the portside. It was time to return. He'd had this conversation with Adele many times before. Team Logic.

"Exactly. Consider that. Each chance you can." Ruby rubbed the back of his neck with his hands and took another deep breath of the sea air.

"Official business. This is your Captain speaking. No sunsets tonight, Ruby. You wanted to see it. Sorry. This is your unofficial wish, unfulfilled. It would have been in this direction. The direction of those storm clouds - that don't' usually head in our direction - from that direction - but they are tonight. No good, by the way."

One bank of gray storm clouds was forming quickly and appeared dense with thick mist. Jacob marveled at its magnitude. "We're going to have to steer clear of the weather ahead, Ruby. It's closing in fast. Can't say I've seen a storm like that before. But I haven't been here that long. Time to head in." Jacob shrugged, then steered away as the clouds formed quickly and chased the retreating yacht.

"Smells like rain," Ruby said.

"Looks like trouble!" Jacob quickly replied.

Ruby interrupted, "Looks like opportunity! Can we go out just a little further?" He asked and gave Jacob a big toothy smile as the salty air blasted the yacht, swaying the mast to the side and rocking the craft with force.

"No, I'd stick with trouble. And sorry friend, unfortunately, no. We need to turn back. Time to return."

"What do you say we go venture into the unknown?" Ruby was holding on to the railing as the yacht rocked. "One more time. How about that way?" He outstretched his arm, and as the power yacht rocked in the increasing waves, his finger pointed as much up as over and into no particular direction out to the horizon.

"That is not the direction we'll be heading."

"You say. Captain Jacob Columbus Paisley. Traded the concrete jungle for the middle of the Pacific. Boo-yah!" Ruby was looking toward Jacob, bracing himself from the building rock of the waves and chuckling.

As Jacob steered the yacht away from the approaching storm toward the harbor, the ship went in the opposite direction – toward the storm.

Paisley looked at Ruby, winced, and looked away toward the dark clouds ahead. He looked at the forming calamity that loomed ahead and said it out loud, but mostly to himself: "Fuck me...here we go again."

"Fear may be our companion, never our master Mr. Paisley!"

*****

She had been crying. Holding the baby, rocking it in its light blue swaddle, Kerri tried to wipe her cheeks with one hand using a corner of a fuzzy baby blanket. Seated in the aft, the back of the boat, she watched him out of the corner of her eye as she cared for the small infant's next need.

It whimpered while sucking on the pacifier but was falling asleep.

Cutter took a break from screaming at her while he used the remainder of the fire extinguisher to squelch the remaining smoke from the galley. One cloud was replaced by another, with the dry chemical soon settling – trading black smoke for white. The ammonium phosphate base had no smell, but the oak wooden trim from inside the small sailboat did.

A thirty-five-foot Sloop at sea was no place for a two-month-old baby, nor a meth lab. Filled with a host of dangerous chemicals, battery acid, phosphorus, benzene, sulfuric acid, and iodine crystals among others – Cutter had traded the small-time pushing in Manhattan for minor-league drug production in the Pacific. His buy-in was for the small craft and materials procured off the books, from random Sand Island manufacturers and importers. His new product, methamphetamine for Oahu was his concoction of a new market for the cartel – and a by-product from watching reruns of Breaking Bad.

The problem was that he was no Walter White. He was no chemist and for that matter lacked no knowledge of compounds, agents, bonds, alkalines, or reactions. A periodic table to Cutter was a table used periodically. Perhaps he shouldn't have cut that class from his schedule in the two years of high school he did attend, trading it for botany.

Kerri looked quickly in the cabin at Cutter huffing and puffing and knew he was angered with her more than ever before. She should have turned off the propane when asked. The baby was crying. It was nerve-wracking. Her sleep deprived nights had caught up with her. How do parents do it?

That was Crazy Kerri talking. She'd been away for a while. But now, now she was back and wanted what was hers. It was her turn. And the baby was in the way. Crazy Kerri wouldn't be locked away for seven months again. She couldn't be contained, and it was just a matter of time until she had her fix. Not now, but soon.

"God damn it, Kerri! You're lucky we're alive!" He was angry. So angry. He pulled her hair, "Did you hear me? Or are you not paying attention again - like you weren't earlier?"

She felt strands depart the back of her head where his fist grabbed tightly, pulling her skull backward while holding the baby tightly. It murmured.

"You're hurting me...again." Her face was looking up into the darkening sky. *We should not be out here,* she thought to herself but didn't dare say it out loud. Acknowledging that his project was beyond his scope wasn't a job for Kerri. But Crazy Kerri could pull that conversation off.

It wasn't completely her fault. Cutter did ask her to turn off the propane at the circuit breaker, but he said that he had it at the valve – and apparently didn't. Neither of them shut off the energy source, as a match was lit inside to melt the solvent. Again – Heisenberg wasn't at the helm here, Cutter was.

"Well...what are we going to do?" She finally found courage to ask for the way forward.

"If I can get the engine working, we'll motor in and figure something out."

Cutter was no more a marine mechanic than a meth chef. He couldn't maintain, let alone fix a problem. He beat things with a hammer until they worked. His knowledge of sailing was minimal, not knowing the difference between a Sloop, or a Ketch or a Yawl. There was no reason for a sailboat, other than it came at a steep discount and provided them with a small space to cook in a private location – out at sea. The coincidence was that a 'Cutter', as in the name of a boat with a single mast like a Sloop, was a configuration name for a small sailing vessel. When he saw that, he was in the market for a sail opposed to a small fishing boat - but settled on the Sloop for the price. With the vessel came a small dinghy that hosted a small horsepower motor.

He did not know a great deal about rigging, knot-work, or sail types - or much at all in the effort to perform next-level maintenance or upkeep. He did know some boating basics and was learning enough to motor out and motor back into the marina keeping his secret and illegal operation, a secret. As well, he and Kerri did not know how to turn off the propane collectively or safely either. But he did know how to work a fire extinguisher and drained them both as he overpowered the fire in the galley. The white residue was everywhere inside.

The crying continued. This time it was not Kerri's, but the baby's ear-piercing wailing.

"Jesus, does that thing ever stop?"

"It's just an innocent little baby," she tried not to agitate either of them, speaking quietly to Cutter while looking at the baby who was not taking the pacifier. "He's hungry again. I'll feed him and he'll stop crying." The child continued to cry while she reached for the bag filled with an arsenal of baby items including the premade formula. *A ditch bag for an infant*, she thought as she navigated the contents inside.

Crazy Kerri and Cutter had an agreement: the kid has got to go. It wasn't Cutter's. It was Boomers. The small black baby stopped screaming for a moment, then began again, louder. She thought she'd ask him again to hold the child while she warmed a bottle but knew the response would be the same: *Not my kid. Not my problem.* She changed her mind and continued to search through the bag retrieving the formula herself. It was getting darker and harder to see.

They were idle, rocking gently in the waves and wind. The light pollution from Oahu was in the distant north and a storm was out at sea in the west.

Cutter was rustling around inside the cabin of the small boat, trying to stabilize himself against the increasing swell as he searched for something. He had cut the main power at the circuit breaker earlier as if the fire was electrical. As he flipped the main, some of the outboard lights came on but not all the power was restored. Down below in the small engine room, a beam from a flashlight flitted around. Once it steadied, the sound began again. Metal to metal, accompanied with grunting, the beating of the diesel engine with a hammer continued.

16

Burnished

The vessel had a mind of its own and did not follow his command. It headed straight toward the approaching thunderstorm instead of back to the area it had come from. The more he tried to steer away from the storm, the more it accelerated on the water's surface.

Ruby was shouting into the wind. Paisley couldn't hear what he was saying. His laughter was as if he lived to challenge this storm at this moment. Water drenched them as the craft crashed into ten foot waves spraying the salt water, the hard winds blowing the ocean spray, and the torrent rain pounding relentlessly. It was all they could do to keep their eyes open.

"Sum up some courage that you don't know you have." He screamed as the lightening and claps of thunder began to strike closer, with a deafening force, and more frequent. The beating rain was fierce and continuous. "Crazy good. Right?"

Jacob looked out into the skeins of the unrelenting downpour. The stormy sky found its voice, cracking with flashes of light and quick, deep, rambling echoes of thunder. Flash, boom. Flash, boom. Flash, boom.

Out of fear, Kolohe started barking at the wildness of Ruby and at the storm. He kept performing the wet-dog-shake to avoid the soaked coat, unsuccessfully.

Jacob dug through the deck for ponchos. It was really too late, they were wet from surface to skin. It wasn't cold, but much cooler than normal and uncomfortable. Ruby felt the pointed hood of the rubber poncho and joked that he must be on the wrong ship, because the weather-wear slickers resembled Klan members robes when the wind blew the point of the hood upward. Jacob looked at the bright yellow ponchos with glow-in-the-dark neon green piping running along the arms and quickly discarded that thought.

"Oh God, Dorothy!" Jacob shouted. He pictured her below holding on with all her might as the bow of the boat took the pounding waves. "How in the hell could I have left her alone so long?" The storm-entertainer that was Ruby, screaming in the wind, had distracted him from checking in on the one other soul on board, a Captain's chief responsibility. With much of his strength, he held on to the aluminum rails and began shouting her name as he took small steps toward the parlor below. Jacob steadies himself at the below deck cabin door.

"Dorothy!"

There was no answer. He anticipated a response of some sort from the elderly woman. She appeared tough but did not seem to have the go it alone toughness. The whipping wind speed and the increasing sound from the pounding rain onto the fiberglass of the boat made slight sounds impossible to hear.

Again, "Dorothy?" No sound from below. Perhaps she had fallen. Louder, he shouted down below, "Dorothy, you alright?"

The yacht was built in 2003. Its home port was the slip at the Ko Olina Marina. Aicon's were among the finest yachts built. The care that Paisley's ship was given from nose to rudder, starboard to port, was meticulous. It was getting thrashed and pounded in the storm. The waves it had to overcome were not what even the best sixty-foot yachts were designed for. It creaked and cracked from the violent surf. Several empty dock ropes rung against the aluminum handrails. The carabiners attaching the ropes were clanging with the uneven wind gusts.

Kolohe could no longer maintain balance. He was tossed into the captain's cubby and stayed there barking out of fear. "Ruff. Ruff-ruff. Ruff-ruff-ruff." One bark, then two, then three. One bark, then two, then three. He stopped only to occasionally lick at the deck where water had pooled.

The Aicon had never been tested like this, ever. Some mysterious force caused the windows within the enclosed cabin to fly open. Jacob raced to close what he could. He was frightened. From flourishing to fear, he did everything he could to maintain his grip and balance.

"I'm going below for a few minutes!" Ruby had to shout to be heard. With the rainwater in his face, he somehow managed to slowly creep his way to the steps below inching his way toward the hull. Jacob had to return to the helm to attempt control and couldn't possibly help him and found it odd that Ruby moved slowly yet was steady.

The wind would not stop howling. The rain was so thick he could not see ten feet in front of him.

Ruby was now below deck, with Dorothy for no more than three minutes before Jacob abandoned the captain's chair briefly to check on them. Maybe she fell. Maybe he hit his head.

Ruby shook at the aft cabin door as Jacob entered, startling him. "Only three! I could only get three! You'll know later!" The harder he tried to shout, the less Jacob could understand him.

"What are you talking about? What?"

"Three. You'll know." Ruby held up three fingers.

"How's Dorothy?"

"What?"

"Dorothy! Is she okay? Down below..."

There was no understanding here. Not now. Just rain and wind and a very frightened dog that was clutching on to a life preserver with both of it's front paws, barking incessantly into the wind.

Lightning and thunder drowned out the reply, and Jacob had to rush back to the wheel, knowing that no one was safe, including himself.

The music from the sound system continued to play. Louder, it replayed *Living on The Edge*. Jacob tried to turn it down, but it played even louder. The more he adjusted the volume knob, the louder the music hailed. There was no control in the situation. The rain pounded on the deck and echoed from the cabin. The wind howled louder than Jacob had ever heard before. His ears were crackling with the noise.

The largest swell and water on the floor was what caused the fall. When Jacob fell he hit his head. The painful *thunk* against the captain's window frame caused the unconsciousness. His temple took the blunt *whack*. A quick and acute pain shot to the point of impact. It was so excruciating, it numbed his ability to move his arms and his feet were numb. Before he blacked out, he fell. And before darkness surrounded Jacob Paisley, lying on the deck floor, he knew that things were dire. His final thought was *that's it then*.

17

An Unexpected Discovery

The wind had eased. The enormous waves subsided as quickly as they formed. The sheets of rain became a steady light drizzle. The cruising cabin windows were all open. He was on his back. It was a hard surface. It didn't make sense. He blacked out again and felt himself crawling into a fuzzy state of a recurring dream state similar to when he was in the hospital at Mount Sinai in Manhattan:

The first man asked, "What will keep him company?"

The other answered, "What insulates him and acts as his companion. Chance."

The first man provided a suggestion, "We'd favor that he lose his way." And after some contemplation, asked, "Will he?"

The other answered, "We'll see to it."

The first asked, "And the sense of himself?"

After a lengthy pause, in a soft voice, the second man replied, "Yes."

A third voice spoke softly, "You're hearing this to know what lies ahead."

Jacob barely had enough of a cogent analysis to know he was hallucinating.

All things were black, warm and wet. He felt breath on his face. He opened his eyes. Kolohe. His furry friend let out a whimper, perhaps of relief.

His head hurt badly. He was lying on the floor in a pool of seawater, except it wasn't just water. It was blood and it was his own. The gash at the temple throbbed with his heartbeat. It was a chronic pain in his head. But, when he felt the pulse, it was accompanied with an acute surface pain. His heart beat. Surge. Surge. Surge. Surge. He rubbed left side of his head and looked at the blood on his hand. So much blood. He knew that it acted as a colorant, and a little blood went a long way. *Maybe it isn't as bad as it looks.*

It was indeed Kolohe that woke him, licking his forehead.

"You've been out for a little while." Ruby said. He sat on the interior passenger's bench behind the captain's chair. It sounded like you fell and, I don't know, maybe hit your head?"

Kolohe backed up a few steps and whined. Then shook, jingling his dog tag attached to his collar.

Jacob said nothing, sitting up. He touched the wound gently this time, looking at his fingertips. He used his navy shirt to absorb the blood. Looking around at the deck, the blood loss wasn't as bad as he thought.

Ruby asked, "You alright?"

"I think so. Head hurts. Might not look like it, but I'm OK."

"Well, it was the craziest thing. As soon as you went down, the storm subsided."

"Microburst."

"Say again?"

"We call these..." he winced from the throb within his head, "...microbursts. They're rare this time of the year, but they happen. Can't control Mother Nature. How about you. Are you alright?"

Ruby ignored the question and offered aid saying, "If I knew where the First Aid kit was, I'd help. But..."

"I'll be alright. I think." Paisley reached for a First Aid kit at the bulkhead to fish out aspirin. He moved slowly to the passenger bench seating across from Ruby, lifting the cushion to retrieve a water bottle.

"Sometimes the smallest victories are our largest. We just don't know it at the time." The thin old black man looked into Jacob's eyes.

"How's Dorothy? Is she safe? Is she down there buckled in? I don't hear her."

Jacob looked into Ruby's eyes and saw what he thought was enlightenment. Ruby excused himself. "I gotta' go."

"Where are you going?"

"You know… I'm an old man and I gotta' go. A lot more than I used to. Can't even sleep through the night." Ruby held his hands out to grasp the railing on the side of the deck, clutching the aluminum he moved toward the aft of the craft with small steps. "Don't you worry…I'll check on her."

Kolohe followed.

Jacob watched as he clutched the rail, not looking back. "Ruby, you don't't' know where you're going. I'll help you," he called out – but he didn't go after him. "Ruby!" No answer.

He looked around the ship first, then to the sea. There was something out there. A small yellow light emerged. But, it was far away. The engine was off. Jacob pushed a button to prime the gas line and another to bring the engines to a gentle purr. Jacob turned the ship wheel in the direction of the distant beacon.

It was a single light on the horizon, and other than a mesmerizing arrangement of stars that began to speckle the sky, it might as well have been the only light. Honolulu's glow was nowhere. The light appeared far away, barely visible. The more the Aicon softly sped along in the direction, the light on the horizon seemed to blink on and then off. On for a few seconds, then off again. The stillness of the water was dramatically different from what Jacob thought it was just a short time ago.

His head throbbed. "Ruby – you alright?" Jacob actually wanted him to hurry so that he would be on deck as they moved toward the vessel. "Ruby?"

Jacob left the helm and quickly moved to the aft to find no one. "Ruby? Where are you?" After checking the head, the galley, the hold, and then the deck, he stopped to listen. The waves splashed and the motor softly hummed. However, there was no motion. No one.

For a brief moment he thought he'd check the water. He'd need to grab the spotlight and scan the waves left behind. But he knew that Ruby wouldn't be found there. Once more, "Ruby!"

The light, or what appeared to be a light had disappeared and they were venturing without coordinates into the darkness.

He had to return to the helm as the yacht was venturing to the portside closing a circle tighter and tighter. There was no light to see it, but it could be felt from the force of the turn. There at the helm was the old man, smiling and humming. Ruby gripped the wheel, and looked in the direction of Jacob.

"I thought you left?"

"Oh? Where would I go?"

"Well, I... I thought that I...Dorothy...I need to check on..." Jacob's confidence was missing. His assurance of nearly anything was missing. He did not know how he met this unpredictable and unexplainable moment, but here he was.

"Jacob...there is no Dorothy. Hasn't been for an hour now. Navy Seal, Dorothy, had a ditch bag attached to the bottom of your Aicon. A tough bird she is. Had a military grade dinghy attached to old fishing buoy marker T2149 about three nautical miles from Ma'ili Point. We were a little concerned you were going to hit it. You were so damn close." Ruby smiled while he spoke as if it were all a game and he held the remote control.

Jacob caught himself in a dilemma. Fight or flight? He was cornered. It felt as if he were completely bulldozed. Flight. He exhaled in defeat. He paused in pursuing a volume of detail to understand what his next step might be and absorbed the moment. He watched Ruby's face illuminate. The old man was deliberately driving Paisley crazy.

"Can you explain?" Jacob asked, insinuating that there was a logical story to tell.

"Explain what?" Ruby shrugged.

He was agitated. "Well, cut the shit...please. Please... please just tell me what this is all about. Time for an explanation, don't you think? Don't you think I deserve that? You've been toying with me." Jacob lost his smile and was losing his cool, "Any of your strange occurrences, all of them. Meeting me, falling from the eleventh floor of the hospital onto my car, uh...the codes you seem to speak in, those..." Jacob was fumbling with thought, "...the interactions we've had. Dorothy. Most recently Dorothy. Let's start with the moment."

Ruby looked at Jacob. "You should always begin with the moment, right?"

"It's a start..." Jacob spoke and was interrupted by a Ruby who appeared to have a depth of sapiential knowledge to share.

"I won't answer to all of it. But I will agree to answer to most of it. Let's say that Dorothy is an actress, an accomplished diver because of her experience and rank. She jumps off of your aft deck and gathers the flotation gear that she had attached to your hull. A small trailing vessel picks her up just fifteen minutes later from her EPIRB. That must have been one tough mother of a storm in a small boat."

Jacob had what Ruby was talking about on his vessel. The emergency position indicating radio beacon, EPIRB for short, was a marine essential. He could vision her being identified and picked up even in the conditions which the microburst brought. So far, the story was legit.

He cut to the quick, "So you're playing a part in a network of actors? For what reason?"

"There's more to the story, allow me..."

"Go on," Jacob sought to understand.

"Dorothy has a Seabob scooter with preset coordinates in her dinghy to lure you to a unique location. You follow the lights. That's what we're doing now."

"Yeah, again...why?"

"We'll get to that." Ruby held out one hand, palm up in a gesture of offering something more. "Or - that there's infinitely more to any of this than our simple biased minds can comprehend. We cannot explain all things. There's a presence that plays with us, gently guiding us along as if these bodies that we live within are vessels like this boat. From here to there to somewhere else, our souls indescribably intertwine with the presence. We're one, more than we are parts. All things are connected. And we accept that we cannot explain the presence. We don't always know 'why'. It isn't always about the answers."

Jacob listened to Ruby as he described this alternative version of the mystic interactions with an animated description and a smile on his face. "There has to be an explanation."

Ruby was abrupt. "No. Jacob, there doesn't." After a moment of silence, looking into Jacob's general direction he continued, "Choice and chance. You choose. You choose. You can explain it all away, or you can realize that there are some things that you will not know the answers to. You choose to understand that what you do know cannot compare to what you won't..."

Ruby reached over to touch Jacob's elbow and gently grabbed the back of his upper arm, "You might be surprised at your outcome if you lean in the direction of choosing to play with the presence that surrounds you."

Jacob felt a chill. He wondered how cool the temperature was for just a moment. Then, he thought about what Ruby just said for a minute, but said nothing. Perhaps the chill was something more.

"You're describing divine intervention."

The old man looked at him and smiled. 'There you go. Events will sometimes happen that cannot fully be explained. Our organization works alongside that presence."

"Organization?" Jacob knew there was rationale to the mystic providence or coincidences that Ruby was propositioning. Team Logic was still at work here.

"This is where it can get interesting. I'm going to make a believer or a non-believer out of you with what I say next." Ruby let go of Jacob's upper arm and looked out at another light on the horizon. "Looks like we're going to need to alter our direction some."

Jacob noticed an additional light further out and steered southeast.

"Keep it at about 125 degrees southeast," Ruby was referring to the coordinates.

Jacob added, "How far we've come in such a short amount of time. You, barking out coordinates."

"Kolohe does the barking around here. I'm just following the breadcrumbs." Ruby held his finger to his left ear. Pinching the lobe slightly. His lightweight clothing was nearly dry.

Jacob had noticed him doing that more often over the past fifteen minutes. There was more to the storyline here and he needed to uncover more detail. "Is it an earpiece you're wearing?"

"Something like that." The old man held his finger to his ear again.

"Two-way?"

"Maybe..."

"How many people are listening to you...me?" Jacob was curious as to why the earpiece and the connectivity were so strong, yet the technology on The Final Trade was so compromised. Before he broke into his next question, his first was answered.

"Four, five, maybe six seven people are monitoring what we're discussing..."

"So much for privacy." Jacob felt that all the personal attention was for the purpose of a staged performance. Yet he needed to validate the statement. "What year did Columbus discover America?"

Ruby lowered his chin to his chest, "C'mon... Really? You're going to begin with the easy stuff?"

"Name a Governor from the State of Ohio..."

"Mike DeWine," fell through Ruby's lips before Jacob was expecting it to.

"What's the name of the river that runs through Columbus, Ohio?"

Ruby paused for one second and retrieved, "The Scioto River, featuring the Scioto Mile which features a string of parks on both sides of the river along with a sculpture garden and a museum showcasing American and European paintings nearby. The German Village area..."

"It's like I'm talking to Alexa." Jacob interrupted while shook his head disapprovingly.

"This AI is legit."

"Where did my high school girlfriend and I go to make out?"

Ruby smiled. "Can't Google that one, can you?" He pulled the earpiece out of his ear, knowing it violated the confidentiality between the two of them and tossed it overboard. To Jacob, it appeared that it was just the two of them now. But that wasn't at all the case. What one ear tossed away, the other kept.

"Just us. What do you really want to know?" Ruby asked.

"So...what sermon do you have for me now?"

"How about that...it sounds like you're getting to know me," Ruby replied.

"Let's hear it," Jacob encouraged. Now he was curious to hear what might spill through Ruby's lips. It was getting interesting. There was more to the story than chance.

"We're bankrupting our world right now. With the systems we have in place, what we're doing isn't sustainable. We have linear economies which are our drivers. We're limited in natural resources which don't get distributed equally. Politically, environmentally, religiously, financially...fundamentally...I'm sure you'll agree the world is not as it could be, as perhaps it should be."

"I follow you so far." Jacob saw the light in the distance growing closer and maintained the slow course heading to the beacon.

"We influence the influencers. We enable the potential for change to happen. Our problems...governments won't solve them, science isn't solving them quickly enough, religions and denominations as we know them today won't solve them, consumer demand can't solve them, activists...give me a break..."

Jacob weighed in, "Hell, politicians make our problems worse by division and shame toward opposition."

"They can't stop talking long enough to hear themselves reason," Ruby chuckled as he said it.

"Then what is the answer that you..."

"Choice. Collective choice will solve problems. Collective. What's best for mankind? Choice, some of them anyway. Outside of the management systems we have today, a new organization which can impact equality and a better world is what's required and what we've designed." Ruby sat listening as

Kolohe returned from deep cover to sit next to the old man. His black and wet nose and brown eyes were nestled next to the man.

"You keep saying an '*organization*' and have referred to it as '*we*'. In what way? Those few people that were listening to you and helping you out with Google-like answers? What part to you play in all of that?"

Ruby looked directly at Jacob in the dim lighting of the yacht and smiled, "I'm a recruiter."

"A recruiter...?"

"I seek and recruit talent - like you."

"Me?" Jacob didn't understand. He reached into his khaki shorts for a final and soggy treat to give to Kolohe. The dog didn't mind and chomped the small soft morsel in several bites, seeking more by smelling the air. With a pat on his head and a scratching of the ears, he knew no more treats were being presented and licked Jacob's hand in appreciation.

"You've been in and out of my life quite a bit, haven't you? For what reason, to check me out to see if I can add any value?"

"In some ways yes and in others, no. Perhaps not as much as you might think in a physical sense. Some of what's in your head is just confirmation bias."

"What's that? Confirmation..."

"You see what it is you think you need to see. Sometimes you get in your own way with your convictions, borrowed and created." He pointed to his temple, "Your mind plays tricks on you."

Jacob felt like he wasn't doing well at tryouts. Where had he dropped the ball? What was it that Ruby didn't like in him?

Ruby rubbed his palms and the backs of his thin hands against each other, it seemed admiring work they had done, and continued, "Yes, I've had to take acting classes...so many acting classes...and play many parts. Some which I was honored to play and some which I didn't want to partake in."

"How so?"

"Working your project was very gratifying to..."

"My *project*? What does that mean?"

"Working on your project for the potential of the organization..."

"There's that reference again."

Ruby paused.

Jacob thought he was holding back information, or hesitating and prompted him to divulge, "C'mon old man, what do I need to know? You know me."

"Probably shouldn't but, here it goes. There may not be as much of an agenda as you might think. But we are social engineers. We guide and build guidance for outcomes. We provide options, transitioning from an owning economy to a sharing economy."

"You sound like a bunch of well-intended do-gooders." Jacob watched the light in the not-too-distant waters dim. Another one, further out lit up. "Should I keep chasing these prompts?" He looked over at Ruby, shaking his head slightly.

"Wish it were that simple. We're more than good Samaritans. We're middle-men. The middle persons I should say. We stay out of the news. We're the change-makers under the radar. The greatest things we do...you don't know about."

"Middlemen? Middle people? I didn't mean to sell you short, and I don't want to sound like I'm not buying the bullshit you're selling, I am, but also...also, you're giving me some of the picture...not all of it. You know I need the architecture to build..."

"Build. That's the architecture you need. We're bridge builders. All things require succession. Succession. The coming of one person or thing after another in order, sequence, or in the course of events. But... But better. We all need progression or a succession..."

"Succession. One of my favorite wines. The Pinot is rather tasty." He paused, and switched gears, no longer speaking of varietals, "I still need to own the thought of your thing in my head..."

"Stop yourself there. It isn't about owning, it's about sharing...collaborating...debating...positive conflict. Positive conversations...not meathead managing situations for basis-point outcomes. Your need to know everything and control it is what has kept you from coming into the fold for a while now. I can see we've got a little more work to do here."

Jacob was quiet, absorbing the criticism. He remained that way for two full uncomfortable minutes. Then, couldn't help himself, joking, "See...I can shut up and listen."

"You're like a little schoolgirl, seeking playground gossip, aren't you? You can't help your..."

"Exactly. Never saw myself in that light, but I'll go for it if it gets the job done..."

"You are as bold as your past. You must be as bold as your future. Your results – they're a fraction of your true potential."

"A-gain...what does that mean...exactly?"

"You have a gift. There's money in money. You know how to make it multiply handsomely."

"And...?" Jacob wanted to hear it but interrupted himself with another comment, "I don't' need money, I need purpose." He paused, listening to himself brag about his wealth.

"I know what you might be thinking. We don't want the money you have in your accounts. We may want to utilize the knowledge between your ears. There's more opportunity for sustainable wealth creation there."

Jacob squinted, having to say it, "I don't want to sound pompous here...I really didn't it to come off that way."

"I get it. We don't need purpose, we already have that. We need money to fund the purpose. That's the part you could play. You contribute. You help finance our operations. Simple stuff. But it's not like you're just setting up an offshore account and feeding dollars into the slot machine. We need directed and active involvement. Not passive intervention. It takes diligence and rigor, mass funding to do what we do. We're always looking for talent to help finance our endeavors. People who genuinely care about what we can do.

Jacob watched him talking about the organization. The 'we' kept coming out of Ruby's mouth. *Who is this we?*

The old man continued in his tribute, "Compounding. It isn't just a financial term. There's compounding in wisdom and knowledge, in relationships, in talent and skill." He was excited to talk about it. "And in possibilities. Potential compounds..."

"What the hell are you spouting about?"

"We seek like-minded people who care about what we care about. We believe..." Ruby paused, "We are a people who believe that we are here to serve others, not our personal ambitions, but collective objects to do a greater good. You know... the same boat, rowing in the same direction."

Jacob revved the engines as a teaser. They didn't respond as he had hoped, which indicated that there might be fishing line entwined around the propellers, but they did churn and propel them forward. "I already have a boat."

"That's it. I am the worst recruiter ever."

"I'm joking..." Jacob looked at Ruby shaking his head in disgust with himself.

"I know you are. I am too. See? Told you I took acting classes."

Jacob had a question he was particularly interested in having the answer to, "So, not being able to smell, or hear, and obviously you can see..."

"Fake. A part played..."

"What about the body in Manhattan? At the hospital. How does that...?"

"I didn't agree with their decision there, but we haggled and leveraging a cadaver for the purpose of... I just, not proud of it, I just went with it."

"How many?" Jacob assumed a dozen, or dozens of members of Ruby's clandestine organization. He aimed for the high side of how many others were in-the-know of the consortium. "Dozens?" Jacob noticed the first sign of Honolulu's light pollution. North. It verified with the direction he thought that he was cruising. He looked at Ruby, who was clearly contemplating the answer.

"Hundreds upon hundreds. Don't know of an official headcount number, but it's many upon many of us."

"Hundreds...upon hundreds?" Jacob was surprised. He didn't receive confirmation from Ruby.

They looked at each other. Ruby was carefully considering what he said next. He squinted, breaking the silence and disclosed the mystery Jacob so desperately wanted and needed.

"Ellipsis. That's what we refer to ourselves as. The Ellipsis. The intentional omission of all of the speech or writing of words." He waited for Jacob to say something.

"Like the grammatical punctuation marker?"

"Something like that. Similar to what you may see on a phone while you're awaiting a response."

"Ellipsis." Jacob said it aloud.

"The plural is ellipses, but let's keep it simple. Ellipsis. The go-between. The answer that has not yet arrived, from the query or question asked. An anticipation. Something yet to come...from something else."

Jacob thought of Adele, and said it to himself, but loud enough for Ruby to hear, *'Some things happen for a reason. Team Hope. Some things happen because of reasons. Team Logic.'*

"Exactly." Ruby replied.

Jacob wasn't sure how Ruby knew what he knew but didn't discard him any longer. No more. The old man was clearly resourceful and knowledgeable beyond comprehension.

"Ellipsis."

"Now...you need to keep that to yourself, young man." He pointed his index finger at Jacob emphasizing that it was a tightly held secret.

"I'm not that young."

"Young enough."

Jacob needed more of a confirmation. "Who is this 'we' you refer to? What kind of code of conduct is at work here? And who is it you're so commonly recruiting?"

"Lots of questions there Mr. Paisley. Let's just say for now that we are guided by the modern-day pillars I've been mentioning. But there's a little more to that. There are principles, and powers, ethics and guardrails. Standards and even mathematical formulas we adhere to."

"Math?"

Ruby looked at Jacob and squinted, searching for the correct theorems, "Sure, Probability Mass Functions, and the Markov Chain, and the Poisson Distribution. Conditional Probabilities. Bayes' Theorem."

"Also known as timing the situation?"

"Something like that." Ruby rubbed the back of his hands again and slid them down his trousers to his knees. "A diverse gathering of talent, I'd call it. Then, again, I brought many of them into the fold. Teachers, lawyers, coaches, wizards of their trade, IT technicians, security consultants and specialists, private investigators, people with a unique form of intelligence or a profound way of getting to it. Social media managers, special forces, government agencies... People who have unusual resources and ways of leveraging that unique knowledge."

"A roster of top-of-their-game and talented MVPs?"

"That's right." He paused knowing that he'd said enough for the moment and intended to shift gears.

But Jacob asked, "Results. Have you done anything I know about?"

"That container ship that was hi-jacked in the Port of Long Beach last summer, we brought that to a close, not the SWAT Team. The active shooter in Philadelphia, we helped the negotiations in his hostage crisis. We've returned twenty-something missing persons and have a dozen cold cases thawed and solved. You remember the hack of the national healthcare database a few months ago? We launched ransomware within the bitcoin tokens to freeze out the hackers. That was risky, but it worked. Our doings. The vigilante that captured the mall shooter in Houston, it was *our* special ops team...."

"I get it. Page one and page two newsworthy things, not bad."

"There's more, but I've said enough. For now. Don't' want to bore you. We may be small when compared to an agency but thinking big. And the red tape doesn't get in the way if you know what I mean."

Jacob said nothing for a minute, then added, "So you're perfect planners?"

"Hardly." Ruby rubbed his chin and smirked at the thought, "Far from it. We all deal with the acts of God. Acts of God...they involve tragedy. Reminders that we are all vulnerable." He paused in his assessment as though he'd lived through a few situations. Then, he began again, "But those unfortunate situations are also the reminders that we're supposed to be cooperative. More so than competitive. We're intended to be a compliment to each other with compassion and need to serve one another." He breathed deeply the salty air wafting through the slow-moving yacht. "Most of the time things work out. Some of the time we're surprised at just how well things came together."

Jacob was wrapping his head around the possibilities of an off-the-charts organization with a goodwill agenda of its own. In the age of digital awareness, how could it remain hidden? Then it occurred to him, evil. The heinousness always drew the attention. The news cycles never attracted viewers with acts of kindness or goodwill. Everyone would surely tune in to learn of the body counts from an active shooter. People wanted to know of the tornadoes which wreaked havoc on an Oklahoma trailer park. The public was fascinated by the celebrity divorce and deviltry and corruption from a C-level public figure. They weren't as impressed with virtues and grace and distinction.

Ruby looked at Jacob, "Change. It takes dollars to make change happen. It'll take funding. This is your specialty."

"I can...on momentum...double money. But the VIX is in my head, I'm good for ten percent in bull and bear markets. The lift..."

"I don't know what 'vix' means..."

Jacob realized he was speaking financial district gibberish, "The Volatility Index. If things are going to shit, it's like catching a falling knife." He paused, allowing Ruby to catch up. "If I had a million, in a good upturn I can double it. If the bear market is running, I can capture ten percent. Slow growth."

"Say I granted you one hundred million dollars to begin with." Ruby looked over at Jacob after he said it, seeking a reaction.

Jacob tilted his head to the side, "You have some serious intentions with one hundred million dollars. As a jumping off point?"

"Let's just say anonymous billionaire philanthropist seed money."

Nothing more needed to be said. Jacob knew that his millionaire's club standing was found wanting of the billionaire's club. They were royalty. Old money, new money. Billionaire playgrounds were where the millionaires went to feel rich: The Golden Triangle, Portugal. Lugano, Switzerland. Antibes, France. La Condamine, Monaco. They reminded themselves that there was always room for more and that goodness was the enemy of greatness. They allowed themselves to be deceived of their own fortunes and accomplishments by the bigger boats, exotic cars, younger wives, and deeper secrets they absorbed.

He was generalizing again. Looking down at the tanned toes of his feet which used to wear expensive dress shoes on the sidewalks of Manhattan, Jacob frowned. His score keeping was migrating and he shook his head, amazed at how aloof he had allowed himself to become.

"How's the head?" Ruby asked, knowing that Jacob was in there somewhere, wrestling deep in thought.

"Hurts."

"Say, Captain Paisley, do you remember those pillars of potential we talked about?"

"God...has anyone ever told you that you talk a lot? Preach much? That you're a bit wordy?" Jacob felt another sermon from Ruby on deck.

"I get that from time to time. No ramble here though. Stay with me," Ruby had his point to make. "Do you?"

"I do. You can be convincing. I remember them well. First it is beliefs, or faith if you prefer. Then, it's perspective – how you see it all moving forward. Next is feelings. Some of us are better there than others. And finally, the thoughts and the words that accommodate. The transition from the internal to the external."

"You're right. Couldn't have said that any better."

"Actually, you probably could have said it differently and it would come across more effective to some people, because their perspective is altered from mine."

Ruby acknowledged Jacob, "Well said. Two final pillars that round out our potential. And they're actually the easiest for you, since you do it all backwards."

"I wouldn't necessarily agree with..."

"Hear me out. Actions and results. These are the final two pillars of potential."

"I am correcting my earlier assessment of myself and agreeing with you. Actions and results – now that's good livin'. Talk away, old man. I prefer to thrive within those pillars."

"Yeah," Ruby paused, "Lots of business people do. And as a result, they create some of the greatest conflicts of all – diminishing the other four pillars: faith, perspective – which can be respect for diversity, and feelings, and the transition points, our thoughts and words."

"Beliefs...perspectives...feelings...thoughts...actions...and results." Jacob recited the points made because of their encounters. "If it were only that simple."

"But really? It is. Some of us live on the left side, those first three, a little more than others who live on the right side. And that adds mystery and some drama and some suspense to our lives."

"I suppose it does."

After several minutes of silence and reflection, Jacob's tone was different. "I want to thank you...Ruby. Thanks... for helping me."

"Perhaps you just needed a little nudge to uncover what your own possibilities might be. To help yourself. And by the way, I'm the one that will be grateful one day. I just want to put that out there now." Jacob frowned, not understanding the comment.

Ruby lifted his chin to feel the ocean breeze, taking a deep breath of the fresh air. "Three words to describe yourself friend".

Paisley remembered the challenge question originally posed in the hospital two years earlier. He took much more time answering, thinking about his transition. "That's a little tougher than it used to be."

Ruby smiled broadly.

"I'd say," Jacob paused: "Lucky..." He reached over to put his hand on Ruby's shoulder, and looked off into the dark distance. The wind had died. They were close. He didn't speak loudly. There was no need. It was almost a whisper. "Lucky and...Comfortable."

"Comfortable." Ruby repeated, "That's a – " He stopped speaking for several seconds. "That's a good word. And?"

"Lucky, and comfortable, and..." Jacob was blank. He could normally snap off judgmental descriptive articulations. Not now. He thought without interruption. Other than the breeze, it was quiet for a while. "Incomplete."

Ruby chuckled some. "How about that. The man that had it all figured out is self-describing himself as *incomplete.* Sounds as if you've found yourself in a place you didn't know you could go to." He looked toward Jacob's direction, yet over his left shoulder and spoke softly, "I believe in something that Albert Einstein said. Goes something like this: *The most beautiful thing we can experience is the mysterious. It is the source of all true art and all science. He to whom this emotion is a stranger, who can no longer pause to wonder and stand rapt in awe, is as good as dead: his eyes are closed.*"

Paisley thought about it for a moment. He remembered sitting in the hospital bed, with arrogance, stating that he was *competitive, creative, influential.* Those were distractive descriptions. He thought about how he was changing. It was a short time ago that he believed there was much less mystery. He saw a shallow self in the man that once was. A man that leaned hard on what worked, not what could be. And he saw himself as he was now and *anything but balanced* came to mind. And it was joined by *happier.* When he looked into the palms of his hands, he saw potential. "Incomplete. Maybe... the most wonderful word. A beautiful word. There's an immeasurable sense of wonder that accompanies it. Lucky, comfortable, incomplete." He looked at Ruby and felt appreciation and sensed a new evolving wisdom which he felt a need to share. "We find happiness when we own less, judge less, and seek to understand more, don't we?" He was seeking agreement more than asking a question.

"Jacob, there are a finite number of people that actually impact your life. A limited number that have the means to do so. And I'm not talking about influencers. This is about those whom can dramatically change your outcome. This is going to be somewhat hard for you to swallow. These people, my people, now your people – the organization - they arc the flatline."

"What does that mean? They...arc the flatline?"

"They truly uncover potential. We can see them from a distance as parents and my teachers, mentors and leaders that have had a profound role in changing our course. These people who arc the flatline, that do both great and small things, they may or may not even realize their outcome. Their influence is...eternal, so to speak. And at other times, it's intended. Let me describe it this way - as you know, light doesn't bend, but offers and optical illusion of bending through refraction. These people that I'm describing – they're that kind of force. They, well, the point is that they find a way to bend light."

Jacob did think of Ruby's mystical presence in and out of Jacob's past and a grin faded from his face. The crinkles in his eyes eased. "Fundamentally, light doesn't bend. But, I can almost glimpse what you mean. They find a way to change the outcome."

"That's right. They can arc a position because they have a way to sense what's beyond the horizon. This is the way it was described to me, and the way that I've tried to influence the lives I've encountered. Most things appear normal, but just enough isn't to add a value of cryptic wonder to some moments."

Jacob sat silent for a moment looking into the direction of Ruby and off into the dark sea. The waves were calming yet still splashed gently against the hull of the ship. "From the moment we met, I've been puzzled, baffled...at times bewildered by what has happened. And because of that, this isn't too much of a stretch. But, to convince me...it takes a little more than a magic show. I'm sorry. Where I come from, well...ambiguity is for amateurs."

Ruby placed his hand on Jacob's shoulder. "Like I said earlier, we have more to do. You're hearing this to know what lies ahead."

Jacob winced at the comment. It was recurring. "What do you even mean by that?"

The old man was speaking low "Venturing beyond the horizon, altering an outcome, bending the light, arcing the flatline...it's the work of wizards. And you, Jacob Paisley, may very well be one. One of us, that is."

"Ellipsis. I. I'm..." he was struggling with comprehension, "...It's enigmatic. It's obscure. It's all so elusive."

"Perhaps that's just one of the reasons why we found you," Ruby said. He was looking in Jacob's direction and was as surprised with the revelation as Jacob was. "Perhaps that is why we found you."

"How and why?"

Ruby shook his head with his own kind of wonder, and was about to speak as the radio suddenly crackled with static and came back on. Israel Kamakawiwo'ole's version of *What a Wonderful World* quietly played from the second stanza.

Jacob confirmed, "Need an affirmation here. Ellipsis, like in dot, dot, dot?" His fingers poked at the air in front of him.

"Dot, dot, dot," Ruby verified. "It sure seems like you're far away from where you were, doesn't it?" He was solemn in his comment.

"It does. I went from leading a five-year strategic plan for my company's direction, to a five-month plan of scrambling together an exit from Manhattan strategy, to basically focusing on the five-day forecast. I traded the concrete jungle for the sunshine. What a bizarre twist of positioning."

"Life can be funny like that. Leads us in many directions. Sometimes, we just don't know where we're heading. There are times when we have all of the answers. And there are times when we simply need to live with the questions."

Jacob thought about that for a moment, closed his eyes and clearly saw the cardboard sign that homeless Mary in Manhattan held:

SOMETIMES THINGS
JUST DON'T TURN OUT
LIKE THEY WERE SUPPOSED TO

"Hell of a three-hour tour, right? If you provide a shitty Yelp review or complain and the foundation wants their money back, we'll understand. No problem." He tried to make light of their deep conversations. Ruby didn't answer. Jacob assumed he was calibrating a next step or that there was more to the unanswered story.

They continued to move through the sea's breeze toward the light.

Jacob needed to apologize. He didn't like to do it, but if felt necessary.

"Knowing that you know so much about me, what I've done...I'm a bit embarrassed by some of my actions. If you *really* know, then I'm *really* embarrassed. I allowed myself to be deceived in some of my actions. I was swayed, manipulated..."

"That's why the world is round, right?" Ruby injected a reprieve in Jacob's sort-of confession.

"I don't follow."

Ruby chuckled to himself more than at Jacob's hazy apology. "The world's round. You just keep on going. Eventually you'll end up where you need to be, where you're supposed to be, even if it's back where you were, all the way around. Keep on going. It's called forgiveness. Forgiveness is spherical, it's circular, it's..." His words stalled and he contemplated just how special forgiveness was. "Its powers are mystical."

Jacob shook his head slightly, looking at his deck mate's moment of reflection.

"Adele will be worried about you." Ruby spoke softly in the direction they cruised.

Jacob hesitated, then asked, "How well do you know Adele?" There was no answer. He looked at Ruby, intentionally looking away, out into the depths of salty nothingness.

"I have some talent I'm looking at tomorrow. There's something there. A young man, local guy, Hawaiian island man...but doesn't live here any longer."

"Oh yeah?" Jacob was focused on the dim light ahead as the engines churned a small wake behind them. The sloshing of the water was the only thing breaking the silence of the late night which was becoming an early hour's morning.

"An athlete. Or...former athlete anyway. Always looking for potential."

Whoosh.

Suddenly, the small light burst brighter with a bright and hot yellow flash. He heard what sounded like a buildup and rush of propane when ignited while bursting through a burner.

When Jacob could finally make out what it might be, he said it for Ruby to relate, "I'm not sure what that flash or noise was, but it looks like a thirty-to-forty-foot sailboat." Squinting in the umbra of night, "Maybe single mast, with the sails dangling and...perhaps...shredded or...maybe burnt." The light on the deck bobbed slightly with the gentle waves.

Under the Aicon's dodger, Ruby stood. "One last thing..." the old man said softly. He smiled and his eyes creased with kindness when their glances met each other.

"Uh...last thing?" Jacob repeated, asking curiously.

"One last thing, my friend." He took another deep breath of the sea breeze, "The potential that you continue to discover within yourself is just a tiny light in a dark sea. The capacity that you help uncover within others is a more important and infinite possibility – that brighter light that we're all challenged to uncover."

Jacob returned to watching the approaching craft, while listening.

The black man standing next to the captain's helm was humming while they moved closer. "How far away is that?" he asked.

When Jacob looked his way to answer him, Ruby was smiling. He had the look of the cat that ate the canary.

"Time for us to kill the speed – well, what speed we have that is. We'll coast in slowly for less wake. I can make out a man, I think. Waving his arms. I think...I think he's either happy to see us or needs... help or both." Jacob moved from the helm to the edge of the beam to see better. Moving away from the cabin lighting helped him focus.

Ruby moved to the side while Jacob made the engines purr, causing the yacht to slow in its approach. He put his hand on Jacob's shoulder. "I don't remember where this came from but, it fits the moment," Ruby spoke softly while looking off into the distance at nothing: "*I didn't ask for it to be over. But then again, I didn't ask for it to begin. For that's the way it is with life, as some of the most beautiful days come completely by chance. But even the most beautiful days eventually have their sunset."*

Paisley was back at the helm looking at the instrument panel. He thought for a few seconds and added, "I know that quote. It's from an Iranian physicist. Ali Jarva...or Javan...or something like that. His invention in the gas laser eventually led to fiber optics and the foundation for the internet." He flicked his fingers on the instrument panel making a clicking noise on the glass housing. Several of the gauges were not responding to the toggles that would command them into action. Some of the lights of yellow and red and green had not come on. The RPM gauge barely responded when he pushed the engine throttle forward.

Ruby looked at Jacob with a broad smile, and then continued in a whisper, bringing his mouth closer to Jacob's ear, "Just as much can be said within a whisper as with a scream. I can see that things will be different now. Until we meet again, my friend."

"Wait...I..."

"Oh, I won't need my shoes. Size ten. Maybe you can use them." Ruby winked and turned to face the Pacific.

While steering the Aicon toward the approaching craft, Jacob turned to seek understanding and realized that Ruby wasn't in sight. He was gone.

Kolohe whined.

He heard no splash. He looked around the deck and toward the bow of the boat. No Ruby. It made little to no sense. However, with the mystery that constantly surrounded Ruby, Jacob decided that the mystery may unravel later. He began shouting for him. "Ruby!' Seconds later, "Ruby, where are you?" Followed by "Ruby...say something...anything."

Silence followed.

Jacob continued looking around the Aicon for his acquaintance and potentially new teammate. He shouted his name a few more times.

Looking forward to the craft he was approaching his said to himself, *'Ellipsis'.*

From the short distance away, cries rang out: "Hello! Help us! Hello, hello! Please, please! Please help us!" A man continued waving his arms at Jacob. A light atop the deck was repeatedly switched on and off signaling some form of distress.

In response, Jacob switched his light atop the bridge on, off, on, off, on a few times as well. The two boats were no more than fifty meters apart. "Ruby?" Once again, Ruby had disappeared. "Ruby!" No reply. No where, no one, nothing. "Ruby?" The old black man had vanished.

Jacob lifted the spotlight slowly and directly toward the motionless sailboat to assess. Approaching portside, clarity and definition were available. The craft's masts were ripped, and the deck was scorched. Black soot probably meant fire. It appeared to be darker inside the cabin. It was a probability that that was where the fire originated.

Now he could clearly see a young man, perhaps late twenties or early thirties, who appeared to be alone on the other boat. The young man had shoulder length light brown hair. He waved his arms, appearing frantic. "Please, please help us."

Us? Jacob scanned the craft and saw no one else on board. He shouted, "I'm throwing you a line." He heard a whine of a kind and looked for Kolohe's heavy panting nearby.

What is that? Crying? A baby?

Cocking it's head to the side, the yellow lab barked once.

The two yachts came to a close. The Aicon was twice the size of the other. Jacob could see the young man clearly and a woman suddenly emerged carrying a baby against her chest.

"Fire?" Jacob asked.

"Yesterday, we've been at sea for two days stranded. My girlfriend had a baby. Please, we need your help."

"I'm going to toss you a line. Brace yourself and pull tight to draw us our boats closer. Cleat it first, then draw yourself in if you can,"

Jacob did just that. He threw the thick rope to the man in the scorched craft. He heard crying. "Can you climb aboard?""

The woman was sobbing. Jacob determined that these were either tears of joy or relief from what was probably hopelessness just several minutes earlier.

She spoke softly as she approached the side of the stranded vessel, "Thank you, thank you, oh God thank you so much."

"Kerri, here, let me take it," the young man said. The baby was wrapped in a light-colored blanket and slightly whimpered in the handoff. *It*, Jacob thought. *Odd.*

Just then the young man said to the woman, "I'll hold him, you get the bag." He looked at Paisley, "Man, I mean it - thank you. What luck to find you out here in the middle of nowhere at a time like this. What are the chances...?"

"I'd say one in a million." Jacob looked at the baby.

"Cutter, can you help me out here?" The woman, apparently named Kerri, was holding out her hand while trying to balance between boats. There were no formal introductions, so Jacob offered one.

"My name is Jacob. Here, let me help you out." Paisley reached for the bag and her hand to bring her aboard. He looked at the baby, and at her, at the baby again, and at the young man, at the baby once more, and back at the mother. Silence passed as Jacob made a few assumptions.

In an awkward moment, they looked at the burnt boat and then at each other. White male, white female, black baby boy, yellow lab, and a confused Captain Paisley. He looked at the liquid foundation, the sea. It offered no traction to navigate from.

Jacob asked, "Need anything else? I don't know what our coordinates are here. So, if you'd like to retrieve supplies or..."

"Nope, we're good," Cutter interrupted with his reply, "Let's get out of here Thanks man. Thanks." They were sizing each other up, crafting unsaid opinions at this point. Man, woman, man, baby, dog. Several observations were made, many questions unasked. They didn't introduce themselves, but Paisley gathered their names anyway: Cutter, Kerri, baby.

"You sure?"

"We're good." But, only the man spoke for them.

"Then, we're off." Paisley looked at the woman for a confirmation, however she didn't provide one. Her eyes were down, looking at the dog. The couple with their small child sat down on the deck's bench and exhaled. They weren't looking at the child, they gazed off into the darkness. Jacob gunned the engines, and as he sped away from the couple's craft felt a drag in performance. He thought the twin engines were misbehaving. There appeared to be a lack of responsive power. He was thinking: *I'll have to ask one of the boat mechanics at the marina to have a look.*

"You alone out here?" the young man asked. The whites of his eyes were more bloodshot than white, more wild than excited, more evil than kind. When he spoke the right side of his mouth moved more than the left.

Jacob didn't know how to reply. He simply gestured a 'yes', saying nothing. Ruby had a way of appearing and disappearing. He looked at his dog, and then nodded again.

Over the increasing sound of the engines, the baby cried, and the mother held him closer to her breasts. Kolohe was curious and crept closer to check the contents of the bundle. The infant became quiet as he sucked on his mother's pinky.

They were no more than two hundred yards away from the scorched craft when it exploded. It was an epic: *ka-boom!* Neither Jacob, Cutter, nor Kerri was looking back when the blast happened. They were looking forward. The sound caused them to quickly turn to the burst of flame.

"Mother Fuckers," Cutter said when he sprung around to see the black billowing smoke ascend into a dark night sky.

It was a reaction that made no sense to Jacob. He felt the warm burst from the exploding fire, the bright yellow and orange flames were spewing car-sized clouds of black smoke, whirling in the air and lighting the night. Kerri gasped, looking up at Cutter with a sweaty expression of exhaustion and despair.

Wincing, Jacob had to ask, "Is there more to the story?"

"More to the story," Cutter replied abbreviating. He was less than appreciative this time. He pointed his finger into the dark night. "That way, I believe. Cutter looked back at the burning boat. "Awe...man... There goes my buy-in..."

"That's the look of a liability-only insurance face." He gave Cutter a good look from head to toe. Even though the black tank top he was wearing was black, it appeared grimy in the low light. It was probably from a couple trips into the scorched cabin or a crawl through the small sailboat's engine compartment. It had a printing on the chest reading: Aloha Beaches. It was white lettering filling the front torso of the shirt which was soiled. His shorts were denim cut-offs and as was typical on a boat, he wore no shoes.

Finally, "Yeah...liability only."

"Me too," Jacob added quickly. *Too soon*, he thought, smirking to himself. It was far from the truth. He was seeking common ground, out here, in the Pacific.

Cutter looked around the well-appointed craft with its high-end furnishings and the shiny command center Jacob kept turning on and off. Even though it was dark, and the lighting was dim, in the deepness of the night he knew this was the premium vessel it was.

"Do you know what time it is? My phone stopped working."

"Got somewhere you need to be?" Jacob asked, but there was no reply.

"I lost some of my nav and power with the storm, and a sense of direction. I think the light pollution of Honolulu is this way. The instruments were spinning inconsistently and blinking." Jacob pointed to the control panel and moved his index finger in circles to mimic the disruption. "So, to answer your question, not really."

Jacob found it unusual that neither this man nor this woman felt more attached to their burning boat. It was odd to be focused on forward, than the fire behind them.

"I have a slip at the Ko Olina Marina. I haven't seen you two, you three, or your boat there..."

"We're...down in Waikiki." The young man may have been wrestling with the loss of his craft, but Jacob who was not necessarily new to boating, but not uninformed knew that there was no marina at Waikiki. Perhaps he meant Keehi, or Ala Wai, or even Hawaii Kai. It was unusual not to call out the marine center you were cleated to - unless there was something to hide, or you truly didn't know what you were doing.

The man, Cutter, looked at the woman, Kerri. He shrugged his shoulders in a despondent manner. It wasn't a comforting shrug. "Can we go any faster?" he asked.

"Normally, yes. But for some reason, right now, that's a 'no'." Paisley answered the young man, then asked himself. *Where's all the Aicon's power?* Something was not right. As a matter of fact, something was definitely wrong. He had to press the issue with Cutter, "By the way, your yacht just exploded. None of us are alright with that. Who are the *mother fuckers*?" Saying this reminded Jacob of the cold dark December ally in Manhattan. He thought of the same gunmetal grey revolver locked in the safe in the ship's cabin. It made the trip from New York to Oahu.

"Just some dudes that tried to run us around. Pirates." He was animated in describing *dudes*. His eyes were wide, and reminded Jacob of the greasy skinned kid in the New York ally botching a holdup. It wasn't a straight answer, and didn't sound the least bit convincing.

"Let me ask you again. Who are the..."

"We gotta' get out of here man! Like now!" Now he was convincing, Jacob thought – believable in a motivated way. "Gun it!"

"Not really how it works when we're trying to determine if something might be caught on the props or the rudder." Jacob throttled up and down, getting the same result. The engines churned without much torque. "I need to go for a little swim." He checked for bars on his cell phone. Still nothing. He'd call Sea Tow or BoatUS if he had reception. Nothing was working. The radio just crackled with static. Channel 16 was flashing on and off. Without a connection, he'd have to go it alone in his troubleshooting.

They both knew that the lack of responsiveness couldn't lead to anything good. They were too far from land to think that lighting a flair would signal help. Checking again, their cell phones and the radio landed no signal.

The utility closet at the captain's helm held an underwater light. It was 100 lumens and would work. Jacob looked into the black sea and began stripping off his shirt. He stood there bare-chested.

Kolohe turned his head. It wasn't like Jacob to swim from the yacht at night. And to not invite Kolohe?! "Ruff. Ruff-ruff!"

The child began to cry. But it wasn't in Kerri's arms. It was lying in a blanketed bundle, alone on the white poly passenger bench.

Jacob hadn't noticed that Kerri had gone below. She called out, "Um, I think we have a problem!" He heard splashing. She climbed the steps from the cabin. Her feet sloshed the hardwood steps. "There's water down there. That's not supposed to happen, right?" Her voice echoed from below.

"How much water?" That was the last thing you wanted to have to ask, Jacob thought to himself. A fracture of any sort wasn't a good thing, especially on a boat.

"Two inches. Maybe more."

'Well, isn't this just great'... Jacob said to himself.

18

The Edge

"Go faster!"

"No!"

"Go faster!"

"No!"

"Go...!"

"No!" Their banter increased in volume, ending with Jacob killing the engines completely and reverse throttling. "We're snagged, we taking on water, and we're just going to make it worse unless we get it figured out quickly."

Without a response, he tossed the same line that he used to bring their ships together overboard, grabbed a waterproof flashlight and a facemask. He stripped off his shirt and was down to his boardshorts. Holding the nylon line, he jumped in. Nearly one minute later, he surfaced, breathing hard, and had a two-foot piece of the mast from Cutter and Kerri's sailboat.

"This is yours; I believe!" he shouted from the water. But that's not it. There might be a stress fracture drawing in water."

"I'm going to start bailing!" Cutter shouted back, not offering to extend a hand to Jacob in the water.

Kolohe barked once.

"You do that." Jacob said to himself, reaching for the outboard ladder steps.

Once on the deck, Jacob glanced around seeing Kerri holding the baby, rocking. He wasn't sure whether it was more comforting for the baby, or for herself.

Kolohe sniffed at the blanket's edge and wagged his tail. Light was just beginning to prevail in the east. The sun would quickly diffuse the directionless dark.

How long had they been at sea? It was surreal. His head hurt.

Cutter was bailing water with a one-gallon bucket found in a utility closet. It looked more effective than it actually was. Splash, pause, splash, pause, splash was the sound of the seawater being tossed from the floor of the cabin out the cabin window, back into the Pacific.

Jacob had hoped that it was the water heater or his freshwater supply that had ruptured spilling into the body of the yacht. The reality didn't coordinate with the desire.

Unfortunately, if the hull had ruptured with the pounding in the storm, and saltwater was seeping into his beautiful Aicon, the two bilge pumps would have triggered and started the expulsion of seawater. That wasn't happening.

"We need to shed weight." Cutter called up from below. Splash, pause, splash, pause, splash, pause.

Jacob looked in the direction of the command and maintained course. With the approaching dawn, he only needed to tweak his anticipated direction slightly. They were heading north-northwest. He reached into the bench locker to retrieve binoculars. Peering in the direction that the craft was heading, searching for the Waianae or Koolau mountain ranges, he was left wanting.

Seeing the Diamondhead crater would place them twenty miles from the Ko Olina. They could dock at Sand Island or the Kewalo Basin Harbor. They could even get in close enough to Ala Moana Beach Park to inflate the life raft and paddle in if necessary. He tried the radio again, but it only hissed static. The GPS was a black screen.

Pause, splash, pause, splash. With labored breathing, Cutter called up to Jacob again. "Did you hear me? We're too heavy."

Jacob ignored what he heard. Splash, pause, splash, pause.

Cutter stopped bailing. Soggy shorts sloshed on the steps up from below. "I think we've taken on another two inches. Tell me you see Oahu."

"I don't see Oahu. She's not there."

"Are you sure you're taking us the right way?"

"I'm not sure of anything other than you're better off with me, than on that sailboat I pulled you off of a little while ago."

Cutter rolled his eyes and returned to the hull.

Jacob considered him a drama queen.

Splash, pause, splash, pause, splash. Not more than two minutes later he slowly sloshed back up the steps carrying a portable safe. When he set it down, he lost his grip, and it cracked the deck with a 'thud' sound. He was hunched over it, straddling it while on his knees unsuccessfully trying to catch the heavy metal box as it fell. "Sorry. This weighs what...sixty pounds?"

"Maybe forty or fifty. You've seen this in a movie, or something. It doesn't work like that. You don't just start tossing things overboard and lighten your load." At this point Jacob actually thought they were going to make it to shore in the condition they were in.

"You bail for a while," Cutter commanded while panting shallow breaths.

Jacob looked at the portable safe on the deck sitting between himself and Cutter. It contained $250,000 in cash, a passport, the distribution package from his PPCM severance package as a memento of getting fucked by his own company. It also held the handgun that was used against him on his termination day in Manhattan. *Hands up, muth-u- fuck-a!* He briefly thought, playing it again in his head.

They traded positions at the helm so that Paisley could go below to assess the situation. Jacob looked at the safe again, thinking about the hidden stacks of pastel spring green hundred-dollar bills, carefully wrapped in paper $10,000 bands and stacked neatly under the velvet liner. Five stacks of five aligned a burrowed-out section in the base of the safe. The balding, thin-lipped Benjamin Franklin stared at the holder of the stack with a smile-less stare.

Kolohe followed Jacob as he descended the stairs. He didn't expect to find six inches of water sloshing around in the belly of his Aicon. It was alarming. Dogfood was floating throughout the seawater. Kibble of pink, orange, green and brown. It was the least of his concern, but he found it amusing that he was as disappointed that dogfood was floating within his ruptured craft as he was disappointed that the ship was taking on water. He could hear the twin Caterpillar engines purring while in the cabin. A sound that he wasn't familiar with.

He picked up the bucket and scooped ten gallons out the oversized window into the Pacific. Splash, pause, splash, pause, splash, pause. He stopped to catch his breath.

Kolohe stood on all fours away from the water and wagged his tail when Jacob looked at him. Jacob found a smile within a grim situation and rubbed Kolohe under the chin. "If you had thumbs you could help too."

Jacob looked around at the heaviest items within the cabin. Stoneware sink, refrigerator, microwave, granite countertops. It wouldn't buy much time if any at all.

A pump. He needed a pump, a hose, and suction to siphon the water while bailing. It would work.

Just then the engines throttled loudly. Jacob was tossed to the aft of the vessel against the galley's bulkhead. His head struck the stainless-steel refrigerator in the same position and began throbbing again.

He held his hand on his head while shouting, "Kill it! Kill it! That's not going to help us!" It was then that Jacob saw the leak. The fiberglass hull had been breached on the portside and water streamed and bubbled into the hull from the acceleration. He didn't notice it before, but being in the salon while the engines were pushed, he noticed water seeping in as they moved with force through the water.

Jacob now sloshed up the steps, angrily shouting, "'God damn it! Kill the engines you moron, we're taking on more water!" Kolohe followed.

Reluctantly, Cutter pulled back, returning the twins to their gentle churn.

"Please. Please just bail." Jacob asked Cutter to help with eliminating what was already entering the vessel while he toyed with the instrumentation panel. Perhaps the navigation screen simply blew a fuse.

"We need to shed weight," Cutter bellowed.

Jacob reached for the binoculars. "You're not helping me here Cutter. We don't need parallel thought streams. I need you to bail."

Cutter asked where the pail was.

Jacob held his hands out to show how empty they were. *Not in my hands, and not up here, you moron.* With a degree of sarcasm he replied, "Where do you think?" Jacob clicked at the radio once more. More crackling static was returned. He tried to power on the global positioning system. Nothing worked.

Where was Kerri in all of this? It was one thing to acknowledge that Ruby had appeared and disappeared, but she was no Ruby.

Where was the child? The child's cry broke the moment. It screamed loudly, as if to pierce the thought of wondering where the adorable little baby could possibly be. Kerri and the infant were tucked down low in a low sitting deck chair in the aft of the craft.

Cutter huffed and moved toward the stairway to return below deck.

She entered the open Captain's deck with the child in her arms neatly wrapped in a blanket. "It's still so dark out there, when will it be light?" she said softly. It was a stupid question.

"When the sun comes up." He didn't know how else to respond.

Cutter sloshed up the stairs with the stoneware sink. It was heavy and he struggled to carry it. Jacob looked around at the storm's wear on the yacht. The water in the hull had begun to slosh around to the point it could be heard from above. They were taking on seawater faster. He shrugged, "If that's what you got to do, then that's what you've got to do. I won't stop you."

The young man heaved the heavy sink overboard and it made the sound that a perfectly performed cannonball dive would make: a deep *ker-plunk* arose from sea-level. Cutter marched back down below to retrieve heavyweight items. Jacob heard prying and beating sounds from below. He left the helm briefly to assess the demolition from below. When he arrived into the galley he noticed the deck head stripped away. Wiring and pipes were exposed from the captain's deck above. Wires were pulled out from the conduit to the command center. They hung stripped and idle, without connection.

"Did you do this?" Jacob asked, judging Cutter.

"No."

"I'm going to ask you once more before I deck you. Did you pull these wires from this navigation housing?"

"I didn't do it. I didn't do it. I didn't do it." He was agitated. "I'm just fucking getting rid of the heaviest items."

For a minute, Jacob tried to picture Ruby fumbling around in the belly of the yacht, searching for the navigation control wiring. It didn't add up. Then he pictured Dorothy's time alone below deck. *Wasn't feeling well, my ass.*

Then, he replied to Joe, "You're actually delusional to think what you're doing is making a difference. The keel is cracked, and the fiberglass hull has been compromised, it's fractured. We going to take on water and we might need to life raft it ashore. Just sayin'. Shedding a few hundred pounds does nothing to advance our situation". Paisley sloshed away toward the steps to the deck in the water that was a foot deep.

As he was splashing away, he heard Cutter reply, "It's your situation."

Jacob was slow with a response, "You're right." He looked around the craft, considering that they were now probably three or four hundred pounds lighter, and thinking of the water displacement, summed up the words, "It is. Oh hell, maybe shedding weight might do some good. I don't really know. Like I said, do what you got to do. Bail or toss watery shit overboard. I don't care."

When he was back in the captain's seat, he saw Kolohe and Kerri sitting with the child. She had a bottle prepared, feeding him. He didn't notice that in the exchange with Cutter, that the child had stopped its crying.

"Do you know how to care for a baby?" she asked softly.

He shook his head slowly, "I don't have any idea how..."

"That's too bad." She replied quickly. He thought it was an awkward response. *These are just kids.* Jacob thought. *And the baby's clearly not his.*

The safe hoisted by Cutter up from the master stateroom sat on the deck between them. Jacob left the captain's seat for a minute to look at the baby sucking from the bottle. "Cute."

"Thanks. Three weeks early. Two months. A lot of work. A lot of work. Too much, really."

"His father?"

"Cutter was away. He...he...he was nice to me. I needed it, the kindness I mean..." Her eyes filled with tears and two streaks fell down her cheeks. With her arms cradling the child, Jacob reached to her face to wipe them away. Tears were followed by more tears. He knew that the salt from the tears on her cheeks was of the same amount of salt in the water Cutter was bailing.

These two. They're not together, they're not a pair. The child isn't his. I've invited trouble into a troubled situation.

Cutter squeaked with each step as he climbed back above carrying a piece of the granite countertop. Overboard, it made little splash, as it slid into the sea. A few minutes later, another slab of rock was tossed and delivered a more productive.

"Cut the anchor." Cutter demanded. "What is it two, three hundred pounds?"

"Are you fucking crazy? It's aluminum. They don't make 'em like they used to."

"What about one of the engines?"

"That we're using to get us to Oahu? They're inboards, like yours. They're encased, custom, not top fixed outboards." Jacob reached for the binoculars as Cutter stormed off toward the bow of the boat. He hoped to see land break the horizon. Knowing that the wires to the communication deck was ripped he clicked the radio handset once more for no more of a reason than that's what he had been doing. The unit received power, but the connection to the satellite was compromised.

Cutter approached Jacob, "The safe."

"Just a minute." He kneeled down to roll the tumblers right three times to settle on 14, left twice to settle on 9, right three times to land on 2. Retrieving the handgun, pulling up the velvet underlay and a large black metal box hiding the $250,000 in cash and his passport, he said, "There you go."

Cutter was sweating. He appeared slimy and had sweat from the bailing and stripping weight from the yacht. After looking at the handgun, then at Jacob, then at Kerri, he knelt to hoist the safe to his waist and shuffled it to the edge to push it overboard. It made a deep and perfect cannonball sound. Ker-plunk , with a large splash. Not knowing the contents of the black metal box and while Jacob turned away, Cutter also tossed it into the sea. Unknowing its contents and in a total state of one-mindedness, the quarter of a million dollars was tossed.

Jacob, once he realized what Cutter had done, ran to the starboard side watching the black metal box sink slowly, releasing tiny air bubbles as it descended. *Goodbye old friend.* The box was lead-like in weight. $250,000 only weighed five and a half pounds. He thought of the 2,500 one-hundred-dollar bills submerging into this unknown location.

He took a deep breath - and screamed at Jacob. "Where's the life boat located?"

"Why?"

Cutter picked up the gun and pointed it at Jacob, "Because we're splittin' up!"

Assessing danger and tone, Kolohe started barking.

The baby began crying.

Kerri looked in the direction of Cutter, still sobbing quietly with tears on her cheeks in the morning's pre-dawn.

Jacob took a step back and held his hands up to his head.

The Aicon's engines sluggishly churned the water, causing a small wake of water sloshing behind them.

With the noisy distractions in the quiet Pacific, the safety made a small click which was the loudest noise of all.

19

Arcing The Flatline

Brian slipped on his neon green Brooks running shoes. *They'll see ya coming,* Laki told him, as he opened the early present. He was too kind to tell her he could have had them given to him by the local sales rep if he had asked. Perks of the sporting goods industry. Their kids were never going to have to know want for the latest gear if things continued.

The Waianae mountains were towering above concealing the eastern side of the island's dawn where the light was just beginning to penetrate the day.

He liked getting in his running early. And he had most of the morning to summon the endorphins from the runner's high. It felt good again, to get in the minor mileage at a decent pace without pain. The beach walk at the Ko Olina was the perfect place to capture the uninterrupted workout. It was already two hours earlier in the day in Oceanside where Laki was. He texted her that he loved her deeply and would be home soon. Hearts and hibiscus flowers tattooed his text message.

Uncle's small pickup truck was old, but reliable. Two decades ago, he rode in the back up and down Farrington Highway. It was once white and shiny. Now it was weathered, scratched, a grayish white and dull. The Nanakuli way: *don't nix it, fix it.* The keys were clutched in his fist as he quietly exited the hale and headed for the carport where it lived. He learned to drive in this old truck. His smile was as broad as his shoulders. *It purrs just like a kitten* he thought when he turned the engine. *Kind of. Maybe not, as a slight squeal came from the timing belt.*

The morning commute from westside dwellers into Honolulu had just begun. Red taillights were building from traffic light to traffic light. Then the run the Ko Olina exit provided Brian to re-remember Uncle, the gentle teacher, talking in pidgin about turn signals, and rights of way, and how to change a tire or the oil. He took the exit below the speed limit, making the exit ramp serve as the break from the highway speed.

Once on Aliinui Drive at the entrance of the resort, he slowed down at the Aloha Gate to see if he recognized anyone. A young man threw him a shaka, but he was skunked and didn't know the guy. The resort speed was 25 miles per hour, and he tried to get it perfect on the speed devices measuring the small trucks speed.

He turned right and rolled into the Beach Park parking lot ahead of the other early morning traffic. Several of the Kupuna were gathering to strum their ukuleles for Kanikapila. He looked at his watch which would count his steps and register mileage. 7:02am. The elders began playing a song he knew growing up, playing ukuleles with his friends and cousins. The words and the music were that of Jerry Santos, Ku'u Home 'O Kahalu'u. He knew most of the words. They were in English. He hummed those he didn't.

Strolling over their way, they were finishing.

"Aloha Aunties and Uncles."

Most of them replied, "Aloha." They were gathered in a large oval, nearly fifteen of them, all with ukuleles of assorted sizes. Some were of dark koa Hawaiian wood, other were the cheap swap meet or Costco kind, but they sounded almost as sweet playing the island songs too.

One of the Kupuna not playing an ukulele, but playing a pakini bass, which was a stick with a thick string attached to an old red gas can, asked him, "Hey bruda, you got song you sing?"

Brian knew the pidgin well and had no problem interpreting, or joining in for a bit, "Oh...can you do Sweet Lady of Waiahole?

"Shoots den," one of the Uncles replied and several of the Kupuna checked the legend, when one of the Aunties shouted out, "One tree eight, ode book." They scurried to locate page one hundred thirty-eight in their four-inch binders filled with songs. More Kupuna continued to arrive and set up their black aluminum lightweight sheet music stands barely able to support the thick books jammed with paper.

"Second line of Hui first," one of the Uncles called out. He also counted them in, in Hawaiian, "Ekahi. Elua. Ekolu. Eha..." They began strumming. He had slipped his sunglasses on, not because the sun was shining, but because he made an assumption as to what would happen next. Brians eyes got teary hearing the old people play the song they had played for years and perhaps decades. It was a song from his boyhood, growing up local here, before any of the resorts were risen by the cranes along the seashore. Another one of the Kupuna limped over to Brian to offer an ukulele. He simply could not turn down the offer and jammed with them. They asked if he was Hawaiian boy and he admitted to living in Nanakuli, playing football with the Golden Hawks, that his Auntie and Uncle still lived here, but unfortunately, he had to move away from Oahu as he went to college and now worked in San Diego supporting a family of his own. They had much to say, and he knew that he'd get pulled in for lengthy talk story session if he chatted much more, so he requested just one more song.

"Ulupalakua?"

"Oh brudah, you in for spesha treat," one of the Kupuna joked, and three of them arose from their folding chairs to hula inside the circle. They were charming. *Hula from da Kupuna.* If nothing else happened today, his day would have been made from their kindness and sharing their Aloha with him. He smiled and blinked often to conceal the teary eyes hiding behind his sunglasses. At the end of their hula within the song sung by the others, he threw them all a shaka and a loud "Mahalo and A-lo-ha," as he left their melodious circle of love and friendship.

Listening to their next song he walked toward the pavement of the beach walk. Three extra-extra-large Samoan boys were unloading contents from their large black SUV into a blue wagon. Makua Rothman's, *Beautiful Life*, was playing loudly and competing with the Kupuna's soft songs.

What a life, living here in Hawaii. A day at the beach with their families was apparently in order. A large cooler and some reusable grocery bags containing island grinds was carefully moved to the overloaded wagon. A football fell from the trunk and onto the asphalt near where Brian was walking. He picked up, clutched the pigskin, and launched it toward one of the large Samoans. "Mahalo," they called out to Brian. He just nodded.

"Hey Tiny...way da poi?" One of the Samoans called out to another.

The largest one, apparently named Tiny, replied, "Da coola."

The first looked in a red and white Rubbermaid cooler.

"Da udda one. Check in... uh, check in Moni's coola, Tink it's deya somewhere..."

Linemen, Brian thought to himself. They too, looked like locals and probably knew all the Hawaiian songs which he knew. *Big boys. Ono grindz.*

It was time for Brian to attempt to get a few miles under his toes. He punched a few buttons on his phone, drumming up a play list of his favorite beachside running songs. The guitar strumming from Jack Johnson's, *You And Your Heart,* played in his ears as he skip stepped into his light jog warm up.

*****

With one arm, Cutter handed the black child to Jacob. It wasn't a careful handoff. The sweaty young man had the handgun in the other. The baby whimpered as Jacob landed on his butt in the inflated yellow raft. Two plastic unassembled yellow oars were roped to the side with fifty feet of one inch thick nylon. “Boat in a Bag”, the description of the lift raft proclaimed.

“She was going to give it up for adoption anyway.”

Kerri was crying uncontrollably.

Cutter tossed baby items and supplies from inside a diaper bag to Jacob in the life raft. Formula, diapers, a bottle, a blanket, and a few baby care items that Jacob didn’t know existed. They bounced around inside the vinyl inflatable as they landed, scattering.

“Why can’t he just have the bag?” She was sobbing and distraught and she found it difficult to work the words from her mouth.

“I’ve got coke in the bag.” His tone to her was now condescending. He was gone for a minute.

She sat looking at the child without more words.

Jacob Paisley was questioning the reality of this moment. He thought that it must be a dream, and he didn’t know his next move. The former money manager sat idle with the child in his left arm.

Kerri Latch was certain that this action, sparing the child from herself, was the protection needed from Crazy Kerri and her dominant need to use again.

There they were, face to face, sharing the breath of life with the baby between them. Little did he know that this was the same woman that fell to the floor of a drug store the day he was released from Mount Sinai. Little did she know that a disturbance at a hospital across the street two years ago was the event this same handsome man was involved in. Their paths were intertwined yet not crossed.

Cutter returned to the deck and tossed two bottles of water to Jacob. He fumbled receiving them and they fell inside the small floatable.

Kolohe. Where was Kolohe? Jacob thought. The yellow lab appeared to the aft of the craft, with its tail wagging wildly. He whined once and sprung past Cutter to the wobbly inflatable from the stern of The Final Trade. K-9 paws were not ideal for a life raft.

"Here's the deal. We'll call for your rescue when we land somewhere. After we're clear." The man with the gun was calling the shots.

"Drugs?" Jacob asked.

It wasn't met with a response as Cutter turned his head. He set the handgun on the bench which would have normally been filled with happy Veterans excited to see whales or dolphins or turtles but wishing for mermaids. Or perhaps couples from the Hoku foundation which he began supporting, taking a break from hospice to count one of their final sunsets together, might normally be sitting where the gun rested. It wasn't a bench seat on a luxury yacht intended to host drug trade shenanigans or a drug-yielding punk's initiatives.

Kerri quickly retrieved the handgun from the seat under the dodger, where Cutter had set it down. As he reached for it from her grasp it bounced on the hardwood deck once, and the edge of the lift raft once. It bounced toward Paisley in the air, and he caught it with his one free hand. Once again, with one hand holding the child and with the other capturing the gun in midair, he was looking down the same barrel – this time he knew it was loaded.

"What the hell do you think you're doing!" Cutter scolded Kerri.

Jacob heard them arguing about something else, but it was short lived. Cutter was curt and yanked her hair at the base of her skull. She cried out in pain.

He assumed that there was more in the diaper bag than cocaine. But here he was, the shiny revolver in hand. The power had shifted…or equaled. He now had the handgun.

Cutter ran to the helm.

The baby began crying. Jacob looked at it wrapped inside the blanket. In Kerri's handwriting, she printed the child's name:

GABRIEL HOLLINS

"This name…" Jacob asked in a panic. "Why? Why does it say Gabriel Hollins."

Kerri acted as if there were two of her. It was odd. She spoke in a different way, and confidently. "Some old dude on a park bench. Said that's what he'd name his child if he had one, which he didn't."

"A black man. Somewhat charming..."

"Yeah, that's the guy. Back in New York."

"You're from New York."

"City. Why?"

Jacob was as shocked as he wasn't. "Manhattan?"

She shrugged, not at all acting as if she cared about the baby. There were two of her, "Hell's Kitchen. Sat on a park bench, gave me an envelope that had a thousand bucks in it. Said he had it saved for his son's or daughter's college fund, but then never had kids. Asked me to put it to good use. So, I bought some doctor H." Kerri showed him her arms. Scars of needle tracks left dots and blemishes on her skinny white arms where sharps ruled. "Users gotta' use, man."

Jacob was speechless.

One tear ran down her cheek. One eye produced no tears.

Finally, he found the words for their brief connection – the three of them – Jacob, Kerri, and this impostor willing to give up her newborn child. "I'll take care of him for now...you'll find him later...this is temporary..."

"Yeah, yeah, yeah...that's why he's wearing the name, dude. You'll do the right thing."

Jacob thought that all she cared about was her next fix but that somewhere inside of this crazy version of herself, the timid mother, Kerri, was dying from loss, and shame, and vile actions of this charlatan.

How could something like this happen? And even though the situation was as far away from his distinguished New York life just a short time ago, he thought of the need of Victoria. It too, was like a drug. An unrelenting desire which in the end delivered no good.

Cutter ran to the captain's deck and loudly fired up the engines. The twin Caterpillar's roared to life, churning a white and frothy wake from under the vessel, rocking the yellow rescue craft haphazardly. Jacob could tell that forward thrusters were engaged and the yacht, slowly at first, then with a draw from normal operations, forcefully speed off. Jacob watched his yacht depart with a sluggish as well as a robust response. It moved away gaining speed as it departed, causing the small yellow life raft to toss wildly in the wake and the surf. White seafoam grew in a departing V shape as the craft quickly moved far away. Even though it was dark, it was light enough to see the despair that had arrived.

Jacob could see moniker: The Final Trade on the back of his yacht. Then, he noticed Kerri looking back.

Something didn't fit. Why did she ask if he knew how to care for a child? It was a puzzle of pieces that didn't come together. He looked down over the right edge of the small inflatable and as the seconds became a minute, found an easing surf, void of wake or waves.

The connection to the prized vessel was waning. As the yacht was nearly out of sight, when he could no longer make out that it even was an Aicon, he thought about the nice surprise they'd find in the metal black box that was probably sliding across the teak deck right about now. $250,000 in cash wasn't something you didn't usually miss, even if you were Jacob Paisley. Perhaps they'd throw that overboard too. The safe, too much weight, was another thirty pounds - and a burden which Cutter, who seemed to make one bad choice after another, would likely toss overboard.

For some crazy reason, Jacob thought about a bad day in Manhattan. *How could this even compare*? The sky was still more night than early morning, but he could tell that it was peppered with white puffy cumulus clouds. The December Pacific was usually a deep and inviting blue. This moment, however, was too deep and uninviting.

Only five minutes had passed. The wake of the million dollar yacht was long gone. "How did we end up here?" Jacob asked Kolohe. Kolohe whined. The tiny black child was rocked asleep in the gentle rock of the waves. He looked as far left as he could without turning his body, then as far right. No land.

"They're not going to make it." He wasn't sure who he was talking to. It was Kolohe who understood more than the two-month-old. Perhaps the lab was his audience. The words were for the light breeze and to satisfy his acknowledgment of judgment. "There was too much drag. Hope they can both swim." His consideration changed the more he thought about it. "Hope she can swim." A look at the small child in his arms, thinking that he would need a mother sooner than later, but maybe not that mother – at least at this point in her life. "I have an idea of how she ended with you. What I don't know is how did you end up with her? Is this Ruby's idea of divine intervention? Perhaps your name is what he means by the power of a suggestion. And maybe, just maybe, it's all randomness and meets one of the mathematical formulas. Conditional Probability or the Markov Chain. Or..." he hesitated, "or we're not done yet."

He remained silent for a minute. "Ellipsis."

More moments of nothingness other than floating passed. Jacob watched the morning light encroach upon what was a dark and mysterious night.

An hour of floating had passed by. He wondered if the small craft had found an ocean drift and if so, was it toward land or away. It wasn't a comforting thought. "Eventually, I'll show you both my rowing skills." The small bright yellow folded rows were still just that, folded.

Kolohe wagged his tail occasionally. The child slept.

The sun broke the sea's horizon creating a beautiful orange haze. Clouds reflected reds and violets.

Kolohe was lying at Jacob's feet with his overly expression-filled eyebrows asking Jacob 'what they were doing there?' Jacob imagined a thought bubble coming from the top of the dog's head: *Where's my boat? Where's the Ko Olina? Where's Adele? This is boring. Got a treat?*

"I know, boy." With one arm holding his newfound precious cargo, with the other he scratched one of the ears of his dog.

Two birds flew over the raft. They circled once and moved on in the same direction they were originally heading. "We can't be that far from land, boy, not too far off course. What do you think?" Jacob talked with Kolohe as if he was expecting dialogue. "Those birds. Either they're on the way to breakfast or they just came from it." He knew otherwise. Birds could travel hundreds of miles. He doubted that that kind of distance was between where there were and Oahu.

Jacob had drifted asleep. His waking thought was of the final comment that Ruby had provided before he disappeared: *"You're hearing this to know what lies ahead."*

He jerked as he awoke. The seawater was unusually smooth and gentle. His movement caused some ripples. The child was whimpering but not crying. As he looked in each direction, he saw nothing. Then all hell broke, the baby wailed. Jacob reached for a bottle. It was cold but he had no idea of how to warm it other than sticking it under his armpit for a minute. He put it in the baby's mouth, but it was rejected time and time and time again.

"Oh God no, please. You need a diaper change, don't you?" Jacob had an idea about how to do it, but this would be his first. He did what he thought should be done sorting through the things which had been tossed his way as they were ejected from The Final Trade. When the contents of the diaper were revealed, Jacob found religion. "Good Lord! That was inside of you? How can you live like that?"

For the moment at least, the child stopped crying. Jacob used the adhesive from the diaper to wrap itself tightly shut and nudged it with his toes to the other side of the raft. He could still smell it and nudged it two inches further away. "Yeah, I'd cry if I had that in my pants too." Holding the small baby, he leaned back. Sunshine was beginning to command the morning in between the cloud breaks. He kept the little one from the sun's direct rays.

Then, there was something. A disturbance in the quiet moment. It was Kolohe which first drew his attention.

"What is it, boy? What do you see? Help on the way?"

It was the sunshine on the water's surface that illuminated and reflected light from the dorsal fin. The grey shark's fin was gliding across the glassy surface. Kolohe was standing up causing the inflatable to bounce and rock uneasily. The dog's tail was not wagging and his ears were down. Jacob had never seen this before.

"Down boy."

Kolohe didn't react to the command.

"Kolohe, down."

There were two fins. He didn't notice the second until the first altered course. It was a quick turn showcasing their fierce agility and strength in the water.

There appeared a third. Jacob sat up straight. The child began to cry. Kolohe barked. The provisions from the baby bounced around as Kolohe moved from one side of the inflatable to the other. "No Kolohe, no!"

The yellow lab jumped out of the unstable yellow inflatable into the sea toward the fin. It caused the raft to rock and seawater spilled over the eighteen inch parameter into the dry area. Most of the baby blanket was drenched. The child was crying wildly.

"Kolohe! No! No, Kolohe. No!"

The dog paddled away from the raft and quickly turned to return. Jacob laid the child down carefully and jumped to the edge sticking his hands into the water to retrieve the lab. "Come here boy!"

The fins spun in the direction of the dog. Jacob felt the front paws of Kolohe in his hands and then the claws on his forearms. Still swimming forward with all four legs, Kolohe pulled himself onto Jacob's arms and onto the ridge.

The baby's cry added distraction to the moment. The lead shark appeared to breach the surface but missed the dog's hindquarter. Instead, it nipped at the raft and fell back into the ocean. For one second, Jacob went eye to eye with it. Grey, sleek, evil, fast – the sharks sensed the danger and the prey, and the game was on.

The fins were submerged. But he knew that with the dog's scent in the water that they were below, scheming an attack. The baby was taking breaths and gasps to cry louder. It caused Jacob's ears to buzz. He picked the infant back up in his arms. The handgun was underneath the child's wet blanket on the raft. Jacob bent over to see if the safety was on. The child continued to cry, but it wasn't the disturbance that Jacob thought.

Hissing.

He heard a small hissing noise that was as much of a high-pitched whine as it was air escaping the life raft.

The shark had bit into the inflatable and a stream of bubbles created a humming noise from the underbelly of the wet edge. "No!"

Kolohe barked six times, then shook. The saltwater lightly sprayed Jacob and the baby. *This cannot be happening*, Jacob thought. He said it out loud to confirm its reality. "This cannot be happening!" It came out of his mouth with more volume than he thought – and his words were rooted in fear.

"Kolohe, No!" The dog didn't stop. It couldn't. Its natural instincts to protect were engaged and its claws scratched the rafts edge making the streaming bubbles larger.

The gun, Jacob thought. *Six shots. Think. Think.*

The child wailed, the dog barked, the bubbles appeared to grow larger the more they left the small craft. *The plastic oars.* Jacob looked at the few provisions. The handgun, two bottles of water, two bottles of formula, wet diapers, a wet blanket. With one hand, he felt for any contents within his pockets – his wallet and cell phone were on the Aicon. *What good would they do anyway?*

What he saw was what he had. His thoughts shot through his head of all the moments he favored most: the money, millions of dollars, the fame, power, control, admiration, stock tickers floating through his head, traders barking buy and sell orders on the floor of PPCM, earnings calls, cigars, fine dining, bottles of champagne, opulent clubs, the women, Victoria's irresistible charm, Adele's compassion, the Manhattan penthouse, Central Park, Manhattan, hotels, limos, private jets, arrivals and departures. He thought of all of his better-elsewhere's.

Was this it then? Is this how it will end? One disappointing descent into the sea?

The sharks were back.

Kolohe barked at the circling fins, smoothly gliding on the surface. The child continued to cry. The bubbles splashed as Kolohe moved around the inflatable causing disruption.

His flashing thoughts of what he'd done adjusted to what he must do. He must fight. He'd put his hand in the water to feel the rupture. The fins tightened their circumference. *Bad idea.*

The gun. Jacob reached for the gun. It felt foreign in his grasp even though he just held it earlier. This time he was using it to kill. He looked at the largest fin. *First*, he thought. *You go down first. Six shots.* He aimed, then withdrew. Wait. He listened to the bubbles, the child continued to cry, Kolohe continued to bark.

He reassessed his time. He processed the situation. He took it all in and made some sense of it. That's what he did.

And he came to an unfavorable conclusion. *Three shots. First, it'll be three shots. Three shots, first. Then three to spare.* Fear and stress throbbed through him. His chest hurt. His hand holding the gun was shaking. He looked at the dog, he looked at the child.

The small bubbles signaled fleeting time, like the last few grains of sand through an hourglass. He thought: *How much time? How much time do we have left?* He asked Kolohe, "How much time do we have left?" Kolohe stopped barking for a few seconds to turn and look at Jacob. Then, continued to bark at the relentless orbit of fins. "Time is on their side," Jacob said. He watched the grey dorsal fins circle in a vengeful cadence. Their precision in the water would be flawless. They wouldn't stop until they had what they wanted. He tried to avoid the thought of the pain and the suffocation.

A sacrifice? Could he do it? Could the child be enough? Could Kolohe serve as the offering? He listened to the bubbles. No.

He looked at the child and the dog. "This isn't going to end well."

The raft was half of what it was. Listening to the bubbles, Jacob retreated to the flashes of his life's memories: his parents, life as a kid growing up in the Midwest, his grandfather's farm, shoveling snow, college campuses, Adele, Ruby... *Where are you now, my gentle companion?* He thought of the conversations that they had. His mind was racing through anything thought about Ruby's pillars of potential: "*That's life's game, friend,*" Ruby would have said.

A shark bumped into the inflatable.

Kolohe barked and reached one paw toward the water. The sides of the raft began to dimple from the dog's weight. "No, Kolohe, no." They wouldn't last long. He raised the handgun toward the water's surface. Three shots for three sharks. He laid the crying child down. Kolohe stopped to sniff at the baby for one second, then continued to bark.

He fired. The gun caused more response than he anticipated. It was loud and caused Kolohe to tuck his ears and whimper. The first shot was disappointing. It missed the fin by two feet. *Anticipate. That's what you were good at.*

A loud bang. The second shot was much closer. But it missed. The three dorsal fins disappeared below the surface again. The bubbles from the hole in the life raft had diminished slightly. They were the markers for their remaining seconds, heartbeats, moments.

Two of the fins reappeared. Bang! The third shot also missed. Again, the fins retreated by submerging. The gunfire caused Kolohe to whine, but the baby continued to cry.

This was the moment. The one that alters the course of existence. The one moment that changes everything. A decision. An exchange between what might matter most and what happens next.

Jacob knew what needed to be done. The suffering and the pain from the potential of the next moments would be intolerable. He had three shots remaining. Three for me? One for the dog, one for the child, one for me? The bubbles continued to mark fleeting minutes. The sharks would return. This was their territory. They'd have their way. "A shark's going to do what a shark's going to do." It rolled across his tongue like he'd said it before. He thought of the times in Manhattan that his mean-spirited style of leadership used that sentence to disregard another man's existence. Competitive, creative, influential.

That man was dead.

His eyes began to well with tears. He took a deep breath. Time was drawing to a close.

Kolohe lay at the bottom of the raft with his paws covering his ears. Jacob aimed the gun at his friend. "I'm so sorry, boy. I am so sorry."

Two streams of tears fell from both cheeks. He aimed the gun squarely at his dogs forehead, extending the gun away from himself and the baby.

Then, he quickly moved his gun-holding hand and arm away - facing the water. Click. Misfire.

Quickly, and without further consideration, Jacob held the gun to the infant child's forehead. He moved his forearm away from the back of the baby's head.

He couldn't do it. Before he pulled the trigger, he moved the aim to the sea. Click. Misfire.

"Oh God," he cried out. He sobbed at the agony of living, and failing, and being placed in this desolate moment of despondence.

He looked at the child. It's eyes were wide while it continued to cry. He held the gun to his mouth. His right hand was on the trigger. He smelled metal.

The barrel of the gun was in his mouth, his finger was on the trigger, his eyes caught the stare from Kolohe and the child before he fired.

And he didn't. He pulled the barrel from his mouth, aimed it in the direction of nowhere, and for the sixth time pulled the trigger. A hollow click.

The handgun gave a ringing sound as the empty chamber was struck by the firing pin. He opened the carriage with one hand and the fingers also holding the child as best he could. Three shells. Only three empty shells were available. He held his hand over the edge of the raft and the pistol slipped from his fingers into the Pacific.

Where did the other three rounds go? He had never fired the gun before.

The circling fins disappeared. *They're in pursuit of the sinking revolver*, Jacob thought. It probably reflected the sun and looked like a fleeing fish as the metal sank away. *But they'll be back.*

He sat up and dried his eyes with his on his damp shirtsleeve. The bubbles continued to count remaining minutes. The baby was exhausted from crying and was finally beginning to ease in the vocal assault.

Ruby. Ruby was babbling about *three*. Something like, "*...could only get three.*"

He looked at Kolohe. The yellow dog yawned a nervous yawn. The bubbles were growing louder. Remaining minutes. How could that have happened? The gun was locked.

He remembered Mount Sinai. Hospital volunteer. Ruby sat in the corner of Jacob's room and must have listened to Jacob calling into his account at least twice. Jacob was obsessed with the fluctuating amount and called several times each day. Columbus: 14, 92. Columbus, fourteen, ninety-two. Columbus: 1, 4, 9, 2. Columbus: 14 – 9 – 2. It was a number that stuck. A number that someone who's middle name was Columbus would remember. He kept what could be simple, simple – because his life had an affinity to attract complexities. 14, 9, 2. The combination to the safe. Either this conclusion lent itself to an outcome of *perhaps* or *of course*. The riddle didn't matter.

The code of this mystery didn't deserve any attention and would remain unsolved. The child only whimpered now and it began to grow quiet. Jacob heard the sound of the seas breeze against his ears. A gust would toss his growing hair. He hadn't paid much attention to the elements.

The fins were still below the surface.

His mind went blank, his final step had been taken, his energy extinguished. He tried not to think of what was next. Instead, he listened to the growing noise from the bubbles. The air was depleted from the raft to the point that if Kolohe moved to its edge, Jacob would have to choose to not bring him back in. So, he sat still and didn't speak to his friend. He'd continue to toss remaining items overboard to distract the sharks while minutes would become seconds. The child stopped crying completely.

Lost at sea. That's how it would sound.

The bubbles continued to count down moments. It was all he focused on for nearly a minute.

Ruby. He looked at the child. Ruby. He remembered Ruby at the bar in Bobby Van's, *"My father tried to kill me once. Pulled the trigger, just once. The gun didn't go off. Lots of things can always turn out different than they do. That's the capacity of change."*

He looked at the baby, "It was you."

Kolohe sat up.

"No, Kolohe! Down! Down!" The yellow Labrador stood on all fours and wagged his tail happily. "Kolohe, no!" Water seeped into the raft. The dorsal fins appeared for a second and darted below the surface.

Kolohe wagged his tail and barked. The bubbles grew louder. Jacob looked into their direction to see why they were seemingly louder. But, it wasn't the bubbles from the sinking craft that drew an increased volume. Jacob tried to steady the dog while watching the water's surface and listened to what he could.

It was an outboard motor. It was Kito.

Kolohe's attention at the approaching fishing boat was the distant noise that caused the bark. *Ruff. Ruff-ruff. Ruff-ruff-ruff.*

Kito pulled alongside the sinking raft, "Aloha, brah." He assessed the few seconds before the seawater would engulf the inflatable and offered his hands out to take the baby.

"Quickly. Kolohe...No!." Jacob had desperation in his voice. But the dog didn't obey and jumped causing the water to pour into the life raft

"What do you..." Kito watched the yellow inflatable begin to submerge, wrapping Jacob. Three shark fins that were away from the boat altered course toward the yellow rubber. Jacob's eyes become wide.

Kito scrambled to the bait locker and tossed a handful of tiny baitfish away from Jacob. The sharks again changed course, quickly darting toward the bait.

Paisley reached for the rail of Kito's small craft and pulled himself up. Kito extended his hand and they both fell into the Japanese fisherman's vessel.

Jacob remembered his opinion on sharks. The kind that swam on Wall Street. *A shark does what a shark has to do.* Jacob began to laugh.

Kito was lying underneath him, and didn't understand the humor of the moment. He smiled a toothy grin and looking up at Jacob said, "Dis my best catch ever."

Still on his knees, Jacob looked at the fish locker. The biggest Ulua he had ever seen was protruding from the white cooler at the back of the boat. Its tail was sticking out.

Kito began to laugh with Jacob. "What story dis make - old Japanee fish-man like me...I once caught a man, dis big." He held out his arms to indicate size and Jacob reached over and hugged him.

The child remained quiet, nestled in the Captain's chair. Kolohe wagged his tail at the welcomed sound of the laughter, and licked at Kito's fishy smelling knees.

He retrieved the few floating items from the water with a net.

Kito pulled the single outboard motor to life with its hand crank - and they were off. A peaceful wake split the deep blue calm sea.

Not today sharks. Jacob thought as he looked back at the formidable moment and the last look at a small piece of the yellow life raft still clutching to the surface.

*****

Brian's legs had an extra and unexpected burst and bounce. He'd found his mojo at the first lagoon where many of the tourists were on the way back to the fourth lagoon - where many of the locals congregated. It was ideal running weather. The morning was perfect - not too humid, not too windy, not too listless. Light breezes from the Ewa plains had increased as the sun continued to rise in the lapis blue sky, lightly bending the coconut fronds above. Puffy small white clouds moved quickly across the early morning sky from land toward the sea.

In a quick assessment of 'go, no go' he found his inner rocket fuel and turned the burners on. He felt no pain attempting to finish strong as he approached the common area green lawn of the beach park. There they were, the Samoans he'd seen earlier, tossing the brown leather football to each other. Standing twenty yards apart they were throwing it easily but missing the catches more than seizing them. They were just a little encumbered in the agility department. But their size, Brian noted, could stop a truck from getting a first down. *Linemen.*

They stopped and began talking among themselves while walking toward the water. There was a disturbance of some sort.

It was a scrawny man, hitting a thin and helpless woman. She recoiled as he continued shouting at her and was unrelenting with his strikes. They both appeared to be soaked from swimming as their long hair was wet and clung in clumps with the haphazard strikes.

Her cries were matched with shouts from the Samoans for the man to stop. She covered her face with her hands. His blows struck anywhere. Her torso, her shoulders, her ears, the hands that covered her face. In several seconds he landed as many strikes as possible. Then he stopped, screamed at her more, and began again. He wanted her to carry something, or perhaps her name was Carrie, Brian thought.

He stopped. He was breathing heavily. Looking around the beach park quickly he saw the Samoans which were still cautiously walking in the direction of the repulsive hits she was enduring. Others, near the showers and at the beach, which had settled on towels to devour breakfast or sip morning coffee had taken notice and were informing their small gatherings of the disruption.

But few were doing anything to prevent the assault at the moment.

He watched. It was unrelenting. She held her hands across her face and torso as he pulled her hair and continued to strike her. The Samoan brothers were yelling and shouting as they walked quicker in the direction of the young and scrawny couple.

Yancy. Just like that. It wasn't Yancy, but the thought of Yancy harming Leilani drew a gametime rush of Adrenalin. *No,* Brian thought, *it's wrong, no. No. Leilani had no one to protect her as she was made a victim of a beating. That could not happen today, not if Brian could help it.* Fifty yards separated them.

Without any more consideration he began sprinting past the Samoans toward the two. Five more strikes. Six. Seven...

Before the man with long hair and a black tank top was able to hit her again, Brian leaped into the air hitting him in the ribs with Brian's shoulder. It was a perfect tackle. Cracking sounds were heard as the two of them flew five yards to the ground. A grunt from the would-be-Yancy, the woman-hitter, a haole, the gaunt white man was heard.

Brian felt no pain as they crashed to the grassy ground. He had never tackled someone so light. Even the smallest wide receivers had thirty pounds on this scrawny haole. Perhaps it was the man's ribs, perhaps it was vertebrae, Brian didn't care. His target, he was out cold. No movement at first. Then, a small groan as the three massive Samoans surrounded him. *The Linemen have you now...you bony punk.* His breathing was hard as he had just sprinted half the distance of a field which he once commanded to stop the assault from continuing. He felt out of breath, and it felt wonderful.

The woman continued to cower, covering her face with her hands as if the attack were ongoing, and was weeping. She fell into a fetal position on the lawn and began rocking herself while lying on the ground weeping. There was torment in her soul as she seemed inconsolable in the wretched moment. Two women attempted to calm her, but their calming words were useless in the moment.

For a small moment Brian thought to himself, *what did I just do?* It was overcome with a quick conviction of: *I did the right thing. I stopped it. Had to.*

Minutes of sorting through what had just happened with the Samoans, while the attacker continued to groan, were soon followed by the beach police arriving, a man and woman officer They quickly assessed the situation and radioed for backup. In a minute another car rolled up. The lights were blinking a bright blue from the two vehicles in the parking lot. Two additional vehicles arrived, and it was officially a commotion. The static of police radios could be heard, as the attempt to resolve the situation was happening fast.

You don't hit a man when he's down. Why don't you stand back up so I can take you out of the play again... That was just one hit. I've got a game in me, man. Let's go... Brian thought as he looked at him. *You're not so tough now, are you? You may not be Yancy...but the broken parts inside of him are inside of you too.*

Brian was soon approached, and answered several questions, as did his new Samoan teammates. The young man that had been striking the woman was now sitting upright, hands cuffed behind his back. A skinny young man, not fit like Brian had always been. One male police officer remained by his side, asking questions, and taking notes. He often used his black shoes to keep the attacker's legs separated. Once out of sight, the policeman's work might not be as gentle as it was in public view. Another joined him, flanking the bully punk. Bringing him to his feet, assessing whether he could walk, they hauled the offender to the closest squad car and tucking him into a caged back seat, the sped off.

The young woman who had taken the brunt of the strikes was taken away, separately, and without restraint but rather with the care and concern of two female women in blue. They offered a towel from the trunk of the squad car to her to help dry her off. Bottled water was provided. She remained sullen, looking down at the ground in front of her, clutching the edges of the towel wrapped around her just under her chin. Clumsy steps were taken. Each officer held her skinny upper arms and elbows as they proceeded to their car in the parking lot.

It was over quickly. Brian had a minute to himself now - to digest what had just happened. This would make for an interesting conversation with Laki. He found a green bench facing the water and sat. One of the Samoans, the largest one, named Tiny, walked over to Brian carrying the football.

"Brah..."

"Yeah," Brian replied.

He held out the football. Thinking he wanted to play catch, Brian shook his head.

"Game ball, brah..." He continued holding the ball in Brian's direction. "You MVP." He nudged the ball in the air in Brian's direction. "Play of the day."

He didn't want to take their football but reached out to hold onto it. It had been a minute since he was rewarded with the game ball. *Go Golden Hawks,* he thought to himself. "I don't want to..." he held the ball out for Tiny to take back.

"For reals, brah...you got skills. Should've played ball."

Brian couldn't help himself and chuckled. "Mahalo, brah." He held up the ball and nodded his head to the big man who had already turned and was walking away. Sitting back down on the bench, with the leather ball at his side, he thought that the hit may have made his high school coach proud. Maybe it would have made Friday Night Highlights. He repeated the quick event in his head twice more as he sat on the bench at the sea's side. *Not bad for a shoe salesman from San Diego*, he said to himself.

Before he decided it was time to leave a couple stopped in front of him. An elderly couple, a black man and what may have been his wife were trying to take a selfie with the ocean in the background. She was encouraging her companion to take the shot, and he was insisting it wouldn't take. The elderly black man had a veteran's hat with stars and bars and proudly arched VIETNAM across the crest of the cap. She was dressed plainly, wearing a skirt.

"Bill, just push that white circle," she taunted.

"I'm pressing it. Where's the lens?"

"Can I?" Brian offered.

"Oh...thank you so much. He's so kind," the old woman said to Brian first, and then to her companion.

"Make us look pretty now," the old man joked.

"There you go. Took several." Brian looked at the man. He hesitated, then said, "You look familiar. Maybe like Morgan Freeman's kid?"

"Me? Well...don't know..." the old black man mumbled to himself and could be heard saying, "I do get that occasionally. Guess it wouldn't be a good thing if you were in a police lineup, would it?" He chuckled, mostly to himself, and gave Brian a look. It was a stare. "Instead of driving Miss Daisy, I'm a drivin' Miss Dorothy." Then, the man clutched onto the woman's arm as she thanked Brian once again.

They took small steps together and away from Brian Kehahanamanui further on the beach walk, in the direction of the blue sparkly half-circle lagoon girdled by the tawny and sandy shoreline.

20

Precious Cargo

As Kito, Jacob, the baby named Gabriel Hollins and Kolohe approached the first buoy to the channel, in the distance, closer to the rocky shore, two Coast Guard jet skis approached the scene of the sunken yacht. They had a floating dinghy filled with small bright orange fenders to exhibit caution around the vessel.

There was no mistaking the two white marine radar and radio domes which were attached to the top of The Final Trade. The beacons normally were the lifeline of communications. Their purpose for dutiful determinations such as distance, depth, and distress hadn't failed him. Dorothy's tinkering for the designated outcome or Cutter's carelessness had.

They and an aluminum antenna were all that broke the surface of the water.

"I'm surprised they made it this far." Jacob said it to himself as Kito small craft motored on and approached the second set of buoys. They were close to the jet skis now. The Coast Guard jet skis continued to drop the orange fenders and as a precaution surrounded the submerged yacht with containment booms. They too were a bright orange and floated around the boat as soon as they were laid on the water's surface. There was no smell of seeping diesel.

"Dis no good, Kai Koa," the Japanese fisherman didn't look at Jacob. He didn't need to. It was said to say something that needed to be said in the awkward moment.

They slowed to a whisper of speed drinking in the scene as they passed The Final Trade, or what remained of it, its navigation bubbles. twisting their necks past the turn, including Kolohe, they continued watching the emergency dispatch from the Coast Guard lay the boundaries, occasionally breaking to talk into their radio handhelds.

He was just joking about liability-only insurance earlier in this day – the wee-hours of the morning. He really like the Aicon. The moniker: The Final Trade, was ten feet underwater. The LLC organization he set up to take on the debt to finance the yacht required insurance upon the craft. Since it was leveraged as structured entity and on the balance sheet of his new company and creatively financed, the money meant nothing. It was covered. He loved the lack of risk and responsibility. The two hundred and fifty grand in cash was another story. He could dip his toes back into the market and make that back up in a minute, maybe two.

"This too shall pass," Jacob again spoke to himself.

Home. With his small craft leashed to the marina's floating dock, Kito lifted the lid to admire the catch. Smiling his teeth-missing smile, he spoke softly. "Kai Koa, need get mo ice and dis big boy to feesh mar-ket." He was referring to the Ulua. The small fishing boat rocked. Jacob stood slowly, lifting the child carefully. He'd retrieve what few items for baby care that he was given once off the skiff.

He was first to step out of the small boat onto the dock. Following Jacob, Kolohe jumped from the boat's edge to the familiar safety of the dock.

Jacob turned and in broken phrases asked, "Kito, the fisherman...the one who gave you the tip – of where to catch - the - big fish..." His voice trailed.

"Yeah?"

Paisley paused and smiled. He knew the answer, but for a self-indulged form of amusement asked anyway, "it wasn't a..."

"He not ha-oh-lee like you. Not local. He not Havaiian," Kito rubbed his chin thinking about the question, seeking to understand he paused looking at Jacob carefully. "He not Japanee, like me. Was skinny black man wit freckles on him cheeks. Name, Rudy or someting like dat. Nevah met him before. But, he had him a couple big fish, so me tinks he knows what he knows."

They both looked at the over-sized cooler with more of the fish than the tail hanging out of it.

"Aloha, Kito. Hey..."

"Huh'" Kito said startled.

"Mele Kalikimaka, friend."

"Alo-ha, Jacob." Kito smiled, threw a slow shaka in the air over his chest, and stepped deeper into the boat and to start the small motor. One tug, it purred immediately. Kito and the small craft slowly throttled away toward the slips causing a small foamy wake in his departure.

Jacob stood alone on the lawn near the marina. But he wasn't truly alone. His new companion and his fury companion were with him. He would need to manage to what calamity awaited from the sinking of The Final Trade soon. But this moment, it was his contemplation. It was another opportunity to recount the events from the past night and early morning.

He lost his yacht – and his so-called passengers. Not to worry, picked up a few others stranded at sea, including a newborn. Kito appears out of nowhere to save the day. A quarter of a million dollars in cash had gone missing in the base of the safe. No big deal.

The big deal? His soul sank to the bottom of the sea. He was changing. A transition which he'd merely been toying with was taken hold – like a barnacle on the bottom of a boat. Clutching to the smooth surface until pried off with a sharp blunt instrument and force.

Or just another day in the market. I do not miss Wall Street. Do not. Could I go back to the hustle? Paisley assessed. His thoughts were about the request to raise capital for the cause, the project: Ellipsis.

He recited some of his findings from the past twelve hours to his companion of the moment, Kolohe, who listened intently. Then, shook off the vibes of misunderstanding.

His head hurt.

Jacob recognized that just a short time ago he would have been delusional from the lack of control. The actions and results would have equaled displacement from the intentions. It was a basis to come unglued. Now, he used the moment to seek understanding. He had a secret to keep.

His cell phone and wallet were tiny sacrifices to the great Pacific, but he checked his pockets for their presence anyway. The envelope. A still soggy 'thank you' note was in his back pocket and all that remained as a possession. He recalled Dorothy handing him the envelope and saying, *"It's just a thank you note from a dying old man. You go on and take that. Read it later if you want to."*

He opened the envelope and read the note –

Dear Jacob,

It was you. All along – it was you.

My friend, there was a time during our connections when you thought that I could not smell, a time when my ears could not hear well, and a time that my eyes could not see. Although they were merely deceptions, you've made sense of things for me. And if all went well, as we planned that it would, this is a moment when I cannot speak to you. So, these words will have to fit this moment.

The 'ruby' was within you – The treasure of your potential has nothing to do with the money or accomplishment, nothing to do with fame or recognition. The jewel that is within you has no meaning. It isn't connected to the souvenirs and assets you've collected along your ways.

It does have much to do with finding a new way forward. A new sense of yourself...discovering the capacity that lies within you to touch the lives of others in manners often beyond your comprehension.

You lent your senses to me. I hope that my sense of wonder that I've shared with you offers you opportunities to go out a little further. My father was a wise man. He explained that it was not what we were born with, but what we made of ourselves, and with those we choose to deliver a difference with that mattered most. He told me that it is just beyond our horizon that we discover our potential.

Time is always short and valuable. I must end with an unwritten beginning: knowing you, you'll harvest missed cues and prosper from the worst of circumstances. You'll capture your own dividends with the way forward from this point... And the goodness extended by your capacity and your potential may very well be a prescription for a change that we could all use.

When the time is right, my friend, we'll be in touch.

Jacob thought back and spoke it, but only to hear himself: "You're hearing this to know what lies ahead."

"Ellipsis." He said this one word to himself, thinking of the potential for outcomes which solve real-world problems and do so outside of the harnesses of

A strong breeze blew the flying flags atop the marina. The American and Hawaiian flags, then the Ko Olina marina moniker flapped and the nylon snapped from the aluminum pole. The wind made its way to Jacob's face. He looked up, blinking into the blustery force. His fatigue was setting in. A parent's job doesn't allow for time outs, naps, or predictive pauses. He'd call Adele and take it a moment at a time.

The pressing question was what to do with the baby. Cues from the police would likely put things into motion. This was not his call to make. He had a name, descriptions, a story, and not much else to operate on.

He watched the families and friends in the nearby lagoon congregating and beginning their day. Not far away, a young shirtless man wearing a fedora was sitting facing the Pacific on a bright green bench.

He was strumming an ukulele. Next to him sat a man with a football to his side. They looked like locals sitting there, enjoying another perfect Hawaiian day. They were smiling and enjoying the moment. Perhaps for them it was a moment of potential and unknown possibilities.

Seeing a figure walking his way, Jacob squinted into the sun. It was Adele. Adele was in the distance, on the other side of the parking lot, walking toward Jacob on the lawn. He was as surprised to see her as she was that he was holding what appeared to be a baby.

Kolohe's yellow ears waved with the brisk wind and he raised his black nose into the air.

Looking back at the letter to see the message, and after all that had just happened, Jacob was startled from the unexpected. A strong gust of wind snapped the note from his hand and blew into the sky toward the sea. "No," he whispered to himself.

Proof, Jacob thought. His natural instinct was to document, and capture, and assess with fact. This moment was unnatural, and all of the moments leading up to this one over the past two years were not about proof. But rather, what was beyond perspective. He watched the note dance into the wind gusts and float into the sky beyond sight, well beyond reason, and far beyond understanding.

He then thought of the words that disappeared from Ruby's red binder left behind in the hospital room. And then, quickly resumed his thought to Ruby's most recent comments: '*We don't always know 'why'. It isn't always about the answers.*' And then, '*Choice and chance. You choose.*'

Adele was halfway across the lawn. She was wearing khaki shorts and a navy blue tee. Her hair was pulled back. She was close enough that he saw her head tip to the side and squinting, he could see an inquisitive smile on her face.

The lapis blue morning sky was nearly cloudless on the leeward side, but clouds gathered over the Ko'Olau mountain range down toward Honolulu and east toward Diamond Head. A rainbow began to form in the distance. It grew more vibrant by the second. And a second arc of light joined the first. Jacob held the baby toward the rainbow. "You see that? A double. That's light bending. That's arcing the flatline." He looked back at Adele approaching.

The waves gently crashed on the black volcanic cove breaks. The trailing white and frothy sea foam swallowed the shore. The coconut fronds tickled each other offering a hissing sound. The Pacific's horizon offered an arcing flat line from east to west. He had ventured beyond the edge, and returned with a new attitude filled with less longitudes and latitudes, more wonder and wander. As quickly as the wind came, it died down.

A monarch butterfly bounced awkwardly into the breeze, dancing above them, resting on a leaflet of the Naupaka bushes between Jacob and the rocky shoreline. Then there were several of them. They danced in the breeze and rested on the lush green shrub. The leaves were waxy and dotted with an occasional and inconsistent small white flower. Adele looked at the butterflies, their wings of contrast - bright orange and stark black, then at Jacob.

He looked into Adele's eyes. They were bright and shiny, and looking back, they were glistening with curiosity, a chance, hope, a new way forward. Kolohe's tail was wagging with happiness, seeing her. Jacob smiled as he looked at the child, realizing that their journey had just begun.

"What do we have here?" Adele asked.

"This little guy? His name is..." He hesitated. Perhaps the secret was compromised. Perhaps he'd have to disclose some of his mystery to Adele and she'd think he was officially nuts. There may be quite a few 'prehaps' in the near term. Finally, he finished, "Ruby."

Jacob remembered Ruby's odd departing comment the night before: '*...for the first thing that you gave me, thank you. I can see that things will be different now.*' It made some sense. For now, he'd call the child Ruby. Gabriel, Ruby, Hollins. The name had gotten damp in the calamity but could still be read.

"There it is, then." Jacob whispered quietly to himself. Borrowed words that applied to the moment.

Adele reached for him, wrapping her arms around the bundle, looking at the child and up to Jacob. "Where is his mommy and daddy?"

"Don't think he has a mommy...daddy at the moment." The words sounded awkward and felt foreign to Jacob. Caution entered the picture. What did he know about being a father? A moment later he reasoned, based upon the change he was reveling in recently, what did he really know about anything?

"Hello Ruby." Adele spoke softly to the child. The baby had his eyes closed now. She looked at Jacob and winced, "Your head. That looks like it really hurts." She touched the wound with her fingertips on one hand while holding the child closer.

"I'll be alright." He thought of the fact that it was either dumb luck he was in the moment – or that it was meticulously orchestrated by Ruby and whatever her name really was. *Dorothy? I don't think so. William, Bill, Fetch. We know better now, don't we?*

"Oh...Jacob...is that our boat?" Adele looked at the satellite housings on the command center sticking out of the water near the marinas buoys. The two white bubbles, an antenna in between, and when the surf sunk, the deck supporting them was all they could see.

He frowned at the site of the loss and found more of a shrug, than a response. "Was."

The Final Trade, he thought, was for the knowledge of what could be...or perhaps for the child. He could recant a conversation with Ruby just two years ago: *There is no final trade*, Jacob would say. Ruby would answer, '*That's it then*'. There was just enough humor in it to land another smile on his face.

She looked around the bright green grassy grounds for a different answer. "Hmm," was all she added, sensing a mysterious change.

Looking at the child, "We might need to take good care of him." Jacob said with uncertainty. "Until we get it figured out."

Smiling, she said, "Who ever really figures parenthood out? But we'll do what we need to do. Even if it's just temporary." Adele was always tuned in to what mattered most.

"Why aren't you on your way to see your boys in New York?" Jacob asked.

"Craziest thing. I missed my flight. Westbound traffic on the H1 was gridlocked. Another water main broke on the Farrington, then the microburst... It's not like I could really leave anyway. Pushed it back. I'm going next week, post-Christmas. And then there's you...you were out there in that freak-of-a-storm. I'm glad that you weren't hurt. You could have died." He did what he did best. Took it all in, tried to make sense of it.

"I think, maybe, I did." He looked into her eyes and saw himself: lucky, comfortable, incomplete. And, complete - at the same time. "You...you've probably never missed a flight. Have you?"

"I know, right? Strange. Oh well. Sometimes things happen for a reason."

"Sometimes - they do. Team Logic, learning from Team..."

"There's hope for you yet, Jacob Paisley," she interrupted.

Jacob reached down to scratch Kolohe behind the ears. He was thinking that, like much else, this story was his alone. Or perhaps it was his to share with her. Either way, it was of the truth and the beginning of something else. He considered the Ruby letter - dashed into the breeze and likely basking on the surface of the saltwater. *When the time is right, my friend, we'll be in touch,* it said.

"There's something I've been meaning to say to you,"

"What's that?" she stated as she paused to adjust the weight of the small child in her arms.

"You didn't run."

She turned to see him with a frown which sought understanding, "Run?"

"When I was released from the hospital. When the body fell onto the car. When the world started falling apart for me. You stayed by my side...to make sure that I was safe. You didn't cut and run."

"Well...I never...thought of it like..." They were both thinking that Victoria had taken a different approach in the situation.

"Like a lit wick on a firecracker or a stick of dynamite...you didn't panic and run away."

"I..." she didn't finish. She didn't need to.

Jacob was harvesting the missed cues, the unspoken words within the moments they had shared through their years together, capturing the dividend of their relationship now, instead of then. There was a prescription for change being written. He was the writer of it, eager to prosper from the best and the worst of circumstances yet to happen.

Ellipsis, he thought.

Looking left to the Waianae Mountain Range, and then out to the Pacific, Adele commented quietly, "Just another perfect day in paradise." A deep breath was taken, then slowly exhaled.

Jacob chuckled to himself thinking several things. *Yeah, a bottom-kissing six-million-dollar yacht and a baby in tow. I sure am glad she missed her flight. As usual...don't know what I'd do without her. So much puzzlement surrounded the past twelve-plus hours. The big question in his thoughts stopped him from walking. How did the mystery and coincidences and scrupulous planning from Ruby all align?*

Something occurred to him. It started in the back of his mind and meandered its way to the front. It found a way to his curiosity and continued on its way until it landed in his mouth and spilled it way through his tongue and lips in the form of a question.

"Adele..."

She stopped walking further too. Staring at him while holding the precious cargo, "Yes..."

"You didn't just happen to encounter a good-looking black gentleman named Ruby recently... Did you?" He looked her way and their eyes locked.

Being his Executive Administrative Assistant in New York for years upon years, there was much she needed to conceal from him. It was for his own good, plausible deniability. But she had secrets she didn't want to keep from him any longer. Secrets which she had been permitted to share when the time was right. And this was that moment. The organization, the Ellipsis, had allowed it.

In keeping with the spirit of suspense, she delayed her response, instead holding the child in her arms rocking the baby boy. Finally, she answered, teasing him, "Well, that's a bit of a complex answer."

"Complicated or complex?"

"Com..." she hesitated, "Com...prehensive. That's my answer." She knew the drill.

Jacob looked at her, both impressed by her keeping of a secret and in wonder – for what it was she might say next.

She continued with another pregnant pause, "It was back in Manhattan. The night of your..."

"Demise?" he quickly questioned.

"Arrival?" she asked back slowly.

Jacob quickly thought of the judgement he had generated at the first Ruby, the staged hospital volunteer actor. A bit of an enigmatic philosopher. Then, the second. A glass scrubbing bartender at Bobby Vans. An I-might-know-something-which-you-do-not theorist. Then, the most recent encounter with Bill Fetch-come-Ruby. The apostle of the cause. The great proponent of the cause. The paladin who promised to connect when the time was right.

Playing it back through his thoughts...the instances that he thought there was a fleeting connection, a Ruby engagement, were what...? Confirmation bias? A carefully planned encounter, perhaps. Blind chance? Randomness? Not actually what he thought that they were.

"He spoke favorably of you...really thought a lot of you." She looked at him while a piece of hair had escaped her ponytail and blew into her face. Trying to blow it off of her cheek with a corner of her mouth, Jacob reached over to her and gently tucked it behind her ear. "that's when he had my attention. Hook, line, sinker, bobber, bait. I wanted to see what the mysterious promoter had to say about you. And..."

"And?"

"And...it evolved into a deeper understanding of what we're doing here."

"What are we doing here?"

"It was explained to me...as an...Ellipsis. Like divine intervention, but not that. It's like an outcome-based connector, an enablement architecture. It's the person or the thing that's in between. It's at work to help make things happen. An Ellipsis."

Jacob thought of Ruby. Each of the older Ruby's. And of the undiscovered mystery within Adele's comment. He's the in-between. They're the in-betweens. The enablement architects. They're the ones to arc the flatline.

Jacob broke his own silence, "I've been captive. In my own head for a long time. And then...there was this two years long period of uncertainty. Along came this spirit. An essence. A phantom of uncertainty. Poor choices..."

He looked at Adele to acknowledge that Victoria was a diversion, but then thought that perhaps she, too, was a draw in on the theatrics. Continuing with his assessment of the Ruby-concocted interactions. "It...he...was quite the fisherman, pole in hand – if that's what you'd call it. It's been an interesting run, Adele."

Kolohe ran ahead, barking at a pair of amber colored canaries on the lawn.

"Venturing a guess...making a prediction...calling as I see it, we have some wonderful adventures just waiting to happen." Adele wasn't naïve or wishful in what she said. She spoke with authenticity, a genuine and hopeful appreciation for the unknown.

"I don't know...what's next" Jacob added.

"None of us really do. We take it as it comes, I guess. The last time we spoke was on the phone a month ago..."

"So...you've had plenty of communication over..."

"I wouldn't say plenty, I'd say some...and add *limited.*" Adele added, "He has always been a bit covert...or what's the word I'm really looking for?"

Jacob shrugged his shoulders, "Underground, behind the scenes?"

She tilted her head, "Untold. As if there's more to the story."

"Yeah," he paused, "that's it. Vast."

"He said, 'We'd be in touch...' and that was it." She looked at the child, as if the infant could understand her, "I bet it's time for a diaper change. What do you think about that?"

Jacob was glad that it wasn't going to be him doing the dirty work this time.

They continued walking across the spongy grass lawn, slowly in an attempt to not wake the child.

Kolohe bounced along, panting, and occasionally stopping to sniff.

He thought of the lack of guardrails on the way forward. He was emerging and becoming an optimist at the scene. His flat world was round and interconnected and suddenly and beautifully beyond comprehension. "It's easier to pretend it isn't this way, right?"

"That isn't who you are." She tipped her chin to her chest and added, "You're well beyond easy."

Jacob gathered in the significance of the changes that had taken place over the past two years and absorbed this moment. Adele, the optimist. The live-in-the-now yellow lab, romping into wonder with each new sensation. An unexpected addition to the crew, the baby – salt from the sea. Could Ruby have made winning him over easier? He thought, *probably not.* It really took some convincing. *Well-done Ruby*, he thought.

They walked from the waves splashing their effervescent foam against the ocean's edge, Adele carrying the bundled child, Jacob Columbus Paisley by her side.

He looked at Adele, and then to the child with the hand-written note: GABRIEL HOLLINS, which he recently named *Ruby* in homage to his happenstance acquaintance whom he presumed was to be a friend and ally in what lay ahead. He felt an uncertain newness, and at the same time, repurposed. This dawning insightfulness would unquestionably be filled with a reverence of ambiguity.

"You're just showing off now, aren't you?" Jacob said it out loud but more to himself and as an affirmation of the work of his confidant, Ruby.

Adele, as if reading his mind added, "What do they say...the two most important days of your life are the day you were born...and the day you understand why."

He looked in her direction with contemplation on his face, then down to the pathway in front of them, and finally answered with a small smile on his face, "It really is something like that. The day you understand...why."

No longer was he walking away, but rather forward. Certain that there was a mysterious and playful presence ahead of them, he thought about the call to be the agent of change, the catalyst for things to come, to arc the flatline – one of a finite number of people to gap the differences. It was a new course.

Jacob Paisley, the former version of what he thought of himself, was dead. This new Jacob Paisley was filled with a new sense of wonder and purpose – to deliver a difference, a subtle and well-intended change which would make things better. Known and unknown, the way-forward outcomes they would provide as bridge builders would offer the world more than digits and dollars. Ellipsis. He would be a financier for the cause. The score-keeping changed over the course of the past couple of years. Jacob thought to himself, *what might the next couple of years uncover?* Come what may, together they moved forward, toward all of the unpredictable moments filled with wonderful potential that life could offer – knowing that the possibilities of the past were just the loadstones of implicit and compelling ideals of their time ahead. The days behind them were their anchor, tethering them to reason. The days ahead of them would be their sail – chartering change and liberating likelihoods.

PART FOUR:

NEW BEGINNINGS

ONE MONTH LATER...

21

A Sea Of Dreams

"Why Club Triple Seven?" Jacob asked Adele. She flipped the turn signal of their shiny white BMW to exit the H1 to Nimitz Highway. They were heading toward the karaoke bar in the warehouse district on the Sand Island Access Road. There were half of a dozen traffic lights between where they were and the turnoff. Only the shadows from the coconut trees and the telephone pole wires fell upon their vehicle now that they were out from the double stacked highway. The intense sun was the reason to shut the sunroof blind. Glare still radiated in on them.

Adele wore white capri pants cropped at her calves and a thin cotton cornflower blue top which buttoned down below her cleavage. A white spandex tank, underneath, gave her all the support her killer-Bs needed. Her brunette hair was getting longer and was kept in a tight ponytail, keeping her cooler in the Oahu humidity. She tipped her chin to her chest, looked at Jacob over the top of her sunglass rims, and answered, "Even when you ask Ruby a question, do you really get the answer you're seeking?"

"Fair enough. Something always leads to something else." He was wearing a navy Tommy Bahama camp shirt with khaki board shorts and leather slippers. The almond flip flops were the expensive kind from a boutique, not the Don Quijote endcap loss leaders.

"That's a good way to say it."

"You look nice today. Beautiful...really. You look extra beautiful today." Jacob took a minute to compliment her. "You're one of the lucky ones. People who just get better looking with time."

"That's a good way to say it," she repeated to the different meaning. She accelerated to beat the yellow and needed to quickly tap the brakes behind a Menehune Water truck stopping suddenly. "Oops." Her shoulders shrugged as Jacob rocked forward in the passenger's seat, his own sunglasses spilled from the bridge of his nose to his nostrils.

"Easy there, Kirby," he said softly, nudging them back up to his eyes.

"Kirby...? I don't think you've ever called me that."

"I know, it's usually 'amazing', or 'savior', or 'lifesaver', but I didn't used to be riding shotgun, gimped up like this. He tweaked the volume on the radio, slightly turning up a song about soaking up the sun. Sheryl Crow strummed a beachy tune about soaking up the sun and looking up.

"Better today? Your arm," she looked at the sling around his right elbow and forearm, wrapping his wrist and hand, lifting it for support. It was too big, and Adele offered to tighten it up before they left their condo at the Ko Olina.

"Who knew sailing would be so tough, right?'

"Hey, I liked the power boats better. But, oh no, you had to trade down for the Beneteau. A guy from New York, who knows nothing about sailing, buys a *two-million-dollar* sailboat. Only you, Jacob Paisley."

"Well, remember...I'm from Ohio, actually."

"Yes, Jacob Columbus Paisley."

He drew in a deep breath and slowly exhaled as she turned onto the industrial road, driving through commercial warehouses. Pickups, delivery trucks, and dusty cars lined the street. An occasional business moniker dotted the industrial zone, with its ribbon signage standing out above a customer entrance. A coffee outlet, a candle outlet, a cabinet facing business, and others advertised with their logo that this was the source for their goods. *Of course, all of these warehouse workers would need a place for a cool libation at the end of their day's work*, Adele assumed, Club 777.

"Why did your mother give you Columbus for a middle name? I've wondered, all these years, and have never asked you. I don't know why."

"Two stories there. One, she wanted me to be an explorer."

Adele stuck out her bottom lip some, and shrugged with the shoulder next to him, "Sort of...".

"Two. It was an accident. A nurse listed Columbus as the city in which I was born within the child's middle name area. When she saw it, she came up with story number one."

"That's where we're slightly different. You see, I call that fate, something in the universe playfully screwing with intentions. You call it logic, someone simply screwed up."

He was looking at warehouse workers changing a tire on the side of the road as they made a turn. Jacob spoke softly, facing the window, "Team Hope versus Team Logic. Enter randomness."

"What's that you say?" Adele kept her eyes on the road. "We're going to need a car-wash after this boondoggle."

He just shook his head slightly instead of answering her.

Adele saw him fidgeting with the over-sized sling, "Did you take anything this morning?"

"No, I'm off the juice. Don't call in for another prescription. Please."

She didn't respond, she just glanced in his way and looked at the navigation screen which commanded them to turn left.

"This is one sketchy area."

"Leave it to Ruby, always in character – recruiting talent or working a gig."

The X5 slid on the gravel to a stop. Dust plumes rose around their SUV gently dissipating as the breeze blew them away.

Adele tapped the brake and pushed the button causing the BMW to turn off. "I'm not hungry, like at all. Are you?"

Jacob shook his head 'no' slightly. He removed his sunglasses.

"You going shy on me? Hello. Are you in there somewhere?"

With his left hand she reached up to her face, embracing her cheek. He stroked away several hairs which escaped her tieback, tucking them behind her ear. She held his left hand to her face with hers, locking their eyes in the moment.

"I always like the way your eyes look at this time of the day. Maybe it's the refraction or the spectrum, I don't know. Even in the towers back in Manhattan, and I never told you – I never could – I loved looking into your eyes as you were working a deal, or asking me to schedule you away somewhere, or even aligning with her...you know who. It just never got old, looking into your soul through your occasional glance. I saw so much."

"Let's have this conversation. Let's... No," Jacob looked out the windshield at the lineup of warehouses down the street. Ahead of them was the hole-in-the-wall joint Ruby asked them to meet. Adele was attending under one pretense. Jacob was attending for quite another.

She sensed the depth of what he wanted to tell her. "Hey. It's Happy Aloha Friday. We can rum it up at MonkeyPod Kitchen and tell each other what we need to say at happy hour tonight. You can get the ahi poke tacos."

"Two MaiTai's max. Two and you're comfortably numb. Three? Well, three and you start speaking in tongues."

"Three and you're in the 'let's make bad choices' category."

"Three, and you wonder what you bought on Amazon."

"That lilikoi froth – we've got to figure out how they do that," Adele marveled.

"The pineapple slices – that's cut on a mandolin, right?"

"Uh-huh."

"Three – and the shenanigans begin," he quipped.

Together, they giggled – wiser from their experience with the island delectable.

Jacob returned to what needed to be said. "Now. We have a few minutes, because you're Adele and you're always prompt."

She smiled at his recognition toward her efficiency. But she wanted the conversation to lead toward something else, perhaps something more. And maybe even something wildly more.

"I need to get something off my chest. Victoria."

Adele removed her sunglasses, cradling them on the dash. Shifting in her seat to face him more she added, "Victoria. Long lost Victoria."

"That's just it. She vanished. The power and the title, they go away, and so does the girlfriend experience."

"The girlfriend experience?"

"The girlfriend experience. Not a hooker, not a call girl, not a mistress – just someone who was in it for an experience. Me, the sucker, the misjudging suspect with deep pockets and a vast armada of resources..."

"I don't know if that's the way I saw everything happening..."

"Exactly. Victoria - with an agenda that played to her motives, whatever they may have been, living on the edge,"

"Of a knife!" Adele added.

"Pulling me over a horizon that I never would have ventured beyond..."

"Are you praising her, or...?

He shook his head fiercely, "I'm not praising her. What I'm saying is that I was lost in a sea of dreams, thinking that something was everything. Lost. Not all dreams are nightmares, not all dreams are sweet. And you cannot explain many of them. But that was a point when I was in a state of being misled."

"Like when she talked you into a trip to Morocco and you got mugged." Adele had a fierce lineup of situations she bailed Jacob and

Victoria from. Following the incident, Jacob was deeply thankful, and Victoria was flippant.

He piled on, "Or like in the Jets suite with her risqué friends – or at Kukrumazushi – "

"You do not do that with caviar! Gross." Adele shook her finger, knowing of the naughtiness the vixen drew Jacob into.

"Or on my desk, New Year's Eve..."

"Uh. I can never un-see that," she said as she crossed her arms.

"What I'm saying, what I'm trying to say is that the trade was a dream come true. There is a sea of dreams out there. Trading what I had at the time, for what I want most – to spend my days with you...here...or anywhere... That's what I want to have happen. I am sorry for having put you through it all."

She uncrossed her arms, "Do you think about her often?"

"I think about her. I do. Less all the time, but let's face it - she was a shiny object of my imagination. She had an allure which wasn't something I turned my attention away from - for a long time. I don't know if it was Ruby, or that the power and title were gone, or that she sensed trouble and cut and ran back to her old self in Miami. The ghostly disappearance troubled me at first, then...suddenly I found my sensibility and it didn't."

"Hmm..." Adele watched him grovel in open thought, looking for the next thing to say. It was as if he were childlike, searching the couch cushions for a quarter as the ice cream truck drove by – its metal tingly sound blaring out nursery tunes from an old speaker atop the van.

He looked at her, "I'm sorry I put you through any of that, knowing that the resolution you provided was a form of torment for you."

"I didn't always want to be in her shoes. The bail in Nashville, that night chaos in Dubai – you're lucky you're not in an Emirates for-ever-jail, and how about the morning at The Palazzo in Vegas – who sunbathes in the nude in Vegas and gets locked out of the penthouse suite?"

"Yeah, the Vegas trip...well, at least it was the penthouse," he shrugged, slowly turning to her to seek the glaring scrutiny.

"She didn't even wince when I unlocked the slider. She stood there with her perfect fake tits standing at attention as I let her in. The courage it must have taken to pour herself a whiskey, invite me to a spa day with her saying that you'd send us to the best, and then ask me if she should get dressed..."

"Yeah, I..."

"You're right. Better to air it out now. Happy Hour is for happiness. With that woman...I – I – I'm at a loss for words."

"It's in the past." Jacob sensed the anguish Adele had to deal with. The tomfoolery and the buffoonery she dealt with was enough for any Executive Admin to grapple with. Finding out that Jacob had line itemized "entertainment funds" on PPCM's ledger must have flipped her out.

"Is it? If she reappeared, would there...?"

"There would not. I'm not who I was. And you – more than anyone will know that. You were with me at the beginning. You were with me at the end, the only one at the end."

"I cried, Jacob. I cried that last day at PPCM until I had no more tears. I thought you'd disappear. I waited until I couldn't wait any longer and I had to find you – to let you know that I was still there for you. Walking into Bobby Van's – running into Ruby, knowing that you were there...and then you weren't. That was tough. The toughest point – the loss of you." Her eyes found salty tears pooling. Quickly she used her shirt to blot them, sniffing a few times.

Jacob needed to affirm what he was trying to convince her of. "He's gone. I didn't know that I could transition like I did. But the skylarking and the desire for the seductress and the enough-is-never-enough man that I was - has changed. He transformed.

With a final quick sniff, she added, "I believe you. I'm still here. Since I saw your rise, and rise some more, and rise up some more –

then fall, I know what you're capable of. Almost anything. And I believe in you."

"It was floating in despair, out of sight of land, with baby Ruby in one arm, Kolohe flailing in and out of the sinking raft, the revolver in my hand that I was at that point of no return and of mindfulness. I saw the light of day and the depth of the night. I can't explain a desire to change any more than wanting to no longer exist was...it was...it was that cognizance of transformation that I needed."

Adele placed her hand on top of his, resting on the leathery console armrest between them.

He said nothing, respecting her words and her silence as he usually did.

Adele found a small smile, and shook her finger in his direction, "And no more workouts on the dock. Do your exercising in the gym or out on the lawn or something."

He wiggled the arm in the sling a little, and replied, "No more showing the young bucks at the marina how the old man gets jiggy. You got it."

"Let's go see what Ruby has up his sleeve today." Adele opened her door first, allowing the air conditioning to begin seeping out of the vehicle.

"Hey!"

She turned before she climbed out to see what he wanted.

"I got you." Jacob reached to her cheek with his warm hand again, tracing her cheek softly. His look was sincere.

She shook her head just once and replied, "I still got you."

They walked into the seedy lunch diner by day, karaoke bar by late afternoon and early evening, and wondered who might venture here late into the night.

Arlo was cheery. He sat at the bar nursing half a Foster's Lager from a heavy mug. Frost was melting from its surface. The fans moved the air in the diner by day, karaoke bar at night establishment but did not cool it. His cell phone occupied him. A rugby match played on the screen to which he occasionally pumped his fist and shouted "*Tackle,*" or "*Ruck,*" or "*Touchline!*" His enthusiasm was the first thing that they noticed while they were waiting for Ruby.

"He said noon, right?" Jacob asked.

"And don't be late." Adele added.

The Australian looked at Jacob with his arm in the sling and Adele sitting next to him. They had no waiter attending to them for several minutes.

"G'day mates. No service in the day, nor can you say there's much at night either." His accent identified him to the two of them. His E in 'either' was pronounced with an I. There's a menu up here with a few items. Help yourself. They'll be out soon enough," and then he shouted toward the kitchen, *"To fill my empty mug!"*

Once heard, pans and dishes clattered from a door to the kitchen and a heavy Samoan appeared. "Brah – you got beer in that mug I jist bring you."

To which the Australian chugged the rest of it. "No, no I'm afraid that I don't see no lager in there. Do you two?"

Adele and Jacob looked at

The barkeeper, cook, waiter, and likely owner held his hands on his hips and approached Arlo, grabbing his mug for another round.

"Don't ordah the feesh sandwich. The bloody tail will steel be wig-glin', and the chips – they're raw."

The Samoan walked over to Jacob and Adele, sliding a menu in front of them. There were three items on it. "The French fries are like McDonald's and the fish is grilled and fresh caught Mahi. Never mind him, his Brumbies aren't winning against the Rebels."

"Uh, we're waiting for one more." Jacob watched Arlo.

Arlo was clutching his fist shouting, *"Oi! Oi! Oi!"* at the phone's screen

"Water while you wait?" the Samoan asked them.

"Sure, that'd be nice," Adele added.

"Want me to tell him to chill?"

Jacob smiled into the distance and said, "He's not bothering us."

"Just wait a while, he will."

A quiet continuous sound spilling from the kitchen was KINE, a local radio station. Often, more commercials than music, a cell phone service provider ad was followed by a public service announcement about drinking and driving, not to be outdone by an insurance company's clowning attempt to showcase bundling home, auto and boat for savings. An iconic radio personality's voice proclaimed that now that the bills were paid, they could play music. A guitar intro was meticulously picked by Randy Lorenzo before the strumming about his Hula Girl was strummed.

Ruby walked in as the Samoan left their table and dropped into the seat across from them. He looked at them, saying nothing at first, and then smiled broadly. "Jacob Paisley and wonderful Miss Adele!"

They met his smile with theirs and before three waters made their way to the booth with a smudgy table a conversation broke out about what they had been doing with their time on Oahu.

Ruby stopped himself in describing his trips back to the mainland to address the Australian at the bar. He tipped his head, "Hey Arlo. Sounds like your boys are playing? How they doing?"

"Hey, old man. You can say they are getting their bloody asses handed to 'em." Arlo stammered, "Oh, oh, oh," a moment of game-playing suspense was followed with a disappointing, "Crikey!"

Adele, a little surprised, cocked her head and asked Ruby, "Come here often?"

"With this gig, you go where the gravity takes you." Ruby shook his head just once.

"You've put some weight back on since I saw you last." Jacob was looking at him, "You were scrawny back in December. Those guava cookies good, or what?"

"Love those things. Keep taking them back with me."

The waters finally made it to the booth, when Ruby added, "Sorry Maleko, we'll have one more join us today."

Maleke, the owner, cook, bartender, waiter rolled his big round brown eyes and returned for one more water to round out the booth.

"One more? Who?" Adele looked to Ruby, seeking the storyline.

He didn't say anything. Looking at Jacob and then a cheap watch on his left wrist, he repeated, "One more."

"Blimey!" was shouted from Arlo, clutching the phone with one hand and his forehead with the other. The mug which contained the beer was empty again.

She snuck in and sat at the booth next to Ruby before Adele saw her arrive. "Hello there. You must be the wonderful Adele which I'm hearing about..." Her Georgian draw was pleasant to hear.

Adele reached across the table with her hand, "I am. And you are?"

They shook fingers more than hands.

Jacob's turn. "This is Dorothy. Or...was Dorothy?"

"I'm Dorothy," she said – still playing a part.

Jacob tilted his head unconvinced that it was her true name, "Meet Dorothy. She's the Navy Seal from the Aicon's three-hour tour."

Adele's eyes grew wide, and she only added an "Oh, wow..."

Ruby looked at Dorothy, then at Jacob, then addressed the table, "I don't think we have a lot of time. You..." he pointed at Dorothy, "You play it cool." He looked at Adele, "You, you do nothing." It was Jacob's turn, "And you, you do what you need to do, moneyman."

Jacob nodded. Adele didn't understand. Dorothy slumped her shoulder's because she had to sit. Ruby watched Arlo sway behind the bar and pour himself another Foster's, returning to where he sat as the froth spilled over the edge of the mug onto the floor.

As in on cue, in walked another patron. A seedy haole, dressed in workman's coveralls. A name patch on his right-side chest read '*Jason*'. The young man had lengthy hair which teased the back of his neck like Jacob's. Unlike Jacob's clean-shaven face, a goatee wrapped around his lips.

He found the four of them sitting at a booth and pulled up a chair to join them, riding the back of the chair with his elbows. The Jason character said nothing, reaching for Adele's water. Taking a long drink and setting it back in front of her, he looked over to Dorothy and spoke, "Well, well, we meet again."

"What do you want this time?" Dorothy was cogent in character. She acted timid and frightened.

The tough guy and dirty-uniform-wearing Jason, said glibly, "I want what I wanted last time. I want what I told you to have for me this time. You think this little crowd surrounding you is going to scare me off?"

"I didn't know they were going to be here..."

"Do you, have it?"

Dorothy faked her fear, "He didn't give it to me. He said I owed him something else and I don't know what he wants..."

Jason looked over at Arlo. He was still more interested in rugby and beer than dividing his attention into any barroom drama.

"My attention only goes so far. You know what I do when I run out of my interest with you?"

"No. No, what."

Do nothing. That's your part, Adele thought.

"I make one last request, and then I get mean enough to do bad things." He reached into his coveralls and removed a small handgun.

"And he's got a gun..." Adele couldn't help herself. It just came out of her mouth like – *how about that; there's a situation here; address it; deal with it.*

"Is this necessary?" Ruby added. He acted somewhat passive, as if he were a hospital volunteer who lost his sense of smell - or a bartender with one bad listening ear at an upscale establishment in the financial district - or a victim blindness caused by cancer, enjoying what was left in life.

"Oh, yeah – this is very necessary." Jason moved the gun from close to his chest to under the table, pointing his right hand with the piece in it in Dorothy's direction. "So, when?" He looked at her and shrugged. The grease on his uniform was more on the chest and the shoulders than the arms. Adele assumed that he worked on small pieces and parts in close proximity, not extending wiping grime on his arms or thighs if he had to. She looked around the table for the next move.

Finally, Dorothy said something, "What if I can't get it. What other kind or arrangement could we make?"

Jason rolled his eyes, "Are you stupid or something – he's got the goods, he's got the intel on me, and I will do anything to avoid going back to Halawa."

Halawa, the correctional facility wasn't Aiea's touristy destination. It's the place criminals wanted to avoid. It was better than the long-time inmate option though.

"If they have enough on me, they'll ship me off to Arizona or California. Then I'll never get to see my baby girl." Jason looked at Dorothy as if he needed her to come through with the intelligence on his misdeeds - as much as she needed it to avoid what might come next.

She didn't act threatened enough.

Jason waited for silence. He cocked the firing arm. They all heard the metal pieces engage in the snubbed revolver for the trigger to be pulled.

A small gasp was sucked in by Dorothy.

"So, this is me being nice before I get mean enough to do bad things. When?"

Jacob removed the sling around his right arm slowly, revealing a slightly larger handgun than Jason. "There's four of us, and one of you. Who isn't to say this doesn't go well for you here, now?"

Adele's eyes were wide with astonishment that Jacob had been acting. Did his arm even hurt? Really? Was he, the moneyman on the Ellipsis tryout team, in on this stunt all along with Ruby? With Dorothy? *Do nothing. That's your part. Play it,* she told herself.

"I see. So, to be continued..." Jason shook his head. "Disappointing." He seemed uncomfortable that he had found himself here, threatening the elderly black woman. He appeared disappointed in her, but in himself also. "What's your name?" Looking at Jacob with the gun, cocked and loaded pointing at him, he was surprised by the answer.

Jacob spoke lowly and slowly, "It's a lot like yours. But it doesn't represent a hollow man that would be filled with regret if he pulled that trigger. Get out, now, while you still can. Forget the threat. It'll go away. We know things that you don't. We know that your daughter is going to grow up needing a good father. We know that your wife still believes you're a good man, despite that weapon you pointed at her." Jacob was referring to Dorothy, who sat as instructed, doing nothing other than clutching herself as a helpless victim.

Jason unclicked the mechanism and tucked the small handgun back inside his uniform.

"We know that your lack of scruples isn't all your fault. You need help in making choices. The compass is missing. But it isn't always your responsibility. You need some help, and we can do that."

Jason was breathing heavily. He looked toward the bar and at the exit and at Adele whom he had just met, Dorothy whom he had threatened with his small piece, the quiet black man in the corner, and at Jacob – doing all the talking. His eyes were becoming teary, "I... I don't know what scruples are. I need help..." Jason reached to his eyes with both hands to hide the tears.

"Hands in the ruck!" was shouted from Arlo, completely clueless to the drama of the conversation at the booth. He drank another, supping the slow-moving foam from the bottom.

Jason wiped his eyes again with one hand and nodded. "Help me. Please. I don't know what to do."

Ruby spoke, commanding the next steps required, and the emotions Jason was showing, "How about you do nothing and the problem goes away. Your need to act is a complication which will not help your predicament. Be patient. I know it's hard. But by doing nothing, your problem will disappear. You must trust us. We have our fingers in your situation."

He stood and awkwardly didn't do anything. Then, finally, with hesitation departed their table and Club Triple Seven.

Noises came from the kitchen, made by Maleko, the Samoan. More grunts and clutched fists were made at the bar from Arlo, the beer-drinking Australian. The soft-speaking Georgian Navy Seal looked at the menu as if nothing eventful just happened. The moneyman from Manhattan took off the rest of the sling wrapping his shoulder and elbow. The master of disguises and the architect of change reached for his phone.

Adele laughed. She looked around the table as they continued doing what they were doing, occasionally looking her way with a wry smile. "Is anyone going to address what just happened?" They all joined her in a good chuckle at how careless they played their parts.

She looked at Jacob, "And you...You? I just said to you, out on the street in our SUV that I know what you're capable of..." She squinted at him like a schoolgirl fending off teasing on the playground. "I take it back. I *often* know what you're capable of. I *sometimes* know what you're capable of."

"Here's the backstory on the dude," Ruby addressed the table. His father is a congressman, a Democratic congressman who's strongly against gun violence. Funny, right – seeing him pull a weapon on us?" Ruby's eyes grew wide, then he shook his head. "He, his dad, is going to retire – not running again next term. We want the vote to ban automatic rifles and to continue to ban bump stocks for the ARs in Hawaii. When the potential gun loving challenger takes his father's seat, we might have a bigger challenge, but for now we're just seeking Hawaii to remain one of the sixteen states that disallow the bump stocks. His son, Jason, got mixed up in a get rich quick side-hustle."

"And the side-hustle went a little south," Jacob assumed.

"And the side-hustle went way south," Ruby corrected. "As happens in the quid-pro-quo world, somebody had a little intelligence on someone that wouldn't serve them well. Then, the tradeoffs begin, followed by the actions our momma's and poppa's might not be proud of - the lying and stealing and threatening and all that nonsense. We need Jason to clean up his act, get rid of his damn gun that goes with his "

"So, he wasn't really...?" Adele found a glint of faith in humanity.

Ruby winced, "Well, he did threaten us. That needs to be monitored, but he needs to protect his father's lawmaking decisions without causing the family embarrassment and wrecking his own future. Work to do here. But for another day."

"You've got your fingers in a lot of pockets. Meddling and interfering and influencing, don't you?" Jacob was intrigued at the obtrusive and brazen actions which Ruby caused or reacted to in an effort of sizing someone up. "Not cavalier, but almost. A quenchless curiosity you just must have answered."

"If that's the way you want to see it." Ruby answered. "I believe we're helping people in ways that they could, couldn't or should not be helped. We're helping them find their potential with some known and unknown actions. Ellipsis has some of that Dexter-syndrome where we judge the good and bad. Sometimes it's easier to see if you invite yourself behind the scenes. Is bugging someone's home a good thing? Not necessarily. Does it cut through the clutter of what we blindly have in place – a law enforcement system which is somewhat shackled in formalities – perhaps. Does it infringe on rights? Well, rights are not necessarily a balanced scale. Do we prompt actions? Hell, yes. Are we lordly? We try not to be." Ruby didn't break eye contact with Jacob as he spoke, sharing his perceptions and perspective of the Ellipsis outcomes.

Jacob looked down to his hands, resting on the table between them. Then at Ruby's hands. He questioned the work of his own hands and of Ruby's - during a lifetime, what had their hands accomplished? It made him want to test further his own potential.

"And addressing Adele's question," Ruby continued, "wasn't really a bad actor. Not all that bad, anyway. Showed us what he's capable of though. He is troubled by a give-and-take. Eliminate that or expose that and it's surprising how a man can come around. That isn't always the case, unfortunately. But it was here. A good outcome. "Hopefully," he had an ounce of doubt within his calculation of the situation. "We'll steer him to a safe harbor."

"Rooster one day, and a feather duster the next. The porch lights on, but nobody's home." Dorothy looked at Ruby, "Anything else for today? I'm going to head back to the base. Hankering for a tomato sandwich, or some comfort food, or somethin'."

"They have food here," Ruby put up the defense, pointing at the scrawny menu.

"Don't eat the feesh – " Jacob had to add in, attempting to accentuate it like Arlo, the Australian.

She looked at the empty bar area, spare the Australian, and added, "Nah, it's been a month of Sunday's since I've had some good Southen' cookin'. Get me some sweet tea. It's hotter than blazes. And...and I'm plumb tired." Dorothy looked over at Jacob and Adele, sitting close to each other. "I do have a question for you, and please do pardon me if it's forward, but what are you two to each other?"

Jacob smirked, "Well, we used to work..."

"Can I?" Adele interrupted Jacob. He simply stopped speaking and wanted her to put her words out into the air for him to hear. "He was my boss. It wasn't a creepy thing. I know that's the place most people go when they hear that. He hired me, was my employer, and we had tremendous respect for each other. We don't talk about it, but there were moments when I thought, well...we thought...there's something there. But I went my way and Jacob went his ways and we had a tremendous admiration and appreciation for each other. The friendship became...uh..." she looked at Jacob looking back to her. Adele continued, "Well, it became friendly. And then there was a moment of separation when we didn't work together – torture. I missed him, and obviously he missed me. You don't know what you've got until it's gone. Out of the blue, Jacob calls and asks if I'd come visit him on Oahu. He picked up a condo with a place for me to stay. I did. We found out that our friendship was a little more than friendly, it was friendlier – and that's fun. And that's probably a good way to tease the tale of Jacob and me."

"Hmm...lookin' forward to hearin' more of the story someday. Do tell. Thanks for lettin' me poke my nose where it don't belong. Anyway, tired as all get out. I'm out, ya'll," Dorothy looked at Ruby, looking back at her.

Ruby gave in. "Thanks. I'll call you. I'm heading back to New York on Sunday. Or how would you say it, *over yonder on the Lord's Day of Rest.* If there's a reason why we don't connect..."

"I know," she reached over to touch the old black man's face, "Aloha to you too – you pretty as a peach man." She looked at Adele, "Ma'am, you don't have a ring on that finger yet," looking at Adele's left hand, and then glancing at Jacob. "This man is one smooth talker." Pointing at Ruby, she added. "Watch yourself around him, since you're not completely taken." Dorothy looked at Jacob, "Just yet."

Adele watched the comfort between them, her and Ruby, play out.

He had to know. "Hey Dorothy...before you head out. I've been meaning to ask you, how did you alter the rudder on *The Final Trade*, on the Aicon, my boat?" Jacob asked, genuinely seeking an answer to the reason why the engine didn't obey the helm.

"Yacht Controller. The thing cost us twelve thousand dollars. We had a time crunch in installing it while you two were down in Honolulu and stopped at Costco and Safeway in Kapolei. Operates off of a joystick when in operation. Wireless. Through a VPN we had dual band control. They have them for stern and bow thrusters too." She looked at him with some compassion. "We tweaked the communications, but the storm, that microburst? Well, that was just Mother Nature doing her thing."

"Yeah, there's that," Jacob said, "but the intervention and playing with the wiring harness and commanding a vessel with outside technologies - you know all of that because...you're a Seal...and Ellipsis is leveraging a sophistication beyond what us normal people know?"

Careful not to divulge more than she was permitted, she looked at Ruby. Dorothy touched his shoulder with her fingertips and gave them a gentle wave goodbye without saying more walking toward the sunlight outside of the simple establishment.

Ruby looked at Jacob and then at Adele. "She's a hundred-ton Master

Captain. Not exactly sure what that means but it's a thing, I guess. She was truly sad to hear about your boat."

"Yeah, that makes two of us."

"Three of us," Adele added, seeing Jacob out of the corner of her eye, she pouted. "The Coast Guard was rigorous in getting her off the rocks, getting the pumps in, five of them at a hundred gallons per minute capacity, lifting it with the yellow Kevlar balloons. The stress cracks were so wide, I could stick my pinky in them."

"It's a shame. I'm sorry. Insurance cover it?"

"Like we said, still tying up loose ends on that but I'll be upside down, one way or the other. A net-net loss, but..." Jacob shrugged, "but I know how to make money."

"That you do." He looked at Jacob

"Time to transition from luxury yachting to really learning how to sail."

Adele excused herself for a trip to the lady's room which left the two of them alone. "We'll reconnect next when you're back in Manhattan. Lay a little groundwork that should help you out. It will help you understand things. And you'll meet a few others. Seems like everyone wears a few hats. Their duty, and how they can transition to other talents and skills. Make sense?"

"Not completely, but I'll go with the flow."

Adele reappeared quickly, "Never mind. A gas station might be twice as nice."

Ruby gave her a grin, knowing the restrooms were perhaps the last thing to be cleaned and infrequently at best. Then turned his attention back to Jacob, "How's the arm?"

Jacob rolled the shoulder around a few times, peering at Adele out of the corner of his eye, "Never better. And nice to be out of that sling."

She made a fist and punched him lightly in his shoulder. "Punk. I'm going to beat you up when we get home."

"Home. About that. I just mentioned New York to Jacob. Listen, nice to be here, it's Hawaii. Can't think of a better place to get your chill on. But it'd be even better to have you two back in Manhattan. How could that happen?"

Adele and Jacob looked at each other.

"You want to fill him in, or should I?" Adele asked Jacob. He wanted to hear how she pitched it. "I will, Mr. Loss for Words. She began explaining their intentions, within the coming months and in the year ahead.

He reached over to look at the menu again. Only three items: burger, fish, chicken. Under the drinks it said: beers, wine, good wine, stuff that'll make you sing. The simplicity of the choices caused Jacob to think waiting for a real Happy Hour with Adele back at their blue lagoons might be better.

As Adele told Ruby that they were enjoying checking in on the infant, and that they felt honored that the placement office with the county had included them in the vetting process, they weren't ready to cut and run back to New York today. She told Ruby that the insurance company was settling for the Aicon and that there were a few tasks that would need to be completed. Her explanation about the condominium at Coconut Plantation needing to go into a monthly rental pool opposed to a weekly rental was a zoning regulation. Some of what she said, Ruby was in-the-know on. Other things were a cause-for-pause with him.

After a few other excuses, Ruby spoke, "This new island home of yours...it's nice. And if this is ultimately what you want..."

"We're moving to Manhattan." Adele interrupted him. "There's a new project we're taking on. It's in the Waldorf Astoria. We need to wait for the buildout. 25th floor, two beds, three bath. Eighteen hundred square feet. For Jacob it's a step down. For me, it's a step up."

"Waldorf. Isn't that a glitzy hotel?"

"They have residences too." Jacob chimed in. "MidTown East. Adele is moving there from her apartment in Brooklyn, I'm...well, you know where I live."

"So, no Billionaire's row for you?"

"I was never a billionaire. It's the M's, not the B's for me."

Adele adjusted her spandex crop top, thinking of her cup size. They were not C's or D's, and she didn't care. They were real. Seeing her fidget, Ruby and Jacob didn't address the innuendo.

"Millions instead of billions. You should hear yourself talk about your first world problems. Well...all good – staying here a bit longer. What's here will take you some time. Within Ellipsis there's a lengthy vetting process. A few small trials to ensure it's not only right for the organization, but also right for you."

"Let's talk about that." Jacob furrowed his brow, "Where's the governance in all of it? Where are the checks and balances coming from? When does the inducement of something happening receive verification that it's the choice of...of Ellipsis?"

"Wow. The genius of generating wealth who got run from his own company is asking about regulations?" Ruby had a spine. He wasn't just the scout, drawing talent into the team. His player development included bringing the right ambition, core strengths, and collaboration into the culture of the organization.

"I'm in the wrong. I apologize."

"You have every right to know. And I have a responsibility to explain. To both of you. But not today. I have someplace I need to be, and something I need to do.

"Okay..." Jacob was left wanting. "Soon?"

"Soon. Like my next trip to Oahu in a couple months soon. You two enjoy each other's company and tie up the loose ends and oh, I don't know...Live Aloha – as they say." He smiled. It was a warm smile like the daytime high – right as the sun turned its corner high in the sky, heading for the horizon, making the water sparkle silver bursts of light.

When Ruby was gone, Jacob and Adele sat there in the diner by day ordering nothing. They talked about occasionally returning to check in on the child.

Adele told Jacob that there was a military family seeking to adopt and that she was invited to ride along for a site visit next week.

He told her that he really thought that he was really getting the hang of sailing. It was easy to remember everything. The big clippers and schooners were even easier to sail than the small ketches, sloops and yawls. He lied. But it was a little white lie.

She had been around the marina just long enough to know it. She had also been around Jacob long enough to know when he was teasing too. Sensing bullshit was one of her superpowers. It was a nice surprise today that he had the ability to stun and ruse her.

The afternoon had slipped away. Standing to leave, "Oh shit," Jacob expressed.

"What? What's wrong?"

"Four o'clock on the H1 heading West on an Aloha Friday."

She winced at the thought of paradise's highway congestion. "The wine is in the fridge. C'mon, let's go. Home away from home. There's a sea of dreams for us to gaze at out there. A bottle of red for you, and a bottle of white for me."

22

The Dream Of The Potential

Several months after their last conversation with Ruby, Jacob and Adele needed to work with a design consultant at the Waldorf Astoria Residences in Manhattan. It required their presence. Other than the arrangement of care for Kolohe – they were free agents, deciding to make a ten-day trip across the six time zones separating Hawaii from New York.

The posh amenities and status of the property served as home to world leaders, royalty, movie stars, and music legends. Security was meticulous. The vetting process was absolute. They were bathed in the history of the joint venture between the historic Waldorf hotel and the iconic Astoria hotels which were like palaces to the growing American capitalistic empire in 1893.

New York's unofficial palace experienced its grand reopening in the early thirties as the largest and tallest hotel in the world. The Art Deco style catered to cultural luminaries with 24/7 room service, offering palatial suites and grand public spaces for captains of industry, presidents and royals to gather.

During the Golden Age, celebrities such as Frank Sinatra and Ella Fitzgerald frequented the property. It served every U.S. president from Herbert Hoover through Joe Biden, apart from the one that had a hotel brand in his own name. American icons of music regularly sang in the Starlight Roof ballroom. Galas honoring greats of all kinds filled the social calendar.

It was part exoneration – the parade of misconducts which Jacob caused Adele to endure from his maneuvers with Victoria. It was also an untainted beginning for the two of them. There would be no 'did you and your ex live here in this Brooklyn neighborhood together?', nor would the 'is this the same bed she screwed your brains out in?' questions which might haunt them. There was enough of the runoff to fill their curiosity. The questions didn't need to be fed with dismissive and adulterated explanations.

She had learned to live a little simpler when on Oahu. Gifting much of her wardrobe to women's charities in the area, she added a few classic pieces to what her new small walk-in closet would be. Dressed to impress, although she didn't need to, she was wearing a V-neck black halo dress, with patent leather heels and a matching Saint Laurent flap-pouch bag. A long classic strand of pearls hung loosely around her neck and dangled from her ears. Jacob wore what had become the standard uniform for him – nice jeans, a dress shirt, and a jacket – all ensembled in a variety of flavors.

Together, they looked around the lobby area. A Turkish-travertine ceiling was balanced by a raw umber marble so glossy it looked wet. Gold moldings ran across the walls and accents of bronze and copper dotted a bookshelf with the covers of the books all falling within the sepia color pallet. The furniture was deliciously soft leather, in dark mochas and russets and beaver browns.

"I love it here," Adele said to Jacob. "Or I think we're going to."

"At three thousand dollars a square foot, we'd better." Jacob felt the creamy texture of the leather couches arm. "I want to come back here after we're finished and take a nap."

"I know, so comfy." Then she asked him what she really wanted to know. "Will you feel sandwiched, not having the penthouse floor?" Adele authentically wanted to know if there were any regrets before they closed on the unit.

"Not at all. We've got all the space we really need. Learned to live with less in Hawaii, right? And we're far enough up and away from most of the street noise, and..." he looked at her all dolled up, and smiled finishing his thought, he whispered the rest, "it's so quiet."

"I know. The acoustics and soundproofing is incredible. We're going to have to play music all the time, it's so tranquil."

"Maybe the management doesn't want the middle of the night call from Bill and Hillary: 'hey – can you ask the yahoos in the next unit to take it easy?' Or something like that."

"Yeah, Keith Richards or Mick Jaggar might need their rest for the evening's performance at the Garden," Adele joined in on the star-power roster, referring to MSG, which was round but for some reason unknown to her was named Madison Square Garden.

"Or Prince Albert and Charlene are hosting a ritzy dinner party and can't hear themselves speak above the rockers jamming out down the hall."

"Who?" Adele's brow expressed curiosity.

"You know, Prince of Monaco, son of Grace Kelly..."

"Nah... Simple me," Adele said to herself, "maybe I'm way outclassed here," she was seeking reassurance that she wasn't going to be the blight of the 25th Floor.

"Chill. Remember, live aloha. You and me – we're just happy to be here in the middle of freaking all of '*this*'. You help charities. I'm in private equity. End of story. It will all come together nicely." Jacob's confidence in knowing twenty percent of the answers and spewing bullshit for eighty percent of the answer was strong.

Adele was the opposite. "If you say so. We're probably going to have to hear about the preservation of the history, and inspiration of the heritage and sophistication, or maybe take an oath to live the values of responsible representatives of artisans work toward the magic created..."

"Did you take your medicine today?" Jacob teased. Listening to her overthink the moment was his queue to ask her to relax.

She gave him a spicy look. "I'm going to hurt you later."

"Ooo, promise?" he shot back.

"How much was the real estate back on Oahu?" Adele pivoted back to the costs. She'd never been involved in something...anything so expensive.

"Nine hundred thirty-seven bucks a square foot."

"Damn!" she said, "What a difference. Is that why we're keeping it?"

"Well..." Jacob shrugged his shoulders, "that and we need to see if the you-know-what project works well for us."

"Once we're in here, I'm never leaving. Like never."

"Not ever?" he asked.

"Nope."

"Who are we meeting with?

"Cassidy somebody..." Adele looked at the brochure she'd carried in with her, lying on the stone foot table. "Cassidy Quinn. She'd better not be pretty. I don't want you flirting with her in front of me."

"Cassidy..." He checked the face of his phone for what he thought was a ping. It was a high wind warning for Kapolei where the sailboat sat. Small-craft advisory. He looked up with a puzzled look on his face, "I don't know any Cassidy's."

"We're going to be tight on time." Adele was looking at her phone briefly too.

"Ruby will wait. This is important..." It was then that the door opened to the design studio. A beautiful woman, taller than Adele, shorter than Jacob spoke clearly and bubbly, "Hey guys...! Thanks for waiting, you two. I'm Cassidy. I've been looking forward to meeting with you to assist you with your design selections." Cassidy appeared a bit rushed, perhaps from a prior client's appointment running long. She held out her hand for a firm shake with each of them. A diamond bracelet too large for her wrist draped into the air. Her hair was long, auburn red, and in a Dutch braid trailing down her back to her buttocks. Green, emerald eyes with flecks of caramel and gingerbread surrounded her pupils. "Shall we begin? Ready to be blown away?" A perfect smile graced her face, high cheekbones and wide bright round eyes which drew you in like Her silky low-cut sea-foam colored dress hemmed to the middle of her thighs floated in the air as she spun toward the door she arrived from. She glanced briefly at Adele as they shook hands. Her look into Jacob's eyes was much longer, looking at his strong hand clasping hers, then brightly back up to his face.

With Cassidy's hand reaching for the door, Adele spun to look at Jacob watching her, looking at the trailing braid of red hair running down her spine. She pointed her finger at Jacob and mouthed the words with no sound coming from her, *'You behave yourself!'*

Jacob used both hands to swat the air in opposite directions in front of him. *'No, not me,'* was equally silent – mouthed by Jacob to Adele as they followed the attractive Design Consultant from the lavish waiting room through the heavy door and down a corridor of pricey offices.

Cassidy led them down the hallway which was equally impressive. "Full coffee bar, teas, waters, juices are here." She pointed to the kitchenette which looked like an advertisement in an *Art of Elegance* magazine. "And there is an open bar with the top shelf liquors. Too early for a cocktail? I will if you will. James will get you whatever your heart desires."

He tucked his hands in the tops of his jean's pockets. He felt comfortable navigating within the affluence. *Money lives here*, Jacob thought.

As they walked, her fingers drummed on the pricey printed brochure with amenity teasers about their design center meeting. It was a time to be immersed in a new world. *Money lives here*, thought Adele, *and so will we.*

"Jacob," she whispered in his ear. "I want to come here more often. This place is gorgeous. Can we?"

He felt her rum-scented breath near his ear and got an electric sensation of sensuality from her lips against his earlobe.

Adele and Jacob absorbed the warm colors or maroon, olive, caramel browns, yellows, and the palm trees lining the dark wooden walls of the bar. They saw him leaning back comfortably in a tapestry armchair. Gentle music was playing softly on hidden speakers. The tunes were crisp. Michael Bublé sang a song about *Everything.*

Adele listened to the words of the timely song as the bridge began, and a broader smile found her face. She looked up at Jacob scanning the area. Only a few seats were taken at this time. He began walking, and she followed him a step behind, observing his shoulders sway confidently as he walked across the lobby, as he'd done countless times before – on the way to a deal, to have a discussion with potential talent, or to grease the wheels of capitalism with a cocktail. *"It's crazy how things come about"*, the optimist whispered to herself.

"Really? Back to those old red suspenders, checkered shirt, scuffed up shoes and brown trousers?"

"Well, hello there, Mr. Park Avenue." Ruby stood up slowly and shook Jacob's hand feverishly, smiling broadly at seeing him again. "Where are your board shorts and flip flops?"

They chuckled as Ruby reached over to give a deep, hearty hug to Adele, softly saying, "I'm not letting go," while they embraced.

Soft pop and rock music played in the background, barely detectable.

She tossed her little shiny handheld bag on the cocktail table of the lobby and collapsed into the plush sofa in the bar area. "Ahh... What a day, Ruby."

"We just made an eight-million-dollar investment a nearly nine-million-dollar investment."

"Hey – if ya got it, flaunt it, right?" Ruby knew that their amenities and superfluity meeting was before their cocktail hour. "Can I order you up anything?"

"We started without you, Ruby. There was an extravagance bar at the design center. Over two hours, we're three ahead of you."

"We needed one of those in-house bars at PPCM." Adele was reapplying her lipstick. The blush-pink was a good color for her.

"Well, I might need to catch up with a couple then," the old man chuckled to himself.

"We got this. I'll have one and I'm done. Adele?"

"Sure, why not. It's a day of saying 'yes' isn't it, Jacob? You said, 'yes' to anything she recommended." Adele gave him a character-questionable glance from what had just taken place with the design consultant.

"She?"

"Cassidy, our smoking hot up-seller...asked one hundred questions about upgrades. Jacob said 'yes' for two hours. At least she didn't ask you if you wanted a blowjob."

Jacob shook off the jab with his hand panning across his airspace, "She was all twaddle. I knew what I wanted when we walked in there."

"Uh huh, you knew what you wanted when we walked out of there too. Miss Quinn." Adele looked at him, squinting evilly. "What am I going to do with you?"

"Well, hopefully something nice. I did just buy you a pimped out glitzy condo in MidTown."

Adele teasingly shook her finger at Jacob. "If I was any nicer to you, would we be down in Tribeca?"

"Say...why do they call it Tribeca? I've always been curious, when I want to ask someone where that name came from, I forget what I was thinking about." Ruby was more astute than anyone his age. Clever, knowing, sharp-witted.

Jacob saw what was happening. He knew that Ruby was directing their conversation to his desired outcome, taking precautions and allowing a guard to be dropped. Typical Ruby.

It was Adele who filled in the answer to the question. "Tri Be Ca. The triangle below Canal Street."

He shook his head slowly up and down. "Ah. I do remember hearing that once or twice. Dang." He shook his head twice. Ruby remembered looking at her hands in the seedy karaoke bar in Honolulu. No ring on her finger then, no rings on her fingers now. In fact, she was quite simple when it came to her dress. This was as gussied up as Ruby could recall seeing her. But wearing rings and bracelets and expressing money in lavish ways just wasn't Adele's thing. The road of extravagance was led by Jacob.

An Asian bartender wearing black pants, a crisp white shirt, and a grey herringbone tie tucked inside where the buttons met the loops approached them taking their drink orders. He was in his mid-thirties, wore glasses which made him appear smart, and made sure he had the orders correct, repeating them twice, confirming Jacob's order one additional time.

After he left, Jacob twisted his head in the direction the bartender ventured away to and then looked back to ask Adele and Ruby, "Did you catch his name?"

"Jacob Paisley... That was Sammy. He worked with us for several years. Until Goldman Sachs sucked him in, that is. Smart. Super smart. We liked him. That was a loss."

"Shit. Sammy. Hmm." Jacob was lost in thought. It was with Victoria. Sammy... Victoria and Sammy.

They were in a corporate suite at a Yankees game. Victoria and Sammy were talking. Jacob was attempting to listen to the two of them while holding a conversation of his own. He heard Sammy ask her where she worked and what she did. Victoria mentioned something about the services industry. She said something about a concierge service model for high-net-worth clients. Sammy asked her about the Yankees – something about if she attended many games through the season. She could hold her own. Jacob didn't need to run interference. It was Sammy – one of the best, one of his favorites.

Jacob remembered the moment in detail. It was a hotdog eating contest among the invited traders. Victoria. Dressed a bit risqué for a ballgame. Adele wasn't there. Sammy...questioning Victoria about regular things that any two people might talk about.

She pulled Jacob aside, *"That one. There behind me. Don't look. The Chinese looking guy in third place right now..."* ...Yeah...what about him?... *"He's freaking me out. He won't stop asking me questions. It's like an inquisition. What's his deal? Make him stop."* Vic...c'mon, it's a ballgame. Make him stop showing an interest in you? He's one of my favorites. Maybe not my top pick to win the hotdog eating contest, but one of the best and brightest on our team. Why not go sit down in one of those nice seats, I'll top off your chardonnay... *"you'll top off my chardonnay? Really? That's what you'll do?"* Yeah, yeah...you want something else? *"Well....well, you're not getting any tonight..."*

"Jacob? Jacob?" Adele asked. "Where'd you go just there?"

"Oh, sorry. Sammy. Was trying to play out his departure in my head, and was struggling some..."

"That's what I was just telling Ruby." She pressed her lips, wondering where he really went, "Sammy was a rising star, a high-valued asset, you called their CEO out of disgust."

"Yeah, Solomon. What can I say, frenemies. He took my calls some of the time." Jacob wanted to be off topic.

It was Ruby who spoke next, "And here comes Sammy the former Goldman Sachs and PPCM trader with our drinks."

He arrived with the three crystal tumblers with three different colors of amber sparkling between the clear ice cubes. Setting them down gently on the glass tabletop, hearing the glass touch the glass with single clinks, Sammy asked, "You want me to open tab for you, Mr. Paisley?"

Jacob's bottom lip protruded. "Sure, Sammy. Thank you. Would you like a card?"

"For you sir, not necessary." Sammy provided a small bow of respect toward Jacob, followed by two mini-bows to Ruby and Adele, to which he also gave a slight smile and a glance.

After he departed where they were sitting, in the lobby of The Bowery, Adele offered condolences, "Awe... Sammy. We liked him.

Can we give him one hell of a tip, please?" She looked at Jacob hopefully. "I'll pay. I've got this one. I'll do it."

"Nobody's going to pick up the tab. Maybe next time, but not tonight guys. This one's mine."

Jacob and Adele looked at Ruby who looked nothing like he belonged in the trendiest place in downtown NYC – against the wood-paneled walls, leather armchairs, and quirky artifacts surrounding the age-old establishment.

"To a date with Ruby night!" Jacob raised his glass. The whiskey swirled in the glass, reflecting the dimming light of the day and the growing amber lights on the walls and lamps throughout the bar. The fireplace was alive with flickers of flames and warmth wafting across the hearth to them, sitting nearby.

"To Ruby, to Jacob, to saying 'yes!'," she squinted teasingly and jealously toward Jacob with that, "and to, I don't know...come-what-may!"

They clinked their glasses, knowing that this segue was why they were meeting tonight.

"Dearly beloved, we are gathered here this evening..." Ruby said as they finished the first swallows.

"Sounds like a wedding," Adele included.

"More of...perhaps an engagement." Ruby looked toward the bar at Sammy and raised his glass.

"You know him too?" they simultaneously asked, looking at each other with frowns for the potential coincidence of the three of them knowing Sammy.

"Aye...let's say I come here often." Ruby shrugged. "Back to the engagement party."

"Wait a minute." Adele asked, "Did you know that he, Sammy, he – that one – worked for Jacob/"

Ruby took another drink. A little deeper and slower long sip, buying an extra second to process the question - like a teenager asked a question in which the answer was already known, but the teenager didn't know that the answer was known. He swallowed, trying to buy more time, "Huh? What's that?"

"You heard me."

Busted, Ruby admitted to the exceptional recruiting pool, "Well, let's say there were some cascading skillsets at PPCM. You always interviewed hard so that you could manage easy. There was a little of you in anyone we picked up." He raised his glass to Jacob.

"Maybe," Jacob said, "but that was money-motivated talent."

"There's some truth to that." Ruby clinked his glass, setting it down against the half-inch thick glass protecting the darkly stained walnut beneath it. He looked at Jacob and shrugged his shoulders, "We picked up a few, we lost a couple. That's that. NYC's Fin-Dis - it's a relatively small circle. The size of a dime, some would call it. Everyone knows everyone's business, then acts surprised when something happens. You all have parts on Broadway if the Financial District gig doesn't work out."

"Bravo, old man." Jacob raised his amber colored glass, reflecting a soft yellow lamp behind him. The daylight outside was waning.

"Let's get down to it," Ruby looked directly at Jacob. "You, my friend, have a gift."

"I do?" Jacob smiled. Hearing some version of this before, he didn't know if it was stock-picking prowess, understanding value opportunities, M&A, navigating the derivative markets, or his people leadership skills which Ruby might address.

"It is..." Ruby paused, "her." He pointed to Adele. "She is an unexpected gift."

Jacob sat up straight in his low and cushy leathered seat looking at Adele across the cocktail table. Ruby, in between them allowed it to sink in before he continued. "We knew what we were getting when we sought after you. But the two-fer? Adele?" He paused, looking for an analogy within the penny-colored drink. "Kind of like signing Michael Jordan and getting Scottie Pippen as a bonus."

Adele looked directly at Jacob wondering if he was going to say anything, adding with a raise of her glass, "Go Bulls." Taking a sip, she lowered it, holding onto the crystal goblet. A single clear chunk of ice floated near the surface.

It was a moment to respect Adele. It was a time for humility. This was not The Jacob Paisley Show. This wouldn't be their moment without the 'them', which meant Adele, his backbone, his fixer, his fortress, his enhancer, his treasure, and now...his grace. It was now his responsibility to serve and indulge and adorn her for what she had done for him and in what they had accomplished together.

"Listen, I dig it - the money you gifted to that woman down in Battery Park a while back. Jacob, what was the name of the charity she, Mary, set up with the million dollars?"

"I...I don't know." Jacob replied.

Ruby pointed to Adele and snapped his fingers.

"Mary's Meals, eight soup kitchens in lower to mid-Manhattan." Adele looked toward Jacob, "Mary wanted to call it 'Gordon's Grub'. At least I was able to talk her out of that." She shook her head and added, "Everyone eats in NYC. Mary's...well, she's a bit of a hard pill to swallow."

Jacob, embarrassed that he was nothing more than the checkbook, sheepishly looked at Adele. Her eyes were flickering around this place she said she wanted to return to, remembering the conversation that she, not Jacob, had with Mary and her small child, Marcy, following Jacob's dismissal.

"There's good here. These are the principles we seek within Ellipsis. Whether it's funding it," Ruby pointed at Jacob. "Or administering it," he then pointed at Adele with the same finger. "You two are the epitome of the one-two punch. A knockout combo."

Jacob raised his glass to Adele, running low on the amber-colored fluid, attempting to be charming, "Summa Cum Laude!" which in Latin meant, with the greatest distinction.

"Allow an old man to salt your game just a little more, Captain Paisley, the charity in Hawaii?" Ruby was targeting, snapping and pointing at Jacob again.

"Pau Kahana Cruise Company?"

"Thank you. It was set up as...?" The finger snap and point were in Adele's direction this time.

She was slow to answer, but did, reluctantly, "Set up as a tax write-off, to absorb the cost structure of the slip rent, expenses, fees, and what-not."

"And...and 'what-not', she says..." Ruby was acting as the AG prosecutor here in the SDNY." He looked at Jacob, "This is why, as your Attorney General for the Southern District of New York, I ask you the jury to find the defendant, Jacob Paisley, guilty."

Silence passed between them with only the background music playing slightly louder on the bar's sound system. Sting sang about *Fields of Gold*. With the filtering light from the outside world diminishing, shadows broadened with meaty yellow lighting causing the red colors of the lobby bar to burst, the oranges to gleam, and the earthy browns to wink their luster.

It, the words not the colors, sank in. The new Jacob received them. The old Jacob would have deflected them.

Ruby was gentler with what he said next, throaty words which were above a whisper, "Listen, Adele has a heart of gold. Yours? More like a heart of glass. But you came around. We don't need the prima donnas. Check the ego at the door. Adele is the selfless contributor here. You can be a little more like her a little more often and it'll do you some good."

Jacob thought that this would be an onboarding session.

Adele thought that this would be a Paisley parade.

Ruby knew where the conversation was heading. "You asked me 'why', and I didn't answer your question with as much content as maybe I should have."

"Why – what?" Jacob's puzzled look on his face led Ruby to state the question he'd been asked before.

"Why the intricate and convoluted interactions. Why so much planning and complicated confluences," Ruby reminded him.

"Ahh, yes 'why' indeed? Even if you did answer the question kind of, sort of, I'd like to hear it again. Adele wants to hear it." Jacob glanced at her, prim and proper on the couch, sipping at The Boss Hog bourbon. Her eyes met his as she slowly pulled the drink from her lips.

"It's a distinguished few. I wasn't sure you were one of the fold. Your interests were edgy, selfish, left of center. And then we began talking about 'what-not', and I found a kind soul within a crusty exterior. Probably what Adele saw long ago." Ruby peeked over to Adele studying Jacob. His pride had been ruffled. "I got to know more than the money magnet. We shared stories and a few secrets and in the manner of getting to know someone – I found the assurances and trust in you for something more. I wanted you. The others did not."

"The others?"

Ruby slowly supped the classic Old Fashioned. "Ellipsis – the others which were required for me to convince and to vote you in. It takes three votes of confidence for you to be drawn in. The recruitment process wasn't going well. The boat, your yacht on Oahu...damn strange thing that storm. We thought it would be storm and it would be a test of character, yes. But the severity of the...well, who knew."

"And the child? Out there on the water?"

"That worked out well, wouldn't you say?"

"A half-loaded gun, a crying baby – a newborn, a dog swimming with sharks...?" Jacob's forehead folded with uncertainty and doubt. "Yeah – I guess. Sounds like a Wednesday on Wall Street. Maybe..."

"Lucky." Ruby interrupted Jacob's summation. "You described yourself as lucky when I asked. Kind-of, sort-of crazy how luck has a lot to do with anything."

"Fate," Adele added quickly between sips, swirling her drinks to see the ice cube dance and reflect the dimming light.

Jacob glanced at her . She was looking over Ruby's shoulder.

"We took you two together. Jacob along with Adele. No-she, no you. That's what we all agreed upon. She's the heart, the elixir, that loadstone. You build off of Adele's foundation. There's no telling what you two can do together."

He wasn't sure if what he was hearing was to build her up, or to bring him down a rung. *Okay*, Jacob said to himself, *there was a lengthy vetting process. All good things require a deliberation and some healthy debate. At first, you date. Then you get engaged. Then there's the marriage.* He glanced at Adele thinking of the roundtables he held at PPCM, running his organization. She would wait in silence, offering her opinion last. It was often the one that stuck to the situation.

Ruby softened his statement with what he said next. "Listen, I know it's all odd when it starts out. There are so many things happening, and you might not be aware of the careful considerations behind them. Ellipsis has a few agendas like any organization. You can't be everything to everybody, but you pick and choose your battles. We nurture locations, and communication. We direct actions and outcomes. We have careful coordination to provide solutions. But then there are elements that sneak into what we do or what we try to do. Unexpected things happen. And when they do, you pivot. The crazy part is the things that deliver actions which were unexpected but make people do the shit they do."

"Like?" Adele asked.

Ruby continued, "Like your imagination, your faith, someone's perception and perspective. People's biases. They do a lot of the work." He paused looking into the distance as if remembering miracles he had experienced. "It's the dandiest thing, seeing good come together from - what was sure to be evil."

"Well," Jacob lifted his glass to Ruby, whom he had experienced his own unexplainable adventures with, "I'm grateful for the hospital volunteer, the bartender, the passenger in the Pacific. And now...for you as my friend."

"Crazy how it all comes together, right?" Ruby asked Jacob. Their eyes met and locked. "There was a bit of osmosis at work, maybe. Me, rubbing off on you. Adele, rubbing off on you. At times I thought you weren't all there."

"Mutual," Jacob said, not taking his eyes off of his friend.

"Fair enough. I thought you needed to finger your anger, find that fury within yourself. That void you were trying to fill..." Ruby didn't mention the name, Victoria. But you followed the trail of bread-crumbs nicely. You got off of that hedonic treadmill you were on. You found that compass within yourself which carried you to where you needed to be. Not many can say that about themselves. You tested your human potential and realized something."

Jacob looked at Adele, and then back to Ruby, "What's that?"

"That is...that it isn't about 'you'. It's about 'us'. You listened. You listened to a calling to right some wrongs out there. The world can be a selfish place. You, you two, you and Adele – you were able to migrate from the selfish to the selfless."

"We told you we just bought a ten-million-dollar condo up the street, right?" Adele reminded him.

Ruby smiled, and added, "Well, you gotta' have a place to lay your head at night." Chuckles surrounded the table top between them.

Sammy came over to ask for the next round options, interrupting the stale and weightiness of Ruby's declaration.

Ruby raised his index finger, "How about one more for them, and three more for me? Could we do that Sammy?"

He smiled and nodded respectfully, "As you wish, sir." Retreating with backwards steps, Sammy moved to another couple which sat down in a seating arrangement close to them and the fireplace. The blazes were of natural gas, but there were still golden flickers resembling flashy sparks.

Finally, to break the stalemate between the three of them, and in an unfeigned approach toward understanding, Jacob asked Ruby,

"What would you like to see more of from me?" His ingenuous question was sincere, unpretending, and simple.

Adele was muddled by Jacob asking for coaching. Tumbled, and tangled, and tousled – this was her icon of confidence asking an old black man how to be a better human. She desired him all the more with his mussy vulnerability.

Ruby looked long at Jacob, swallowing the last of his first drink with three on deck. "Time to go to school, young man!" His energy was boosted. "We have a partnership. A few sustainable development goals we align to. SDGs - a time to learn about what's good for all – not what might be good for some. It's a black out period, a waiting period, a time for understanding that we ask of you."

"SDGs?"

"Ellipsis is closely aligned to a few principles, values, and directives which through charters and..." Ruby shook his head and smiled some, "and off the books agencies makes a difference, a true difference, where governments and companies and well-intended charitable organizations cannot deliver our difference. We're not solving world peace here. It isn't a campaign to end poverty, or for green energy, or greenhouse gas reductions." He glanced at Jacob and Adele to see if they were still in on his soliloquy. They were, hanging on to the 'and then what?'

"This...globalism...isn't what we see on cable news..." Adele added to his broadcasted proclamation.

"Dear Lord, don't get me started on that mind bending crap. No."

Jacob added, "Again, how can we best help the organization?"

Ruby took a deep breath, "Delivering a difference is...well...it's different. It isn't for everyone. You're going to need to identify what solution you two might want to solve for. It might take some time. But, just like an Ellipsis...that waiting between something happening...the void...the expectation of something...anything...action...happening, you can choose to act upon the potential you see." He summarized his thoughts, "What can you do, you ask? Take a breath, take a little time, give some thought to your cause, and when the bell sounds, come out of the corner swinging. Fists drawn, ready for a fight. And we'll be there with you. We'll go do good things together."

Sammy surprised Jacob and Adele, walking over to the three of them, carefully setting down one drink in front of each of them as requested. Then, he sat two on a side table near them, but not in front of them. He dropped himself into the cushy chair, and declared, "I'm off the clock, boss, Thirsty."

Ruby giggled. He looked at Sammy. "Giddy up, then," and raised his glass.

Adele looked at Jacob, acknowledging that surprise shouldn't be discounted with Ruby at the table.

The Chinese American former trader turned bartender-human rights advocate raised the glass of libations to his lips, looking at Jacob raising his eyebrows as he sipped the caramel bourbon. "Ahh... It's good to be us, isn't it? So much opportunity to do good."

Jacob smiled. Against the backdrop of another high-hat establishment in Manhattan, straddled by an old black man with the best of intentions, a new and former acquaintance, and Adele – the one who meant the most to him – Jacob realized that change, real change wasn't easy but was essential and favored those who embraced its unrelenting progress.

Adele smiled when she saw Jacob doing the same. Within this cozy bar, watching a man she adored change as the clock ticked, Adele was much more than along for the ride. She had her hands on the steering wheel. She felt that good things, the best of things like hope and goodness and love were in front of them.

Sammy smiled when he saw two unfinished drinks in front of him.

Ruby smiled at the speculation – the risky ventures ahead and the outcomes they may offer. He saw potential. The potential of what had taken years to assemble was coming together. It could be the best of all things. The imaginable as well as the once unimaginable. What potential could this new ensemble and emerging league of well-intentioned custodians of rectitude deliver? Potential. It was his purpose: to bring possibility together with need. He watched the flicker of the flames in the fireplace tickling the keystone at the hearth, while listening to the white noise surrounding him. Younger souls, with days ahead of them to dream and to delve and to do. Potential. Like the splashing sparkle on the sea's horizon, encouraging one to go out just a little further - to touch the horizon. Arcing that flatline - between the known and the unknown, potential was the dynamic driving his rectitude.

Another song played softly. Van Morrison's, *Into The Mystic*, frolicked with a horn-filled message. In its suggestion, there were magical forces at work. Spirits, greater than souls with flesh, were acting upon an agenda to push us into the unknown. A concept hymn, a man on a sea voyage, returning from an elsewhere, waves crashing about. A magical presence love song.

Jacob gazed into the warming colors in the distance, tipping his head away from the others. He was here together with them and, at the same time, alone, allowing the music to do the talking in his head. He listened to the whispers of an unsaid intimation – encouraging him to venture out, a little further. It was an obtrusive companion within him – a buoyant passenger, a yearning, a graceful cheer for change.'

BENDING THE ENDING

THE FUNDAMENTALS FOR *ARCING THE FLATLINE*

Afterword

What if who you became wasn't who you should have become?

All your preparation, education, experience, talent, and skill – misguided. Mis-intentioned. Not properly allocated. Something amazing could have happened, but since you missed the cues, didn't. You pumped the brakes instead of gunning the gas. Or perhaps something did happen, because you took that step that you should not have taken. I'm not trying to make a point about second-guessing anything. This is just a hypothetical about reaching into yourself for more or less. I've always thought that we're really a little tougher than we think we are. And perhaps a little more vulnerable too.

Arcing The Flatline is a story about a man who has tremendous aptitude and aspirations for one thing, transitioning into something else that is slightly foreign and uncomfortable. He realizes with time that his life will be about so much more than the results that he seeks. The net worth, numbers, quantifiable results that he once crafted was merely a component of his capacity.

When I first charted a course for *Arcing the Flatline*, I was on a beach on Oahu. I felt lucky to be there. There it is: lucky. One of the words I often use to describe the life I've been given. Lucky. I'm just a poor shoe salesman from Ohio. Really. So, everything is lucky. And grateful. I'm grateful too, to have experienced all that luck.

As I looked out at the sea's horizon, I thought I was the luckiest guy I knew. Surrounded by so many beautiful sights. Deep in contemplation of my "what's next?" for a long time, I declared a moment of redirection. It was simple: I wanted to be there. Permanently. Who wouldn't and why not? Leaving all the worldly thoughts and things behind was always an option. Right? Many of us have this fantasy while in a beautiful place, away from our responsibilities: *Does this fit? Sure. What would it take to trade what I've got - for what I want?*

Sure. Let the fantasy begin: Millie and I could live in the nearby condo community, Coconut Plantation. I would convince my company that I'd step down into a Territory Sales Manager role. We'd sell IT gear, software and services throughout the Hawaiian Islands to local small and medium-sized businesses. We didn't have a physical presence in Hawaii yet, and the information technology market share was ours for the taking. What an opportunity to dial it back some, and at the same time to build a market – to create.

That's it then, this moment and this place was my finish line.

But that wasn't real. My reality would have to be different. There were quotas to retire, quarters to conquer, people to lead, a pending implementation of a new order transaction software system, and brain-drain to fend off, as competition was stealing talent each week. The reality was that there was a mortgage to make, friends to keep, a life back in Phoenix to maintain.

Surprisingly though – it was mostly about work. The addictive grind that had become mine. That was the way it was.

I like to believe that I was influential in making things happen back at headquarters. I felt required. It's hardly the place to cut and run when you're needed. My way forward relented to my way back. I boarded Hawaiian Air flight 36 back to Arizona. Once you digress into your seat on the plane and open your laptop to tackle an eternal surplus of email and dig into the quota deficient spreadsheets, the waves don't tickle your toes anymore. The trade winds get traded for Monday morning, the next staff meeting, a recovery plan for attainment, and providing solutions toward problems. Returning to the grind wasn't bad though – it was good. I liked the people I worked with, my boss, the company leadership team, and what we were accomplishing. I'd flee my idea and get back to reality, because what I was doing was my purpose...or so I thought.

That thought of missing my opportunity to shake things up never left. I dwell on the subject matter. Why do we stick with what we stick with when we reach that certain point in our lives? Complacency? Comfort? Fear? Family? Obligations?

As I became somewhat obsessed with why it is that some folks take those risks, and others don't – I decided to capture some of the comments from business associates and friends that I asked my questions to. A researcher of sort, I'd ask that same questions to broad groups and compare their answers. Hundreds of conversations took place, notes taken, output cataloged. The silly and simple questions ranged from, *who is the happiest person you know?* to *how many pairs of shoes do you think you own?* Turns out, the questions and the answers weren't so simple and silly after all.

One meaningful question that I asked: *Why do you think that some people seem to be capable of doing just about anything, while others struggle so much?* As you can imagine, the answers were various. Culture and physical proximity topped the list. Genetics and family were next. Many of the responses were about education, ethnicity, demographics (like physical proximity, but more about choice), and family history.

But the replies that got me twisted most were those that cited fate. Fate – as some things were meant to be. There is a wide range of unfounded spirit around whether it's (our lives) all happening in a scripted sense – or we're charting our own course. Nearly half of the people told me that life is meant to be, while the other side would indicate that we're making it happen.

With 91% of all people replying to a PEW research project that some form of God exists, a higher and divine being, how did in my research – they come up with the conclusions that *it's supposed to happen this way*, or *we're in charge.*

This led me to some of the common denominators people take to draw their conclusions:

- We all Believe in something.
- Our Perceptions aren't always our own, but we can often do much to change what we might see from where we might stand.
- The Feelings we choose to take on may be divine. They are also optional. There's much diversity within how we choose to feel.

- Thoughts are wide-ranging and the transition from the interior person that we have become to the person we might become. Thinking is that catalyst from the grey-matter deep-rooted stuff to getting it done.
- Those steps from concept and strategy, Actions, are the visible bi-product of the first four categories of our delivery. Actionable items are a delivery mechanism.
- Results. If you can deliver them, you're precious. If you cannot – and like it or not, your value is questioned a little more often than you might like.

Let's take a checkpoint here. This is what I like to refer to as a six-point list of 'pillars' that often equally build toward our human potential. When they separate, we work hard to draw them together. When they touch – we can easily migrate from one toward the next.

And there it was: the idea. When the six pillars of potential are strong enough to carry us on, when they are close enough for us to leap from one to the next, we thrive. When we cannot make the leap, we need help. We need the bridge - to compensate the difference or help in transitioning from one to the next. We need to travel the arc, that line toward what we do not yet know.

I set out on a quest to understand in general terms why we fall short of our capabilities. Why do we settle? What prevents us from pursuing more or less? Why do we fear the change? Why had we quit? Why do we believe enough isn't enough? Why we miss the mark, and as well - why do we sometimes go too far? All roads led me to the descriptions of human potential. In business, in sports, in relationships, in life.

Sometime later, from social media, someone shared this with me, and it had to be included because I found it relevant:

"So many people live within unhappy circumstances and yet will not take the initiative to change their situation because they are conditioned to live a life of security, conformity, and conservatism, all of which may appear to give one peace of mind, but in reality, nothing is more dangerous to

the adventurous spirit within a man than a secure future. The very basic core of a man's living spirit is his passion for adventure. The joy of life comes from our encounters with new experiences, and hence there is no greater joy than to have an endlessly changing horizon,
for each day to have a new and different sun." --- Into the Wild

I wanted to tell a story, then un-tell it. So, here we are. I took some of those thoughts that I gathered to construct a character: Jacob Paisley. A fictional story of a period in the life of one man able to alter his course, to transition a good life into something potentially even better, yet far from where he thought he was heading.

Unraveling the character and providing a glimpse into some of the experiences that I've had the good fortunes to gather, here are those six pillar touchpoints that, to me, attempt to explain some of our steps toward, *What's next?*

BELIEFS

"My religion consists of a humble admiration of the illimitable superior spirit who reveals himself in the slight details we are able to perceive with our frail and feeble mind."
--- Albert Einstein

Each of us believes in something. Those beliefs allow us to evolve, flourish, and cope. If you believe that the car on the other side of the road will stay within the yellow lines that contain it, you might be likely to climb behind the wheel and drive. If you believe that in time you can generate money from money, you may be likely to save or invest (even small amounts) and yield from a portfolio many years down the road. If you believe that good actions generally deliver rewards and bad actions can cause consequences – you're likely to live within the laws of the land. If you believe that you can get away with something that perhaps you shouldn't, you may be likely to break those rules for an advantage or personal gain.

Those basic beliefs are often borrowed – accumulated in our formative years. And as we age, we continue to accumulate beliefs that are pertinent to our timeframes.

As parents and guardians, we believe that we should expose our children to the same doctrines (or completely different values) we experienced as children. As we can, we send them to schools, churches, summer camps, the arts, crafts, sports teams, and any program that might provide them with the tools to live a balanced life and to thrive. As parents and guardians, a result which we deeply value will alter their futures. All based upon our own beliefs, we've impacted the beliefs of the next generation.

As a captain of a sports team, we believe that communicating our strategy will help the players behave in a way to score points. So, we call the play. We believe that practice will build the actions to win. We work hard, we sweat, and sometimes even bleed to achieve our victories. Ever been on a winning team? Sure, you have. Ever been on a losing team? Sure, you have. There's often a glaring difference at how we go about posting those wins and losses. If you believe you can win, you might do anything. And if you believe you're going to lose – you might just cut your losses and do nothing. But your beliefs in your team's potential might be more borrowed than you realize.

So, there's the rub. We can't take forever to determine the outcomes, favorable or unfavorable for each step. Paralysis through analysis gets nothing done. But we can always take one moment to decide how we got to the point that we've approached. Whose beliefs are at work: ours, others, or a healthy combination?

The accumulation of what we believe ultimately takes on other forms too. As we look at religious doctrines and theology, beliefs are gathered masterfully into faiths. Faith is what we collectively believe in. It's the knowledge handed down from one generation to the next. It's the scriptures that are preserved, interpreted, and shared with explanation or, in some cases, interpretation. Faith is sometimes believing that the impossible is possible. It's seeing the path ahead that is not within sight, knowing that you don't know it all, realizing that something is at work behind the scenes – mightier than all that we can collectively comprehend.

According to several polls, more than 9 in 10 people believe in God or some form of higher power. Beliefs are something that we generally do not trade. Religious distinctions can cause us to challenge our faith, to lead ourselves into wars, to define generations, or to firm and form our direction. Wiping out or replacing our fundamental beliefs and convictions is never as easy as it seems.

Unfortunately, there are numbers of people that have had their faith shaken due to a crisis or condition. Their foundation, all that they've stood for, was in some manner altered. And then, there are millions that kept their faith at a convenient arm's length, only to encounter some reason to later embrace it.

A transition sometimes takes place. Those convictions, borrowed, can be given back, and those that are earned, can be worn with a resolve. The evangelical, bible-beating, good churchgoers can find themselves become indifferent. And a fervent Atheist can rotate their faith.

The point made here is that faith, what we believe and what we do not believe in, serves as a loadstone. Its foundation closely aligns to the other pillars that follow.

What's known and what's unknown, what can be seen through words and deeds, may be a product of just one moment or a countless period of time considering or convincing. Think of the extensive thought process it might take to re-engineer your core.

We're most likely to change little.

Personality tests can often measure the inner core. A wide variety of products, such as the commonly known Briggs-Myers, determine probabilities toward key factors like extroversion; conscientiousness; openness; emotional stabilities. Correlated traits are derived through a series of questions and the answers provided. Perhaps you've participated in one.

I have had the opportunity to learn and to leverage several of these assessment tests (DiSC, Self-Awareness Management Training and Predictive Index) through my working years. These were used to hire, train, or to modify my behavior to seek team results or an individual desired outcome. The truth? The truth is we don't change much. During a lifetime, how we are out of our formative years slows dramatically. And we don't mold much after that. Over the years, we may look back and assess all the changes that have taken place.

But, often, the greatest drama is everything that has changed around us.

I'm old enough to have had a secretary. Not today's more politically correct term: an administrative assistant...she was my secretary. Her name was Adele. I adored her efficiency and her competencies. Her talent and skills greatly helped me thrive and I'm grateful for the team of managers that reported to me loved her. She enjoyed her work and was much the backbone of our successes.

Growing a sporting goods chain from a regional to national level takes high-quality people just like Adele. Affirmative, outgoing, detail-oriented, visionary, understanding. I traveled from Southern California to Florida, from El Paso to Seattle. It takes a firm foundation to win in any competitive environment. It takes a degree of trust in knowing that the people you support, and those that support you have the same outcome in mind. It was a form of faith.

Adele was that faithful foundation that I could build with. I went about building a team, identifying talent to operate sporting goods stores, furnishing them with products and marketing to grow faster than any other district of stores within other markets. As a city would establish enough stores, we'd spin it off into another district. Adele did what she did which made me look good. Better than I was. We called our district The Dream Team. The run of good fortune led us to dollar and percent-leading performances. The Dream Team swept the top honors at one of our annual sales rallies. We were unstoppable. Or so it felt at the time.

A funny thing can tend to happen when you're focusing on the regional and micro-market issues. The macro factors change. It was good living in the West. But, not so much in the Central and the East markets. The company had swelled quickly, and, in some markets, stores were glutted with slow-moving inventories. In a cost-cutting maneuver, secretaries were to be suddenly replaced with technology. It may sound like an investment. But I lost Adele for...yes, a Dell. It was a box with wires coming out of it. Adele for a Dell. Not a trade I wanted to make, but one that was a necessity. There are times when you must accelerate to the future. But Adele had left a lasting impression on me.

Indeed, all of us face the challenges of accelerating change, but none of us do more-so than in industries such as technology, consumer discretionary, logistics, security, and transportation. Imagine flying an aircraft and not reacting to changes in weather. Think about not pulling the trigger on options at the bell's open when there are orders that must be placed. Or a surgeon taking her time with you on the table...flatlining. Any industry touching maniacal moment-by-moment change as the product from which to generate profitability or to protect life is exposed to being forced to make tradeoffs. You can argue that each industry offers the same stresses. But you'd be wrong. Some industries must move at the speed that outpaces others.

The cost-cutting changes continued. Store personnel were slashed, salaries were frozen, travel and expense restrictions were chartered. This ran a course for more than a year.

Oh no. The changes didn't deliver the expected results. The senior managers were replaced. A new leadership team was summoned to right-size the organization. Inventory levels were reduced by more than fifteen percent. Furthermore, stack rankings were to take place to identify the bottom ten percent. Those that were in profit-losing stores slotted for closing were to be dismissed or repurposed. But the preference was to eliminate the non-essential positions.

How do you eliminate people that have given their best working years to your company? Professional and difficult choices, no doubt. Not buying into all of the fundamentals, I questioned my faith in my employer. Many of us have had to make those tough decisions. At that moment, I was still on board, but questioning each move made. The newly crowned executives expected to be driven around in Lincoln

Town Cars and only stay at five-star hotels. I was offered a $75/night target for my personal hotel guideline.

And then, suddenly, I wasn't "in". It was a Monday morning. I was instructed to fly to Texas to fire so-and-so. After my rebuttal, I was instructed to "fly to Texas to fire so-and-so. What's the problem?"

That was the question I needed to be asked. What's the problem? I'd been placed in numerous situations to walk in to take the keys away from the store manager. It was always easy to recite that the Fair Employment Practice Department had reached an unfavorable decision. It was easy to swallow terminating someone when an ethical or criminal law had been broken. It was even easy to cite poor performance when well-documented with stacks of store visit reports and performance assessments. If it was about money, it was about money – when you don't make enough, you reduce your headcount. That was acceptable.

But, to eliminate tenured and valued teammates for little to no reason? It was becoming illogical. It was the fundamentals that didn't add up. I resigned Tuesday morning. With a wife and four school age children, a mortgage and credit card debt, with a bad attitude and an opinion that I was employable, I quit. It was completely unlike me. It was liberating.

That period in time ended well for me. I got picked up quickly and transitioned into a similar role in the technology sector. In other words: I got lucky. Some lessons learned in hindsight. I was unwilling to change what I stood for. And as for those erroneous executives? They were dismissed within the year after I left. Vindication comes in a variety of forms.

The point: if you want to thrive in today's world, you'll need to be comfortable with de-synchronized changes taking place that will impact you and those that you love. We like calling it "transformation" and "disruption."

How this relates to our beliefs is that we're accelerating our pace away from what we knew. As we age, as we live longer, as we connect with other people around the world – we're exposed to letting go and taking on more. But the connection to what matters...well, matters. And we're likely to see those that change well coupled with those who struggle with the pace.

Another and more important lesson learned was that respect and dignity are not prone to the same pace of change. It isn't unfashionable to respect diversity and doesn't hurt to treat everyone with dignity.

Will the faith that you embrace and the beliefs that you hold dearest be exemplary for others to follow? Will they manage you, driving you toward your potential – and the potential that can be uncovered in others that you share your moments with?

I arrived at this point - our beliefs will firm and form our direction. They may be challenged as well as honored.

PERCEPTIONS

"The most difficult subjects can be explained to the most slow-witted man if he has not formed any idea of them already. But the simplest thing cannot be made clear to the most intelligent man if he is firmly persuaded that he knows already, without shadow of doubt, what is laid before him."

--- Leo Tolstoy, 1897

"You have cancer."

"What?" The phone's reception was crystal clear. I was suspended in disbelief, not really missing those three words that changed my perspective. '*What?*' is a common pause mechanism that places the moment on hold while we process.

My doctor said it again, in a matter-of-fact tone, "You have cancer. Your pathology biopsies came back positive for cancer. Listen, I know that a phone call doesn't do this conversation justice. I'd like you to come in with a loved one next week to discuss your treatment options." He said other things too. There was something about slow growth, a comment that I had time to consider options, that my health and age were in my favor, and that I should limit my concern at this point.

I could see him in his white lab coat on the other end of the phone, sitting at his desk talking with me. Doctor Bob. We said other things, he provided me with several websites to research within the week ahead, and then we were done talking. I hung up and sat there in silence, absorbing it.

I looked at the wooden table in my office that I was sitting at. It was the same as it was before the call. My hand ran over the grain, feeling the lemon oil glide under my fingers. The same. Looking down at the gold-colored carpet under my toes - it was the same. The books on the bookshelves, aligned by genre and author, were no different. The computers that displayed spreadsheets and presentation decks sat there idle. No changes. I looked up at rays of sunshine streaming through the alabaster blinds. That was the same too. But something was definitely different then, and not better.

My first thought within that quiet point where apparently the only thing that changed was my perspective about *everything* was of nothing. My first thought was about how everything was really the same. Nothing was changed.

I must admit, '*That's it then. That's how I lived and died.*' Those thoughts found a place in my head for a minute as well. But, as I looked around at the office, the surroundings remained unchanged. And that stable environment was comforting. Only my thoughts were altered. "Lord, I'm in your hands now."

Sitting at the desk, I said that out loud.

Cancer. The word: it frightened me. Facing fear and uncertainty, doing something felt good. My doctor met with me offering surgery. But he also wanted me to meet with a Radiation Oncologist and a Robotics Surgeon to explore the option that would be best for me. My perceptions and knowledge of cancer were about to change. There were to be moments in which I discovered human kindness I'd never known. And there were moments, deniability, in which I walked into a room filled with fifty patients and family members and would say to myself, "*Look at all these people who have cancer. Oh, wait a minute, I do too.*"

DaVinci was the name of the treatment option I chose. Robotics: six cuts, small in size, lights, camera, action. It wasn't the technology that swayed my decision, it was the surgeon. Dr. Bigelow could have operated on me with a plastic spoon, chopsticks and a butter knife and I would have gone with his option. When it's possible, you do want to have some sort of connection with your doctor. His ego, okay we'll call it confidence, was larger than mine. I loved the competency he ensued. And we hit it off. His humor humbled my concerns.

"Years ago, when they asked me to test the system it had a few kinks in it. I thought that I didn't see a long-term solution. So, wasn't interested in the company's $10 stock. R&D, precision, additional enhancements for the mechanics, it's an evolved system. As of this writing, the stock trades at $450 a share. To think about it this way, if I jumped in – you may have someone not as experienced." Kevin Bigelow had performed over 900 DaVinci surgeries and trained numerous others on the procedure.

He continued in his conviction: "Mike, I'm a much better surgeon than I am an investor."

"I'd hope so," I replied.

Cancer-free. The term meant that I was lucky. Lucky to have taken the advice to have a physical. Lucky to have followed up on the high PSA numbers that the bloodwork produced. Lucky to have had the uncomfortable biopsy. Lucky to follow up on all of the advice I was provided with. Lucky to have met Dr. Bigelow. It was also a term which meant that my perception has been altered. Cancer-free means hope can be found and is always alive within the dark moments which may swallow us.

We often do things because we've done things. There's predictability, stability within traditional and acceptable behaviors. Mature companies, countries and cultures prefer a conservative pattern of growth. In control of the numerators and denominators, they build upon their successes. Erratic behavior generates degrees of risk, and because there is much to lose, risk is often managed out.

Perspectives can cause all sorts of things to happen such as relationships, legislature, wars, bull markets, bear markets, reactive policies, irreversible actions, moments of triumph, mergers, divorce, and the list goes on and on.

Timing, and intelligence, and resources, and experience, and character, and talent are some of the bones that frame up how a decision is made based upon how we see our world. Therefore, how we act within it.

Ask yourself this: Just how bad would things have to get for you to change *your opinion*? Test your limits. Ask yourself, how bad it can get from your first thought. Test your limits again. To change your *thought process*, how you would think of that situation the rest of your life, what would it take? The point I'm making is that we are so very naturally behavior based. Our natural instincts cannot always be denied. But, as we evolve – as a species – we have the ability to contemplate and understand our situation with the assistance of knowledge, history, enlightenment, and so many other assets and talents. We're provided with an opportunity to be competency based as well. Our perspectives can be altered in any situation. With any approach toward any circumstance, we have the capability to see things differently.

To think, act and produce a different, more favorable, or constructive result, we simply need to consider the consequence or outcome. Back to the human potential *Beliefs* question: Are you willing to trade what you want now, for what you want most? Short term, long term. The choice is yours. Free will is one of our greatest gifts. We're all dead in the end. But is the snapshot of your life one that someone would want to see? We have a gift – to add value to this moment and the next. And to contribute to others beyond our own boundaries.

I'm sure of this: interpretation is one of the most important forces in our lives. Our languages, our understandings, what we sense, how we deduce, when we realize. One interpretation after another. It lends itself to our evolution.

We're all doctors, aren't we? Finding ways to affirm life. Whether you've got your hands in someone's chest, or you drove the ambulance to the hospital, or you served lunch to the nurse, or you laid asphalt for the ambulance to drive upon, or you helped provide electricity to make any of that happen...your part contributed to the circle.

We're inherently resilient people. Even after we do everything wrong, we'll do something right to improve the end result and drive progress.

FEELINGS

"Too often, feelings arrive too soon, waiting for thoughts that often come too late." --- *Dejan Stojanovic*

There are a number of psychological or philosophical classes of explanation for the emotions that we encounter. Labeled, categorized, and in some schools of thought, even color-coded, the feelings distinctions are generally divided into two dimensions exposing the initial input (positive or negative) and the output (action or inactive response). This visual mapping affords a wheel that migrates from happiness to sadness, encompassing basic emotions such as anger, fear, elation, and disgust. From there – it can become much more complex. That's complex, not complicated. The attempt to explain how we generally might feel reminds me of a tool to manage behavior that was once shared with me.

Predictive Index, or PI Worldwide, is a professional theory-based assessment and measurement of work-related behavior. Used for the purpose of talent acquisition, development, change management, or growth, PI offers several tools to assess behaviors and qualities which may or may not align with drivers for job performance impact. In its simple format, a descriptive test is taken before work begins asking an applicant how they feel that they are expected to act by others. 86 words - from passive to audacious, fearful to eager, daring to careful.

Following the first round of self-assessment, the same words are offered requesting that the applicant check boxes really describing their style. Managers are offered classes to understand the purpose of the work style classification exercise, and more importantly, how to leverage the diversity in the workforce.

The words used to describe potential employees are to measure how they may behave and are categorized into theaters such as dominance, extroversion, patience, and formality. Depending upon the range of words checked or left blank, the tool offers a prediction as to the motivating needs, drives and aptitudes of the employee.

As adults, we're still formative. However, it takes more effort to change. Our drivers have become entrenched. PI is an attempt to describe, explain, and to predict behavior. However, to control feelings and behaviors in workplace adults is not the use of the tool. But rather, modifying a leader's behavior to attempt to select or leverage work styles to align for the job at hand is more the motive.

Predictive Index system is used to assess the potential of an individual, considering information gathered from the interview, personal history, experiences, or observations. The application has been used by thousands of professional clients, all in an effort to benchmark and drive results.

Feelings, simple in their nature and complex when in motion lead to an outcome-based result. Now, or later. Ask any therapist. There's a burden, hidden or exposed or both, in managing feelings. A control-mechanism, or lack of, allows the emotions to migrate to the parameters of awareness, often acknowledged by others. Or, to remain centralized - and perhaps unpredictable.

The feelings are also often without a framework. Timing, as it seems, is inconsistent and action arrives too early or too late. And occasionally, at just the right moment. Isn't it a common denominator in a love story for 'I love you,' to be spoken too soon or not at all?

One of the most acknowledged and basic feelings is fear. Fear of the unknown..."What happens next?"...is a driver across our experiences. In business, sports and in relationships, fear lends itself to a variety of outcomes and we tend to rationalize our way to conclusions.

As if translating feelings isn't difficult enough, the complexity deepens when we consider the representation of mental, physical, and real or imagined combinations that distinguish those sensations.

Categorized and questioned, our feelings are better understood. But really, who takes the time to consider the comparisons? Is hope to you the same as hope is to me? When your neighbor talks of pride, does it trigger a similar response with you? Relief and Disappointment may be cousins, just as Gratitude and Envy are. The interpretation is vast. And that's what often makes emotional intelligence a product and workplace predictive behavior indexing an industry. Defining and understanding those annotations and their representations lends itself to our evolution.

Our virtues – toward self-control, efficacy, respect, and kindness – lead us or cause us to stray from our limitations. Our potential is tested in regards for our humility as well as our courage. I think that on occasion, when we realize it or not, that there are others that place their hands on the wheels of our lives and turn the dial a little. It sometimes seems, with just enough of a crank, miracles happen.

We all have the capacity to be larger than ourselves, to be bigger than the moment. How we feel about the moment is relatively temporary. Thinking collectively about our character, overall, is a more lasting, beneficial, or consequential glimpse of impact.

Years ago, I ran sporting goods stores for a national chain. At first, I sold shoes. Then, I operated stores. And with much luck, was promoted to the rank of district manager. It was customary that within the first few weeks on the job as a district manager, the regional vice president, and a veteran DM or two to tag along for the purpose of offering guidance and basic onboarding suggestions.

My regional VP was especially well-liked. He was admired as a mentor, coach, and an extraordinary ambassador for the god-loving, hard-working, middle-class that we fell into.

Day one. "Mike, you'll be a successful DM when you learn to hate!" He went on to explain that hating poor performances was the loathing that he was referring to. Apparently hard work could cure poor performances – and as a result, if a sales manager of a store or the team in place delivered poor performances, a component of laziness or apathy would be nearby.

Learn to hate. And so, I did. I hated poor performances. Throughout my district, we learned to hate. Haters. All of us.

A measurable key performance indicator at the time was the increase in the items sold within a single transaction. Units Per Transaction, or UPTs for short, became as important as revenue, profitability from the P&L (profit and loss statement), and as important as loss prevention. And any manager with a poor UPT percentage to sales would receive a lengthy sermon on the do-better how-to's. Unfortunately, words don't always get the job done. UPTs became a metric of promotion to market-leader, a metric toward attaining a larger volume operation, a metric of respect within the team and the region.

Praise, a low-cost currency, was leveraged on a daily and weekly basis to highlight the best of the best. Not to be mentioned was failure.

Naturally, the sale of like-style items was the target. With a football, you sell receivers gloves. With shoes, you sell socks or laces or cleaners. With a pool cue, you sell chalk. But...selling rain ponchos with rollerblades? Sure thing. Ping pong paddles with baseball gloves? Absolutely. Soccer shin guards with baseball cleats? Of course. UPTs were the new metric of a successful sales rep and of who would be promoted next. Salespersonship soared to new levels.

Or so you'd think. We had created a simple lever that grew complex. But more on that in a minute.

I had one manager's team that ranked constantly and markedly low on the stack. After several conversations about effort and pride and discipline, a surprise visit was in order. I traveled to the store on the managers day off to view the team in action. What I saw was typical. Sales reps, trying hard to do the right thing. Occasionally, they were successful. Most of the time, not. When the tape was run at the day's end, as slight uptick was realized. Yet, nowhere near the district average. I stayed an additional day. The manager worked that next day. My reminders of hating poor performances were relentless. However, our conversation led to an interesting point. The were no games played on this manager's team. No manipulation of data. No discounting of extremely marked down items or no-charging to attain the benchmarks.

In other words – cheating was widespread. Across the district, store-to-store communication was exchanged as to how to avoid a poor performance review. At the same time, an investigation was underway. Discounts were at record levels. Auditors crawled all over the journal tapes seeking the manipulative method to drive old goods out, UPTs high, and capture the desired outcome. We had all gone too far in hating poor performances. And this certainly isn't as complex as the financial instruments used in bringing the bubble from our nation's real estate crisis to light.

Unchecked emotion had driven the behavior. As in so many things, left to its own demise, the hatred of poor performances ran wild. And it took the courage of one manager to step in and say, *no cheating*, to draw a light on exactly what a good performance consisted of.

Emotions: love, hate, fear, and happiness are divine and define us. These internal forces are contained until they aren't – managing our actions or years later managing other deeper feelings. I guess that sometimes it takes an honest loser to help you realize that winning is almost always more than a number.

THOUGHTS

Whether IBM's "THINK" motto coined by Thomas J. Watson back in 1911, or Apple slogan, "Think Different" – Apple's supposed decades-later response, thought is the necessary DNA within the information technology industry.

Google was no different. Perhaps it was better.

I had the opportunity to experience Google early on. As early as 2000, Y2K as we called it, while in the capacity of an IT reseller sales leader, I had the opportunity to visit the campus. Before the Googleplex came to be, they were in a nearby business park. Traveling in with one of my favorite reps, John, we planned to meet with everyone we could speak with. Our primary contact said that if we wore red socks, he may be able to arrange a meeting with one of their chief architects. "Okay," I thought, "they're probably hazing us, but I'm down for that." Picture a navy suit, crisp dress shirt and yellow power tie with bright red socks. I borrowed my son's little league stirrups. They were bright red. Looking like a clown when I walked or sat down, we moved from meeting to meeting.

Across a maple conference table were discussing basis points with a procurement guy who leveraged purchasing knowledge he garnered elsewhere, "If you have two coins to rub together at the end of this transaction, that's one coin too many." The piercing blue eyed former-commodity broker knew he had us where he wanted us. He knew the value of a nickel. And we were all-too happy to make money on every other quarter million dollar order of hard drives, processors or memory.

Venture capital money fleeced their balance sheets. This was a time before they were public. They thought through everything, spreading the Sand Hill Road money as thin as they could. The result: they were building blades before anyone. Collocation units filled with thousands of servers, blinking and buzzing, to support the ever-expanding World Wide Web. It was impressive. We were in awe of the expansion and the talented thought behind Larry Page's and Sergey Brin's architecture of their darling, Google.

But my thoughts led to the bottom line. How are they going to make money? Who's in charge of that piece of their pie? His name was Urs Holzle. I was told that Urs was Google employee number eight. And that he was the chief technology executive working on their pay-per-click project. "What the heck is that?" I thought.

"Hey Urs. There's a guy wearing red socks I want you to meet."

Around the corner comes a massive black Mastiff. Google is a dog-friendly campus. I thought it was going to eat me. And the master followed. He appeared to be a gentle man, wearing jeans, a checkered flannel shirt, and of course, red socks – and I don't know exactly why but looked freaking smart.

We exchanged pleasantries and I asked about four pieces of paper taped together on the wall in the hallway next to his office.

"This," he said, "is code. Search code. These are bundled within industry." He pointed at what appeared to me as a spider with legs. A daddy long-legs. On each of the long lines away from the body, were batch gathering web addresses. "These are knowledge-based searches. These are Commercial purchase application, or dot com. Education searches, or EDU. These are for Government, or GOV."

"And what about these three, Urs. They have red crayon circling them."

"That's porn."

"Excuse me?"

"Pornography," he said matter-of-factly.

Pay per click meant advertising revenue. In an instant, I knew that when this company went public, I needed to be in on the IPO. To think that the minds at Google had our curiosity on tap and an evolving plan is impressive. I am quite sure that Google had absolutely no intention on making money through any form of exploitation. Their corporate motto was...Do No Evil. But pay per click was emerging at that time and they were way out in front of what "search" would become. I was simply honored to see it in its development stage so early on. Who's coattails might one rather ride on?

Those ideas, our thoughts, and what we choose to do with them are the difference deliverers. Investing in time to think is always a valued "tuition". Thoughts, the transition between the internal and external forces can predicate volumes of action.

<u>ACTIONS</u>

"Self-restraint is a manifestation of greater power than all outgoing action." --- Vivekananda's Philosophy on Karma Yoga

The first marathon that I ran was in 1990 when I lived in Houston. After I finished, I said that it was the stupidest thing I'd ever done. Not running the marathon, but rather not training for it. It was originally Thelma's idea. At the suggestion of one of my assistant managers in a sporting goods store I worked at; I sent in an application to run the Houston Tenneco Marathon nearly four months in advance of the event.

She asked me each week about the distance I had accumulated. When I delivered my inadequate number, she'd shake her head and offer her number of miles logged that was always four or five times greater than mine. And then, Thelma would add, "You do know that it's 26.2 miles, right?"

I knew that she questioned coaxing me into it when I would tell her that I'd gut it out and not to worry about me. She knew that I wasn't taking it seriously, and because she had run marathons before also understood that I wasn't properly preparing.

Cross country, which I did run in school, was not a marathon. But we did log miles to build our endurance. Running track and cross country at Clay High School which was in a suburb of Toledo led me to nothing more than 13 mile runs. The rationalization was, *OK – just two of those makes a marathon. I can do that.* Reverting back to the present: at that point, living in Texas, working 60-hour workweeks, a husband and father of four, the question was posed well after I agreed to run – when was I going to train?

I embellished the answers to the training and mileage questions that Thelma would ask. When I ran 10 miles within a week, I'd answer 20. When I reached 15 miles, I'd say 30. Her raised eyebrow looks of concern diminished as I exaggerated the miles. Race day rapidly approached.

And then it was the middle of January. An early Sunday morning: time to run. We met before the start of the race to talk about pace and the course and whatever carb-loading we'd taken part in the night before. In a crowd of thousands, the starting gun shot out and we were off. Thelma lagged. And I couldn't help myself when we were winding through the streets of downtown Houston. Volunteers and cheering fans shouting out. Air horns and cowbells ringing. Cheerleaders chanting encouragement. I sprinted ahead with adrenaline and lost Thelma. Mile 4 became 6, 6 became 8, 8 became 10. Discomfort arrived earlier than I had anticipated. My lower back ached. It felt as if the water stations, usually just after the mile markers, were becoming further apart. They alternated the beverages, water, and Gatorade, in tiny green cups at each station. At mile marker 12, I thought it was water and I doused my face with it. It was lemon-lime – and in my eyes not all that refreshing. Where was Thelma? Was this a joke? Was she only really going to run some of the race? I needed to stop and walk.

And then she passed me. Just before the halfway mark. *Good for you, Thelma*, I thought. Now I was in her rearview mirror. My long strides quickly turned into a shoestring shuffle as the pain grew from my lower back to my legs. It surprised me that my shoulders and neck hurt as well. I began to think about what didn't hurt as 15 became 16 and 17 became 18. This was ridiculous. What's wrong with quitting? Why did I think that I needed to finish? The answer became clear quickly. Because whether I quit or whether I finish, I still needed to get to the finish line where the car was.

When I approached mile 22, I began to reverse engineer the outcome. I originally anticipated that it would take 4 hours to finish. That was wild guesswork on my part. At that point in the marathon, 4 hours had already passed. Just 4.2 miles to go. *Perhaps 4:30 for a finish?* Pain consumed me from head to toe. And I don't remember anything else about those last 4.2 miles. But I do remember finishing. When I crossed the line, a giant timeclock overhead read: 5:15:15.

Not knowing it at the time, but reading it in the newspaper the next day, an American had won the race. Paul Pilkington, a junior high school teacher from Utah with a time of 2:11. And for the women's division, Maria Trujillo from Scottsdale, Arizona finished first, posting 2:32. It took me twice as long as she to complete the race.

Thelma dusted me by more than an hour. Preparation – the mother's milk of marathon training.

My wife was sick. She had the flu. When I returned home to her, she was in bed, yet in a sweet but groggy voice she asked, "Honey, how did it go?"

I replied, "That was the stupidest thing I've ever done. I'll never run another marathon."

That declaration later became a concrete-consuming project. Years later, work became stressful. And I took to the streets to run away from the stress of the job. I found difficulty in managing people's poor choices. Why wasn't my charm or inspiration enough? It once was. The company that I worked for was on the hunt for one of my managers. I had difficult decisions to make in defending him. Then, there were two. Then there was another. What we had built was falling apart.

The laces on my sneakers were drawn tight. I ran away from the moments with miles of asphalt. But then a few miles weren't enough. The 5Ks became a 10Ks. And before I knew it, a thought crept back into my head: *Why not just run another marathon*?

Time had passed. It was now seven years later, which meant that I was seven years older. But seven felt like twenty.

Since I began mentioning that I ran my first marathon, you may be assuming, correctly, that there was at least another. From Lake Tahoe to Los Angeles, Phoenix to Philadelphia, Cincinnati to Albuquerque, Big Sur to San Diego – they accumulated in one personal-best producing race after another. 3:27. Three hours and twenty-seven minutes across twenty-six point two miles. It wasn't enough. I needed to shave 7 minutes from my overall time to qualify for Boston.

Years ago, and at this same period in time, at the church that my family attended, our 8th grade students were required to participate in a project in the summer between middle school and high school. With much planning, the support of their parents and sponsors, and through rigorous and diligent coordination – this team of people were going to build homes for homeless within Mexico. The border cities of Tijuana and Tecate were the sites that were developed.

The group of graduating 8th graders would, with much support of their parents, however without power tools, lay foundation, erect 500 square foot homes, roof and stucco the structures within 5 days. When the project first began, it was nearly 20 people and one home. Then, with scale – it became two worksites and two homes. A year later it was a home and a school. Then, a church and two homes. I attended five of these projects.

This year that I'm referring to involved over 60 kids and 20 adults. The campsite that we were to take was better than years past. There was no running or clean water, but this one had stalls – boys on one side, girls on the other. The banos (restrooms) had no spiders or snakes. The area to pitch tents wasn't rocky or on a hill as in years past. This was as good as it got. It wasn't a night at a JW Marriott. But the evolution of this trip over the years had become enjoyable. Perennial participants traded stories of the sophistication of the later trips compared to the earlier.

Something from nothing, never loses its charm. In business, in sports, in relationships and in life – creating a situation from the ground up and remembering its foundation can lend itself to much favor.

This was good. Perhaps you could stretch and call it some of Gods best work. But I had a problem. How was I going to run the San Diego marathon that Sunday morning, and then get to Tecate early that afternoon to meet the caravan traveling down from Phoenix? 3:27 ended up being part of the answer. I'd just have to run fast. The logistics of turning in a rental car consumed minutes that I didn't have. If I missed the church caravan at the border, I'd have to sort out where they were. I don't speak Spanish. Well, a little: *un poquito.*

I'd have to run fast. Turn in the car. Get a cab. Then, I'd fork over a hefty amount of cash for a taxi through the Southern California wilderness to Tecate. Still sweating from the run, I dashed into the finisher's tent to pick up a bagel and a banana. I raced to the rental center to turn in the rental and hailed a taxi.

The driver questioned my destination three times until I forked over half of the estimated fare upfront. Perhaps because I was ripe from running, the driver opened the windows as we rolled along winding Highway 94.

With 15 minutes to spare, I arrived. The U.S. side of the border is nearly desolate. There was a Cash-n-Carry where I was to meet. The kids and the adults, vans and tool trailers, and my weeks' worth of pre-packed bag of work-clothes would make a pitstop here before the border crossing.

There are times when you must arrive in order to finish. I had arrived at the thought that I didn't need to run anymore. Forget the seven minutes. And in a Forrest-Gump-like moment, my days of running were over. Twenty marathons, countless halves and 10Ks, thousands of training miles of preparation went into running away from stress. It had manifested itself into the challenge and math of activity. There was always a *different* or a *better* to compare one race to another. I drew a conclusion that I'd reached a destination.

Change begins with one single moment. For me, it was a simple suggestion to run a marathon long ago. Sometimes there are these hard, lifelong small pieces of an equation that can lead to broader achievements. It sounds like: *We could, I can, What if...*

I've learned that at the mercy of those forces beyond what we accomplish, or as a benefit to it, what we achieve is never really ours alone. But it sure feels like it, doesn't it? I've also learned to pay attention to these calls to action. They move things forward.

RESULTS

"Remember how far you've come, not just how far you have to go. You are not where you want to be, but neither are you where you used to be."

--- Rick Warren

In the end, we sometimes tend to think about the beginning. What was the original plan? Did the course change direction from the original intention? How was the launch? What milestones were met along the way? What tools were leveraged? If you're running without reason, you're merely running with the wind. Ahead of it...or chasing it.

SOMETIMES THINGS JUST DON'T TURN OUT LIKE THEY WERE SUPPOSED TO

I was on a business trip to Tucson, Arizona many years ago. As I pulled up to an intersection, I saw an apparent homeless person holding a carefully printed cardboard sign that read "sometimes things just don't turn out like they were supposed to". I'm being honest here, occasionally in this situation my thoughts would be, *I wonder how they got to this point.* Other times I might think, *how can I help here?* Sometimes, I'd offer them a dollar or two. More often, at that point in time, I thought, *oh crap – another panhandler - don't look in that direction.*

I know. I admit, as a humanitarian – I've got work to do. Maybe we all do. But I did look. I saw a young woman, perhaps in her early thirties. From where I sat, she was very attractive, but looked worn from the heat of the sunny day. She had long straggly blond hair, big and bright blue eyes, high cheek bones, was wearing jeans, and a dark tee-shirt. But a pretty face. There was something more. What was it? I'm not sure if it was a look of despair, or exhaustion, or hopelessness.

The more I looked at her, the more this beautiful woman seemed out of place. Indeed, *sometimes things just don't turn out like they were supposed to*, or for that matter...belong.

I was third in line at the light. The car in front of me rolled down their window with pocket change for her. She approached the car to thank the driver. They talked for a minute. I thought the light would change quickly. It didn't. Longest red light ever. As I waited, I looked at what I originally thought was a duffel bag.

It was a little girl that looked like the homeless woman, her mother. Perhaps she was five or six, sitting on the dirt in the median, playing with a couple round stones, attempting to stack them. She looked up with the hot sun shining on her face. Cute kid. My thoughts were: shouldn't be in the median, sitting on the ground, playing with rocks. I strummed my fingers on the steering wheel. Still red.

The mother looked in my direction. My finger stopped strumming. I motioned her to my car. I knew my wallet was hungry, but reached for it, and opening it only saw a ten-dollar bill. She could have it. As the window opened and I looked at her, she appeared even more out of character. "It's all I have on me, I wish I had more," I said.

She accepted the money, and after looking at the bill, making eye-contact with me said this, "Oh sir, Thank you. You are a blessing. This is lunch today." She looked me in the eye so that I would know that it was for food, not drugs or booze or cigarettes. Her voice was soft. I think she enjoyed the cool blast of air-conditioning from the open window because she stood there for a moment.

I felt compelled to do more. So, I asked, "Are you safe? Do you have someplace to go?"

She answered. Not what I was expecting, "Yes, thanks. We all do." She reached down to briefly touch my forearm with her hand. "God bless you." She looked tired, but her eyes were bright and blue and sincere.

That was it. A horn honked a few cars back, and I looked up at a green light. Indeed. *We all have someplace to go.* She was safe. And I assumed that little girl with her, who I assumed was her daughter, was too. I took the ramp onto interstate 10 heading west to Phoenix, thinking about her well-being occasionally on my drive home – and in years to follow.

We all have some place to go.

Some of us don't venture far from home, or far from what we know. Some of us are travelers that experience as much as we can. Others are fearless in their ventures and go beyond – into the unknown – beyond their imaginations. They take that step. They find that place that they didn't know existed. And it's called love, or adventure, or knowledge, or achievement. If we're lucky enough to live many good years, it's called experience, wisdom, or peace.

It was the sign - that handwritten cardboard sign that stuck with me most. *Sometimes things just don't turn out like they were supposed to.* Sometimes they don't match the plan, or meet the intention, or align with the preparation. And in some moments, we find that they just might be better.

It's just as much about the journey as it is the results, isn't it? Few questions or comments may define our remembered points-in-time as well as these:

I love you.

Will you marry me?

Mom, Dad – we're getting married!

I now pronounce you husband and wife (or whatever your preferred arrangement)

It's a boy! It's a girl!

I want a divorce.

Please forgive me.

Time of death...

These moment-makers capture the day or the hour, but I like to think we strive for (or against) the idea of it. And we thrive in all the time preceding or following life's announcements and declarations. The results matter, really. It is as important to live well without wins and losses. The fabric of each moment weaves together a life well-lived.

Our lives are constantly ruled by randomness. At the same time, passions and proposed purposes pursue the way forward. When these two meet at an intersection, a difference is delivered.

Last licks:

God-willing, one day I'll be an old(er) man. I have a responsibility to care for that old man that I'll become – a purpose – perhaps to give him something to be proud of, something to be ashamed of, something to giggle at. That old man that I'll become needs a few stories to tell. He will know things beyond my comprehension.

In the end, I'm his best friend and he knows it.

He's my best friend, and I'm barely learning that as I go.

Using all that I believe and perceive, feel, and think, attempt and do – I owe it to him to reach for my human potential. Even knowing that I may not reach it, I owe it to him to try my very best.

You are not your history, your reputation, your net worth, or your things. You are not a byproduct of the stock market, your checking account balance, your 401k, your debt, your equity, or any measure of capitalism that mankind has created. But there's nothing wrong with creating – even creating wealth because money can and will help solve some of our problems. We should encourage each other to gainfully produce and generate as much as possible. And then to save, invest, and share.

No, you certainly aren't measured through economics – unless you choose to be. It's what you choose to do with your bounty and productivity that matters greatly.

You are not a scorecard of how many friends you have or how few you have. You are not worthy or unworthy based upon the car you drive, the neighborhood you live in, the school you attend or the church you might choose to go to.

You are real. You matter. You count. Each single moment of every day. If your moment hasn't happened or isn't here – perhaps it's coming. When you've made a difference, you'll know it. You are the challenges you constructed, the jobs you generated, the relationships you built, the smiles you caused, the mouths you fed, the lives you saved –

You are the possibility within yourself, and the possibilities within others that you helped uncover. Until you're a cadaver, you're moving. You're an open book, an unwritten story, an unsung song.

Whether you're completely stressed out or experiencing one of life's triumphs; surrounded by brick walls, or on top of the world; at your very edge or taking a leap of faith – you have human potential. You can do miraculous things for those around you. Your spirit extends well beyond your perspective. Remember, it's the things we don't know that sometimes matter most.

As American Author, H. Jackson Brown, Jr. reminds us:

"Kind words and good deeds are eternal. You just never know where their influence may lead. " ...and, "*Most of us know what we need to do to make our lives more fulfilled and useful, but sometimes we forget.*" He goes on to touch upon what we're all capable of: "...those simple things which, if done well and in a spirit of love, can significantly change our lives."

Sometimes, just beyond the parameters of what you know lie your greatest journeys. There's a world of invention and unmet questions to answer.

Your life – the journey...is one of discovery within the confines of what you've got and what you're seeking to get.

In any comprehensive sense, is there a Human Potential blueprint? No. A wide variety of beliefs and perceptions, feelings and thoughts, and actions and results serve us as roads that lead to free will. Our journeys experienced, intelligence gathered, ambitions taken, and unique human and divine talents charge their way forward into what lies ahead.

Come what may, there's just a beautiful flat line at the edge of the earth, at the edge of your imagination, at the edge of your life. It can represent all things known and unknown - an explorer's horizon, an artist's canvas, a capitalist's accumulation. Anything and everything are possible if we open up to the vast potential and girth of our capabilities.

There may be no final trades, but rather an accumulation of their timely worth. If you're lucky, you trade innocence for experience, you trade ambivalence for intelligence, you trade your time and interests for acquired skills, talents, and everlasting relationships.

You'll probably recognize the famous Spanish painter, printmaker, playwright, and poet who summed it up like this -

The meaning of life is to find your gift. The purpose of life is to give it away. --- Pablo Picasso

Similarly, I've always believed that life's purpose is simply to uncover your potential. We work at that – and occasionally are exposed to a good look at what it really might be. Maybe there are a lot of little reasons why those big things tend to happen. And maybe there's one big thing that causes those little things to happen. The biggest factor is that we try to not go at it alone.

Aren't we all unique, amazing, and capable of practically anything? We just forget that we are. Let's face it, when it's all over, it's the horizon that wins in the end. It outlasts us with its eternal circumference. But the beautiful illusion of meeting its end, of an agenda filled with discovery, of capturing that one mesmerizing moment – these are the fruits of our spirit – our potential.

Cover Design

The artwork for the cover of this book was created exclusively for Michael Woodruff. It is an original watercolor that was painted by Beth Stephano, a professional watercolor artist living on the island of Oahu. bethstephano.com

Beth Stephano

As they say, the journey of a thousand miles begins with a single footstep...

Originally from Erie, Pennsylvania, following a fine arts training both through grade and high school at the Erie County Vocational School and with private teachers and at the Erie Arts Center. Beth earned a scholarship and attended the Governor's School for the Arts at Bucknell University in the summer between her junior and senior years of high school. She attended and graduated from the Art Institute of Pittsburgh. Her art courses were both commercial and fine art-based. After graduation, Beth relocated to Philadelphia to begin a career in advertising as a creative on the art side and later, arriving in New York City and working for many top advertising agencies.

As a painter in oils, Beth participated in First Fridays in Old City, Philadelphia and exhibited in different galleries. Also, she has exhibited in many artist shows and craft shows over the years.

Beth is known for her florals in oils which she has been painting for many years. Each has a unique perspective and fades into the dark field of the background in one place and differs in each work. It is always the game that she plays, not knowing where the point will be that fades into the background till she starts working.

Her watercolors are studies of the ocean and the cloud banks which travel across the horizon in many different variations of color, time of day and light. Trade wind clouds raining into the ocean at the horizon or the ocean at night with white clouds passing by. Different iconic landmarks on O'ahu also are a new interest. Recently, she has started painting on silk.

Currently, living on O'ahu, Hawai'i. A member of the Hawai'i Watercolor Society and have participated in the Members Show at the DAC center. Featured pieces in the Members Show 2023 and currently 2024. (www.hawaiiwatercolorsociety.org/)

Beth was selected as one of the top 10 Artists in Hawai'i at the Park West Competition November 2022. (www.parkwestgallery.com/made-in-hawaii-2022-top-ten/)

Surrounded by beauty, inspiration is all around her. She pulls her visuals from her experiences on O'ahu. It is her work every day to create her best piece next - hoping that her artwork brings happiness to someone else - in their home and life.

About The Author

Michael Woodruff

Michael Woodruff is a poor shoe salesman from Ohio. He began his seventeen-year run through the footwear and sporting goods industry working with a national chain. From Ohio to Michigan, then Texas to Louisiana – he eventually arrived in Arizona. Transitioning to a career in technology, he led sales teams in the capacity of a sales manager and director of sales, and later supporting many of the largest Fortune 500 and most well-known brands in the tech industry he led brand teams as a senior partner manager of strategic alliances.

His collection of experiences, lived and embellished, trickles into the pages and creates the loadstones for his storytelling. Lessons learned, adventures attained, and possibilities proposed, his fables are suggestive in that there's an alternative to each potential outcome. He still lives in Arizona with his wife, Millie, and has four adult children and grandchildren.

Arcing The Flatline is his first publication in an emerging series of novels. These fables and the reasons why they have been written question a bevy of topics through the actions of the characters and may have some similarities which align to the real world we live within, such as how we might choose to transition – why testing our potential is essential – what turning a blind eye could do – where our known and unknown triggers possibly reside – when to act or when not to.

Let's face it – our world is not, in innumerable ways, the way that it should be or could be. His work here and in the unfolding fictional character of Jacob Paisley and a band of serial reciprocity actors is merely to challenge the status quo and take on the topic of delivering a difference.

www.ingramcontent.com/pod-product-compliance
Lightning Source LLC
Chambersburg PA
CBHW020302030826
48979CB00027B/1992/J

* 9 7 9 8 9 9 1 8 4 9 7 1 5 *